THE OXFORD POT

ISBN-13: 9781728976327

THE OXFORD POT

Elizabeth Longrigg

1

In large red letters the poster enquired:

HAVE YOU SEEN THE LATEST OXFORD PHENOMENON?
ON VIEW AND ON SALE IN THE THURSDAY MARKET,
GLOUCESTER GREEN
MAKE FOR THE STALL SHOWING THE OXFORD POT!!!

Robert Taylor stared at the poster and wondered how a pot could possibly be a phenomenon. He continued walking down the High Street and saw another notice:

STUCK FOR SOMETHING TO GIVE YOUR FRIENDS AS A WEDDING PRESENT?
BUY THEM AN OXFORD POT AND THEY'LL REMEMBER YOU FOR EVER!

Robert was amused. Not only a phenomenon but also a memorable one. He crossed Carfax and went on into George Street where two more notices were displayed.

One read: Everyone owns a mobile phone. Get something more upmarket to own - The Oxford Phenomenon!

And the other: Be daring! Be original! Buy your friends an Oxford Pot and they'll never forget you!

His curiosity was aroused. Moreover, he was in need of finding a difficult wedding present. His colleague Nigel

Nethercott had not only invited him to his wedding but also asked him to be his best man. It was Nigel's third wedding and people who are about to marry for the third time usually have a good supply of household necessities, and if they are not already in possession of the affordable luxuries it's probably because they don't want them. 'Nigel's got all the material things,' Robert mused; 'what a pity he couldn't acquire some of the more lasting values that would keep a marriage going, things like patience, fidelity, and understanding. Not that I should preach' said Robert to himself, 'not being married, but they do say the onlooker sees most of the game.'

Robert turned from George Street and went to the market, glad to have been so near to it on a Thursday. He was soon aware of a press of people jostling each other in front of a stall. A long strip of cardboard showing the words THE OXFORD POT hung from the awning above it. There was a roar of laughter from the gathering, though a small, thin, desiccated-looking woman fought her way out of it muttering, in rather a loud mutter, "Disgusting, I call it. Really disgusting. I've a good mind to tell the police!" She marched off angrily in the direction of George Street.

Robert was tall enough to see what was happening even from quite well back in the throng. He heard a woman's voice – one of those very audible upper class voices, quite powerful for a woman – declaiming, "Be daring! Be original! Buy your friends an Oxford Phenomenon for Christmas, for a birthday, for a wedding-present!" The voice went on. "Now you ladies; now you girls. Freud talks about us suffering from penis envy. Most of it's complete nonsense, but there is just that one thing we do envy: men can pee anywhere – standing up! NOW you can do it too! Are you travelling? Going to the Continent? Worried about loos you wouldn't use or no loos at all? Just use the Oxford pot and you're home and *dry*! No splashes, no damp underclothes. I'll show you ….let those little girls come up to the front, you chaps….” Robert got in a little closer and craned over the crowd. He saw a tall woman, somewhat middle-aged looking in face and feature, but clad in a trendy black trouser-suit of a neat, slim fit. She held up a receptacle made of pottery. Robert knew about pottery and identified it as slipware. It looked like a rather large gravy boat. With a flourish she spread her legs and held the vessel between them. “You see?” she said. “This is all you need to do – apart from lowering your garments, or raising a skirt if you're wearing one – and you can pee into the Oxford pot and you're home and *dry*! Just empty it anywhere; well, anywhere suitable. In Scotland a few hundred years ago you could just shout ‘Gardy lou!’ and toss it on to the passers by, but they're a bit strict about that sort of thing nowadays. Still there are plenty of drains and the canal's not far away.” Repeated bursts of laughter were heard during this performance and there was the odd shout of, “Show us again, love!” “Go on, show us how you do it properly!” “That'll do, you chaps!” the woman countered. “*You're* not the ones that need to know how to use it. Buy them for your womenfolk and there are small sized ones for little girls, too – and no more problems when you're out in the countryside, or in some benighted place abroad where the loos are gaping holes with a footprint on either side!” Marvelling at this blatant display of vulgarity coming, as it did, from a speaker with a decidedly up-market accent, and wondering briefly if perhaps it was Lucinda Lampton, that dedicated describer of all things lavatorial, Robert pushed his way to the stall, where a much younger, very beautiful woman, wearing vaguely ethnic clothes and flowers in her hair, seemed to be in charge of selling the objects.

"How much?" he asked.

"Ten pounds each, the full size ones; between £9 and £5 for the little girls' sizes. Add two pounds if you want a smart, handy, bubble-padded carrier bag."

"Thank you. I'll have a large one with a bag." Robert handed the exact money.

"Many thanks, sir." The young woman smiled graciously. "I hope you'll enjoy watching your wife use it!"

Robert smiled a little wryly. It had been on the tip of his tongue to say he hadn't got a wife, but he refrained for fear that would be the occasion for more ribald comments, however politely expressed. His purchase was handed to him in a colourful carrier bag with THE OXFORD PHENOMENON spelt out in large letters. As he left the stall he saw in the not very far distance the desiccated, muttering woman approaching the market in the company of a large, impressive policeman

2

Melissa Marjoribanks clattered up the spiral staircase, which was the only means of entering the flat - the owners called it a 'maisonette' – above the Speedysave grocery shop. She brought up the post, which the postman insisted on delivering to the shop below. Her daughter Cassandra was sitting at the kitchen cum dining table, pensively smoking a roll-up.

"Look, darling!" said Melissa. "I've got a letter from Oxford."

"Who do we know in Oxford?"

"I can't think of anybody," Melissa answered.

"Come to that," she continued, "who do we know anywhere? Since you will insist on potting pottery in the wilds of Devon one does get rather out of touch."

"It's cheaper in Devon," Cassandra murmured absently. They'd had this conversation before. Melissa opened the letter and scanned it rapidly.

"Heavens!" was her comment.

"Who's it from?"

"She signs herself Cousin Agatha. Listen: 'My dear Mrs Marjoribanks, Owing to the long-standing feud between our two branches of the family, we know almost nothing of each other. I have only succeeded in tracing you through the efforts of my solicitors. I wish to see you and your daughter. As I believe you live in poverty even more dire than mine I enclose a cheque for £100 to defray your expenses. You must book into this bed-and-breakfast on the outskirts of Oxford.' She gives the name and address and telephone number. 'It's not far from Huntsfield House, where you will find me. Please write immediately. They try to tell me I'm lucid only at intervals; this is quite untrue. I'm totally lucid all the time. Yours ever, Cousin Agatha.'"

"Sounds a bit bizarre," Cassandra commented

"Positively weird," her mother assented. "I think I remember my mother meeting her, she'd be that generation."

"Anyway, are we going to see her?"

"If we don't we'll have to send back the cheque. And that would be a pity."

***

It was late in the afternoon when Melissa and Cassandra arrived in Oxford.

"Well," said Melissa with relief. "We've got here."

"With a bit of help from the AA on the way."

"Well, that's normal. The older the car the greater the need."

"Now, we're in Banbury Road. Keep your eyes open for the B&B. Oh Look! Dripping with hanging baskets and busy lizzies everywhere; that's got to be a guest house."

"Oh Lord! I hope it's less ornamental inside!"

They drove in and stopped in the only space not totally devoted to dazzling displays of flowers. A kind-looking woman with prominent teeth and a sentimental manner opened the door. In tones of deepest sympathy she enquired about their journey – "*such* a long way, *so* tiring, I'm sure you would like a cup of tea. Come into the lounge and I'll bring you one while you get your breath back." They sank into deeply over-upholstered armchairs. Cassandra noted with dismay that there were signs everywhere saying: 'We are a smokeless zone', and 'No smoking permitted anywhere in the house. Smoke alarms fitted'.

"Oh *dear*!" she muttered drearily.

***

After a good – very good – breakfast Melissa and Cassandra got into their car and Melissa studied the map while Cassandra thankfully rolled a cigarette. "It's only ten miles out of Oxford," Melissa said. "It's on the ordinance survey map; it looks quite big. We should be able to find it."

Cassandra relit her roll-up, which had as usual gone out. "Mmm," she murmured doubtfully. "Would you like me to drive?"

"Oh no. Finish your fag. You can navigate."

Cassandra followed the map with a little less difficulty than usual. They skirted a high stone wall, and then came upon a pair of vast wrought-iron gates.

"They look awfully…. shut," said Melissa doubtfully. "The grass seems to be grown up all round them as if they hadn't been opened for years."

Quite a long way off, across the rough green of what should probably have been a lawn, stood a substantial brick house in the style of Queen Anne. Thinking it might not be the right place but was at least worth a try, they followed the wall round and found an opening, without gates, leading into a kind of courtyard with outbuildings to the right and the west side of the house on the left. To the south there was a low balustrade and more wrought-iron gates leading to a path across the grounds and over towards what was, apparently, a ha-ha beyond which there were fields with grazing animals. There was an ordinary looking door in the side of the house.

"This must be the tradesmen's entrance. Let's ring the bell, anyway." The bell resounded satisfactorily and was immediately answered by feverish barking and yapping. After a matter of minutes the voice of an elderly woman called out angrily: "Who are you? What are you doing? What do you want?"

"Are you Cousin Agatha, Lady Egerton?" Melissa called in reply. The answering voice was still angry. "Yes, but who are *you?"*

"Your cousin Melissa and her daughter. You wrote to us. You invited us to come and see you!"

"When?"

"A couple of weeks ago."

"I don't remember."

"We can show you the letter. Can we come in?" There were sounds of fumbling on the latch.

"I can't open this door. You'll have to come round the south side to the french windows. I'll let you in there."

Melissa and Cassandra looked at each other. "Seems odd having french windows in a house like this. Oh well, can but try."

They walked round and found the french windows but they were behind a jungled heap of garden furniture: tables, benches, and deck chairs.

This can't be right!" said Cassandra, puzzled. But a large figure appeared behind the glazed doors, the figure of a woman with unkempt hair and a strange assortment of loosely fitting clothes descending to a pair of huge gumboots. As she opened the door Melissa and Cassandra between them removed a large bench from the tops of two tables, pushed some chairs aside and squeezed themselves through the rest of the furniture and in through the doorway to what appeared to be a very large dining-room with furniture and chandeliers covered in dust sheets. Cousin Agatha didn't impede their progress any further but still eyed them suspiciously. "*Who* did you say you were?" she queried.

"Your cousins: Melissa and Cassandra Marjoribanks."

"Silly names!" Cousin Agatha pronounced definitively. "Can't help it, of course. *Your* side of the family!" Melissa was less put out by this remark than relieved that it showed a germ of memory and recognition.

They progressed into a much smaller and very crowded room, which seemed to contain bedroom, sitting-room and kitchen furniture all vying for space. In front of a noisy gas fire was an even noisier dog whose yapping had not ceased since the doorbell was rung. "Treasure!" said Cousin Agatha, indicating the animal with a sweeping gesture. It was a sorry-looking creature standing on its front legs with its bandaged back legs trailing uselessly behind and most of its hindquarters wrapped in a nappy.

"Paralysed!" said Cousin Agatha. "Half of it paralysed. Perfectly happy, however, perfectly. They say I should have her put down. Refused, of course."

"Ah!" said Melissa. "Of course." She drew out her cousin's letter but lacked the nerve to thrust it under her nose. "It was so very kind of you, Cousin Agatha, to write to us. I did write back. Perhaps you may remember…"

"Remember, remember," Cousin Agatha intoned, "they say I don't remember, but I do, far more than they think…far more. Have a cup of tea!" This *non sequitur* was delivered without extra breath or change of tone as her eye fell on a trolley in a corner, piled with a jumble of cups, saucers, teapots and a kettle, none of them clean.

"Oh no, we wouldn't dream…wouldn't put you to so much trouble…" said mother and daughter simultaneously.

"Sherry!" said Cousin Agatha, as if summoning it to appear. She waved a hand around the room. "Somewhere!" she said. Cassandra located it after a slight search and even found some glasses on the bottom shelf of the trolley. At least alcohol had an anti-bacterial effect, she thought.

It had quite an effect on Cousin Agatha too. She became more lively, more coherent, less suspicious and increasingly *compos ment*is. Melissa was almost convinced that she knew who they were. Their popularity certainly increased to the point of their being offered biscuits in addition to sherry.

"Shouldn't drink without eating, I always say! Come to that, shouldn't eat without drinking, either, what?" Melissa and Cassandra joined in comradely laughter. "There's a good girl now!" Cousin Agatha addressed Cassandra "Fetch the biscuits would you. Over there; in a tin covered in Santa Clauses. Ghastly vulgar thing but that's what one gets for Christmas these days."

Cassandra located the tin without difficulty but with some misgivings as to how many Christmases ago it, and presumably its contents, had been received. Melissa was on the point of declining the proffered refreshment but was forestalled by the insistence of Cousin Agatha, who gratefully helped herself to a biscuit and a half.

"You know I'd forgotten about these" she mumbled over a mouthful. "Takes a drop of something in the right company to make one think of these things."

Cassandra took a mouthful and decided that the tin and its contents must date from at least several Christmases ago.

"Is it all right to let Treasure have some biscuit?" she asked tentatively. "She's looking so---so path---I mean interested."

"Jolly good idea!" Cousin Agatha looked beamingly gratified. "Never thought of it before. Used to give her dog-biscuits but she can't eat them now. Managing that all right though." Judging from the limp, damp state of the biscuit in question Cassandra thought this unsurprising. "I think it's just the thing for her," she rejoined brightly, feeding the last morsel to the appreciative animal.

"Now have some more sherry----and I will too."

Cassandra hastened to fill Cousin Agatha's glass but declined any more for herself, pleading the necessity of driving.

"Never worried about that in my day," said Cousin Agatha with spirit. "Wouldn't worry about it now but they won't let me drive. Last time I drove was down a very narrow street in Summertown. Very crowded. Damn cars parked on either side of me ran into me! All the way down. Said it was *my* fault. Won't let me drive now unless I pass a test. Hmph! Never taken one. None of that nonsense when I started driving. Anyway I do drive when they're not looking. But they don't know that."

Melissa finished her second glass of sherry without undue haste and rose to make appropriate departure noises.

"Sorry you're going," Cousin Agatha sounded genuinely regretful. "Enjoyed seeing you. So did Treasure. I'll remember about the biscuits"

They went out through the french windows and round to their car. "Pray heaven it starts!" said Cassandra. "If it doesn't she might come out and offer to drive us home!

3

On the window-seat of the large bay window in the Senior Common Room of Chester College, Oxford, sat a group of dons drinking their after lunch coffee and reading newspapers and magazines. Suddenly a guffaw came from one of them. Robert Taylor, among others, looked to see what he was reading, expecting it to be *Private Eye.* In fact it was the Oxford Mail.

"What's so amusing in the Mail, Richard?" he asked. "A howler?"

"No, look!" Richard Holdsworth showed a picture of a stall in the Thursday market under the heading *A Storm in a P...Pot.*"

"What does it say about it?" asked Nigel Nethercott.

" 'Stall holders in yesterday's Thursday market,'" Richard Holdsworth read, " 'narrowly escaped being charged with public indecency when a bystander called the police to complain about the explicit demonstration of the use of a new product of the Oxford Pottery advertised as The Oxford Phenomenon or, more succinctly, The Oxford Pot. A relative of the stallholders, fifty-year-old grandmother Mrs Marjoribanks….'"

"Marshbanks!" Nigel interrupted angrily. "Marshbanks! Not 'Marjorie Banks', for heaven's sake!" The angry tone of Nigel's interruption, somewhat unnecessary in the context, was actually due to his having himself fallen foul of the pronunciation of that particular name as a new undergraduate, with the additional mortification of overhearing the possessor of it, a languid Etonian, remark to an equally languid companion: "Oh well, what can one expect from a grammar school geographer?" Unable to doubt that he was the 'grammar school geographer' in question Nigel had harboured a residue of anger, which now belatedly showed itself.

"How do you know? Are they friends of yours?" said Richard in tones of defensive sarcasm.

"*Everybody* knows that!" Nigel retorted.

"I'll bet they *don't*!" Richard responded vehemently. "Samson!" he called to a colleague just approaching from a distance with a careful tread necessitated by his concentration on the wobbling coffee cup in his left hand. "Samson!" he repeated. "If you put that cup straight on its saucer it might stop wobbling."

"Oh! Yes!" Samson gratefully adjusted the cup and beamed at the success of the operation. "You scientists have your uses," he remarked kindly.

"We need your help," said Richard. "You've got a funny surname nobody can pronounce. How about this one?" He held out the newspaper, underlining 'Majoribanks' with his forefinger.

"Oh! 'Marshbanks' – is that the one you mean?"

Richard was still suspicious. "How do you know?" he growled.

"Oh, well you know, one simply does," replied Samson.

"Does what?"

"Know these things."

"Then why is it that hardly anybody knows how to pronounce *your* name?"

"Ah well, I'm afraid mine has rather more literary than aristocratic connections," Samson sighed, "and literary connections which are less eminent than formerly. My lineal ancestor Robert Southey was Poet Laureate in his time, but one hardly hears of him now, except as a lesser associate of his more lastingly successful contemporaries."

Samson Southey was a slim, slight, almost excessively mild-mannered man of indeterminate age. He always insisted on being addressed by both syllables of his Christian name, which seemed to have been bestowed upon him by his parents on the grounds of least possible suitability. The only particular in which he could be considered remotely to resemble his Biblical namesake was in the length of his hair. Any interest he might take in the charms of a Delilah could be reasonably supposed to be of the most objective and academic kind. Nevertheless he always persisted, with an impeccably polite but essentially steely determination, in correcting anybody who called him 'Sam' or 'Dr Suththy'. "*Sow* thee," he would say, *'Sow'* as in female of the porcine species, or indeed as in *south*; not 'suthth' as in 'southerly'.

Richard Holdsworth had no further wish to draw attention to the story of The Oxford Pot and indeed his own relish for it had been decidedly soured. He departed to spend the afternoon in his laboratory, leaving the Oxford Mail on the window-seat. Robert Taylor edged towards it as unobtrusively as possible. Simon and Samson were still talking about names. As his fingers reached the newspaper Simon turned to him, saying, "Like yours, for example, Robert'"

"Like my what? Sorry, I wasn't listening."

"Your name. We're talking about parents almost never getting it right, even when they choose the plainest, most ubiquitous and unnoticeable of names, like yours."

"Yes," sighed Robert Taylor. "You're quite right. What could be more ordinary and unexceptionable than 'Robert Taylor' – and then it has to be the name of a famous film star with whom one's always unfavourably compared. But yours must be relatively trouble free, Nigel, and yet distinctive into the bargain."

"Well yes," Nigel replied with more than a touch of smugness. "But of course I always have to spell 'Nethercott', and sometimes find myself addressed by some very strange variations on it. Can't really complain though."

Robert mused privately that Nigel's smugness, often increased to arrogance, was a main source of his general lack of popularity with his colleagues. Another, of course, was the fact that apart from breaking up two of his own marriages Nigel showed a predatory attitude towards the wives of colleagues, with some success as far as the women were concerned, to the considerable chagrin of their husbands. These affairs – if indeed that is what they were, it was doubtful if they went so far – usually blew over with rapidity as Nigel sighted a new object for his very temporary affections, thus rendering himself at least as unpopular with the abandoned wives as he was with his colleagues, their husbands.

"Now about this wedding," Nigel was saying as Robert emerged from these musings on his character and propensities, in which he'd been too engrossed to notice the silent departure of Samson Southey.

"What? Oh, yours. You haven't told me much about it, apart from the date. Quiet and select, is it?"

"Well. ...actually....I suppose we've reached a sort of compromise. Effie and her family want the full works, you know, church, choir, everything. Effie's mother's main objection to her marrying a divorcé is due to her not being able to have a 'proper' church wedding. So we'll be having a service of blessing in the College chapel a day or two after actually getting married in the Registry Office. That'll be just the family and then lunch in the Randolph."

"The Randolph?" Robert asked in surprise. It was not the kind of place greatly favoured by the majority of Oxford dons, its clientele being generally supposed to consist of American tourists and the nouveaux riches.

"Well, yes." Nigel sounded apologetic. "Sort of place Effie's mother likes; she describes it as 'smart'. It's her favourite adjective, generally to be equated with 'expensive' and 'showy'. But after the chapel service the reception will be here."

"Really Nigel, I don't know why you bother!"

"It's for the bride's parents to bother!" Nigel sounded rather defensive.

"I don't mean with the reception and the trimmings; bother to get married at all is what I meant."

"Not the kind of remark I expect from my best man: I hope you're not going to put it in your speech! Unlike you I *need* to be married. It keeps me out of trouble.

4

Melissa Marjoribanks removed the pots and pans and related debris from the hob of the cooker, wiped it over carefully, turned the electric oven on full leaving the door three quarters open, and placed a large, upright clothes-horse in front of it. She then took a very wet sheet from the clothes-basket beside her and draped it successively over the eye-level grill, the oven door and the clothes horse. "That'll make a nice fug," she murmured aloud.

There was a clatter on the iron steps outside and Cassandra elbowed her way in, impeded by the bulging shopping bags hanging from each hand. Her mouth was closed over the edges of an assortment of envelopes.

"Dahling!" exclaimed Melissa, "I would have helped you!"

"Oh – i aw eye," came from behind the envelopes. Melissa removed them from her daughter's mouth and was rewarded by the elucidating, "It's all right." Cassandra hoisted the bags onto the table. "I'm used to it. There's an oddly long envelope among the post. Looks rather legal. No more dreadful debts I hope." Her eyes lighted on the sheet-draped cooker. "You know that's a frightfully expensive way of drying the washing!"

"Oh darling, don't *worry.* At least it provides us with some warmth at the same time. Did you get my faggies?" Cassandra put them on the table. "Good. Now let's sit down and have some coffee and open the post – oh, I suppose you want herbal tea. Well, whatever."

The kettle had already boiled and the steaming mugs, unique pieces of slipware made by Cassandra, were soon on the table and Melissa happily lit one of her cigarettes while Cassandra rolled one of hers. Before lighting it she looked through the mail. "The electricity bill," she said accusingly, looking at her mother, "and appeals from charities. *They've* got a hope!"

"Let's open the legal-looking one – it's addressed to both of us," Melissa suggested, not too eagerly.

Cassandra lit her roll-up. "You open it," she said.

Melissa drew out some large, obviously official papers and a letter, which she opened. She gasped and dropped her cigarette, fortunately into the ashtray.

"What is it?" asked Cassandra anxiously.

"Cousin Agatha!" Melissa replied.

"Not from her, surely?"

"No. She's dead. I can't believe it."

"Why? She didn't seem far off it when we saw her."

"No. It's the house."

"Well that looked pretty dead too."

"She's left it to us."

Cassandra's roll-up went out. She was too shocked to speak.

Melissa scanned the solicitor's letter again. "There's a proviso," she said. "We can't sell it or any of the contents for ten years and we must provide a home there in the house and proper care for Treasure 'for the term of her natural life'. It goes on: 'This last codicil' – oh yes, the bit about Treasure, 'could be considered not legally binding as it was added very recently when the testatrix' that's Cousin Agatha, of course, 'might have been considered not entirely sound of mind. The rest of the will, however, dates from some years earlier.' *That* must be why she insisted on seeing us. She wanted to know if we were suitable guardians for Treasure! How bizarre!" Cassandra and Melissa burst into shaky laughter, from a combination of shock and incredulity together with some objective amusement at a situation in which their own part seemed completely unreal.

Melissa topped up the cups with hot water. Cassandra read the solicitor's letter. Melissa opened the copy of the will, rested it against the shopping bags and tried to fathom its complexities. "I can't take it in," she sighed. Cassandra stared into the middle distance, mentally transporting herself into the remembered details of Huntsfield house and its surroundings. "We'll have to go and live there!" she said incredulously. "And we won't have to pay any rent."

"No!" her mother responded. "And there are plenty of outbuildings for you to pot your pottery in. I think we should go as soon as possible."

"Yes." Cassandra came down to earth. "Preferably before the next electricity bill arrives!"

***

Less than a month later Melissa and Cassandra waved their last waves to the back of the large van which had brought them and their belongings and several of their more devoted and able-bodied potter friends from Devon. After several days' stay the potters had departed, with many promises of contact and return, leaving 'Mel and Cass' standing in what they called their backyard, the large paved area bounded by the wall and iron gates leading into the grounds, the main outbuildings and the side of the house containing the 'back door' which had so firmly resisted Cousin Agatha's attempts to open it. It was open now and Treasure was yapping frantically for them to come in as she couldn't venture out any further.

"It was fun having them all to stay," Cassandra remarked a little wistfully.

"Well of course it was, darling. All those strong young admirers of yours!"

"Middle-aged more like!" Cassandra objected.

"Yes, from your point of view, I suppose so. They seem young to me. I daresay they've all propositioned you at various times."

"Yes, but they didn't seem too put off by my negatives. It's so useful being a Catholic; I only have to say it's against my religion and they can't really argue with that. At least I won't have to drive thirty-five miles to go to mass from here."

"No we're barely ten miles from Oxford – remote though it may seem; more remote than a Devonshire village. But we'll get used to it. You'll be happy once you start making pots again. It's very good of Gustaf to let you have his second kiln."

"Well, only on loan, of course. But it will be a start, and if I can sell some of the stuff I've brought with me I'll really be able to get going."

"Yes. We must be positive. There's some of that wine left. Let's fortify ourselves with a couple of lunchtime glasses and then explore."

They started with the attics, if such they could be called. They were immense, without sloping ceilings and with large, shuttered windows. The shutters opened with surprising ease and revealed superb views on all sides.

"We could make several flats up here, you know," Cassandra pondered, "and let them to rich Americans or some such."

"Very true," her mother responded, "they'd be a goldmine. But it's the old story: you can only make money when you've already got some. I haven't any earning power; no training to do anything useful and productive, except run a house – rather extravagantly – and cook. And pottery's not the most money-spinning occupation."

They left the attics and descended two flights of stairs to the first floor. In one of the larger passages there was an immense display cabinet with glass doors.

"What a pity we can't sell some of this stuff!" said Melissa with a sigh. "It must be worth something."

Cassandra rubbed away some of the dust and looked more closely. "It can't be very valuable," she said, "it's only a lot of old chamber pots. Look! The door's not even locked." She opened the cupboard and revealed a not unattractive display of variously adorned and painted vessels. "Oh – look at this one with an open eye in the bottom of it. *Honestly!* Is that Victorian humour? And what on earth are those enormous gravy boats doing in here. Rather out of place, surely."

"Oh no, darling, they're not gravy boats," said her mother knowledgeably, they're bourdaloues. Heavens! It's years since I've seen one – and that was in a stately home. I don't think we ever had one, though my mother knew what it was."

"And what is it?"

"It's a pee-pot for women so that they can pee standing up. Marvellous really. I can't think why they became obsolete. It must have been when gussets were put into women's pants."

"How do you mean?"

"Well, when they were joined up under the crotch. Before that they were just a pair of legs really, each one separate from the other and only attached to a waistband. I used to have some among my grandmother's old linen. Hence, you see, under the skirts, one could just hold the bourdaloue up to the bare crotch between the pantalette legs and pee away. It must have been a bit tricky getting the full pot out again, though it's much easier now with the comparatively scanty clothes we wear. Marvellous for using behind a bush on a picnic – you know how *impossible* it is not to get one's pants wet peeing on to the ground – let alone one's legs and feet. And it's even more ghastly if one's wearing tight trousers...."

"Yes," Cassandra interrupted, "you're always wearing tight trousers ....not always suitably;" but hardly aware of the interruption Melissa was warming to her theme: "and you know those *frightful* loos on the continent where one's simply confronted with a hole in the ground and a large footprint on either side of it! Now just think if one had a bourdaloue. One could simply use it with ease and safety and empty it into the hole. Really somebody ought to...." Melissa stopped and looked thoughtfully at her daughter as if seeing her in a new light. "*You* could do it," she said slowly. "You could make modern bourdaloues and take out a patent on them and market them. That would really start something." Cassandra picked up the nearest of these historic vessels and weighed it in her hands and turned it over with a potter's knowledge and expertise. She turned to her mother with interest and a new respect.

"You might be right," she said; "You might just be right

5

The reporter and the photographer spent a lot of time with Melissa and Cassandra at Huntsfield House, the one asking as many questions and taking down as many answers as the other took photographs.

"What a story!" the journalist enthused as she turned over yet another page of her notebook. "Not only a pottery that produces the famous – perhaps I'll say notorious – Oxford Pot but a stately home into the bargain."

"I hope you won't mention Treasure," said Cassandra anxiously.

"Treas....? Oh! The poor little dog. No – not quite the right note – the animal rights people - - - indignant letters - - - no no, not on the right lines for this."

"Surely the Oxford Pot's the *cause celebre*," Melissa remarked. The reporter wrote 'Oxford accent' in her notebook, and then put two question marks beside it.

"Oh – absolutely," she replied. "Especially after that interesting little incident with the policeman in the market last week. That's what brought it to our attention, of course. But the house and grounds are rather more than a bonus. John," turning to the photographer, "shall we have some of Miss Marjoribanks sitting on the wall by the wrought-iron gate holding up the Pot so that it can be seen against the whole background? We've probably got enough of the interiors. Can you get a corner of the house in as well?"

John was doubtful. The Pot might not show up sufficiently. "Worth a try," he murmured, "after all we don't have to use it." John liked to do things his own way and was of the opinion that the text should be a back-up to the photographs, rather than vice-versa. Cassandra duly took up the required poses and then, with all the charm she could muster, which was considerable, begged to return to her workshop in order to have enough wares to take to the next market.

"Of course once this has appeared," the journalist advised confidently, "you'll have people coming here to see everything and buying pots as well."

"Why, yes!" Melissa was intrigued. "Perhaps we could charge them to see over the house too, eventually."

"*Eventually* perhaps," Cassandra echoed more cautiously. The representatives of the press refused tea and departed. Cassandra sighed. "You know this is not really what my art is about," she complained to her mother. "I don't want to be known as the producer of the Oxford Pee Pot."

"Possibly not," her mother rejoined, "but you're the one who goes on about electricity bills. Didn't you tell me Bernard Leach made flowerpots? If people come to buy your Oxford Pots they'll buy other things too. There's nothing like advertising and publicity. Without it you'll sell no pots and pay no bills, and heaven knows how we'll be able to go on living here – or anywhere! I'm going to get back to my sewing."

"You're being very mysterious about this sewing," said Cassandra. "It wouldn't have anything to do with the next market, would it?"

"You'll see when the time comes," Melissa replied firmly and went purposefully back into the house.

Even before the two-page spread with colour pictures featuring Cassandra and her Oxford Pot and her nearly stately country house appeared in the local paper for all to see, Robert Taylor had abandoned the idea of giving his previously purchased vessel to Nigel Nethercott as a wedding present. In fact he wondered how he'd ever thought it possible. "I would never have the nerve," he said to himself gloomily. He'd toyed with the idea of bringing it into his speech in a way not unsuitable among mature, mainly married or previously married people. "No more tedious waiting outside women's lavatories (the kind labelled Ladies Toilets, of course) while one's partner (safer word than 'wife' these days) spent seeming hours decking the doubtful-looking seat with lavatory paper. She wouldn't need to touch it if she used the Oxford Pot!" It might just have gone down if it had been a really new phenomenon and nobody had heard of it before – but everybody knew about it now. Well, at least he was not averse to visiting the market stall again for a closer look at the young woman he now knew as Cassandra Marjoribanks. "Cassandra," he murmured. Quite a name. A sense of mystery about it somehow. He didn't admit to himself that he'd originally been drawn to her stall by the power of clever advertising, or in fact bought an Oxford Pot for the same reason, totally unsuitable though it was as a wedding present from a best man. He did wonder, however, how many other people had been approached to perform in that capacity. Nigel Nethercott might be attractive to women but he was certainly not popular with men. Of course I haven't got a wife for him to make passes at, Robert mused, and if I'm not exactly a friend I'm not an enemy either. I'm probably about the best he could do. But what on earth does one say in a speech about a bridegroom with two failed marriages behind him? 'Third time lucky' or put it more obscurely into Middle English and say 'Thridde time throwe beste'? Will wives one and two be invited to the wedding? Should one make a jolly reference to continued friendship or lament the fact that Nigel's neither a Muslim nor living in a country where he could, in fact, have four wives at once? Robert had a highly developed sense of the comic and was afraid he was too liable to see the funny side of it all to make an acceptable speech at all. He'd have to make sure he didn't drink too much or there was no knowing what he might come out with. Something like: "Nigel tells me he needs to be married because it keeps him out of trouble. I'm not sure what that means because as far as any objective and unprejudiced observer can see his behaviour is not a whit different whether he's married or not. Or is it the implication that the women he seduces are less likely to demand that he marry them when he's married already?" Robert gave a chortle at the thought of the effect produced by such words at the wedding breakfast, but relapsed into gloom at the prospect of preparing for the reality.

The high table lunch for the dons on the following Thursday was less well attended than usual. Several of the normal habitués were absent. This was briefly remarked upon but without raising any interesting, or indeed interested, speculation. Most of the missing members were, in fact, jostling for position among the crowd round Cassandra Marjoribanks' stall in the open market. Robert Taylor was surprised to see Nigel Nethercott there. Nigel was not particularly pleased to see Robert, especially when the latter asked, "What on earth are you doing here?" What a futile question Robert immediately told himself; from the way Nigel was gawping at Cassandra the answer was obvious. Nigel did his best to compose his features into a look of non-committal objectivity. "Oh – you know," he murmured, "can't believe all you see in the papers…need to see things for yourself, don't you think?" What they could see was Melissa, holding an Oxford Pot aloft and going through her spiel about its advantages. She did not, however, demonstrate its use in person as she had previously. Instead she put it back on the stall and in its place held up a pair of Victorian style pantalettes in white cotton with frilly lace attached to the bottoms of the legs, which were in turn attached to a waistband, and the waistband delicately pegged on to a wire coat hanger with small coloured pegs.

"Now these," Melissa was saying in her high-toned, carrying voice, "these will demonstrate how the Oxford Pot was used in its hey-day. As you see the legs are not joined to each other but are *separate*: look!" She lifted one leg delicately as it were by the knee to resemble a provocative sideways kick making the pantalettes separate in the crotch area. She was rewarded by the close attention of the predominantly male spectators, the odd whistle and sounds of "Cor!" and "Phew!" "Beats black nylon any day!" came from a hefty looking middle-aged man in the front row. "That's Butler!" said Nigel in surprise. Butler heard his name and turned round. He was one of the Chester College porters. Seeing Nigel he gave a large wink before returning his gaze to Melissa and the pantalettes.

"Got any of those for sale, love?" came a bass voice from another part of the throng.

"Now in fact we *are* thinking of marketing these," Melissa replied. "We're willing to take orders. They would have to be made to size, of course."

"How about getting the young lady to model them?" another resonant male voice suggested, soon seconded by cries of "Yes! Yes! Go on, love!" Cassandra gave a smile of great sweetness, lowered her eyes and managed to look demure.

"There would be a price reduction for orders made at the time of buying an Oxford Pot and any other pottery purchase totalling at least £20," Melissa continued, despite interruptions and half joining in the laughter. The general mood was very good humoured.

"Going to buy a pair for Effie?" Robert asked Nigel, who with some reluctance shifted his gaze from Cassandra and said, "What? Who? Oh! Effie – yes, of course."

"Go on then." Nigel moved towards the stall as if mesmerised and Robert saw him pointing to various items, including a Pot, lingering over discussions of price and payment. Melissa had to help behind the stall, selling, wrapping and taking orders, while Nigel continued to monopolize Cassandra. Robert became aware of Butler standing beside him. "Wouldn't have thought to see you here, sir," said Butler.

"Why not?" asked Robert. "I'm interested in pottery."

"Oh yes, I'm sure, sir. That's why we're all here, isn't it?" He gave a leering smile. "Except Dr Southey over there. Now he's a different matter. A *real* scholar, that one." Robert's reaction was divided between amusement at the college porter's views on real scholarship and astonishment at the sight of Samson Southey, whom he hadn't noticed before. He went over to him, partly to escape the attentions of Butler.

"Hullo Samson!" he said, more in surprise than in greeting. "What are you doing here? Apart from peering under your hand as if looking for a ship in the distance!"

"Interesting," remarked Samson without actually replying. "Very interesting. Quite a number of these rather upper class women have a flair for making and selling things, despite the fact that they've been brought up to despise trade. There's another one in this market: paints leafy designs on mirrors and sells them for inflated prices. She's a kinswoman of the Mitfords."

"You must point her out to me," said Robert politely.

"Mm…yes. Not like this, though. Doesn't advertise in this blatant sort of way. That's what's so fascinating here. Draws quite a crowd; and once drawn, of course, the daughter holds them. Clever."

"She certainly seems to be holding Nigel," Robert commented.

"Ah well. Easy prey there of course. He *does* seem to be buying a lot."

"Well, he's getting married again soon. Perhaps he's restocking the house, replacing the crockery that got broken in the rows with wife number two."

"Indeed?" Samson showed something like an academic interest. "I had no idea."

"About the remarriage or the rows?" asked Robert.

"Oh, the remarriage, of course. The rows are no doubt a figment of your fertile imagination. I don't suppose you have a grain of evidence for them."

"Quite true," admitted Robert. "But I do know about the wedding. He's asked me to be his best man."

"From the tense you use I gather you haven't said 'No'."

"I don't see what the tense has got to do with it." Robert was mystified.

"No, of course not. The reaction of a native speaker is purely subconscious. If you had used a straight past and said 'He asked me' I would know that you regarded the incident as belonging to the finished past – over and done with, in fact, no longer relevant to the present. As it is, however, I gather you are still thinking about it or have in fact agreed to do it."

Robert reflected for a moment. "You know you're quite right! I'd just never noticed it before. Interesting! I suppose it's what comes of your being a Comparative Philologist."

"Among other things," said Samson happily. "I hope I would have had the linguistic ability to find a graceful reason *not* to be Nigel's best man!"

"Well since I've been so unhappily lacking in that department perhaps you'll help me with the speech."

"Now that *is* a challenge, Robert. But you never know. Look at Nigel still hanging about that young woman's stall, weighted down with purchases though he is. The function of a best man may cease to be necessary!"

6

The following morning Robert Taylor was working in his room when he was telephoned by Samson Southey.

"Samson!" he said in some surprise. "What can I do for you?"

"Well, of course you know that I've never learned to drive a motor car?"

"Haven't you? No, I suppose not." Robert visualized Samson trying to balance a cup he hadn't thought to place properly on its saucer and some similar indicators of a lack of co-ordination and reflected rapidly that such symptoms displayed behind the wheel of a car might well prove lethal.

"No. I feel it's not quite my métier. I tend to be inattentive to very physical things."

"So you want me to drive you somewhere, is that it?"

"Why yes, Robert. How perspicacious of you. Only if and when you have time, of course. I'm so interested to see where those Marjoribanks people live. I have a feeling they might be kindred to a cousin by marriage of my mother's."

"I can take you today, if you like. I've only got one tutorial at ten o'clock. We could have lunch in the country; have a look at the flourishes of nature on this warm spring day." Hell – thought Robert. When I'm talking to Samson I begin to sound like him. I hope he doesn't think I'm taking the micky.

"Yes indeed. Delightful. Absolutely. You literary people do use some strange vocabulary at times. 'Flourishes!' I wouldn't have thought of it…."

"Meet me in the car park at half past eleven then. That should give us plenty of time." I needn't have worried about sounding like a parody; Robert smiled to himself as he put the receiver down. He was in fact extremely pleased to have been jogged into doing exactly what he'd wanted to do but had preferred not to admit to himself. He'd got as far as thinking he could go out to Huntsfield House *some* time in order to look for a present for Nigel. He'd walked away from the market without a proper look at the stall because he'd preferred the company of Samson to the insinuations of the porter, Butler, and also been put off by the crowd of purchasers, including Nigel himself. Samson's request provided just the required incentive. He was immersed in picturing Cassandra beside the wrought iron gates leading into the Huntsfield grounds when his ten o'clock tutorial pair knocked at the door.

***

Robert and Samson drove into the courtyard of Huntsfield. It contained several other cars but there was still plenty of space. Robert pointed at a silver-grey, sporty-looking car with its hood down. "I believe that's Nigel's new car!" he said. "He's not wasting any time."

"Dear me!" responded Samson, who was as mentally perceptive as he was physically uncoordinated. "On the other hand, of course, he could be wasting his time entirely." Recognising the pottery workshop from the newspaper picture they proceeded into it. Nigel was speaking to Cassandra. They heard him say, "If you'd like to, of course," before Robert broke in with "Why Nigel? Hullo! I've come to buy you a wedding present and now that you're here I can consult you about it!" Nigel, who had been too much engaged in his attentions to Cassandra to have noticed them come in, turned a dull shade of red from his neck to his forehead. Samson reflected with considered interest that Nigel's capacity for blushing seemed somewhat at odds with his experience of life's vicissitudes.

"Ah yes!" he said deliberately improving on this already interesting situation. "Nigel! I hear you're getting married again. Congratulations!" The stress he placed on the word 'again' was so slight as to have been barely perceptible to a disinterested observer. It was not lost on Cassandra, however, who took very little trouble to hide her smile of amusement.

"But I beg your pardon," Samson continued, "we've interrupted you and Miss – er – Marjoribanks, isn't it? Allow me to introduce myself, Samson Southey, I believe a cousin of my mother's married into your family. But we can talk about that some other time. I must let you attend to a potential customer – my colleague, Robert Taylor."

"How do you do," Cassandra murmured politely.

"How do you do," Robert responded. "How nice to see you in – er – your own setting. I was rather enamoured of one of those large fruit bowls: such depth – not quite brown, not quite black and that wonderfully minimal edging of aquamarine. How would that suit you, Nigel? Beautiful, don't you think? And by the way, Samson and I are thinking of having lunch in a country pub, would you like to join us?" Nigel looked embarrassed.

"Oh no – not today – I never…"

"Now *please*," Cassandra interjected, "don't be stopped because you've asked me to have lunch with you." Nigel's flush, which had receded, deepened again. "I can't possibly leave the workshop so the answer's no in any case."

Nigel had not, of course, wanted his invitation to be known to his colleagues. Robert was almost sorry for him and went on talking about the beauties of the large black bowl, which Nigel accepted gratefully as an *excellent* present. Samson savoured the scene with delighted interest, considering it not improbable that Cassandra's interjected refusal was an intentional punishment for behaviour quite unsuitable in one of Nigel's almost married status. Decent women didn't approve of, or appreciate, that sort of thing, he'd noticed, unless they were married themselves.

The bowl duly purchased, Robert and Samson set off for their pub lunch. Nigel left at the same time but still declined to join them. He reversed his car and turned it in the courtyard with a kind of snorting haste, which clearly expressed his annoyance, despite the superiority of his sporty vehicle over Robert's rather old and very ordinary Fiat. Melissa, who had been unseen but not entirely unseeing during Nigel's visit, went from the house to the workshop.

"That fellow in the sports car was the one who bought all those things from you at the stall, wasn't he?" she asked Cassandra.

"Yes, I'm afraid so?"

"Why afraid?"

"Because he had an entirely ulterior motive. He came today ostensibly to change one of the bowls but actually to ask me out to lunch."

"You don't like him?"

"No I do not."

"Pity. Can't you just lead him on a bit until he's bought a few more pots?"

"Really, Mummy, I think you're completely unscrupulous at times. You're developing a passion for making money that's quite taking you over."

"It's something our family can do with, we've always shown a tendency in the opposite direction before."

"A passion for spending it, you mean."

"Well yes, or just losing it. The men of the family were very good at that. But as it is we seem to be doing quite well at the moment. I think you should employ an apprentice. They could make Oxford Pots and you could concentrate on the things you really like doing."

"Oh – I don't think I'm quite up to having an apprentice."

"Well - what about a school leaver for the summer holidays as a start? Lots of them do pottery at school nowadays. I'll start advertising."

"I must admit you're remarkably good at getting on with things these days."

"Yes," Melissa replied musingly. "I think it's all those years of your father being so high and mighty and secretive about his business affairs and regarding me as the empty-headed little wife who knew nothing about such things. And of course I couldn't know anything when he kept it all from me. I had no idea he'd gone bankrupt until the cheques began to bounce."

"Well, you were much younger than he was, being a second wife."

"Be warned by my example, darling. 'No example like a bad one.' *Never* be a second wife!"

"Now that's another thing about Mr Flashy-Sports-Car-lunch-invitation whom you want me to 'lead on.' Not only is he engaged with a wedding soon to come but he's been married before!"

"Did he tell you this?"

"Certainly not. The two men who arrived later were colleagues of his and they made it very plain – greatly to his discomfiture. It was actually very funny. Somehow I felt they wanted to warn me, but they were not at all averse to embarrassing him in the process. So you *see*!"

"Yes, I do see." Melissa looked thoughtful. "Frankly, my darling, I'm even *more* inclined to think you should lead him on. It would serve him right. And you could well be the means of preventing his unfortunate fiancée from making a frightful mistake into the bargain. Think of it as a humanitarian venture. If only I were young enough to do it myself – but alas!"

"Oh, Mummy. I'm sure you have lots of admirers."

"I used to think so, but it's hopeless now. Once they've seen you I might as well sink into a black hole."

"Well I don't suppose Mr Flashy-Sports-Car's likely to come back anyway, so we'll have to leave his fiancée to her fate."

"We'll see," said Melissa placidly.

***

Robert and Samson had found a particularly pleasant pub in Tackley and were enjoying their lunch in its courtyard.

"I've never been here before," said Samson. "What a pleasant place: such an attractively shaped village green with totally original stone houses on the two sides of it. The church is superbly placed to overlook them from the hill, too."

"Quite a few dons live here, you know," Robert remarked. "It's got a railway station and you can get into Oxford by train in about ten minutes. It might suit somebody like you who doesn't drive, Samson."

"Oh, I think not. I prefer to live in Jericho and walk everywhere."

"I'm afraid you didn't get very far with you enquiries about kindred and affinity as things turned out."

"Oh, enough to act on, I think. There's not exactly any urgency. But I fear our hopes of there being no call for a best man for Nigel are unlikely to come to fruition – from that quarter anyway."

Robert laughed. "It was worth it to see Nigel's face, wasn't it?"

"Well, if you think so. I certainly do. But then I'm not in the unenviable position of having to make an acceptable speech at his third wedding."

"I wish I had the nerve to make an unacceptable one. Besides…" Robert suddenly became inarticulate.

"Besides what?" asked Samson. Robert didn't know besides what; he was only dimly aware that he'd felt Cassandra should be alerted to Nigel's propensities.

"The Nigels of this world deserve to be shown up," he finally concluded.

7

Richard Holdsworth was in the Senior Common Room of Chester College reading the Guest Night Book. Chester College was not one of the richest of the Oxford Colleges and Guest Nights were normally held only once a week. Dons taking guests to these august occasions were required to fill in, well ahead of time, a form for the night in question, giving their own name and the name or names of their one or two guests (maximum permitted, two) together with the status and occupation of the guests or any other information deemed relevant in helping the Vice-Principal to decide where everybody was to sit at dinner and at dessert afterwards. Richard rarely attended these dinners himself. He was not very highly developed socially and saw little point in making the effort to talk to people he would probably never encounter again. He preferred talking about practicalities to people engaged in useful activities like repairs and building work. He was reading the names written down for the following week mainly because somebody else had already commandeered the copy of *The Sun,* which he wanted to look at. Almost all the daily papers were available in the Senior Common Room, but there was rarely, if ever, more than one copy of each. So instead he scanned the list of professors, the head of a college, an author he'd never heard of and some other people whose inviting hosts or hostesses had put them down as impressively as possible and at the end of the list saw Samson Southey's name alongside Mrs and Miss Marjoribanks and Nigel Nethercott's plus a Mrs Somebody else who seemed to have no status or occupation, and Robert Taylor down to attend but with 'no guest.' Richard had reason to remember the name 'Marjoribanks' since he'd so ignominiously got it wrong, but at first failed to identify it with the purveyors of the Oxford Pot, who'd been written up as *almost* guilty of indecency in the open market. Richard had rather more than his fair share of inquisitiveness, which he and his admiring parents considered to be the sign of an eager and enquiring mind showing a thirst for knowledge, and which Samson and his kindred would cursorily dismiss as vulgar curiosity. Richard would question builders on a working-site as to what was to be erected there and why. Seeing anything approaching a throng in a street he would ask anybody prepared to listen the reason for their gathering. Seeing any strangers in the college he would have to find out who they were and why they were there. So he pondered on the names of Mrs and Miss Marjoribanks and the reason for Robert Taylor's going solo to the guest night, hoping that either Robert or Samson would appear and enlighten him. Robert unconsciously obliged him by coming in a few minutes later. Richard hailed him.

"Robert! I want to ask you something."

"Just a minute. I'll get my coffee."

Robert tried to hide a slight sigh. Richard Holdsworth was not really one of his favourite people. Nevertheless he took his coffee and went to sit beside him on the window seat with as good a grace as he could muster.

"What is it, Richard? Crossword puzzle clue?" Richard liked doing crosswords of the more basic synonym kind; he was quite good at these and only stumped when he came across something literary.

"No, it's about next week's guest night. I notice you're coming on your own and Samson's bringing these people, whose name looks familiar." Richard pointed to the entry reading – 'Mrs and Miss Marjoribanks.' He now knew it was pronounced 'Marshbanks' but was unwilling to say it.

"Oh yes," Robert replied. "Samson asked me to come in and help look after his guests. It seems he's related to them in some way, rather distantly."

"I seem to know the name." Richard was fishing for more information without actually asking for it, which indicated a degree of subtlety unusual for him; none the less his purpose was obvious – obvious enough for Robert to be annoyed at his beating about the bush and to be determined *not* to mention the local papers or the Oxford Pot. He found Richard's typical guffaws over the subject distasteful.

"Perhaps you should come in yourself," he said rather acidly, "then you can find out for a fact who was telling you the truth about the way to pronounce it."

Regarding this as a parting shot Robert left Richard Holdsworth, who almost immediately grabbed *The Sun* just as its previous reader was putting it down, and went over to Nigel Nethercott, who was sitting by himself on a sofa. "Now Nigel," he began, "you simply must tell me more about this wedding of yours. It's not as if I know your family, and I've never yet set eyes on your fiancée. You've got to tell me how many people are going to be there, what sort of age group and so on."

Nigel looked gloomy. "I don't know a lot about it myself," he said. "Effie's mother's seeing to everything. There'll be far more people from her side than from mine."

"Will your two previous wives be there?" asked Robert blandly. 'I'm in good form today,' he smirked inwardly to himself. 'I don't usually let myself go to this extent when I'm annoyed with my colleagues.' Nigel looked nearly as discomfited as Robert had hoped he would.

"I – er – no; I haven't put them on my guest list – I think as things are, I mean it's not as if Effie's been married before; I think her mother – her parents – well they'd probably, well certainly, prefer their guests not to know" – Nigel trailed into silence.

"So you'd rather I didn't mention them in the speech?"

"Good God, no! I mean you mustn't! You weren't intending to, were you?"

"Well if they were to be there I'd thought some small gesture in their direction might not be inappropriate; you know, something about the friendliness and cordiality between you all showing how you must have already proved yourself to be a very pleasant husband on many occasions. After all, I believe it's the custom to display my knowledge of you in your past life, and I didn't know you before you were married."

Nigel had begun to hope that Robert might be teasing him, but he looked perfectly serious, and what he said about the length of their acquaintance was perfectly true. Nigel was, on the whole, a literal minded man and the subtlety and irony of Robert's sense of humour was quite alien to him.

"Oh hell!" he said.

"Never mind," Robert responded kindly, "I don't suppose it's too late to do something about it. You could give me a CV of your life up to marriage, complete with quaint sayings and childhood aspirations. Perhaps I should meet your parents and talk to them about you?" Nigel was not too sure about that; his relationship with his parents had soured somewhat after his second divorce. He said as much to Robert.

"Well, yes, I can understand that," Robert responded with every appearance of sympathy. "Your mother in particular may well be of the opinion that to lose one wife might be considered a misfortune, but to lose *two* looks very *decidedly* like carelessness!" Nigel had a vague idea that Robert might be quoting something, but Eng. Lit. dons were always quoting, as were their Modern Languages colleagues. Classicists were even worse. Of course he could get the gist of what the Eng. Lit. people were saying, though he was aware of there being an extra dimension of meaning behind the words. He smiled rather uncertainly: "That's true, I'm afraid," he admitted.

"What about your student days? That's the sort of thing that gives a best man some excellent ammunition." Nigel sighed. He'd in fact been an exemplary student, up for breakfast every morning, working solidly in the library all day, perusing his Geography books and writing his essays. His evening companions had always been girlfriends; girlfriends who had in fact discarded him because of his dullness, until he met Ellen, who never looked at or for anybody else and to whom he'd become engaged in the middle of his second year.

"I seemed to spend a lot of time with girls," said Nigel.

"That I can imagine. But you must have known *some* chaps!"

"Well there were Jack and Scott. Scott was going out with Ellen's best friend Margo, and we often went out all four together. They got married soon after we did and he was my best man then and I was his. But when we split up of course they took Ellen's side and I haven't really seen them since."

"What about Jack?"

"Well he was my second best man."

"Couldn't you ask him again?" Robert sighted a very minute grain of hope.

"Hardly! He met up with Scott and Margo and Ellen again shortly afterwards and he and Ellen got married two years ago." So that scuppers that! said Robert to himself. "What a pity," he said aloud, "that you're so against inviting them to this wedding. You could have made headlines in the Oxford Mail at least - 'Bridegroom's first wife's present husband is best man at third wedding!' You could become a great modern example of how to maintain amicable relations after divorce. Why don't you write a book about it? I'm sure it would sell awfully well these days."

"If this is your idea of a joke, Robert, I don't appreciate your sense of humour," Nigel responded stiffly.

"I'm sorry Nigel, I got carried away. 'He jests at scars who never felt a wound.'"

'Another bloody quotation,' thought Nigel. 'I expect his speech'll be full of them. Better than some other things he could say, though, and I can't imagine Effie's family understanding the quotes.'

"But I'm serious, in a way," Robert was continuing. "After all, think how fortunate you are to have had three women all consenting to marry you. Some of us haven't had any."

"That's a point!" Nigel's expression came near to assuming its normal smugness, which had conspicuously deserted it during the previous conversation. "Quite a lot of women have wanted to marry me, in fact enough to be a nuisance at times. It was only after I was married to Ellen, when I began to – well – *notice* other women; then they began to notice me and that's how it's gone on really." Nigel paused, looked at Robert as if he'd never quite taken him in before, sank his voice and said, "You're not a" (whispered) "*closet gay* are you Robert?" Robert shook his head. He'd been asked that before. There was no point in resenting it, not these days.

"No, no. I'm totally hetero. I've had relationships with women. I was even engaged once."

"Oh? What happened?"

" I got cold feet."

"Why?"

"I wish I knew. But it's a while ago now. Not something I'd like to go through again, though. I'll need to be very sure before I ever propose to anybody else. But I see you're coming to next week's Guest Night. Who're you bringing?"

Nigel looked a little apprehensive. "I'm afraid it's my future mother-in-law," he admitted. "Pressure," he added succinctly.

"But that's *excellent*!" Robert exclaimed. "Ask for her to be beside me at dinner or dessert and I can find out all about the wedding!"

8

"I'm beginning to wish I hadn't said I'd go to this dinner," Melissa mused aloud over the noise of the sewing machine on which she was running up yet another pair of pantalettes. "I don't think Oxford intellectuals are quite my cup of tea."

"Well, I don't want to go on my own," Cassandra replied, "and he actually seems very nice, our distant kinsman. It's you he's asked particularly; I'm just an extra. You can always talk about the family."

"It might be interesting finding out more about the Southeys and the Egertons, I suppose. But I can't spend the whole evening talking family to Samson Southey, and I haven't had a privileged university education like you."

"Well hardly any women of your generation have, have they? Unless they come from very academic families."

"Or unless," said Melissa over another long whirr of the machine, "they were considered too plain to marry and either they or their parents decided they'd need a career. In my youth the sort of girls who went to universities looked like old maids by the time they left school. All that education put them right outside the marriage market. Speaking of which, I wonder how dressy it is. I've still got a few decent things I bought before the cheques began to bounce."

"Wear one of the dresses," Cassandra advised. "That very plain, very elegant black with just a small diamond brooch. You haven't sold any of them, have you?"

"Certainly not. I brought them all away with me. They weren't part of your father's assets. Anyway, what're you going to wear?"

"Oh, you know." Cassandra gave a shrug. "Something ethnic with flowers in my hair. I haven't got anything else. Between us we'll probably be sufficiently over and under dressed to strike a balance. Don't worry. It may be rather ghastly but at least it's a free meal."

"Apart from the petrol to get there and back," Melissa countered gloomily, "I hope you're going to drive home."

"Of course I am, Mummy. You know I drink far less than you do."

***

Cassandra's car bore her and her mother to Chester College without any reluctance other than that evinced by the emission of menacing black clouds from the exhaust. Samson Southey duly met them at the lodge; fortunately he could be relied on not to see the car at all. He took them over to the Senior Common Room where hosts and guests assembled for drinks before dinner. Most noticeable among the guests was a small, slightly tubby woman standing next to Nigel Nethercott. Cassandra and Melissa looked at her, looked away and looked at each other.

"I see Mr Flashy-Sports-Car with a companion to match," Cassandra whispered to her mother.

Samson saw to their drinks, proffered from a tray held by a waiting maid in black and white, and then steered them in Nigel's direction. He was amused at the contrast between Nigel's guest and Melissa, who must be about the same age. "Ah, Nigel!" he exclaimed. "Let me introduce my guests, Mrs and Miss Marjoribanks – the latter of whom you know, of course, as we all saw her at her pottery last week." Nigel's companion gave him a sharp look; his responding smile was a little forced.

"Yes of course – pottery – things for the house," he murmured by way of explanation. "Let me introduce my guest, Mrs Fraser."

"Norah Fraser," the short lady announced with a smile full of teeth. "I'm his mother-in-law-to-be. Pleased to meet you."

"My colleague Samson Southey and Mrs and Miss Marjoribanks."

"How do you do," murmured Samson and his guests to another 'pleased to meet you' from Mrs Fraser who immediately went on to complain to Nigel: "Here's your colleague with *two* guests, a mother and daughter! Now why couldn't you ask Effie too?"

"It's just not done to ask wives, partners, husbands, fiancées," said Nigel in a tone that implied patient reiteration of a point made before. "Is it Samson?"

"Oh, certainly not," replied Samson reassuringly.

Mrs Fraser looked Samson up and down, uncertain what to make of him. His voice sounded as if it belonged to somebody *smart,* she reflected, but then his clothes looked really scruffy. She herself was wearing a short black dress whose background colour was at least two thirds covered by swathes of gold and silver sequins. Melissa endeavoured to converse. "So you've also got a nubile daughter," she said graciously.

"I don't know what you mean by 'nubile'," said Mrs Fraser suspiciously as if she found the word offensive.

"Oh – of marriageable age, I mean," Melissa went on without so much as a blink at her own insincerity, "one would hardly think so." Mrs Norah Fraser beamed contentedly and patted her red-into-auburn hair in confirmation of her youthfulness. Dyed, of course, thought Melissa and mentally regarded her own brown-slightly-silvering-into-blonde head with satisfaction.

"Oh yes, our Effie, who's engaged to Nigel. Yes. People take us for sisters sometimes. Your daughter's very like you, isn't she? I mean the same bony face, though she looks so much younger of course."

"Of course," Melissa echoed, as gracefully as if she'd been paid a compliment. Nigel, painfully aware of Norah's rudeness, felt he should make amends but was somewhat awed by Melissa's classy accent and elegance and instead looked helplessly at Samson as if seeking aid. Samson realised that Melissa would never be anything but amused by a woman like Norah Fraser and forbore to intervene. Nigel was relieved when Robert Taylor appeared. At a glance he took in Norah's sequins and Nigel's discomfiture and decided, once greetings and introductions were effected, to compensate somewhat for his former nastiness.

"Oh Mrs Fraser!" he exclaimed. "I'm very happy to be able to talk to you. I want you to tell me all about the wedding plans and help me to be the *best* best man!" Oh dear, he thought immediately. I hope she doesn't think I meant the best of the three! Really, the more I try not to say the wrong thing the more I manage to do it. He needn't have worried. Norah Fraser was not well attuned to subtleties and had anyway decided on seeing and hearing him that if he was not exactly *very* smart he was more presentable than Samson Southey and might look quite smart enough once they got him into the right clothes.

"It's morning dress, of course," she said as she thought of this: "all the bridal party's wearing morning dress, well and the guests too I hope."

"Oh, of *course*," replied Robert, as if he'd never imagined anything different. "And your daughter's having a long white dress and a veil and so on?"

"Oh yes naturally. The dress is ordered already: *very* expensive material and a *top* dress salon. Well of course an Oxford college is quite a smart venue, isn't it? Though I sometimes think we'd have rather had a *really* smart *hotel*,

like Hartwell House or the Manoir o Cat Seasons…."
Dinner was announced and Robert, who was to sit beside Norah, helped Nigel to shepherd her into her place at the dining table as quietly as possible. He had no anxiety about a dearth of conversation but was rather in doubt that there would be enough pauses to enable him to ask pertinent questions or receive any really relevant answers.

"Why aren't we sitting down?" Norah Fraser enquired. Are we waiting for somebody important?"

"For the Principal to say grace," Robert replied.

"Oh really? I haven't heard of anybody doing that for years. Of course we used to say it when I was a child, well my grandparents did, but I thought it had gone right out by now." Norah was puzzled. Her memories of saying grace were to do with old-fashioned people who were chapel rather than church, very unsmart people. The Principal made a bang with the gavel and said "Benedictus benedicato" to the immediate response of a scraping of chairs as everybody sat down. "Was that Latin?" Norah asked.

"Yes," Robert replied. "Still used for grace in most colleges – all the ones I know, in fact."

"Oh! Catholic!" said Norah.

"Well originally perhaps, though all the post-Reformation colleges, even the newest, use Latin. Traditional, I suppose, would be nearer the truth."

"Well I suppose that's all right then." Norah had been about to say that a grace in Latin might reasonably be considered quite smart, as long as it wasn't Catholic, but for once she hesitated to use her favourite adjective.

Nigel turned his attention to her. "I hope the college comes up to your expectations," he said.

"Well really, Nigel – oh, is this the starter, thank you – I mean I thought I'd see really *smart* people in a college, and there's nobody here I'd call *really* smart, except just that lady, Mrs Marsh, is it, the one with the daughter in those cotton clothes with the flowers in her hair – I mean she's not smart of course – and Mrs Marsh is wearing a very *plain* dress, but it is quite smart and do you think that brooch is real diamonds?"

"I hadn't noticed," Nigel replied untruthfully, "but I'm sure she can hear you, she's only on my other side."

"Oh no, she's busy talking to that thin young man. Did you say his name was Samson? Tee-hee-hee!"

Nigel was aware, with embarrassment, that Samson, across from him, was able to take in every word of this conversation though conversing with Melissa at the same time. Uncoordinated-looking Samson might be, but his brain-power was formidable. "Do tell Robert more about the wedding," Nigel urged, "he's so keen to discuss it with you." Norah turned to engage Robert's attention and, greatly relieved, Nigel turned to Melissa at the end of the table, as she and Samson paused in their conversation to take a sip of wine.

Nigel had some difficulty in reconciling his vision of Melissa as the lady of the Oxford Pot with her open-market earthiness that would have shocked his mother, and this elegant person he instinctively regarded as 'classy'. To his mind classiness and earthiness belonged to opposite extremes. He found himself unable to think of anything to say to her. Melissa, however, turned a gracious smile on him and said, "Now you're the young man with the very beautiful silver-grey sports car, aren't you? I saw you at our house last week."

"Did you? I didn't see you."

"No, I was inside the house, but I could see out, of course. Cassandra tells me you're quite a connoisseur of her work; in fact I also saw you buying a good deal of it in the market. It's not everybody's taste, of course. People have to *know* about pottery to understand it and appreciate it properly, but I can see that *you* do."

"Oh I know…." Nigel checked himself. His usual 'I know what I like' seemed inadequate. He improved on it. "I know something beautiful when I see it." Melissa knew this was no doubt truer of his appreciation of Cassandra than of her artefacts, but as long as it resulted in his buying large quantities of the latter the distinction was immaterial and the sentiment to be encouraged.

"Those large bowls," she murmured, "though perhaps I shouldn't praise my daughter's work, are exceptionally fine. I know they're expensive, but they have such depth, such *impact.*" Nigel wasn't sure what she meant by 'impact', except that it could have little to do with the usual sense of the word.

"Yes, *indeed,*" he agreed fervently. "In fact Robert Taylor, my best man, has bought us one as a wedding present." Blast, thought Melissa. He won't buy one himself now. Oh well, perhaps he'll know how to praise it to other people and spread the word about its beauty and desirability.

"I'm sure your visitors will envy your possession of it," she said, "and it's not only ornamental but useful. But of course you already know all this; tell me about your*self.*" This was a theme well suited to Nigel's taste and he found Melissa a most interested listener who appeared to regard his teaching and writings on aspects of Geography as the most fascinating occupation she'd ever heard of. He even found himself telling her of his worthy though uneducated parents and their delight on his getting into Oxford. Melissa was hoping he might get on to his marriages but before that could happen the gavel struck again, everybody rose for the final grace and guests were instructed to bring their napkins with them and proceed to the dessert room. Nigel was almost startled to be addressed by Norah, of whose existence he had been mercifully unaware while he was involved in the heady pleasure of talking to Melissa about himself.

"What's all this about, Nigel?" Norah was asking. "Why have we got to take our serviettes? We've already had dessert."

As it was necessary to explain this to almost every guest unfamiliar with the dining rites of Oxbridge Colleges Nigel managed, with less suppressed impatience than he generally felt in answering Norah's questions, to tell her that 'dessert' was not, in fact, another name for pudding.

"*Pudding*?" Norah interrupted. "Oh, sweet, you mean. We never call it *pudding*."

"Well – either, but anyway – ." Nigel was thrown out of the rhythm of his practised explanation. "Dessert means fruit and nuts and chocolates and so on, and we have it with port or Madeira, and you must always pass the port to the left.

"Gracious *me*!" was Norah's response. Samson Southey, behind them, smiled with delicate amusement at what he considered a singularly inappropriate application of the word 'gracious'.

9

At dessert Robert Taylor was placed between Melissa and Cassandra, and as Melissa was early and inescapably engaged in conversation by an elderly professor on her left Robert was free to devote some time to Cassandra.

"I know you're a potter," he said, "that you live in a wonderful Queen Anne house and that you're fast becoming an Oxford phenomenon yourself, quite apart from your products."

"Oh if there's any truth in that," Cassandra replied, "it's my mother who's the phenomenon. I was quietly potting in Devon, barely making ends meet and living in a cold flat above a grocery shop when my mother came to live with me and things seem to have been happening ever since."

"Such as?"

"Inheriting the house is the main one of course."

"Were you brought up in Devon?"

"Oh no. My father was in business, well – businesses – and we lived mainly in Tours, but we had flats in Paris and London. I was educated in England."

"Oh, where?"

"St Mary's Ascot. You probably haven't heard of it."

"Indeed I have. We have entrance candidates from schools all over England and beyond, and St Mary's Ascot is well known to be a good one. It's Roman Catholic, isn't it?"

"Yes. My mother was brought up a Catholic herself but she lapsed when she married my father, who was divorced. Like many Catholics who've deprived themselves of their faith for one reason or another she didn't want her child to be deprived of it too."

"You're her only child, then?"

"I've got two half-brothers, both much older than I am and one's in America and the other in New Zealand. They were brought up by their mother and I hardly know them. But my father apparently said three children were quite enough for him and he was too old to cope with being kept awake at night by another one."

"Is your father still alive?"

"Well…." Cassandra paused wondering how much to say and finally ventured, "He seems to have disappeared."

"How long ago?" Robert was intrigued.

"Just over a year now."

"Where was he last seen?"

"In Tours. Just after…." Cassandra stopped.

"After?" Robert prompted with interest.

"Oh, it's unimportant."

"There have been missing person searches and all that, I suppose."

"He was reported missing, of course, but to be honest Mummy's none too keen to find him. She says if he's still alive and hears that she's inherited Huntsfield House he'll come and find *us* soon enough."

"Really! So he may be alive. I suppose….Oh, do forgive me. It's none of my business but one hears of these things happening and only half believes them. I've never before actually met anybody who's lost a close relative - in such a way, that is. I find it fascinating."

"Oh please don't apologise. He was always a rather remote figure in my childhood. Even when I was at home and not at a boarding school he was hardly there; he was either away on business or working very late. I don't exactly miss him. Do tell me what it is that you 'suppose'!"

"Oh, just that things like withdrawals from his bank account after his disappearance were checked - I believe that's part of the procedure."

"Possibly. But in fact there can't have been any withdrawals from his bank account because there was nothing in it; he'd gone bankrupt. That's one reason why my mother's so angry with him; she knew absolutely nothing about it until her cheques began to bounce. When she found out the reason there was a terrible row and he walked out of the house and never came back. So she packed up everything of her own she could possibly manage to carry and came to stay with me. She even had to borrow the money for the fare from a sympathetic friend. It was the same friend who told her soon afterwards that my father had totally disappeared. We've heard absolutely nothing about him since."

Nigel was flanked at the dessert table by a female colleague on either side, each of whom was also adjacent to somebody else's male guest. Nigel had always had very much less success with female colleagues than with the wives of his male ones, probably because they'd seen him in action for too long and knew him too well. Younger women dons joining the SCR were always warned about him, albeit in a jocular fashion which made clear that where women were concerned he was something of a college clown, only to be taken as a joke. A better deterrent could not have been devised. As one senior fellow, an ex-nun turned Professor of Theology, put it: "The devil, that proud spirit…Satan cannot bear to be mocked." The French fellow on his left, Dr Muriel Thwaites, turned from conversation with the gentleman on *her* left to say, "Nigel, I've been asked the identity of the 'elegant lady in black with the wonderfully understated diamonds' and as you always know all about women I'm sure you can tell us."

Nigel beamed with the double satisfaction of being paid what he considered a compliment and of in fact knowing the answer.

"It's a Mrs Marjoribanks," he said immediately, " she and her daughter have two claims to local fame: one in being the owners by inheritance of Huntsfield House, a listed Queen Anne building set in Capability Brown grounds, and the other in being the purveyors of the so-called Oxford Phenomenon. You must have seen the write-ups about them in the Oxford Mail."

"Oh, I never read the local papers," said Dr Thwaites. "Do tell Dr Kissinger here about it; he's dying to know."

"Thank you, I heard." Dr Kissinger's South African accent was clearly audible across Dr Thwaites. "What's this Oxford Phenomenon then?"

"Well, it's not quite formal dinner conversation," Nigel replied. He found himself somehow unwilling to associate the Melissa he'd been talking to over dinner with the graphically advertised Pot in the open market. Besides, his mother had always been very strict about the kind of things that should not be talked about 'in company'.

"Oh the Oxford Pot!" Dr Thwaites exclaimed. "That I do remember, though more from hearing it talked about in Common Room than from the papers. It's a bourdaloue, of course. I'm in fact rather interested to know whether they'll be able to patent it as of course it's not their own invention. But I suppose patents hardly existed in the eighteenth and early nineteenth centuries when the objects were popular, mainly in France of course."

Dr Kissinger was intrigued to know more and Nigel felt that a French name made the thing sound a lot more respectable. Nevertheless he was relieved when Dr Thwaites took over the explaining.

"It's named after a Jesuit priest, Pere Bourdaloue, who preached such long and popular sermons that the ladies who attended them – they were very fashionable – didn't want to miss anything by going out to answer calls of nature and therefore took these pots into the church with them and used them there. The French were always very sensible and down to earth about such things."

"Whatever does it look like, this Pot?" asked Dr Kissinger.

"Like a very large gravy boat. I'm always hoping for the day when I go out to dinner and the hostess has one on the table. It would be so tempting to point out its original use."

"Now that would really make a dinner party go with a swing!" Dr Kissinger laughed. "I can think of dinner parties that could have done with something like that. But am I going to get a chance to meet this interesting lady?"

"Nigel! Will you introduce Dr Kissinger to Mrs Marjoribanks if they stay for coffee and drinks after this? He can't wait to meet her."

"Oh certainly. Delighted." Nigel beamed, conscious that it would give him a reason to speak to Melissa again himself.

"And who," Dr Kissinger was asking further, "is that *incredible* woman with the dyed red hair and the sequins?" Nigel heard the question but not the answer as Dr Thwaites, who knew it was his almost mother-in-law, replied in the lowest possible tones, no doubt accompanied by a grimace of warning as Dr Kissinger was then heard to say, "Oops! Sorry!" and "I'd better stop asking about people."

On his right, Dr Bowker, Medicine, said, "I couldn't help listening to that fascinating conversation Nigel, especially as it happens that the gentleman on my right has just been asking about the young woman with the flowers in her hair. I gather she's the daughter: there's such a similarity in the bone structure. Both very beautiful, aren't they? Samson Southey's guests, I think. Surprising!"

"Oh, not really," Nigel informed her, "I gather he's distantly related."

"That accounts for it then. He usually brings in the most donnish of dons, especially if they're female. You're going to be busy over coffee. *My* neighbour here wants to be introduced to the daughter. I hope Samson doesn't bring them in too often. The rest of us can't compete!"

The port having been round three times and the other rituals of dessert completed the company trooped downstairs again towards the Senior Common Room, many with what the euphemistic called 'comfort stops' on the way. As she stood in the inevitable queue for the women's lavatories Dr Thwaites was heard to say: "Now if only I had a bourdaloue I could leave this queue, nip into the bathroom next door, use the capacious vessel and empty it into the basin!" Few of the others in the queue had any idea what she was talking about, but the older History Fellow, who did, remarked to nobody in particular that French was not such a refined language as we are often led to believe and too much use of it could increase a tendency to vulgarity. "German, of course," she added, "is worse."

As the gathering reassembled in the SCR Melissa and Cassandra found themselves the centre of attention. Several glasses of wine at dinner and several more glasses of madeira or port at dessert had overcome a good many inhibitions and male members of the company who had carefully kept their distance at the beginning of the evening were asking Samson or Nigel to introduce them, or unashamedly introducing themselves. Robert Taylor stood his ground by Cassandra's side as well as he could but was hardly able to speak to her. Nigel found himself impeded by Norah Fraser, who was not unreasonably claiming his attention. He could hardly introduce Melissa without introducing Norah too, and he found himself increasingly loath to acknowledge her as his prospective mother-in-law. He'd begun by thinking that it would be infinitely preferable to have a mother-in-law like Melissa, but was gradually coming to consider that in such a capacity Melissa might be rather wasted. She was, he couldn't help feeling, an undeniably attractive woman in her own right. At a demand from Norah to go and look at the drinks trolley, however, he reluctantly relinquished his place and reconciled himself to this necessity by pouring an unaccustomed double brandy in addition to Norah's large whisky and drinking it with some relish.

Having met and briefly conversed with almost every man in the room Melissa decided that an early exit was a strategically sound ploy and told Samson they *really* ought to go, as they had to be at the market early in the morning. She and Cassandra said their gracious goodbyes to a chorus of "Oh you're not going - *yet*!" "You're surely not going so *soon* " etc and departed. Robert Taylor paused only to become conscious of a sense of flatness and loss over the whole room and then left abruptly himself. As Samson's helping host, he decided, he had every right to accompany his guests to their car. He was in time to help Cassandra on with her coat in the entrance hall.

***

As Cassandra drove home – the car had mercifully started without protest – her mother remarked happily: "I think they all realise we'll be in the market tomorrow morning."

"*Honestly* Mummy! I don't believe you do anything or speak to anybody without an ulterior motive!"

"Darling," Melissa replied contentedly, "at my age one has learnt the value of economy of effort."

"Well I hope you'll find it worthwhile to have chatted up Mr Flashy-Sports-Car the way you did. I could hardly believe my eyes and ears. Nobody would have thought you considered it too late to lead him on yourself, as you told me."

"I'd hardly expected to be given such an opportunity," Melissa murmured through a yawn. "You've refused to do it and it was really all too easy. I only had to get him to talk about himself. You seemed to be getting on well with his colleague, what's his name – Taylor. Is he nice?"

"I rather think he might be," Cassandra spoke thoughtfully, "and very unusually he seemed to get me to talk about *my*self."

"Yes." Melissa yawned again. She'd found the wine at dinner enlivening at the time but now it was beginning to make her feel drowsy. "I gather you told him all about your father."

"Well I'm afraid I did. It just seemed to come out in answer to his questions. He gave the impression of being terribly interested. I hope you don't mind."

"Not in the slightest! I don't care who knows about the rotten old sod. All your potters in Devon knew, didn't they?"

"They did, but they never seemed to think it particularly interesting, or even strange."

"Well darling, they do rather come from the sort of background where things like that happen all the time. The odd parent coming or going is nothing very remarkable; some of them have probably done a bit of disappearing themselves. I don't think I met a soul in that place who'd been born and brought up there: they're not the sort of people to have *roots.*"

“I suppose you mean they’re all way out and unconventional and not at all respectable.”

“Oh darling! Only very middle class people are respectable.I’d *hate* to be considered *respectable.”*

“I think Robert Taylor is.”

“Of course. That’s why he finds you so fascinating.”

“Thank you, Mummy. I’m sure that’s the only reason – if he does.”

“Oh, don’t be silly, darling. Of course he does. And a little mystery in the background won’t do you – or me – any harm at all.”

10

Samson Southey surveyed the lunchtime buffet at Chester College anxiously as he tried to decide what to eat. Not soup, he decided. Soup had a habit of spilling. Not spaghetti Bolognese: too difficult to manage. Vegetarian? Oh dear. Spanish omelette, very boring looking Spanish omelette. Vegetables? *No* hot vegetables. Sighing he took a large slice of the omelette and went on to the various salads in the cold section. Lunch was always bad on a Thursday, the kitchen staff having exhausted itself on Wednesday's guest night. He sat down hoping that the company might compensate for the deficiencies of the food. Dr Thwaites came and sat beside him. This, he decided, was at least a change.

"Hullo Muriel," he greeted her as if surprised.

"Samson!" she responded. "You *are* a dark horse. Who would have thought you'd have a couple of women like those up your sleeve."

"Horses," responded Samson calmly, "do not wear sleeves."

"Oh really! What's a mixed metaphor or two. You know perfectly well what I mean."

"I do. You mean that a tediously donnish unattractive man like me is not usually to be seen in the company of beautiful women."

"Oh you are being difficult. I don't mean that at all! I'm merely trying to compliment you on your guests without being too obvious about it. Moreover, I was about to tell you that as I'd been in the Taylorian this morning I took the opportunity to go into the market and see your ladies of the bourdaloue in action."

"And were you impressed?"

"Very. Madame looked almost as elegant as she did last night in a simple black cotton shirt and trousers, and Mademoiselle looked equally enchanting."

"They're not actually French, you know."

"I realise that, but there is a rather continental air about them, and French seems to go with the bourdaloue. How clever of them to market it as a new phenomenon."

"Indeed. Very few people apart from antique dealers and their more knowledgeable customers are likely to know of its origins and earlier use. Did they have many customers?"

"They certainly did. I was amused to see several of last night's dinner attenders there. That Dr Kissinger I was next to at dessert was well to the fore and bought armfuls of stuff. And do you know I think I saw one of the college porters in the throng, though he wasn't buying anything. But they were hardly keeping pace with the selling and the wrapping when I came away."

"You didn't buy anything yourself, then?"

"No. There were too many people. But I did take a card and may treat myself to a drive into the countryside to see them in their proper setting. There's something very intriguing about the whole set-up."

***

Melissa and Cassandra returned home in an empty car having sold out of everything, including Melissa's pile of pantalettes.

"It's wonderful what competition will do," Melissa observed. "Once people start competing to buy things everybody else decides they must be desperately worth having and joins in. So you simply must have an assistant. You can't possibly go on supplying such a demand yourself."

"It's probably only a nine days' wonder," said Cassandra cautiously, "I can't believe it's going to last."

"If it lasts long enough for us to make enough money to start on the flats upstairs that's the main thing. However I have a little plan as regards that: we might just be able to get some help. We haven't even opened this morning's post yet and there could be some messages on the answer-phone. Let's sit over them with a well-deserved glass of wine."

Cassandra picked up the assorted mail as they went in. There was rather a lot of it. Melissa spread it on the table and picked out a superior-looking envelope with a handwritten address and an Oxford postmark. "New I wonder….." she said. "But let's get the wine first."

"It's a bit early," said Cassandra doubtfully. "I'll think I'll have some tea."

"You're so English, darling. I can't think how you manage it."

"*Camomile* tea," said Cassandra.

"Oh well. Much better for you. Too late for me."

"To have tea?"

"To have things that are good for me. Now this letter….." Melissa opened it with a hallmarked silver meat-skewer, property of the house. "Do you know these three hall marks mean George II? Probably worth a bit. What a pity we can't sell it. Ahhh!" She scanned the letter rapidly. "Quite promising!" She read it again and then handed it to her daughter, who read, "'Dear Mrs Marjoribanks, I must confess myself quite intrigued to receive your letter'…..Who on earth…..?"

She turned the page over to see the signature. 'Felix Marjoribanks' How did you know about him?"

"I didn't. I looked up 'Marjoribanks' in the telephone book and wrote saying he might be a kinsman of my husband's."

"Well he certainly seems to think so. He goes into all this 'second cousin once removed' business in some detail. Is it possible?"

"Extremely likely. It's a very unusual name. All the Marjoribankses must be related somehow or other. I never knew your father's family; he was so much older than I was, his mother was already dead and he didn't seem to be on good terms with his father, and of course we had an almost runaway wedding in a registry office because my parents didn't approve and he didn't care about such things – but I've told you all that before. The point is, we weren't very family orientated."

"It sounds as if this Felix Marjoribanks is. Apart from all the 'cousin' details he's keen to meet us: 'I saw the article about you and your daughter in the local paper and it crossed my mind then that we might be related, if only by marriage. I had been intending to enquire further and am therefore particularly gratified to receive your communication and hope we shall be able to meet in the near future' – he sounds a bit pompous."

"Well, I suppose he's being formal. I wrote in a very formal and restrained style. He hasn't actually invited us to go and see him; I'd better invite him here for drinks. He doesn't mention a wife – but then some men don't. There was a business friend of your father's who wrote all the letters and answered invitations to stay and so on and he always wrote 'I' – 'I'll be arriving at six on Friday, I'll be happy to stay until Monday' and never mentioned his wife with so much as a 'we'! I know he was Eastern European, but that's really no excuse."

"And did his wife in fact come too?"

"She did indeed, and it quite threw us the first time it happened. It was just as well the spare room had a double bed. Even so, one makes that little bit more effort when there's a woman coming and I had to sneak in another set of towels before showing them the room"

"You didn't tell me anything about writing to this Felix Marjoribanks, married or not."

"It was such a long shot. He was F.G.C. in the telephone book. He lives in a large house in the very best part of Oxford."

"How do you know? I mean of course you know the address, but how do you know it's the best part of Oxford?"

"Well we used to have *Country Life* sent over to Tours. I remember one house advertised in that central north Oxford area as 'only 41 miles from Eton'. It struck me as very funny. But it's quite *nationally* well known that the bigger houses there are selling for three million or more. So when I was in Oxford shopping one day I drove past it to have a look, and it is one of the bigger detached houses."

"Is it on the main road?"

"No, just down a wide side road. I only had to make a *tiny* detour."

Cassandra eyed her mother thoughtfully. "Is there," she asked, "such a word as 'ulteriority'?"

"No, I don't think so. In fact I'm sure there isn't."

"Well there should be. If there's 'superiority' there should be 'ulteriority'. Anyway I'm going to use it: I can't think of a better word to sum you up!"

"Darling!" Melissa purred. "You flatter me."

The rest of the post revealed little of interest and much that was fit for nothing other then the recycling bin. "No replies to the advertisement for a potter's assistant, so far," said Cassandra, with some relief. She didn't quite share her mother's confidence in being able to pay one.

"They're probably more likely to telephone – from their own mobile!" said Melissa knowledgeably. "We haven't checked the voicemail yet."

"I'll do it," Cassandra laughed a little. "You are getting with it, Mummy: 'checked the voicemail' indeed! Anyway, listen. First message; oh – they haven't bothered to speak. Second message-----" The machine poured a young male voice into the room. "Hi!" it said, "I seen the advert in the paper for a potter's assistant. I done ceramics at school and I'm sixteen – just – and I want a job in the 'olidays. Ring Pete on ….." Then followed an indecipherable number. "Blast!" said Cassandra, "I couldn't make that out at all."

"Never mind, darling. Press the 'stop' button. Right. Now press the button over 'caller ID'. Good. Now wait till it says 'Press Start Key'.

"It's on the screen now. OK. Start." Cassandra pressed the button. The machine obligingly disgorged a slip of paper with dates, times and telephone numbers printed on it.

"How on earth did you know it does all this, Mummy?" Cassandra asked almost accusingly.

"Oh" - said Melissa vaguely – "well partly because the young man in the shop was so keen on showing me and partly because I read the book that came with it, well some of it. It's rather a thick book. But I knew you didn't approve of my buying it so it was up to me to make good use of it. Let me see the ID log. Now if we listen to the messages with this in front of us we'll be able to see which number's which – including the number of anybody who didn't bother speaking. Press Play again." Pete's message seemed clear enough when his number could be seen as well as heard. "Now do ring him back, darling, it's worth a try," Melissa urged.

But Cassandra was listening for more messages. "There are all these calls with no numbers," she said. "The ones where it just says 'withheld.'"

"Nothing to be done about those, I'm afraid," Melissa shrugged. "They'll ring again if they're important. No point in worrying over something we can do nothing about. Would you like me to ring Pete?"

"No, of course not." Cassandra dialled the number and Pete responded promptly. Yes, he was interested in the job and he would like to come for an interview.

"How are you going to get here?"

"On me motorbike, Miss. Well, it's a moped really, but it looks like a motorbike. I got it for me sixteenth birthday."

"Do you know where to find us? Where do you live?"

"In Kidlington, Miss; Garden City."

"Oh that's only about four miles away: we're between Wootton and Tackley."

"Yeah, all right Miss. I'll find it. Sounds big enough and I got a tongue in me 'ead. I'll come tomorrow morning. OK?"

Cassandra said it was, said good-bye and put the receiver down deciding that she liked the sound of Pete and actually hoped he would turn up the next day.

11

A heavily revved moped announced Pete's arrival for his interview with Cassandra. Despite an over-abundance of earrings he was a not unprepossessing young man once the removal of his helmet revealed his features. Cassandra came out of the workshop to greet him.

"You're Pete, of course."

"Yes, Miss."

"Pete what?"

"Smith, Miss."

"Well come into the pottery workshop and let's see what you can do."

Clearly interested, Pete followed her willingly. "Warm in here, Miss," he remarked. "Got the kiln on?"

"Yes, I have, Pete. I've had it on a good deal lately. I've been trying to keep up production because I've sold so much, and of course the more the kiln's on the better everything dries ready for the next firing."

"That's right, Miss," said Pete approvingly. "Do you want me to show you how I can throw something?"

"I certainly do, Pete. Just start with anything you please and we'll see how you get on, then you could try and do an Oxford Pot – I'll be wanting you to do those especially."

Pete sat at the wheel and proceeded to work on a lump of wet clay as Cassandra watched him closely. In a matter of seconds a smooth symmetrical shape rose from the wheel. Maintaining the symmetry, Pete pressed his thumb into the centre and formed the inside shape. Cassandra was agreeably surprised and impressed.

"That's very good, Pete," she commented. "Just do another one, slightly different this time." She wanted to be sure it wasn't just a fluke. If he could keep up such a standard he looked like a natural. She watched with increasing interest and approval as he threw two more pieces.

"Can I try one of them special pots now, Miss?" he asked eagerly.

"Yes, I think you can, Pete. I'll do one and show you first." Cassandra sat at the wheel and produced a largish, round shape, then cut a leaf shape out of the base. She moulded it carefully into a sharpish almost boat shaped oval, made good the diminished gap in the base with some clay from the cut-out leaf shape, then freed the whole vessel from the wheel by passing a fine wire under its base. Pete watched with fascinated admiration.

That's really good, Miss," he said approvingly. "How many o' those can you make in an hour?"

"About ten when I'm going well," Cassandra replied.

"Right. Let me 'ave a go. But I reckon it'll take me a bit longer at first."

Pete's first attempt, if not quite perfect, was remarkably good and Cassandra was by now convinced that he was indeed a natural and would be a considerable asset to her workshop.

"You've got the makings of a very good potter, Pete," she told him, "the job's yours if you want it. But I must warn you I won't be able to pay very much at first."

"Thanks, Miss. I'd like to work for you. And I tell you wot, you got a big place here. Now if I was to stop here, nights like, then I wouldn't have to pay me mum and step-dad for me board and lodging. It's a bit crowded like at home with me step-brothers and all."

Cassandra was even more impressed: Pete showed shrewdness and sense as well as dexterity. Still, one mustn't be precipitate.

"That does sound like quite a good idea, Pete; but I think we'll have to have a week's trial first and see how we get on, and then talk more about you having a room here after that. We've got to think about your food as well, of course. We'll give you lunch, anyway."

"Lunch, Miss?" Pete sounded puzzled.

"Oh – er – you know, dinner – in the middle of the day."

"Oh, yeah, dinner. Right."

"And you'd be able to make your own pots in your spare time and fire them in the kiln and so on. You might like to make mugs for your family and things like that."

"Yeah, I really would, Miss. Thank you Miss."

"So if I give you £75 for the first week and then, say, £45 if you come and live here."

"Thanks Miss! I'd really like that Miss. That's really good. What time'll I come tomorrow?"

"Nine o'clock's early enough when you have to travel, though we'll start earlier if you're living here. But you must need something to drink before you go. What would you like?" Cassandra immediately recollected that they probably didn't have anything he'd like – she'd have to get in a supply of Coca-Cola. "Not that we've got very much," she added.

"Don't s'pose you got any coke, then?" asked Pete with doubtful hope.

"I'm afraid not – but I will get some for tomorrow."

"That's all right, Miss. I doesn't mind a cup of tea. Our mum always gives us kids tea – with lots of milk and sugar."

Pete was duly taken to the kitchen where Melissa was, unsurprisingly, running up pantalettes with the sewing machine whirring noisily. She greeted Pete cordially.

"I'm so glad you're coming to help my daughter," she told him after Cassandra's introduction and information, "it's been hard work for her on her own and I can see you're a good, strong young man."

"He's got the makings of a good potter, too," Cassandra added.

"Not as good as you, Miss. But I'll keep at it. You won't be sorry you've took me on. You'll see." He downed his sweet tea and a couple of biscuits and departed.

"I think you might be lucky there," Melissa observed as the moped roared out of the yard. "Even if he does cost us a fortune in milk and sugar!"

***

Melissa finished sewing the last of the pantalettes she'd cut out and wondered whether to buy some more material on spec. or to sell her newly made garments first. She decided to go to the workshop to seek Cassandra's advice. Always on the cautious side her daughter: no doubt she'd advocate selling first. The earliest garments produced had cost very little as they'd been made out of not-too-old sheets to give them an authentically antique look. By the time she reached the workshop Melissa had resolved to sleep on the pantalettes problem and make a decision about it tomorrow. Cassandra had enough to think about.

"What're you making, darling?" she called as she went in.

"Just a few more Oxford Pots to have in the pipeline, though if Pete comes tomorrow and gets in a bit of practice he should be good enough to do them himself next week. I'd actually forgotten that tomorrow's Saturday, but I hope he comes; it'll give the pots an extra couple of days to dry out, and it'll be good to have an extra day if I have to spend time finishing off his pots."

"Would you like to take a break and go and do the food shopping and post the letters – or would you rather I did it?"

"Oh could you? I'd like to keep going now and I've got some orders for big bowls that I want to see to."

"Have you written to Samson Southey to thank him for the dinner?"

"Oh no – I hadn't thought of it. 'Thank you letters' are not exactly customary among potters. Can't you do it for both of us? It was really you he invited."

"Well, if you like; but you must remember we've got a position to keep up now."

"Oh Mummy! How tiresome."

"Possibly. But I'm sure you'll find it's worth while. Anything you specially want from Kidlington?"

"Oh yes! Some Coca-Cola for Pete. You'd better get as many cans as you can carry. But I could get some more on Sunday on my way back from mass if you'd rather not buy so many. I wish you'd come with me."

"On Sunday?"

"Yes, to mass."

"Oh, darling I'm *terribly* out of practice."

"You don't really have to say anything if you don't want to, or do anything other than stand or sit and kneel when everybody else does."

"Yes, perhaps. But I married outside the church. I'm can't take communion."

"It might well be that you're *not* married now, and you certainly aren't living with your husband."

"Thank heaven for *that*, anyway. Do you know, I might just come with you if you go to the Oratory. Felix Marjoribanks must live in that parish. Of course I've no idea whether he's a Catholic, but there must be some people in that area who are and they might well be worth meeting."

"Mummy! Can't you even consider going to mass without an ulterior motive?"

"Mmmm..." Melissa pondered. "Look at it this way: you've told me a lot of people go there because the music's so good."

"Yes, but...."

"Why should it be worse," Melissa interrupted, "to go because the *people* are the right sort?"

"Because that's your only reason for going at all! And by the 'right sort' you mean posh people as opposed to good people."

"'Posh' is not a word I use; and the right sort of people are not necessarily incapable of being 'good'. Anyway, darling, the prodigal son only went home to his father because he was hungry, and his father never even questioned his motives, he was just so glad to see him."

Cassandra laughed. "You may not have had a university education, but you're too clever for me. Anyway, I'll be glad to have you come for *whatever* reason."

***

Pete and his moped roared into the yard a few minutes before nine o'clock on Saturday morning. He worked through till lunchtime with considerable gusto, fuelled by the odd tin of 'coke'. Cassandra was immensely pleased with his progress and only hoped that his eagerness was not too bubbly to last. She asked whether he'd like the afternoon off, as he'd done such a good morning's work and she hadn't really intended him to have to work on Saturdays at all.

"S'all right Miss," he replied cheerfully. "I like having somethink to do and it's better'n the chores me mum finds me round the 'ouse. But p'raps if I done enough for you this morning I could do a few of me own things after dinner – like you said, you know." Cassandra agreed that that would be a good idea, as long as he didn't prevent her from getting on with the large bowls she still needed to make for a number of orders. Asked to come in for lunch, Pete hesitated. "If it's all the same to you and your mum, Miss, I'd rather eat my dinner out 'ere. I likes to eat fast and I can listen to me radio." Cassandra and 'her mum' were by no means displeased to have lunch by themselves and Pete happily carried his back to the workshop on a tray.

"What a sensible boy!" said Melissa approvingly. "If he doesn't like it he can chuck it out somewhere without being embarrassed. Mind you, he should like it: tomato soup and then steak and kidney pie. At least he should find that familiar."

"Good heavens, Mummy! You'll be doing chips for him next!" Cassandra exclaimed. "And what will that do for us?!"

"We don't have to eat them ourselves," Melissa countered. "I'm glad you've got him to help you and I want to keep him happy. We can worry about his diet if he stays. Shall we take him to the market on Thursday?"

"We could certainly do with an extra pair of hands if it's anything like last Thursday; but it would be something to have him help with the wrapping and loading at this end, if nothing else. Let's see how we go."

***

"What shall I wear to the Oratory?" Melissa asked her daughter on Sunday morning.

"Anything. It doesn't matter. People don't dress up. And almost nobody wears anything on their heads any more; at the most you might see a couple of mantillas and one hat. The hat'll be on a little woman who used to be a Methodist; she's never without one. It gives her a certain air of distinction, wearing a hat; she wouldn't be very noticeable otherwise."

"Well I don't want to look distinctive. I want to blend into the background. What about a plain linen coat and skirt with a slightly casual blouse?"

"Just right. A lot of women do wear suits, now I come to think of it. But we'd better start off in good time in case the car plays up, and then we'll have to find a place to park and we mustn't be late or we won't get a seat or a hymn book and mass book; they usually run out."

The car took only ten minutes to start, but by the time they'd got into Oxford, found a vacant space well down St Giles and fished out the right change for the Pay and Display machine, it was just on eleven o'clock.

"Heavens!" Melissa panted as they hustled up to Woodstock Road. "How awful having to pay to park on a Sunday! What's the country coming to?"

"It's the same in France."

"One doesn't expect the French to know any better. Besides they don't take notice of parking rules the way the English do. The Southern Europeans are not naturally law-abiding like us. Oh is this it? What a strange little courtyard."

They hurried into the church just in time to receive mass sheets, hymn books and mass books.

"Let's sit near the back," Melissa hissed. "One can see so much better."

"See better at the *back*?" her daughter queried. "Oh, of course! You mean see the other *people*!"

Unable to find room for two together they each squeezed into different pews, one behind the other, just as the bell rang, the entrance hymn received its starting blast from the organ and the procession began to make its way up the side aisle: cross, altar boys, incense, servers, priests, lace and shining vestments, birettas and all. Melissa turned round to where Cassandra stood behind her and whispered piercingly: "Gorgeous clothes!" Cassandra mouthed, rather than said, "Shhh!" and raised her hymn book to discourage further conversation. She could not, however, avoid seeing her mother turn round again, mouth something and point with a finger jabbing the air several times at somebody in a pew further down on the other side of the aisle. In spite of herself Cassandra's eyes followed the jabbing finger until their glance rested on Samson Southey. Slightly relieved, Cassandra hoped that contemplation of him would keep her mother occupied for a while. Once the service began in earnest, however, she was gratified to see that Melissa was making an attempt to follow the Latin, clearly audible over the loudspeakers, in her mass book, and indulged in the hope that her own devotions might not be too much distracted by her mother's presence. Now, she sighed to herself, I've got an idea what it's like for people who have to bring children to mass.

The rest of the service was without incident and Cassandra was almost able to relax her awareness of her mother and concentrate on her own involvement, helped by the beauty of the music: Mozart's *Orgelsolo Masse* she noted from the mass sheet, very easy to appreciate, and two renaissance pieces, Palestrina and an *Alma Redemptoris Mater* by Francesco Soriano. Cassandra reflected on how blessed they were to hear such music used for its proper purpose, in the course of a mass as an aid to devotion, rather than in the relatively sterile ambience of a concert hall. She sighed contentedly. High mass on Sundays at the Oratory was coming to be the crown of her week.

As they made their way out, slowly shuffling amid the throng, Melissa managed to attract Samson Southey's attention, to his obvious surprise and subsequent gratification.

"How very pleasant to see you. Are you here for the music or the faith?"

"Both, in fact," said Cassandra, hoping her mother would *not* add 'the sort of people one might meet'. "What about you?" she added quickly, to preclude the possibility.

"Well actually – here, let me hand in your books for you – I'm not a Catholic," Samson admitted, "but I do like to hear a Latin mass and I particularly appreciate the wealth and range of the music here, not to mention the excellence of its performance and the fact that it's in its proper setting and used for its proper purpose."

"Oh! That's exactly what I was thinking." Cassandra was grateful to recognise a kindred spirit.

"Of course," Samson continued, "I do also enjoy going to the cathedral or New College for Evensong. One's so fortunate in Oxford: untold riches for little effort and less expense. Would you like a drink? Or a cup of coffee? The social club's round the corner in what used to be the school."

"Oh yes please," Melissa answered gratefully. "That's *just* what I'd like. Wouldn't you, Cassandra?"

"Yes, if you want." Cassandra was not averse to having her mother meet people in the social club, and she was herself finding Samson more interesting than she had hitherto. They made their way across the old school playground, the asphalt of which still showed a kind of softened, as it were padded, area on which a climbing frame had stood. Samson greeted several people as they progressed, turning to enlighten his kinswomen after doing so: "Fellow of Balliol," he murmured, with regard to the first; "Professor of Philosophy," after the second; but when he called, "Good morning, Sir Felix," to the third Melissa immediately asked him: "Is that Felix Marjoribanks, by any chance?"

"Yes, it is, actually. Do you know him?…No, clearly not, but, of course, same name – I really hadn't thought of it before."

"In fact I believe we are related," said Melissa eagerly, "we've been in contact but we've never met! Of course I knew he lived in the parish, but what a coincidence all the same. *Do* introduce us, Samson, it would be so use… I mean helpful, and interesting."

Cassandra regarded her mother with a slightly wry smile and Samson said, "Oh, certainly, of course," and they proceeded into the club in pursuit of Sir Felix Marjoribanks.

12

Samson found a table for Cassandra and Melissa to sit at and himself went to the bar where Sir Felix was already standing.

"Let me get you a drink, Sir Felix," Samson offered, "and also allow me to introduce you to some ladies who are kindred to both of us, I believe."

"Really?" Sir Felix was immediately interested. Samson indicated Melissa and Cassandra. "Of course! I thought they looked familiar! I saw their pictures in the local paper. How amazing to see them here! And you, too, Samson, come to that. You're not a Catholic, are you?"

"I'm afraid not," Samson replied apologetically. "But I have been coming recently: I like the Latin and the music."

"I'm with you there. I come to this mass whenever possible." They took their four drinks to the table. Samson performed the introductions. Sir Felix expressed himself utterly delighted to meet his Marjoribanks kinswomen in what he termed 'such propitious surroundings'. "I'm only sorry my wife's not here," he continued. "She doesn't often come to this mass: thinks it's too indulgent to the senses, I imagine. Prefers Blackfriars – plainer, more down to earth, you know; full of good works and democratic equality. Puts me to shame. Very involved in Gatehouse and Life – looking after druggy dropouts and what we used to call fallen women. Not that I disapprove, of course. Just not my kind of thing."

"Lady Marjorie is a wonderful example of true Christian charity," said Samson, by way of response to Sir Felix and explanation to Melissa and Cassandra.

"Lady *Marjorie*?" Melissa queried, having expected 'Lady Marjoribanks'.

"Oh yes. Daughter of an earl, you know." Sir Felix explained. "Awkward really, going with Marjoribanks. But she says she would rather be called Lady Marjorie than Lady Marjorie-Banks – which is how a lot of people say it, of course. Good of her to take on a name like ours. Married beneath her, of course; I wasn't even a baronet when we got engaged. But there – she's always been more interested in looking downwards than upwards. Nice woman."

"I'd very much like to meet her," Melissa stated with just the right degree of tempered enthusiasm. "I was, in fact, intending to respond to your kind letter with an invitation to come and have drinks with us one evening. I hope you'll come too, Samson. Would you like to bring the friend you drove out with before? That nice young – well, youngish – man we met at the college dinner: Dr Taylor, isn't it? I'll ring him myself if you can give me his number."

"What a good idea!" Sir Felix was quick to respond. "Let's make a day now and we can confirm or otherwise when I've been able to consult Marjorie. She does tend to say she's too busy to have a social life, but kindred are rather special." The following Friday was fixed on provisionally; pleasantries were exchanged, in the course of which it was learned that Sir Felix had been at Eton and Lady Marjorie at Woldingham. Melissa eventually murmured that they must get back to their car before the parking time ran out; she and her daughter made the appropriate farewells and departed.

"Now that," said Melissa happily as they made their way down St Giles, "might be considered an answer to prayer."

"One might think you engineered the whole thing yourself, Mummy," Cassandra spoke almost accusingly, "though I can't see how you could have."

"Of course I didn't, darling, but as well as making the most of opportunities one must try to contrive opportunities to make the most of. I merely hoped F.G.C. Marjoribanks might be there and perhaps recognise us from the newspaper pictures; but Samson's presence *and* his actually knowing Sir Felix was an immense and unexpected bonus. You know, I think you're right: it *is* time I started going to mass again. After all I'm probably a widow, and I'm certainly not living in sin with my married-outside-the-church husband. Let's get there *really* early next Sunday and I'll go to confession and ask them all about it. 'All things work together for good with those that fear the Lord' as my nanny used to say."

Cassandra smiled. "Somehow I can't quite associate you with 'fear-of-the-lord', Mummy."

"Well perhaps not *obviously*, darling. I must admit it's been down among the deeper of my hidden depths since I married so badly. But my nanny was a sensible woman. She also used to say 'if you go to church you meet nice people', and we've no need to throw any doubt on *that.*"

"I'm not sure that I find Sir Felix particularly nice," said Cassandra thoughtfully, "but we'll see what he's like on Friday, if he comes. I do like the sound of Lady Marjorie."

"Yes, I thought you might. Young people of your generation are rather into good works among the destitute and so on, but it all sounds a bit *noblesse oblige* and lady bountiful to the underclasses to me. She'll probably be far too busy ministering to the miserable to come out to anything so frivolous as drinks before dinner. Still, we'll see; mustn't judge the poor woman before we've met her – if we do."

Cassandra considered her mother's reaction to the little she'd heard of Lady Marjorie to be rather acidic and began to ponder on the possibility of an underlying reason for it:

'some sort of ulteriority' as she put it to herself. She was not, however, averse to the idea of drinks on Friday, or to the inclusion of 'that youngish Dr Taylor', despite Melissa's dismissive remarks about his middle class respectability.

On Sunday evening Sir Felix Marjoribanks telephoned Melissa to accept her invitation to drinks on the following Friday, adding that his wife was very happy to come too. Melissa made the appropriate replies of polite delightedness, replaced the receiver and said, "Damn-blast-bloody-bugger-hell-shit-*fart*!"

Cassandra, entering the room in time to hear these expletives asked, "What on earth's the matter?"

"Lady Marjorie's coming too," was her mother's answer.

"Oh, is that all. I thought you must have hurt yourself or spilt your wine at the very least! Why don't you want her to come?"

"Because," said Melissa with some stress, "if you must know and haven't yet worked it out for yourself, I want to persuade, entreat, or otherwise cajole her husband into lending us the money to turn the top floor into flats, and I strongly suspect that a woman like her, who espouses worthy causes, will consider that money spent on anything else is quite ludicrously misapplied; and anyway, it's much easier to work on a man if his wife's not present. Not to mention that entertaining a woman always demands more effort as regards food and presentation and look of the house than entertaining men. They're happy enough with plenty of alcohol and attention."

"So that's it! I thought there was some ulteriority afoot, though I couldn't have imagined such a degree of it. You really are beyond – beyond – words fail me – beyond *anything,* Mummy!"

“Never mind that. We’ll just have to make the best of it. At least we’ve got five days to get ready. We have to decide what to have to eat and drink, where to put it, and what to do about Treasure.”

“Why ever does Treasure come into it?”

“Is she an asset or a liability? Do the sight of her and a knowledge of our powerlessness to put her out of her misery inspire sympathy or disgust? She’s bound to make her presence heard, at least, even if we shut her away. Yes. That’s probably the best thing: shut her away, explain the barking and the whining and produce her only after due preparation and if she’s likely to have the desired affect.”

Cassandra merely shook her head, not sure whether to admire or despise such premeditation. Her mother moved on towards another decision. “We can’t have them in here, anyway.” They both looked around their kitchen cum sitting room cum everything room, piled with papers and pantalettes and all the other apparatus of living and working with only two chairs of a size and shape denoting any degree of comfort or relaxation. “No, definitely not,” they agreed in unison.

“It might be warm enough to stay outside,” Cassandra ventured. “What about just through the french windows where we first saw Cousin Agatha? We could move some of the outside chairs and tables and just use the best of them; there’s even time to paint a few before then. We could go inside the room if it rains, though we’ll be a bit lost in it if there are only four of us.”

“If Samson and his colleague come there’ll be six, though I’m not sure how well the colleague will fit in,” Melissa mused.

“Oh? Because he’s so middle class, you mean?” Cassandra was not entirely unused to following her mother's train of thought, even if her designs on Sir Felix had been beyond imagining.

"Well yes," Melissa responded, "and he's the only one not connected by any kind of kinship. Never mind. You'll have to look after him while I deal with the others. Come to that, perhaps you could look after him *and* Lady Marjorie."

"He might not come, anyway" Cassandra murmured.

"Oh, I know he will," her mother rejoined, "I'm sure he's dying to see you again. I'll ring him in his college tomorrow when Samson's had time to talk to him. Right! Two decisions so far; the food and the drink can wait. We'll take the dust sheets off the drawing room furniture and replace the smell of must and age with polish and lavender and fresh air, though I don't suppose we dare leave the windows open overnight. It's a project for tomorrow."

13

"To think," said Melissa on Friday afternoon, "this is the first time we've done any entertaining since we've been here. I used to be forever having people in for drinks or dinner or what not, and now I feel quite out of practice. Still, it's not as if we want to give an impression of affluence; making-ends-meet-with-cheerful-determination is probably the atmosphere we should try to convey."

"That won't be too difficult," her daughter responded, "as long as we can maintain the 'cheerful' bit. I don't always find that easy."

"Don't you? Why?"

"I prefer not to analyse it. Perhaps it's got something to do with changing Treasure's nappies."

"We do take it in turns!" Melissa retorted. "Still, I see what you mean. It's not the most worthwhile of nasty jobs, when one knows the poor creature shouldn't be here at all. But we must remember that it's probably because of Treasure that *we're* here at all. Have you spread the cream cheese on the pumpernickel rounds?"

"Yes. Where are the smoked oysters?"

"In a sieve, draining. Over there by the sink. I think you'd better cut them in half and put just a half on each round."

"OK." Cassandra arranged the nibbles on one of her own plates, an almost flat square of pale beige with streaks of brown and blue. She managed to make them look like a work of art. It was fine and warm enough to sit on the terrace outside the drawing room.

"Don't you think it's a bit warm for mousetraps?" asked Cassandra.

"Not if they're small enough," Melissa answered knowledgeably. "Men *always* like mousetraps."

"I'd better cut them in half, then."

"Yes, and turn on the oven now so that they'll do very quickly when the time comes."

"Isn't that rather extravagant?"

"Oh *darling*!" Melissa sighed, "Where did you learn to be so *cautious*!"

"In a flat with other impoverished students I suppose. Though come to think of it some of them weren't very cautious – in any way."

"That I can more readily imagine. Heavens! I can hear a car; surely it's too early?"

"It's nearly six. They may not have known how long it would take to get here. I'll go and see." Cassandra went to the door, looked out and came back hastily. "Of *all* things," she gasped, "it's Mr Flashy-Sports-Car with three other people."

"In a *sports* car?"

"No – it's a Jaguar. Mr Flashy-Sports is in the front passenger seat."

"Is Pete still in the workshop?"

"No, he's gone home. I'll go and see to them. You go on making the mousetraps into *petits, petits, petits fours*!"

Cassandra went into the yard and recognised Nigel Nethercott's mother-in-law standing beside a large-bosomed young woman to whom she was speaking volubly. A wispy-looking man on the old side of middle age was hovering uncertainly between the women and Nigel.

"Good evening Mrs Fraser," Cassandra greeted the short, voluble woman with her own unusual combination of self-containment and unconscious charm. "We met at the college dinner, didn't we?" She nodded in Nigel's direction and repeated “Good evening!” She knew Nigel’s name but preferred not to call him anything. ‘Dr Nethercott’ was too formal for people of their age group and ‘Nigel’ too familiar for Cassandra’s liking. Norah Fraser was in the process of responding. “Oh yes,” she was saying, “but you haven’t met Effie. Nigel said he couldn’t ask Effie to the dinner – well I think that’s very peculiar….”

“Hello, Effie – I’m Cassandra.” Cassandra held out a hand to Effie, who looked rather non-plussed as if not sure what to do with it, but eventually shook it somewhat indecisively.

“Hullo,” she replied in a flat voice. Nigel made an attempt to introduce the hovering older man but Effie’s mother was still talking.

“We’re on our way to dinner; we’re going to the Bear in Woodstock – it’s very smart, the Bear. Have you ever been there? They have a lot of conferences. Businessmen from all over the world…..” Nigel managed to break in and tell Cassandra that the older man, whose presence Mrs Fraser was completely ignoring, was in fact her husband and thus his prospective father-in-law.

“What can I do for you?” Cassandra ventured, determined that despite the unbusinesslike hour this could hardly be taken as a social call. What a ghastly thought! “I expect you want to look at the pottery. Let me show you.” Cassandra smiled attractively and moved firmly.

“Well really….” Norah Fraser followed in her wake, expostulating a little uncertainly, “it’s just that we were out this way, because of going to The Bear at Woodstock, you see, and I said to Ray, ‘now just turn off down there, Ray, because that’s where those ladies live that we met at Nigel’s college – well, at least *I* did because you weren’t there and neither was Effie – and it’d be nice to see their home because Nigel says it's really smart but we can look at the pottery if you like; Nigel says you've got some really expensive things…." As Cassandra opened the door of the workshop and stood aside to let the others enter it, a large serviceable-looking car drove into the yard, closely followed by a smaller one. Sir Felix Marjoribanks, driving the first, called out, "Hullo Cassandra! A bit early, I'm afraid; couldn't remember exactly where it was. Midge!" he addressed his wife. "Here's this lovely Cassandra I've been telling you about." Lady Marjorie was half out of the car. "Hullo!" she greeted Cassandra. "Don't mind Felix. I'm sorry we're early and I'd love to see your pots. Am I right in thinking you've already got guests looking at them?" She glanced at the door of the workshop where Norah Fraser was still talking and the other three hovering.

"Well no, customers actually – I hope," Cassandra replied.

"Marvellous. All the better. Let's go in then. Oh, unless…." She saw Robert and Samson, from the other lately arrived car, approaching them. "Hullo Samson! Guests or customers?"

"Guests on this occasion," Samson answered. "Let me introduce my colleague, Robert Taylor – Sir Felix and Lady Marjorie Marjoribanks." They exchanged hullos and how-do-you-dos and went to join the group at the door. Norah Fraser had actually stopped talking at the sound of names preceded by 'Sir' and 'Lady' and was staring at the new arrivals with wide-eyed interest. "Very pleased I'm sure," she murmured in response to the introductions. Cassandra eased them all into the workshop.

"Gracious me!" Norah Fraser found her normal voice again. "It's very messy. There's mud all over the floor!"

"Clay," said Cassandra.

Effie spoke for the first time; so did her father. "Shut up, mother!" said one, and "Now, now Norah!" said the other.

Lady Marjorie had picked up an Oxford Pot and was delightedly holding it aloft. "This is *absolutely brilliant*!" she exclaimed. "You're so clever to make and market these. We had the odd one at home but only sitting uselessly in cupboards or on display like museum pieces. Somehow it never occurred to us to utilize them. It's particularly apt that they should be reintroduced in these days of female equality." Norah Fraser, who almost never read the local newspapers and preferred to watch the television, which in her house was never turned off, looked in puzzlement from the uplifted pot to Lady Marjorie and back to the pot again and asked, "Why? What is it?"

"Oh, it's a bourdaloue," the lady replied.

None the wiser Norah asked, "What's it for?"

"It's a piss pot for women. A wonderful device, one of those special, brilliantly simple things; gives to women one of the very few things they envy men for: the ability to pee standing up!"

"Well *really*!" Norah was completely nonplussed. As she said – at length – to Ray later she would *never* have expected a real lady, a lady somebody, to talk like that. It was really disgusting. "They were probably used less here than on the continent," Lady Marjorie continued.

"Jolly useful for the *in*continent," Sir Felix chimed in, "on both sides of the Channel." While everybody else laughed Norah Fraser's mouth merely dropped open.

"Well I'm certainly going to buy a couple of these – aren't you, Mrs Fraser?" Lady Marjorie used tones clearly indicating question-expecting-the-answer-yes. Norah was sufficiently perturbed to appeal to her husband: "Raymond!" She generally called him 'Ray' but had a vague misgiving that it might be considered vulgar.

"You don't really want one," her husband replied.

"*I* do," Effie interrupted. "How much are they?" Nigel dragged his eyes away from Cassandra and regarded his fiancée with astonishment.

"I'll get you one," he murmured. "They're £10 I think – but – I mean I never thought…." Effie looked up at him with a fluttering of eyelashes and a smile of intimacy, which he was embarrassed to see observed by Cassandra. He fumbled in his wallet and took out a £10 note, which he silently handed over.

"You're in the Thursday market, aren't you?" Lady Marjorie asked. "I'll come and get a couple of pots then; don't want to mix business with pleasure – though I'm most grateful for a private view. Won't your mother be wondering what's happened to us?" Cassandra gave her a glance of relieved appreciation. She'd been anxiously pondering the problem of separating the guests from the customers, given the awkward overlap of social acquaintance with Nigel and Mrs Fraser. She responded gratefully: "Oh yes, please do go over – just across the yard."

"Come along, Felix." Lady Marjorie took her husband firmly by the arm and propelled him out of the workshop. Samson and Robert were about to follow but Norah had barred their way both physically and verbally by claiming Robert as Nigel's best man and expatiating on the strangeness of his meeting Raymond and Effie in such a way and in fact on the greater strangeness of his not having met them before.

"Well you must come to The Bear and have dinner with us now, you really must, Robert."

"I'm afraid I can't; I'm here with Samson to chauffeur him. We're having drinks…."

"Oh that doesn't matter. Just have a quick drink and come on afterwards – Mrs Marsh won't mind, I'm sure. I mean there's plenty of time before dinner. We don't have to eat early, I mean smart people don't eat early, do they? In fact perhaps we could all have a drink here – your mother wouldn't mind, would she? Norah turned to Cassandra. "I mean a few more wouldn't be noticed in a house this size…." Cassandra looked as greatly aghast as she felt; it had in fact crossed her mind that something like this might happen, but that made it oddly more difficult to believe in the actuality. There was a shocked silence. Then Nigel, Robert and Samson all spoke at once in variously expressed negatives, then stopped, each looking to the others to continue. Samson, the most articulate and least involved, was the first to speak again. "Impossible, I'm afraid," he said smoothly, "Robert's already taking me on elsewhere after this."

"Well *you* needn't come," replied Norah. "*You've* got nothing to do with the wedding and surely the other people could take you!" There was another aghast silence mercifully broken by Effie. "Mother! Will you shut up and stop trying to organise everybody! Me and Nigel've planned what we're doing tonight and we're not going to change it again. We've already come here when we hadn't meant to because you would make Dad turn off down the road. Now come on!"

"Yes, come on Norah," Effie's father spoke up in support. "Leave people to do what they've planned." Norah Fraser opened her mouth to expostulate, but her daughter began to hustle her out and she finally signalled defeat by closing her mouth again and only reopening it to deliver a parting shot to Cassandra: "You really ought to do something about the state of this floor!"

Samson, Robert and Cassandra stood wordlessly in the workshop until they heard the car starting up, when each of them let out a spontaneous sigh and, catching each other's expressions, began to laugh. "I'm glad I got that pot they bought wrapped up and handed over so quickly," said Cassandra, "otherwise I'm sure I would have dropped it."

14

Still laughing over the vagaries of Nigel's impending mother-in-law, Cassandra, Robert and Samson went into the drawing-room, where Melissa and her Marjoribanks guests were still standing discussing the room's décor and *objets d'art*, a number of which Sir Felix remembered from previous visits many years earlier. "It's awfully interesting," Lady Marjorie was saying, "but it can't be quite ideal for you to live among so many possessions chosen by somebody else. You say you can't sell them or dispose of them at all under the terms of the Will?"

"No I'm afraid not," Melissa replied regretfully, "though in fact it's taken so much time and energy to settle ourselves in and arrange Cassandra's workshop – not to mention making enough to live on – that we haven't had time for the more decorative side of life. But you must see over the whole house, well, most of it, before you go. Shall we have a drink and a nibble first? Cassandra darling, the mousetraps!"

"*Mouse*traps?" Lady Marjorie was not a weak woman, but an immediately conjured vision of the passages to the further reaches of the house being impeded by dead or dying vermin was daunting even to the strong.

"Oh dear!" Melissa and Cassandra burst into laughter, to the bewilderment of their guests. "Of course – never thought – must sound so awful…" Cassandra made for the kitchen, saying, "Mummy, you explain." Melissa poured wine for Samson and Robert and topped up the other glasses while explaining "'Mousetraps' are a delicacy from New Zealand, hence perhaps the somewhat down-to-earth name – though as they've also given us pavlova cake and the Australians peach melba and melba toast that's perhaps an injustice. Mousetraps consist mainly of vintage cheese and are considered irresistible, especially to mice, of course. My husband came back from one of his trips absolutely raving about them and we've been making them ever since. We're so used to them we hardly think about their name. But these ones today have got to spend five or ten minutes in the oven so have some smoked oysters or some humous and mushrooms in the meantime – and let's go out on the terrace, if you think it's warm enough."

"Can I help with anything?" Robert asked eagerly. "Carry anything in or out?"

"Oh how very kind, Robert. Perhaps you'd like to see how Cassandra's getting on in the kitchen – down to the end of the passage and on the right, thank you so much." Robert sped away and before the others could move out onto the terrace a faint yapping was heard.

"Oh, have you got a dog?" asked Sir Felix with interest.

"What quick ears you have!" Melissa stalled as she considered how to reply. "We inherited Cousin Agatha's dog along with the rest of her possessions."

"Not that snappy little tyke she used to have – what was it called – Jewel or something equally inappropriate?"

"Treasure!" said Melissa significantly. "Yes, I'm afraid so, poor creature."

"But it must be at least twenty years old!"

"Sixteen, I think. It's very sad. That was another clause in the Will. It's not on any account to be put down. *So* disturbing. We try to keep her out of sight and earshot. Cassandra must have taken pity on her – the smell of mousetraps drives her wild. Oh *dear*!"! Melissa was genuinely distressed as she suddenly thought of the off-putting effect Treasure might have on Robert Taylor.

"Is she in a very bad way?" Lady Marjorie was immediately sympathetic.

"I'm afraid so." Melissa decided to make the most of the sympathy. "Half-paralysed," she continued sadly. "Back legs trailing uselessly behind her."

"But how…?"

Melissa put the uncertain implication of the unspoken question to what she hoped was the best use: "Nappies!" she said succinctly.

"How utterly ghastly for you!" Lady Marjorie pictured her elegant hostess in conjunction with Treasure's nappies and put down an unfinished biscuit with its brie-nestling smoked oyster uneaten, while Sir Felix joined in with, "Oh, I say, that's too bad, that's altogether too bad," and Samson hastened on to the terrace to take an unusually deep breath of fresh air. Cassandra and Robert came out carrying a plate of mousetraps each, all glistening with bubbly browned cheese and crispy bacon.

"Whatever's the matter?" Cassandra looked at the dismayed expressions of the trio on the terrace.

"I've been telling them about Treasure," said Melissa. "Sir Felix remembers her."

"Oh Mummy!" Cassandra remonstrated, mentally adding to herself that her mother had doubtless milked the situation for all the sympathy possible, "you know we cope with her very well, and if you saw the way she's devouring a mousetrap you'd know she's almost as happy as Cousin Agatha insisted she was." Cassandra's cheerfulness dissipated the pall left from the revelation of Treasure's inadequacies and did her no harm in the eyes of her audience. The mousetraps were equally successful in restoring jaded appetites especially, as Melissa had predicted, in the men, who dispatched most of them with speed and gusto. Lady Marjorie had less to eat but more to say: "I'm most impressed by the excellence of your food; it's simple, interesting and delicious. I do appreciate clever simple things. Like your Oxford Pot, Cassandra. I call that a clever, simple thing. How did you come to think of it?"

"We found a couple in a cabinet upstairs," Cassandra answered; "it was Mummy's idea actually. I didn't even know what they were for."

"We can show you if you'd really like to see the rest of the house," Melissa suggested. This was received with enthusiasm and they trooped off, glass in hand, Melissa leading the way with Sir Felix and Lady Marjorie, and a little distance behind, Samson making a somewhat uncertain third to Robert and Cassandra. They were really more interested in talking about themselves and each other than in seeing the house, though Robert did notice that there were central heating radiators to be seen. "I'm afraid it might cost an awful lot to use them," Cassandra sighed. "I can't say I'm looking forward to a winter here. Maybe we'll have to live in the workshop and keep the kiln going."

"Dear me! I hope it won't come to that." Samson sounded genuinely worried.

"If we could only make two or three flats out of the top storey and let them we'd have more people using the house and warming it – not to mention some rent money coming in. But of course…" Cassandra felt unwilling to talk about their lack of capital. Robert, having already been told about the bouncing cheques and her father's bankruptcy understood this and changed the subject.

"What nice people Sir Felix and Lady Marjorie are. I gather they're related to you but that you've only just met them."

"Yes, and we might not have done if Samson hadn't been at the Oratory and introduced us to Sir Felix."

"The Oratory? Where? In Oxford?"

Samson answered: "Yes. It's also called St Aloysius. Formerly Jesuit but now taken over by Oratorians. You must have heard of Brompton Oratory, as it's usually known. It's one of *the* churches for fashionable Catholic weddings."

"I don't think I've ever attended a fashionable Catholic wedding – probably not even an unfashionable one – but I have heard of Brompton Oratory. I believe it has a famously large dome. I've never suspected you of attending Catholic churches, Samson – apart from fashionable weddings, of course." Samson explained his fondness for the Latin mass and music in its proper setting and added that he didn't suppose the subject interested Robert.

"I must admit," replied Robert carefully, with a glance in Cassandra's direction, "it's some time since I've given any thought to church services. I don't quite know why. When I was really young we lived in an Anglo-Catholic parish where there was a priest we called 'Father' and high masses with incense and all the trimmings. I even wanted to be an altar boy, but my parents didn't much like the idea – I suppose they thought it would be a nuisance, and anyway we moved out of that parish and the services at the next one were very low-key and boring in comparison and we soon stopped going altogether."

"Oh, what a *pity*," Cassandra exclaimed as if at a story of real deprivation. Robert immediately began to feel deprived and mentally awarded another black mark against his kind and well-meaning but not very educated parents, who had never quite known how to cope with their surprisingly academic son. He and Cassandra stopped at a high window to admire the wide-ranging, uninterrupted view while Samson, hearing voices in a nearby room, went to join the older group, where Sir Felix was showing a sympathetic interest in Melissa's project for making the top floor into two or three flats. "Very enterprising," he was saying, "an excellent way of using the house, keeping it comfortable and lived in. Just the sort of thing rich Americans would like. And it's not as if you haven't got enough furniture to put in from the rest of the house. Most of the rooms are over-stuffed with it."

"But how long would Americans want to stay?" Melissa queried. "It would need to be longer than a few weeks."

"If I might make a suggestion," Samson ventured, "what about visiting American or colonial academics? They're often here for a year at a time and as long as they could drive a motor-car they'd be delighted to live in a place like this. You could advertise in *The University Gazette*; it goes all over the world. I know a number of American professors – and even Australian ones – who would really be quite suitable."

"What a *brilliant* idea, Samson!" Lady Marjorie was impressed. "What it is to have a brain like yours. Though I must admit I'd never realised you were so practical." Samson shrugged deprecatingly. "Oh," he murmured, "it's just that one meets so many colonial and foreign academics in Oxford. Some of them seem to expect to stay in a college or a superior apartment already reserved for them and are absolutely aghast to be greeted with a casual 'Where are you staying?' when they've made no provision for themselves at all."

"How awful for them!" Lady Marjorie was immediately sympathetic.

"Possibly very useful for us, however," was Melissa's thought.

Downstairs again, they allowed their glasses to be refilled (*Positively* the last, said Sir Felix. "All right, I'll drive," said Lady Marjorie resignedly) and continued to discuss the possibilities of Huntsfield's top floor with animated enthusiasm.

Robert and Cassandra gradually detached themselves from the discussion of flats and prospective tenants in which the other four were so animatedly engaged and eventually wandered over to the workshop where Robert said he *particularly* wanted to see the newest bowls more closely. He was sufficiently knowledgeable about pottery to be properly appreciative and Cassandra rejoiced in being able to talk about her work in a way that she had not found possible since leaving Devon. They were too interested in each other's company and conversation to notice the passage of time and were surprised when Samson hovered into the doorway to say the Marjoribankses had offered him a lift home and did Robert mind? Robert was unconcealably delighted and immediately after Samson's departure invited Cassandra to have dinner with him – or maybe a pub supper, since they'd had so much to eat already. On the way to the house he reluctantly remembered his manners and suggested asking Melissa to come too. "Oh, of course," said Cassandra in carefully neutral tones. Melissa, however, was horrified at the suggestion that she could eat another *bite*, as well as being much too exhausted by unaccustomed entertaining to stir a foot.

With barely hidden gratitude Robert and Cassandra departed unaccompanied.

15

"I'm heading for Tackley," Robert told Cassandra, "unless you know of anywhere you'd rather go."

"I hardly know any pubs round here yet," Cassandra, "so I'm very happy to go to any as long as it's nowhere near the Bear at Woodstock!"

"You can count on me to avoid *that* one, particularly this evening. If Madam Fraser spotted us there'd be danger of my being swept into dinner with her while you were told to find your own way home! Really I can't understand Nigel; it's not even as if the daughter compensated in any very evident way for the awfulness of the mother."

"Maybe there's money in it," Cassandra suggested.

"You may just be right there, though if my fears about Nigel have any foundation it'll be a matter of alimony – or whatever it's called – before very long."

"Perhaps Nigel's hoping to get some alimony himself. I believe the laws are changing in these days of equality! But I gather you're to be best man at the wedding? Surely that's rather a task?"

"Don't remind me; the thought haunts me day and night. Every speech that comes into my mind is either heavily ironical or dangerously near libel. But here's Tackley."

"Isn't it a pretty village? After living abroad so much I find it exceedingly comforting that such picture-postcard chocolate-box-lid villages do actually exist and are not a mere figment of Victorian sentimental imagination."

"I agree entirely," Robert replied appreciatively, "though, you know, I sometimes think that the present appearance of such villages is probably an improvement on Victorian reality with its concomitant poverty. Look!" Robert turned from the main through road on to a widened track skirting the second side of the triangular green. "You see that house on the end, the one called 'The Old Smithy'?"

"Oh yes!" Cassandra took in the contours of the long, low stone dwelling with its casement windows and cottage garden. “And is that wisteria all over it? What a picture it must be in summer!”

“It is indeed, but I’ve got an old photograph of it taken very early in the twentieth century when it really *was* a smithy, and it looks more depressing than picturesque there. The combination of the nostalgia boom and present day affluence, the renewed appreciation of Victorian art and the enjoyment of more leisure and more money have made what used to be a largely pictorial and usually unattainable ideal into a reality. But stop me! I’m getting into teaching mode!”

“Please stay in it. That’s the most interesting observation, and as I think about it I’m convinced you’re right. It’s marvellous to talk to a person with a *mind*: they’re all too rare!”

Robert laughed. “I’m not sure how well my mind will stand up to any more alcohol – let alone my driving, but let’s try the pub anyway.”

“Well actually,” Cassandra admitted, “I was wondering how to broach the idea that I’d really rather drink fizzy water at this stage, without sounding too boring and conformist.” Robert of course expatiated on his opinion of Cassandra’s total inability to be either of such dreary things, ever or in any way! Cassandra laughed. “Thank you, Robert; that of course is just exactly what I was angling to hear; and to show you how true it is I’m going to sit outside and smoke a roll-up while you order ‘sparkling water bright and clear’ and anything else you like the sound of.”

“Wonderful!” Robert was enthralled. “However did you know that old Temperance hymn?”

“‘Sparkling water bright and clear’? Oh, my mother’s nanny used to sing it, apparently, and Mummy quotes it occasionally. But I’m afraid I’ve no idea how it goes on. I don't think my mother finds the idea as attractive as I do. It's rather a point of honour to drink a lot in her generation – and certainly they despise people who don't drink at all."

Robert pondered on this while waiting at the bar to give his order. It didn't square with the attitude of his own parents and their friends; they were not teetotal and on special occasions would drink wine or even whisky, and of course champagne at weddings, but alcohol was hardly a feature of their daily lives. After coming up to Oxford he'd always had the impression that he drank a good deal more than his parents, rather than less. Of course everything was different at Oxford, he told himself, but it was easy to forget that after a few years of Senior Common Room life – even undergraduate life, in fact; Oxford began to seem normal and everywhere else aberrant.

By the time Robert came outside again with two glasses of bubbly water made more interesting by the addition of ice and lemon Cassandra was relighting her second roll-up for the third time.

"I've ordered omelettes," said Robert. "With chips for me and salad for you. I hope that meets with your approval?"

"*Exactly* right. Oh this *is* such fun. In Devon I used to go to the pub with the other potters all the time, but I haven't been since they left here after helping us move. I've been too busy to realise how much I missed it. I drink beer, naturally."

"You don't!"

"Why shouldn't I?"

"I mean I'm delighted to hear it. Not many women drink beer."

"I was on the committee of the local branch of CAMRA when I was a student."

"No wonder you've been missing pubs. I hope this is the first of many."

"I rather hope so too – ooh! Are these our omelettes? Bliss! I'm glad you didn't get chips for me – though I must admit they look delicious. I might steal one when you're not looking."

"You don't need to wait until I'm not looking," Robert smiled.

"I hate to admit to such weakness. My mother may drink more than I do, but even she doesn't go in for fatty foods."

"Is your mother a graduate?" Robert asked.

"Oh no. She didn't come from the sort of family that believed in education for girls. They did secretarial courses or learnt about fancy cooking and flower arranging and generally got married young."

"She seems very…." Robert strove for the right word and being unable to find it compromised with "educated".

"She'd be delighted to hear you say so. She was worried about not knowing how to talk to dons at your college dinner. ""Nobody would ever have thought so. She was a great deal more socially adept than most of us. I'm afraid Oxford dons are by no means versed in the most civilized social behaviour. Plenty of people who come up to the university have never had any experience whatever of formal entertainment. I've had pupils who didn't reply to college invitations because they had no idea what 'R.S.V.P.' meant. Most of us don't use it any more and resort to 'Please return the attached slip indicating whether you will attend or not'." Cassandra laughed. "Funny how different it is from what most people think of Oxbridge. I must tell Mummy. She'll be interested and relieved."

"She can't have found Nigel and his guest very 'ept' socially!"

"She found Nigel easy enough; she just got him to talk about himself. And some of my father's business acquaintances had wives not *too* unlike Mrs Fraser, though probably a bit more firmly kept down by their husbands, especially the continental ones."

"Have you had any news of your father?" Robert asked tentatively. Cassandra shook her head as she bit into the large chip she'd purloined from Robert's plate. "I probably shouldn't ask you," Robert continued, "but I find it so fascinating."

"Probably more so than I do," Cassandra replied. "I'm afraid I almost never think about him at all. I was always so used to him being away, and of course I didn't live at home so very much myself. Tell me about your family."

Robert found himself rather unwilling to say much on this subject, apart from the unsurprising fact that he had two parents and an elder brother and sister, none of whom was academic or had much in common with him. He felt they paled into greyness beside Cassandra and her altogether more colourful background and lifestyle. Fortunately it was getting a little chilly outside and their omelettes – and chips – were finished: time to make a move.

"Would you like to go anywhere else?" Robert asked.

"Only home; I feel a little badly about leaving Mummy with all the clearing up, even if it was very much her party."

"It was kind of her to ask *me*," said Robert.

"I'm glad she did. Otherwise we wouldn't have had a happy omelette at the pub."

"We can easily do that again."

"I'd like to."

"When?" Robert wanted to suggest 'tomorrow' but didn't quite feel on sure enough ground. He was too cautiously aware that all things pall 'med ungemete and overdede' and he inadvertently murmured the words aloud.

"What did you say?" Cassandra asked.

"I'm sorry. I'm mumbling some lines from a medieval poem, rather a favourite. An owl and a nightingale are arguing very amusingly about their respective merits and they come out with some sound truths in the process. This one is that everything palls with lack of moderation – ungemete – and literally 'over-doing' – overdede."

"Everything but one: and that is Godes riche," said Cassandra.

Robert was totally astonished. ""Yes!" he said. "It *does* go on to say that. 'Except in God's kingdom'. How on earth do you know that?"

"One of the nuns at school read English at Oxford. She was particularly keen on that poem and often quoted bits of it and told us about it. Besides, you know, I may be a potter but I *do* have a university degree. It's fairly normal in my generation, even among families like ours."

"I'm humbled and impressed," Robert admitted, "so much so that I won't try to hide the fact that I was quoting the wise words of the owl to stop myself suggesting that we go out again tomorrow."

"Thank you; thank you both for the thought and for the explanation. But I think the owl's right – and anyway pubs are horribly crowded on Saturdays. Let's make it next week."

"How sensible you are! All right. As long as it's *early* next week."

"Tuesday?"

"Tuesday. Definitely."

16

On Saturday morning Melissa came down to find Cassandra already in the kitchen, whistling blithely.

"Darling!" her mother exclaimed. "How wonderful to hear you so happily whistling, even if my nanny did use to say---"

"Yes, I know," Cassandra interrupted, "'A whistling maid and a crowing hen/Are fit for neither God nor men.' But I whistle much more tunefully than I can sing. Tunes often go wrong when I try singing them but as soon as I start whistling the notes seem to fall into place."

Melissa laughed "Well either way I'm delighted to hear you so blithe and cheerful. You were born on a Sunday; not that that's *entirely* to be desired these days."

"Why not? Oh I know: Bonny and blithe and good are very acceptable but you'd really rather not have a child who's gay. Well I'm certainly not that, in spite of my whistling."

"I know, darling, and you obviously had a happy evening yesterday."

"I really did and---oh blast! That telephone's ringing early"

"I'll answer it". Melissa picked up the receiver. "Oh Lady Marjorie! No, no, we're well and truly up and doing------oh, thank you, I only hope you enjoyed it as much as we did--------How *lovely*! I'd absolutely love to; I'll just ask Cassandra. Darling, would you be able to have lunch with Sir Felix and Lady Marjorie after Mass tomorrow? Yes? Wonderful!" Melissa turned back to the telephone and accepted the invitation with suitable expressions of gratitude. Replacing the receiver with a deliberation which amounted almost to reverence she murmured, half to herself; "How *very* useful! I was wondering when I'd be able to tell them about my brainwave."

Cassandra eyed her mother cautiously "What sort of a brainwave?" she asked a little anxiously.

"Well of course I intended to talk about it to you first" Melissa answered. "But it's so *obvious*! I can't imagine why it hasn't occurred to me before; there are all those rooms already furnished----albeit somewhat strangely----on the second third and fourth floors. We could use them almost immediately for people to stay in on a bed and breakfast basis, or even dinner bed and breakfast, and make some money out of them before the flats are ready."

"It might be an awful lot of work," Cassandra murmured doubtfully, "and a terrible tie".

"Well it's not as if we can afford to go anywhere, and I'm sure I could manage. I've got a good stock of pantalettes already made and of course they don't sell as well as your pottery."

"No," Cassandra agreed, "but the way you explain them and the Pot are quite a feature of the Thursday market now. People come just to watch the show. I feel like something in a Punch and Judy sometimes. It was all right putting on the act when we first came and were anonymous so to speak, but I feel much less comfortable about it now that we're getting to know people."

"Darling!" said Melissa kindly. "You mustn't worry. After all, Robert Taylor first saw you at the market stall, didn't he? And it doesn't seem to have put him off."

Cassandra had to smile at her mother's quick apprehension of her unspoken anxiety. "That's true," she admitted "but I'd feel very embarrassed and inhibited if I saw him there now. Still I must admit it draws the customers and there are always some who buy something."

"If we were making money out of rooms and flats we could gradually let the market stall go; public interest can't last forever. And we must remember that even though we're not paying rent there are the rates or council tax or whatever it's called and they'll be enormous."

"I do agree about the B&B idea, but aren't the rooms a bit gloomy? And what about bathrooms?"

"As to gloom", Melissa responded cheerfully, "we've hardly opened the shutters yet; a good clean and a clearing out of surplus furniture should make a lot of difference, though only one bathroom on each floor does pose a problem. At least the lavatories are separate. Besides we wouldn't have many people at first, we'd have to start slowly. And *of course* we'll have an Oxford Pot in every room!"

Cassandra laughed. "You haven't explained why you're so anxious to tell our new-found kindred about your plans."

"Ah, well---," Melissa seemed hesitant to voice an explanation, "if they were to offer, offer of their own accord, you understand, to help us along with a tiny loan…."

"Oh *honestly* Mummy, you really are the *end* ! I see it all now. This is the only reason you tracked them down in the first place. Talk about mercenary! Ulterior! You absolutely take the biscuit!"

"Don't talk about biscuits, darling. They always make me think of Cousin Agatha's Christmas tin. I don't think I've been able to face a biscuit since. And besides, Sir Felix and Lady Marjorie are very nice people even if they never lend us a farthing. It's necessary to get to know the right sort of people when one's a stranger in a new place."

"And of course they're *very* right sort, aren't they?"

"Of course, darling, they're devout Catholics."

"And that's why you pursued them!"

"There's a lot to be said for devout people. They're often kind and unsuspicious. I wish we'd known a few in Tours. That was a shallow life, that so-called 'good life' we led there. Look how it's vanished in the twinkling of an eye. None of the 'friends' we had there want to know me now. I'm happier, poor though we are, since we've been here; even the anxiety about making ends meet is enlivening and stimulating. And as to cultivating the right sort of people, I'm sure I've said before that as well as making the most of opportunities one must contrive opportunities to make the most of! And as my nanny used to say---"

"I'm beginning to respect your nanny."

"So am I. My way of life is less removed from hers than it used to be."

"What did she say, then?"

"Oh! I'm sure I've often quoted it before. 'All things work together for good with those who fear the Lord'. Something like that. Not that fear of the lord is one of my most noticeable characteristics, but it's probably time I started working on it. It doesn't seem to do *you* any harm, anyway."

"Yes I do remember you quoting it, but hardly so seriously. You'll have me going all weepy in a minute."

"No time for that, darling; there's Pete's moped making his presence known. Tell him about our plans while you're working; he probably knows some useful people"

"*Pete* does?"

"Yes. You know, furniture removers or plumbers or whatever."

***

Pete was full of interest when Cassandra outlined her mother's plans. So much so, in fact, that he immediately offered to help. "Can't have you ladies pushing heavy furniture about, Miss! Besides I'd really like to get a look inside. Me Mum's always asking me about what's it like but I haven't seen much past the kitchen."

"That's really kind of you, Pete, even if you have got reasons of your own for wanting to do it. And you don't have to go on calling me 'Miss' you know, my name's Cassandra."

Pete turned pinkly red. "Oh I couldn't get me mouth round a name like that, Miss. I'd feel right stupid. No, I'm happy calling you Miss and your mother Missus if you don't mind, like. Me Nan was in service before the war and I really likes to hear her talk about it. Well, she's me Mum's Nan really, but I always calls her Nan too. She said they had a good time and a lot of laughs and things were better then because there was respect on both sides. I stayed with her sometimes before me uncle got divorced and moved back there, You haven't thought any more about me having a room here have you Miss?"

"Well no, I haven't, Pete. I thought you were happy as things are. But I must admit it wouldn't be a bad idea to have a man about the place if we're going to have paying guests. We can talk about it when we're going through the rooms this afternoon."

***

Directly after lunch Pete accompanied Melissa and Cassandra on a tour of the upstairs rooms, excluding their own bedrooms.

"Though if this really takes off," Melissa mused aloud "perhaps we should move up to the second floor and keep the guests to the first floor."

"That's a point," her daughter agreed, "we don't want them---or anybody---dragging suitcases up any more stairs than is absolutely necessary. Maybe we should move up anyway and make the first guest room the one on the first floor nearest the bathroom. Americans are always fussy about bathrooms---and showers. Oh dear! We haven't any showers."

"That should be a priority, I think" Melissa said decisively, "as soon as we've got enough money we'll have a shower put in." They went into the first floor bathroom and surveyed it with more critical and evaluative consideration than they had ever accorded it previously.

"It's funny how differently you look at things when you're thinking about the way they might appear to other people," Cassandra pondered. "There are some cracks in the plaster I'd never noticed before and it looks rather bare and stark for such a big room, with only a bath and basin in it. A walk-in shower would certainly be an improvement."

"Tell you what Miss, Missus," Pete spoke enthusiastically "I can get some pictures and prices from me uncle, the one that lives with me Nan. He does electrics and showers and that. He'd put it in for you and all."

Melissa smiled triumphantly at her daughter. "How *very* useful, Pete, and we might well have your uncle do our bathrooms, if he can give us a competitive estimate. But we can't quite manage it just yet. Maybe after tomorrow---yes, do bring the pictures on Monday."

Cassandra returned her mother's smile if a little wryly. "After all, one never knows what tomorrow may bring, does one?" she said, in a voice sounding more like her mother's than her own.

"I know you're taking me off, darling," Melissa responded with perfect equanimity, "but it's absolutely true."

They went into the bedroom next door. "Of course it looks terrible at the moment" Melissa apologised to nobody in particular but rather as a justification of her project, "because we moved all the stuff we didn't want in our bedrooms into this room. It hasn't got such a good view as the rooms in the front."

"I never seen so much furniture in one room!" Pete looked incredulous. "Is it like this all over the 'ouse?"

"It's not so bad as you go further up," Melissa answered encouragingly. "Let's look at the corresponding room on the next floor."

They climbed the wide, shallow, elegant stone stairs. On the next floor the ceilings were a shade lower but the rooms still well proportioned and the outlook even improved. Pete looked into the bathroom and the room next to it. "Cor! I wouldn't mind this room, if you don't want it for anything else. It's as big as half our house!"

"But Pete," Cassandra objected, "what about when you go back to school?"

"Oh I'm not going back, Miss. I'm sixteen now. I've got to get out and do something for meself. And the only thing I want to do is be a potter. *Please* Miss!"

"You should go to Art College and do it properly, Pete."

"That sort of thing's all right for the likes of you, Miss, but it's not the same for us. My Mum and stepdad'll make me go and work in Sainsburys or something like that. I'd hate it."

"Surely they wouldn't! They must be kind to you. They've bought you a mobile phone and a moped, haven't they?"

"That's different, Miss. Everyone in our street's got a mobile. We'd be ashamed not to have at my age. And the moped's on HP and I pays a bit towards it meself. But nobody round where I live goes to college---specially not *Art* College!"

"I'm beginning to understand" Cassandra answered soberly. "And you can become a successful potter without a degree from a college. What really matters is being able to make pots and sell them. I know you'll be able to make them; selling them is another matter. I wouldn't have started to sell mine here yet if it hadn't been for my mother's Oxford Pot brainwave. And it does make sense for you to go on helping me and to have board and lodging as part of your pay. Don't you think so, Mummy?"

"It's for you to decide about your assistant, darling, I wouldn't dream of interfering. But since you ask, I'll be only too glad for you to have long-term help with your pottery. It's clearly too much for one. As to Pete's living here, we'll have to draw up a proper agreement and perhaps see his mother; make sure she agrees too. What do you think about that, Pete?"

"I know she'll be pleased. She really needs the space I take up and it's not like I take home a lot of money that she'll miss. But I'll ask her about seeing you. She wouldn't half like to come and have a look round here. An' I'll bring the bathroom pictures Monday. I reckon I can find someone who knows about moving furniture, too. It's easy when you knows how."

"Bless you, Pete, you're a treasure!" Melissa exclaimed. "Oh no! That's a word I can't use any more. I wish Cousin Agatha had called her pooch 'Jewel' or something else less frequently employed in one's everyday speech. Well anyway, Pete, what I'm trying to say is I'm very grateful to you."

Pete's face glowed with a mixture of appreciation and embarrassment. "That's all right, Missus. I likes being here working with you and Miss. I'll be off now. See you Monday." Pete clattered down the stairs and the engine of his moped soon announced his departure.

"He hasn't seen many of the rooms," Melissa sounded surprised.

"No," Cassandra answered, "but he's seen the one he wants and he can't wait to announce the good news to his family. Besides, he's probably not used to such praise and appreciation."

17

Cassandra came down to the kitchen on Sunday morning to find her mother singing over a boiling egg.

"You're the one who's blithe this morning, Mummy."

"That's true, darling. I'm looking forward to lunch; but I'm also boiling an egg." Melissa continued singing

"I don't remember you having a boiled egg for breakfast ever before."

"I don't want to be too hungry at lunch time---dah dah dee dee---or get too dopey if I drink anything---dah dum dum dum. There it's done. Aaaaaaamen. That hymn's got six verses and they take about half a minute each to sing so that if I start when I put the egg in it will have cooked by the time I sing amen. I like a three minute egg."

"You never used to do that. Is it something else your nanny taught you?"

"No, I read about it somewhere. In a letter to *The Times* I think, and I was struck by the excellence of the idea. The only trouble is that I can't always remember all the words of a hymn with six verses ---but I only need the first line of each verse and I can dah dee dum the rest."

"Wouldn't it be easier to set a timer for three minutes?"

"Posssibly; but I haven't got a timer and if I had I might go wandering off out of earshot and forget about it. There you see! Perfectly cooked! Would you like one? They're local free range from that little farm where you just help yourself and put the right money in."

"I hope you do!"

"Do what?"

"Put the right money in."

"Darling! How could you doubt me? *Of course* I do. Or take out some change if I need to. Anyway they've got a CCTV going. But I'm always *most* scrupulous about tradespeople. Anyway, shall I boil you an egg?"

"No thanks. I find a bowl of muesli more sustaining. What are you going to wear?"

"Something very unnoticeable: navy trousers, cream silk shirt, light blazer,"

"I'm not sure about the blazer."

"It's quite old; I think it'll pass muster. Anyway if it's hot I won't need to wear it. Old shoes, too; I'll put a better pair in the car but it's only sensible to wear old shoes to mass---kneeling plays *havoc* with one's shoes."

Cassandra laughed, "Mine don't look any the worse for it; they're bad enough already."

"Oh well, darling, you're an artist; and young enough to get away with anything. But neither of us will be able to wander about in our dressing-gowns when we've got PGs; perhaps not even when Pete's here." Melissa sighed. " Never mind; it's probably a good discipline. One can get very slack living alone or with just one other person. It's too easy to let oneself go."

Cassandra scraped the empty bowl of her muesli. "We'd better start early in case the car plays up and we don't want to park miles away from the church and be too late for a mass sheet or a hymn book. They often run out."

The car behaved perfectly; it generally responded well to warm weather. They were early enough to find an excellent parking place at the north end of St Giles.

"Oh blast!" said Melissa, "I'd forgotten about paying for the parking. Now I won't have anything to put in the plate. Too bad."

"You can have some of mine," Cassandra offered, "though it's all in little bits."

"Thank you darling. How one does feel these unforeseen extras when poor. Never mind; soon perhaps…."

They went into the church, collected mass sheets and hymn-books from a still plentiful supply.

"Now darling," Melissa began.

"Yes Mummy," Cassandra interrupted, "I know you like to sit at the back because 'one can see so much more'!"

"Absolutely, darling. Sitting in the front we've no idea *who* might be behind us."

They genuflected, entered the pew third from the end and knelt to say preliminary prayers. As they settled back into their seats Melissa murmured: "At least being in straitened circumstances gives one something very obvious to pray for."

Cassandra reflected optimistically that even if her mother's prayers had more to do with material prosperity than the good of the soul they might at least keep her relatively quiet and contemplative during mass.

Sir Felix met them in the courtyard of the church as they emerged amid the throng at a quarter past twelve. Pleasantries were exchanged and they were invited to come to the house straightaway and enjoy a drink in the garden before lunch. "Midge'll be there already; she always goes to the 9.30 at Blackfriars. When the children were at home she found it easier for preparing lunch. Awfully *good* people go there; nobody could be accused of going for the sake of the music and the spectacle. I find it all a bit Primitive Methodist; but then Midge has never been a Protestant so she's got nothing of that sort to react against. See you in a few minutes".

Once in the car Melissa adjusted her makeup, changed into her 'better' pair of shoes, put on a pair of dark glasses, consulted the mirror to see the effect and took them off again. “Maybe not” she murmured and stuffed them into her handbag.

“Turn on the ignition, Mummy”, said Cassandra as the handbag landed in her lap, “we do want to see if it starts”. They both breathed a grateful sigh as it did.

So easily did Melissa find her way to the house that Cassandra said suspiciously “You must have been here more than once, Mummy.”

“Not exactly,” her mother replied, “just looked round the area a couple of times; some *very* nice houses; *decidedly* upmarket. Here we are!” They stopped outside a large detached house, which was clearly a first among equals if not too noticeably superior to its neighbours. Sir Felix’s car was in the drive and he himself emerged from the side of the house as they approached.

“Well done!” he exclaimed. “You found us without any trouble.” Cassandra was relieved that they were not required to reply as he went on: “Come into the garden Now what would you like to drink?” Melissa chose a gin and tonic and Cassandra an elderflower .“I’ll have to drive home, of course,” she murmured with a smile, “not that I mind, but one tends to need excuses for not drinking anything stronger.”

Lady Marjorie came out and joined them. “This is very nice of you,” she said, “it’s just us as we wanted an opportunity to talk family”.

“The kindness is all on your side,” Melissa replied, “and we greatly appreciate your interest. We feel so fortunate to have met you. I admit I would never have thought of meeting any of my husband’s kindred in a Catholic church. Is all your branch of the family Catholic?”

“Not a bit of it,” Sir Felix laughed. “C of E and go-to-church-when-you-can’t-avoid-it the lot of them. I converted when Midge and I were married; she wouldn’t have had me otherwise. Some French king or other said 'Paris is worth a mass'. As far as I'm concerned Midge is worth more than Paris. Best thing I ever did, marrying her and becoming a Catholic." Sir Felix beamed at his wife with an uxoriousness that was wholly attractive and Melissa reflected that she was delighted at his conversion because it had very considerably expedited their becoming acquainted, while Cassandra reflected anew on her mother's amazing nose for the main chance.

But Melissa was speaking: "I wish I'd had the same good fortune in marrying a Marjoribanks. My husband was divorced and I married outside the church and of course in opposition to my family. You know, now I think of it, such marriages usually end in disaster. I can count four without any effort to call them to mind and there must be many more."

"Oh you're being too hard on yourself," Lady Marjorie countered, "you surely don't believe it's divine retribution that makes marriages outside the church go wrong."

"Not exactly," Melissa answered, "but it can't be a good beginning to fly in the face of one's family and all one was brought up to believe. Perhaps it puts too much strain on a marriage to compensate for all that."

"I'm very intrigued by what you say," Lady Marjorie rose from her seat "and please don't let our moving inside interrupt." They sat at a large round table in a large room-sized hall with red walls and a red Turkey carpet.

"Just like my grandfather's dining-room," Melissa murmured. "How lovely!"

A seafood and salad starter was already on the table. "Do begin," said Lady Marjorie as they sat down and unfolded their linen napkins, "and do go on, this is a family lunch. Tell us more."

"My husband had two sons by his first wife," Melissa continued, "but they were already in their teens when we were married and they lived with their mother. We saw them occasionally but Fergus, my husband, usually took them away on holiday by himself. That's what he told me, anyway. Now one's in America and the other in New Zealand and Fergus had their addresses of course but I'm afraid I've lost track of them altogether since he disappeared."

"Disappeared?" Sir Felix and Lady Marjorie were too well bred to show too much astonishment or make any stronger enquiries. Melissa explained (with brevity and some slight omissions) about the bankruptcy and how she had become aware of it only when the bouncing of her cheques prompted her to make a visit to their bank manager, after which she had returned home to find that Fergus had vanished without, as far as she could see, any trace.

"How very distressing for you," her husband's kinsfolk murmured sympathetically, "whatever did you do?"

"I'm afraid I packed up everything I could lay my hands on and put into suitcases, borrowed enough money for the fare and came to England to be a burden on my poor daughter, who was working as a potter in Devon at the time. We were there when Cousin Agatha first got in touch with us and of course that's why we're here now, living in the vast house you've seen us in."

"So now, very immediately, it's a matter of what you're going to do with it!" Sir Felix had not previously realised how immediate the necessity was.

"We do have a few possibilities in mind. Obviously we can't cope with converting to top floor into flats as yet, but we could probably let individual rooms on the first floor on a dinner-bed-and-breakfast basis."

“But what an appalling amount of work that would entail for you!” Lady Marjorie was aghast. “How could you possibly manage it?”
“I’m sure I could,” Melissa replied with a brave little smile and only a very slight sigh, “I’m not really doing anything else and I used to do a lot of cooking for parties and have hordes of people to stay in the so-called good days in Tours and in Paris. At least we wouldn’t have the complication of having to entertain paying guests and take them out.”
“That certainly is a point,” Lady Marjorie agreed.
“Jolly enterprising I consider,” Sir Felix sounded impressed. “But how would you get the rooms ready? You can’t move all that heavy furniture.”
“Fortunately Cassandra’s pottery helper is simply dying to have a room in the house and seems prepared to enlist the aid of friends and relations in useful occupations like plumbing and furniture removing if only we’ll have him move in himself. It would be useful to have a man about the place, too, even such a young one. Oh, we’ll manage; ‘nothing venture’ and all that.” Melissa gave a slightly larger version of the brave smile and blinked rapidly to imply that she had no intention of crying. Cassandra put her hand to her mouth to hide her anxiety as to what her mother would say and do next, but their hosts interpreted the gesture as another sign of the brave facing of adversity and were even more inclined to sympathy and admiration.
“I think that’s very courageous and I’m most impressed, aren’t you, Midge?”
“Indeed I am” his wife agreed “and if there’s anything we can do to help----”
Melissa and Cassandra both murmured polite and appreciative negatives while the married couple smiled at each other with a look of understanding complicity.

There was a brief silence, which Lady Marjorie, without obvious haste, put an end to by saying tentatively to Melissa: "I know you married outside the church and so were excommunicated,"

"Heavens, was I? I thought I was just *lapsed.*"

"I don't know when you were married but it must have been at a time when marrying, or as they put it 'going through a form of marriage' outside the church incurred excommunication. But I see you go to mass now and of course you're obviously not living with a husband who's disappeared."

"No, nor shall I if he ever appears again."

"Mummy's been coming to mass to keep me company," Cassandra interposed, rather fearful of what her mother might say if pressed on issues of motivation.

"That's true of course, darling, but now that I've got over the first hurdle of going inside the building I'm beginning to think I should put things right. I'd like to be able to receive holy communion again."

Lady Mary gave a murmur of sympathy: "I don't know how much a disappeared as opposed to an ex husband would complicate matters, but the Oratorians should be able to help you. Was it a Registry Office marriage?"

"Oh yes, very much so, and very informal."

"That should simplify things; I shouldn't think an annulment would be necessary, but you'd have to be divorced first, anyway. That's supposing your husband's still alive, of course."

"Midge is marvellous. Knows everything about the Church." Her spouse beamed proudly. "Most of us haven't a clue about these things, and cradle Catholics can be worse than converts, if I may say so."

"That's hardly surprising," his wife rejoined; "converts are usually grown up and have an interest in such things;

but they're not very likely to be taught to children, even in Catholic schools."

"The children wouldn't be likely to take much interest even if they were," Melissa laughed.

"That's very true," Lady Marjorie agreed, "I only know about it now because a friend of mine at Blackfriars had her marriage annulled and ever since then she's been giving talks on the subject for the benefit of people in a similar position. I'll consult her about your case if you'd like me to. But don't worry; the Church always has an answer and nobody stays excommunicated unless they want to. I know several people who've come back to the Church after marrying outside and repenting of it, which, now that I think of it, rather supports what you were saying earlier about the instability of such marriages. Poor Cassandra!" she turned to her younger guest, "this is a discouraging conversation for somebody who hasn't yet entered on the mysteries of matrimony."

"Perhaps it would be more discouraging if I had" Cassandra smiled "but I certainly won't be able to complain that I haven't had adequate warning!"

The conversation drifted to other topics; coffee---delicious coffee, "free trade" Lady Marjorie told them---was drunk and Melissa and Cassandra took their leave.

Driving home Cassandra found her mother uncharacteristically quiet.

"I don't suppose you found that wildly successful, Mummy."

"Mmmm, " Melissa's reply came as if from a distance, "as to that I shouldn't be surprised if fruit has been borne or soon will be, probably with great subtlety and tact. But that's not what I was thinking about."

"No?"

"No. I was thinking about going to see one of the Oratorians. Lady Marjorie's very inspiring in a quiet way; generous-minded and thoughtful and *good.* It's fashionable to imply that good people are boring and limited, to use words like 'worthy' as a dismissive insult; but really people who think of nothing but how to enjoy themselves and spend their time vying with each other about the costliness of their exertions and possessions are often most tediously limited and self-centred. Lady M really gives the impression that she *feels* about one. I might just enlist her aid in my struggle to get back into the Church."

"Oh Mummy," Cassandra sighed, "I do hope you're not being *ulterior* again!"

"Motivation" replied Melissa cryptically "is a very strange thing."

***

Melissa was still uncharacteristically quiet the following morning.

Cassandra looked at her a little anxiously. "Are you all right, Mummy?"

"Yes thank you darling. Why?"

"You seem so quiet and preoccupied."

"Oh, I'm still thinking about yesterday."

"You certainly put on a good act as the brave little woman, Mummy; I'd no idea you could be so convincing."

"I *am* brave by some standards. It's not easy to embrace a very different life-style at my age; and you must remember I've never been a student and led a classless existence the way you have. It just happens to be fortunate that I actually enjoy it. I don't know that Lady Marjorie would, for all her good works. Of course I may feel different when we've actually got PGs in the house. But 'sufficient unto the day is the evil thereof'.

Cassandra was puzzled. “I don’t think I’ve heard that one before. Nanny again? What exactly does it mean?”

“I suppose ‘don’t cross your bridges till you come to them’ is the commoner way of putting it.”

“Do you mean more vulgar or just more frequent?”

“I really meant the latter, but now you mention it perhaps Lord Chesterfield had a point in being so snooty about old saws. They do tend to be very boring, however expressive.”

“How do you know about Chesterfield’s Letters, Mummy?”

“We had a copy in the library at home. They were quite fun. The nasty old man used to tell his young son which women to seduce!”

“No wonder Dr Johnson said they showed ‘the manners of a dancing master and the morals of a whore’.”

“Oh, did he? That must have contributed considerably to their popularity! But to descend to the level of bridges---in one sense---the next one we have to cross is what to do about Pete’s parents. We’ll have to ask them to come and see us. Do we ask them to drinks or tea or what?”

“I don’t think drinks are quite right, and we can’t say ‘come to tea’ or they’ll think we mean supper. Why don’t we just ask them to name a time that would suit them and offer them tea---or maybe coffee, or beer---and a biscuit when they’ve seen the house and we’re talking about having Pete with us? With any luck they’ll come up with useful suggestions of practical help, just as Pete has.”

“Thank you, darling,” Melissa replied suavely, “when it comes to an eye for the main chance you’re almost as astute as you say I am, though perhaps in a slightly different quarter.”

"Oh dear!" Cassandra exclaimed in tones of mock dismay. "I wonder if that's heredity or merely getting like the people you live with. I hope it's the latter."

"Why, darling?"

"Well there's a little more hope of recovery!"

18

Robert Taylor rang Cassandra on Sunday to see if she still wanted to go out on Tuesday evening. He rang again on Monday to ask where she'd like to go. Was a pub supper the best thing or would she like to go out for a *proper dinner?* Cassandra couldn't decide. It was entirely up to him. The Indian summer seemed to be over so perhaps somewhere with a comfortable interior; perhaps a slightly up-market pub with a fire?

"I know just the place!" Robert responded happily. "Is half past six too early to pick you up?"

"No; I think I can have the clay washed off by then. If not you can always come in and talk to my mother until I'm ready."

"Wonderful! I can't wait---I mean of course I can wait till you're ready. I'll book a table for 7.30 and then we needn't hurry and can have a leisurely drink while we decide what to eat."

"Thank you, Robert, I'm really looking forward to it. See you tomorrow then."

Robert resisted the temptation to say he wished it were sooner, echoed the usual codas and unwillingly put down the receiver. He was surprised to find himself trembling. 'Ridiculous', he murmured under his breath; 'I'm not a schoolboy making my first date. Though I do feel like one.' He tried to get on with some work; useless. He couldn't concentrate. He tried to think about composing his best man's speech; even more impossible. He glanced at his watch. No more tutorials this morning. What could he do to fill in the time? 'Oh God,' he moaned inwardly. 'If I'm like this today what'll I be like tomorrow? I've got to *do* something. I know! I'll go out and buy a mobile phone. Then I'll be able to ring Cassandra if I'm delayed on the way.' He almost ran out of college and made his way into the Corn, where he'd often passed a mobile phone shop with the unlikely but memorable name of Orange and a décor to suit. He'd thought little about such items up till then. Few of his colleagues had them; the university telephone system was free and more than adequate for somebody living in college. But suddenly he felt an urgent need to be able to contact Cassandra from anywhere, from wherever he might be.

***

In the Common Room after lunch Robert couldn't forbear showing off his new acquisition. Samson Southey was rather scathing about it.

"Really, Robert, what on earth do you want a thing like that for? It's a species of showiness I would not have imagined you to indulge in. College telephones are perfectly adequate."

"*I*'ve had one for ages!" Nigel Nethercott chimed in.

"Yes, Nigel, I'm sure you have," Samson rejoined with more than a touch of acidity. "No doubt you talk into it in trains and buses to the considerable annoyance of other passengers, or walk along the street with it held to your ear. Many's the time I've imagined somebody was speaking to me when in fact they've merely been yattering into one of those things. I consider them an abomination; almost as bad as piped so-called 'music' in shops!"

Richard Holdsworth looked up from his copy of The Sun: "Well you've never really come in to the 21st Century, have you Samson?"

"Only reluctantly, Richard, I admit. There are many aspects of it which I deplore, but it is rather a matter of when one was born and when one dies, and one has no control over the first of these and the consequences of exercising control over the second are rather limited."

Richard stared at Samson uncomprehendingly and thought, as he frequently did, that only people properly trained in the sciences knew how to speak sense.

"Of course you haven't got a fiancée either, Samson." Nigel rarely managed to speak without sounding smug. "Effie likes to be able to reach me at any time and vice versa, so I nearly always keep mine on."

"So you like having Effie able to reach you at any time, do you Nigel? I am surprised."

"You wouldn't understand, Samson,"

"Possibly not. And of course she wouldn't necessarily know where you are, even when speaking to you. I did read somewhere---I suppose it was in The Times---that it's possible to have background noises supplied, train or traffic noises for example, to provide an alibi, as it were!"

Nigel's unfortunate tendency to blush exerted itself; he had in fact had occasion to consider such a device worth having.

Robert gave up on the idea of arousing any interest in his purchase for its own sake and instead mused dreamily on the desirability of being able to reach Cassandra at any time. He wondered if she had a mobile of her own; somehow he thought not. Perhaps he could buy her one. How long should he wait before suggesting such a thing? Or simply giving it to her as a surprise? He hoped her birthday might be just far enough away to make it feasible. He became aware that he was being spoken to.

"Come out of it, Robert," said Nigel "you seem to be in a trance. I think I might just know why you bought that mobile all of a sudden. I know the symptoms. But I won't give you away."

Unwilling to hear any more from Nigel, Robert took refuge in the familiar ploy of glancing at his watch, saying "Heavens---is that the time? I must go," and going immediately. Nigel chuckled as the door closed on him.

"There must be a lady in the case," he remarked as if congratulating himself on his perspicacity.

"Actually, Nigel," Samson spoke deflatingly, "though I would not have expressed it in such clichéd terms, even I was aware of that!"

***

Tuesday passed a little more swiftly than Robert had feared it would; it was a fairly full teaching day and most of the pupils were bright enough to prevent his thoughts from wandering too far. Once in teaching mode he felt stimulated and lively and soon lost himself in the interest of the subject. He'd changed his last tutorial from 5 o'clock to 4.00 to give him plenty of time to get to Huntsfield House by 6.30, so his last pair of pupils were gone by 5.15. He had a shower and changed his clothes; all of them. He checked his keys, his cards and his money for the fifth time and set off at 5.45. The main rush hour was already over and as he was going by Woodstock rather than Banbury Road the traffic was moving reasonably well, so of course he reached his destination early. He would have stayed in the car for another ten minutes had Melissa not come out into the yard.

"Hello Robert, do come in. Cassandra shouldn't be long but let's have a drink while you're waiting. It is past six o'clock, after all." Melissa made it sound as if he'd be doing her a favour.

"Thank you. That would be nice, but perhaps I could have something soft; I'm really thirsty and I don't want to start on alcohol too early in the evening. I must remember I'll have to drive back to Oxford eventually."

"Sensible; perhaps you'd like some of Cassandra's elderflower. She often has it, not being as keen on wine as most of my generation. You don't mind the kitchen, do you?"

Robert was very happy with the kitchen, where Treasure was mercifully asleep in her corner. He was equally happy with the elderflower, which he found rather preferable to wine as a thirst-quencher at that time of the evening. He was drinking his second glass and talking about his day's work when Cassandra appeared. She was dressed much as usual, though rather more carefully made up, and looked—Robert paused mentally to find a suitable description---*perfect*, he decided.

"Sorry to keep you waiting," Cassandra murmured with a smile which betrayed the 'sorry' as a mere formality "but I'm sure you've had a pleasant time with my mother. Is that elderflower you're drinking?"

"It is, and very delicious too. I find most soft drinks too sweet and rather cloying, but this is excellent."

"How very nice to think I'm not going to have to drive home tonight!" Cassandra glanced at her mother.

"Yes, darling, I take the point," Melissa responded imperturbably. "You can really enjoy yourself. You young people are so meticulous about drink drive laws; you put us oldies to shame. Have a lovely, happy time both of you. I'll leave some lights on."

"Where are we going?" Cassandra asked as they turned out into the road.

"Well it's only a pub, but I think it's quite a special one. It's not far out of Woodstock, in the village where Kilvert, you know, the Kilvert of Diary fame, got married. There are post cards of his marriage certificate in the church. But I'm being a bore; after all, why should you know about Kilvert!"

"I do as it happens. I read his Diary one vacation when I was in France and feeling homesick for England. It was the perfect antidote; so readable and evocative, and he made Hay sound most attractive. I loved the man himself, too; he was so sympathetic and unstuffy."

"You must have read a good deal even when you were still at school."

"I think I did, being an only child with parents who led a very active social life. But you must have, too, though you had siblings."

"They always seemed to have more in common with each other than with me so they didn't disturb me too much. There was a good library near us and the librarian became quite a friend and used to recommend books I wouldn't have found for myself. I think Kilvert's Diary was one of them."

Thus happily conversing they arrived at The King's Arms in Wootton-by-Woodstock.

"Oh what a pretty village," Cassandra exclaimed, "and it can't have changed much since Kilvert's time."

"I think not, probably, but at least the pub's now got central heating as well as a fire, and the food must be a bit more sophisticated."

They went into the narrow entrance passage, which was bedecked on both sides with an impressive array of framed certificates declaring The King's Arms to be the best pub of the year or to have won great acclaim for its food, its décor and everything else.

"It must be quite something if all these are any guide. I've never seen anything like it. Oh and look at this huge fireplace and excellent fire---and comfortable sofas and armchairs!"

"I knew you'd appreciate it," Robert beamed, "let's sit on a sofa and order drinks and you can drink as much as you like!"

"Let's sit in front of the fire. We only need a little bit of warmth but it looks so attractive. Do you think I could have some beer? It looks as if they've got some interesting ones."

"That's a brilliant idea. Then we can look at the menu and decide what to have and what wine to order."

The beer was very good, well kept at a perfect temperature. They studied the menu.

"Ooh look!" Cassandra exclaimed excitedly. "Samphire! I've never seen the word anywhere but in *King Lear:* ''half way down/ Hangs one that gathers samphire, dreadful trade'. It's in the scene where Edgar's telling blind Gloucester he's on the edge of a dizzyingly high cliff. What a picture; no wonder Gloucester believed him. I've always wondered what samphire was like; I simply must have some. *And* it's going with scallops and trout. Have you ever had it?"

"No, I haven't and I want to try it too, even if gathering it does sound like a dreadful way to earn a living."

"Do people really have to hang in the middle of a cliff face?"

"They do if it's rock samphire, but I hope they have a safety harness nowadays. The other kind's called marsh samphire and it's collected from boggy, salty marshes; which sounds just as unpleasant, if less dangerous."

After ordering they found no dearth of common interests or topics to talk about and were surprised when so little time seemed to have elapsed before they were told their table was ready. The food was as excellent as the framed certificates proclaimed it to be and they both decided that samphire was worth the trouble of gathering.

"It really sets off the scallops in particular" Cassandra pronounced decisively, "they can be rather dull if not hepped up with something a little tangy." Robert, of course, agreed entirely, feeling as he did more elated than he had for years. People who become Oxford dons, especially in the humanities, tend to experience, at least in their early life, a depressing lack of kindred spirits, but Robert felt he had definitely found one in Cassandra.

They dawdled over their meal, partly because they were talking so much and partly because neither of them was in a hurry for the evening to end. Finally, on realising that they were the last people in the dining-room, Robert paid the bill with his card and much heartfelt praise of the ambience and the food, and they went out to the car. Robert held the passenger door open for Cassandra, who reflected that potters were never like this, and sat down gratefully and gracefully. Robert slid into the driver's seat, put his arm round Cassandra's shoulders, gently pulled her towards him and kissed her very tenderly.

"I've been wanting to do that all evening," he sighed contentedly, "and I just had to do it now while I still had the courage!"

"Oh Robert, I don't know the answer to that, but it has been the most wonderful evening."

"Thank you," Robert kissed her again and then started the car as quietly as possible. He didn't want to break the spell.

Arrived all too soon in the so-called back yard of Huntsfield they stayed in the car for another embrace and a discussion about their next meeting.

"Tomorrow?" Robert asked hopefully.

"We've got to get ready for the Thursday market tomorrow, and it's a pretty tiring day; what about Friday?"

"Can I come and see you in the market?"

"Oh no! *Please* don't. I couldn't bear it!"

"Why ever?"

"Because it's all an act. I didn't mind at first, when we didn't know anybody; in fact it was rather fun putting on a different persona; I've always enjoyed acting. But I'd feel totally inhibited in front of somebody who knows the real me, unless I could be heavily disguised and unrecognisable."

"I'd much rather see the real you," Robert laughed. "All right then, Friday since it can't be any earlier. Which reminds me, have you got a mobile phone?"

"No, why? I've got an extension cordless phone in the workshop but I've never thought about a mobile. Pete's got one, of course."

"Pete?" Robert felt a pang of anxiety.

"Yes, my assistant. He makes most of the Oxford Pots now. He's coming to live here as soon as we can get his room ready."

"How old is he?"

Cassandra became aware of Robert's anxiety, and its cause. She was glad the darkness rendered her involuntary smile invisible.

"Sixteen. He's just left school. He's a very nice boy and a born potter."

Robert tried to keep his sigh of relief inaudible.

Still smiling Cassandra continued: "It'll be a good thing to have a male presence in the house; he's a big lad and rather overweight. He could be useful if we have any problem purchasers and he's strong enough to lift things that are a bit much for my mother and me."

"I'm glad to hear it; this is a very large and rather remote house for you and your mother to be alone in. Very well then, I'll keep away from the market on Thursday as long as Friday's a promise. What would you like to do?"

"Go to a play or a concert, if possible; there weren't many possibilities for either in darkest Devonshire and we haven't really thought about such things since coming here."

"Excellent! Oh Cassandra!"

"Yes?"

"Just----Oh I think you're wonderful and I wish I could say all the things I want to say---but I will one day."

"Good! But goodnight now."

"Goodnight." Robert tried to keep the final kiss from being too passionate, without entirely succeeding, and Cassandra slid from the car and went swiftly to the house, waved and disappeared.

19

Pete arrived early and apparently extra happy on Wednesday morning and bounded into the workshop, where Cassandra was already preparing for the Thursday market.

"You're looking very pleased with life, Pete," she greeted him with appreciation; she was feeling rather happy with life herself. "Has anything special happened?"

"Nothing special, Miss, but me mum's coming over tonight after tea to see you and Missus, like. If that's all right, like."

"What time would that be, Pete?"

"Ha' pa' six, seven o'clock, like."

"I expect that's all right. I'll just go and ask my mother." Cassandra went across the courtyard to the kitchen, where her mother was changing Treasure's nappy.

"Oh dear!" she exclaimed at the news of Pete's mother's visit, "What on earth does one offer somebody who's just had 'tea'?"

"Better not alcohol if she's driving."

"Don't say so! That means *we* can't have any either; and at *half past six or seven!"*

"You could have something before she arrives."

"It's not the same. Anyway she might smell it and think I'm an alcoholic and unsuitable for Pete to be with. So what *can* we offer her?"

"Tea and something sweet I should think. Have we got any biscuits?"

"No we have not! Do you have to mention biscuits when I've just changed Treasure's nappy?"

"Sorry. I'll go and ask Pete what she likes."

Pete proved hazy about his mother's taste in after-tea food. "I know she likes jam doughnuts," he ventured after a longish pause for thought. "She gets them at Tesco," he added helpfully. No other suggestion seemed to be forthcoming, so Cassandra duly relayed the information to her mother, along with a reminder to buy some more coke for Pete. Melissa gave a slight shudder at the mention of jam doughnuts and was desperate enough to express the thought that biscuits might be preferable after all. "Try and find out what she's like, darling, it might help."

Cassandra returned to the workshop and continued working for some time until a brief pause for rest enabled her to ask: "Do you know how old your mother is, Pete?"

"Yes, Miss: firty-six; she'll be firty-seven next birthday."

Cassandra, who had unconsciously supposed that all mothers of grown children must be a generation older than she was, imagined that she hadn't heard properly.

"Forty-six did you say, Pete?

"Oh no, Miss, *thirty*-six; she's her mum's youngest."

"So---so when you were born your mother was twenty?"

"That's right, Miss, not that young, really. Me cousin Tracey, now, she's sixteen like me and she's got a little boy going on for one year old. It's all right for girls." Having thus detached himself from the production of offspring, Pete went on with his work. Cassandra decided that any further enquiries as to what his mother was like would be totally unproductive and that they would have to await her arrival with no other preparation than a knowledge of her age and her fondness for jam doughnuts.

"Really it's so tiresome in England" Melissa complained as she and Cassandra ate lunch in the kitchen while Pete was devouring his pie and oven chips in the workshop. "In France and Spain everybody has their meals at the same time, regardless of class. What are we going to do about supper if Pete's mother's coming at about seven? I should be starting to get it ready by then."

"Perhaps we should just fill up on jam doughnuts," Cassandra suggested mischievously, " if you've got enough. How many did you get?"

"Well actually," Melissa admitted rather unwillingly, "I did buy a whole bag full, about ten I think, because it was by far the cheapest way to buy them and we don't want to look mean. And what about some bread and butter?"

"What sort of bread?" Cassandra looked doubtful. "I don't think brown would be awfully popular."

"I did think of that," Melissa sounded triumphant "and I bought a plain ciabatta."

"No biscuits, then?"

"Chocolate fingers. They looked about the least biscuity. We can always feed the remainder to Treasure."

Hearing her name the little dog made companionable noises and Cassandra gave her a few pets' chocolates as a reward.

"It's amazing," Melissa remarked, "how we've got almost fond of her in spite of everything!"

***

Cassandra found the afternoon rather heavy though Pete appeared to be bounding with energy, not to say excitement.

"Oh Pete!" Cassandra suddenly exclaimed, realising the he wouldn't be leaving at five as he usually did. "You'll be wanting your tea, won't you? What would you like?"

"Oh, I dunno, Miss," was the not very helpful reply.

"What do you have at home?"

Pete's eyes almost closed as his face set in a mask of concentration with the apparent effort it took him to register the details of his evening meals at home. "Egg and chips" he finally managed, "cup o' tea; bread and butter; sausages sometimes; burgers. Other times me step-dad goes out and gets fish 'n chips when me mum's not home or she can't be bothered cooking."

Cassandra felt not a little dismayed when she thought of her mother's probable reaction to this list. Why had they never considered it before? Lunches five days a week were one thing and at least Pete didn't mind having them at the same time as they had theirs. But what to do about his teas? He couldn't be expected to wait till eight o'clock and eat the kind of food they had.

"You clear up in here, Pete, and stack the boxes ready for tomorrow, and I'll talk to my mother about it. You must have some tea before---before you get too hungry."

"That's alright Miss; I had a big dinner and it was late, like, so I'm fine."

Cassandra went across to the kitchen to ask Melissa why it was that they'd pondered the problem of Pete's mother's time and style of eating but never considered how they were going to deal with Pete's teas seven days a week. "Perhaps we can't have him living in after all."

"Nonsense," Melissa responded sharply, "we'll just have to reform his diet, that's all. I am NOT providing chips twice a day for *anybody*; twice a week's more than enough. We'll have to do it gradually; but really one does wonder *how!*"

"What about his tea tonight? That's the immediate problem. Are there any chips left?"

"Really Cassandra! At this rate Pete will be making you change *your* diet. Well perhaps just this once: egg and chips and tomato ketchup and bread and butter and tea. Ugh!"

Pete came across to the kitchen having changed out of his clay-begrimed work clothes and washed at the workshop sink. Melissa reflected that he was not entirely unpresentable when clean, apart from the earrings and a little surplus weight. She pondered on the possibility of introducing some fruit and green vegetables into his diet, but for the present set about serving the egg and chips, which he happily accepted.

"Now you can't take your sup---I mean tea into the workshop, Pete, now that you're all clean and tidy. Do you mind just having it here on the corner of the kitchen table?"

"That's all right, Missus. You not having anything yourself, then?"

"No, we'll have something later, but thank you for asking. By the way, what's your mother's name?"

"Mini, Missus."

"Oh. Well I can't call her that. What's your stepfather's name?"

"Morris."

"Oh, so your mother's Mrs Morris, then?"

"Oh no, Missus; Morris is his first name. He's really Morris Miners."

Melissa eyed Pete doubtfully; surely that couldn't be true.

"Yeah," Pete continued, "everybody laughs about it till they gets used to it. His dad was at the motor works and his mum had a sense of humour. 'Course he's always just called Morris anyway; last names ain't used that much."

Melissa hastened to share this news with Cassandra, who was upstairs washing and changing, and left Pete to finish his tea.

At 6.45 a van of middling size drove into the courtyard. Cassandra and Melissa hurried out and immediately saw that it was driven by a large man in a colourful zipped jacket. Cassandra thought ‘Oh Lord! The stepfather’s here too.’ While Melissa thought ‘Oh gladness and joy! Now there’s a chap here we’ll *have* to offer him a drink! There’s some beer in the bottom of the fridge. He won’t want wine but I’ll be able to have some.’

“Come along Pete,” Melissa called, “you must introduce your mother and stepfather.” Pete emerged from the house with an unaccustomed awkwardness resulting from a mixture of pride and embarrassment. Cassandra knew it was futile to expect introductions and said blithely: “Hullo; I’m the potter, Cassandra Marjoribanks, and this is my mother, Mrs Marjoribanks.” Pete found his tongue and managed “Hullo Mum, hi Uncle Morris.” Mum and Uncle Morris took no notice of Pete but simultaneously greeted the ladies with a polite “pleased to meet you.” Melissa, feeling that ‘how do you do’ would be totally inappropriate, replied “and *you*” and made up for the deficiencies of language by shaking hands enthusiastically. “Do come in,” she continued, “would you like a cup of tea ---or coffee---or,” she paused and threw a challenging glance at Cassandra, “something stronger?”

‘Uncle’ Morris, clearly accustomed to being the family spokesman, dismissed the idea for the present. “We got all Pete’s stuff in the van; how about bringing that in first? Me and Pete can carry it ’n we can have a look round at the same time. Not that he’s got that much.”

Melissa, having supposed that the purpose of the visit was to discuss conditions, hours of work and the finances involved, before coming to any decision about moving in or the date when this could happen, was so completely thrown as to be, for once, at a loss for words. Cassandra, however, perceiving the reason for Pete’s bounding morning cheerfulness and actually grateful that a *fait accompli* spared them any haggling over terms, said simply: “What a good idea; bring a few things up and see Pete’s room and we’ll know what else needs to be done.”

They trailed up the stairs in a procession with Pete in the lead and his mother, whose weight, Melissa reflected with distaste, must be at least one stone for every two years of her age, bringing up considerably in the rear. Pete reached ‘his’ room, threw open the door with proprietary pride: “Look!” he exclaimed. His stepfather looked and nodded pleased approval.

“Cor!” was his mother’s reaction, when she finally reached the top of the stairs and the bedroom door, “all this space just for our Pete! Wish we ‘ad a bit more of it at our place. Not sure about all these stairs, though.”

Melissa recovered sufficiently to say: “Some of this furniture might need to be moved out.”

Pete’s stepfather agreed and immediately volunteered to move it. With Pete’s help a redundant wardrobe disappeared into a room on the same floor, the other pieces were put into suitable places and the whole bedroom began to look habitable.

Melissa was full of praise.

“That’s all right Missus; glad to help. Any time. You and Miss here have done a lot for our Pete.”

“Pete’s a great help and we’re happy to have him here. But you must be needing refreshment after this hard work; I’ll make up Pete’s bed later, but we’ve only got old-fashioned sheets and blankets, I’m afraid, no duvets.”

“Oh we’ve brought Pete’s duvet and covers and everything,” his mother demurred in shocked tones. “They’re his own things. He can make his bed with them; he has to at home.”

"That's so sensible; of course he'll feel more comfortable with his own things. But what would you like? Tea? Coffee? Beer? Wine? Gin and tonic?"

Pete's mother opted for gin and tonic and his stepfather for beer. Cassandra took the former into the drawing-room while the latter went to the van to help Pete bring in the rest of his possessions. Melissa went into the kitchen and eyed the jam doughnuts doubtfully. They didn't seem to go with any of the drinks selected. But what to do with ten jam doughnuts? 'Idiot that I am,' she told herself, 'I should have bought some crisps. Oh well, bread and butter goes with anything. The chocolate fingers will keep, I can't face putting them out.' She decided to put the doughnuts out anyway and give any left over to Pete's mother to take home for the other children, not to mention herself, since going by reports and appearances jam doughnuts must play a large part in her diet.

It proved to be the right thing to do, though over-pessimistic about the number uneaten. The immediate reaction was: "Ooh, doughnuts! Look Morry," to her partner as he came in *"doughnuts! Jam* doughnuts!"

"Mmm—mm!" Morry reacted approvingly as he reached for his beer and took a slice of bread and butter, made it into a roll and put it all into his mouth.

Pete came in a moment later: *"Doughnuts!"* he exclaimed. "Look, Mum, I told them you likes doughnuts!"

His mother laughed. "Well that was clever of you, Pete, because it's not just me that likes them, is it?"

"What would you like to drink, Pete?" Melissa asked tentatively, "are you allowed beer? Or would you rather have coke?"

"Coke, please, Missus; beer's a bit sour I reckon, though sometimes I drinks it mixed with cider. But I likes coke better, really." This was an admission Pete was happy to make to 'grown-ups', though he might have said something different to his male peer group.

By eight o'clock there were only three doughnuts left. Realising that departure time would never be decided by their guests, Melissa rose and went to the kitchen for a suitable container. The doughnuts went into it and were duly presented to Pete's mother. "I know you'll be wanting to get back to your younger children," said Melissa "and I thought you might like to take these for them. Am I right in thinking there are three of them?"

"That's right, Missus: Morry's two boys and then our little girl, our Kylie. Thank you, they'll be ever so pleased. Come on Morry; our Pete's got to put his room to rights before he can sleep in it and our littl'un's probably gone to sleep in front of the telly."

Melissa smiled graciously, relieved at the success of her ploy, and led the way to the courtyard where thanks were repeated and farewells exchanged. Pete showed no emotion at the van's departure but went bounding upstairs to take possession of his new room, while Melissa and Cassandra retired gratefully to the kitchen and decided to have another glass of wine and the few remaining pieces of bread and butter as a substitute for supper.

"Don't forget we'll have to dress before we come downstairs tomorrow morning," Melissa warned, "it wouldn't do to set a bad example!"

"Do you think he'll want a cooked breakfast?" asked Cassandra anxiously.

"Certainly not!" was Melissa's reply, more relevant to what Pete could have than to what he might want, "that's one meal we can start putting on to a healthy basis. He's not going to end up looking like his mother if *I* have anything to do with it!"

20

Robert Taylor's colleagues noticed that he was not quite his usual self. He was distant; he was preoccupied; he was silent. Richard Holdsworth thought he was offended about something; others wondered if he was applying for a new and more prestigious job. Only Nigel Nethercott and Samson Southey knew that he was in love. Nigel was more discrete about this than he might have been had he not feared that Robert would, on the least provocation, refuse to be his best man. Samson's discretion was largely due to lack of interest. He knew Robert was in love with Cassandra and considered this quite unremarkable. He wondered vaguely whether it would come to anything, decided it probably would not and largely forgot about it.

Robert was unable to forget about it at all. He was convinced he had found the woman he wanted to marry and spent many pleasurable hours weighing up the pros and cons of doing so and always coming to the same conclusion. She was not only beautiful but intelligent and lively. She shared many of his interests. They had found so much to talk about that he hadn't even shown her his new mobile phone, which he had planned to use as a conversation piece. In fact he'd done nothing but find out that she didn't have one herself. Conversation had flowed without any aid or need of planning. He realised she was a little more upmarket than he was but she was neither rich nor extravagant. He didn't even mind her being a Roman Catholic. He'd enjoyed his childhood venture into Anglo-Catholicism; he'd even missed it briefly when it disappeared from his life; he was by no means against religion, he merely hadn't thought about it for a long time.

Meanwhile he'd make an effort to come down to earth and find out what was on at the Playhouse on Friday. It was a very short distance from Chester College to the theatre so he preferred walking there to telephoning. It was *Charley's Aunt.* Robert had never seen it but it must have some merit to have lasted so well. Robert never made the mistake of despising something merely because it was popular. He booked two seats. It gave him a useful excuse to telephone Cassandra and tell her about it. She sounded delighted. "Oh what fun!" she exclaimed. "It must be amusing because my mother's grandfather, who was apparently the most dreadful old philistine and never went to a theatre, was once prevailed upon to see *Charley's Aunt* and he enjoyed it so much he insisted on going every year. I've always wanted to see it."

Robert basked; he put down the telephone receiver even more happily and firmly convinced that he had found the future partner of his life.

***

On Wednesday morning Melissa and Cassandra managed to get dressed in time for breakfast and to have it set and ready by the time Pete came down.

"Now Pete," Melissa used her kind but firm voice, "there's muesli, apple juice, yogurt, actimel and bran flakes, and would you like a cup of tea?"

Pete seemed a little awed in the strange situation of sitting down to breakfast with two ladies he regarded as rather grand. He gave an anxious glance towards the door to the courtyard, decided escape was not feasible and merely nodded.

"Good," Melissa smiled approval; "you'll like this muesli, we make it ourselves."

Pete realised that this was an order rather than an observation, decided that such a slight downside to living-in was to be balanced against the luxury of having his own room and submitted without a struggle. He liked the taste of the actimel but the first spoonful of muesli tasted and felt, he decided, like sawdust. He took a smaller second one. It had little squares of something like sweets in it; that was better. He made sure of getting several of these on the third one and munched slowly. He managed to finish the whole plateful, to his not inconsiderable surprise. Melissa rewarded him with a couple of pieces of brown toast and a choice of jams and marmalade. He washed it all down with several cups of milky, sugary tea and gratefully escaped to the workshop.

The postman was just as late that morning as he usually was and it was almost lunchtime when the morning's post fell through the letter slot. Melissa heard the thud and went to pick it up. There were the usual appeals from worthy charities, which she threw into the bin as quickly as possible in case the heart-rending pictures of starving or deformed children, suffering animals or tortured prisoners upset her to the extent of making her want to give them something, which of course she couldn't possibly afford. There was only one missive which looked personal or interesting. She took a knife from the table, made sure it was clean and opened the envelope with it. Five minutes later she was running across the courtyard shouting: "Cassandra! Cassandra!" Her daughter downed tools and came out with anxious haste fearing some catastrophe worse than any that had yet befallen.

"Whatever's the matter?"

"It's this letter---but" seeing Pete look out with unsurprising interest "it's nothing bad, just very astonishing---come inside and I'll tell you."

Cassandra felt for Pete, who was clearly almost as greatly consumed with curiosity as she was, and told him everything was all right and not to worry, before she hurried after her mother.

"Sit down," said Melissa, who poured out a glass of wine before doing so herself.

"Have a drink I know I was hoping---but I never imagined---."

"You've heard from Sir Felix!"

"Yes; all expressed in the most delicate and tactful way, he's insisting on lending us twenty thousand pounds!"

"I don't believe it!"

"Well look for yourself: he says he's well aware we could raise a similar loan from other quarters with the security of this house behind us but that the peculiar terms of Cousin Agatha's will might involve us in expensive and time-consuming legal complexities, so it is infinitely simpler for him to lend us the money himself with no fixed date or dates for repayment. He also waives the payment of interest."

She handed the letter to Cassandra, poured herself a 'tiny top-up', as she usually expressed it, and sank back in her chair to take in the news and the alcohol with complementary pleasure.

Cassandra looked up from her perusal of the letter. "I don't know what to say!"

Melissa smiled with more serenity than she had previously exhibited. "It's an answer to prayer."

"Not to mention your manipulation of main chances, of course!"

"Darling!" Melissa was fast regaining her normal poise, "it's like that story about the Irishman who kept praying his hardest to win the lottery."

"And?"

"And the Lord said to him: 'well meet me half way; buy a ticket!' Everybody knows that the Lord helps those who help themselves."

"Of course your nanny always said so!"

"Yes, such a wise woman. Still I am very impressed. I shall definitely go and see the Oratorians as soon as I can."

"That will certainly impress Sir Felix and Lady Marjorie!"

"Darling it's not quite fair to imply that I *always* have an ulterior motive. I'm really very much moved by the immense kindness of those very good people; they're so outstanding against the shallow, superficial, materialistic people I used to regard as my friends; and while I can never aspire to being as good as they are, getting back into the Church would be a big step in the right direction."

"Hmmm! Well, what are we going to do with the loan? That's the next question."

"I've been thinking about that."

"I thought you might have!"

"Well of course; every time I've said to myself 'If only we had---if only we could buy….'"

"Shall we make a list?"

"Excellent idea. Nothing like it for steadying the nerves and coming to grips with reality."

"You make the list, then, and I'll look it over later. I must go back and put Pete out of his misery."

"What are you going to tell him?"

"Just that we've managed to raise a much bigger loan than we expected and will be able to go ahead and get the rooms ready for paying guests. Then he can get his friends and relations working on showers and decorating and all the things we need to have done as soon as possible."

Melissa reached for pen and paper, steadfastly denied herself 'another tiny top-up' and wrote: computer

broadband
car
showers
decorating
front door
microwave.

Then she realised it was well past one o'clock and rapidly set about seeing to the lunch.

Pete was bounding with enthusiasm at the thought of immediate action and offered to telephone his contacts then and there. Cassandra had given up the idea of doing any more work before lunch. "What a good idea, Pete; use the land line. I think showers and decorating are the first things we need done."

"O.K. Miss, I'll just get the numbers off me mobile."

By the time Melissa called them to lunch all the relevant people had been contacted and made interested promises to come and view the 'jobs' as soon as possible.

Pete still insisted on carrying his 'dinner' back to the workshop, where he turned his radio up full blast and enjoyed eating with gusto and no anxiety about manners.

Cassandra studied her mother's list with interest and some approval and without mentioning that Pete had already initiated some of the necessary work.

"I'm impressed you know about broadband, Mummy."

"Yes, well, I've seen it in other people's advertisements. I know it's something to do with computers."

"We'll certainly need it and we'll have to have wireless as well."

Her mother looked puzzled. "We've got a wireless already---not to mention Pete's ghetto blaster."

"Not a radio, Mummy; wireless is a means of enabling a computer to be used anywhere within range by anybody who knows the right code. It's so that our guests would be able to use their computers here and get on to the internet and send and receive emails."

"Oh dear! How confusing. I thought it was simply the word people like us use for a radio."

"No, it can't be used like that any more. I don't think it's very expensive. We'll have to have a printer/scanner/photocopier, too."

"Heavens! It's just as well we're getting twenty thousand. It's beginning to seem a less vast sum than I'd imagined."

"Yes; I'm afraid it probably won't run to 'car' as you've put it on the list."

Melissa sighed, "Not even a second-hand one?"

"I very much doubt it. We'll have to put up with black exhaust fumes and frequent resort to the AA a little bit longcr."

"I think you mean a long bit longer."

"Probably, but at least I'll be able to get a mobile phone to ring the AA from and not have to resort to roadside telephones or help from other motorists. But what do you mean by 'front door' on the list?"

"We'll have to use it for arriving guests. They can't come in this way from the courtyard, or not until they know us. The front door hasn't so much as been opened yet."

"Well we've never found a key for it."

"No; nor thought about how the front hall might look to a new arrival. All that will have to be seen to."

"You really are doing very well. I'll get back to work and leave you to write appreciatively to Sir Felix."

"Thank you, darling; I'll express your gratitude too. And I'm also going to telephone the Oratory."

"Couldn't you just deal with it by going to confession?"

"I doubt it; too complicated altogether."

"Are you sure you're not just being ulterior?"

"Now darling, don't forget what I said to you about the prodigal son!"

"What? Oh, that he only went home because he was hungry."

"Yes; and his father was still enormously glad to see him!"

21

Lunch was in progress at Chester College. Robert Taylor seemed unaware that Dr Muriel Thwaites, the French fellow, had spoken to him. She tried again. "Really, Robert," she complained in jovial tones, " you do seem to be absolutely *distrait* these days!"

Robert felt as if he was descending from a great height and distance. "Mmmm?" he said. "Oh, do I? Sorry."

"Something very important on your mind?"

Robert looked thoughtful. "Mmmmm," he said, as if pondering what to say next, then "Ah."

Samson, always the observer, remarked: "Your customary loquacity seems to have deserted you, Robert; I do hope this is only a temporary *malaise.*"

"Thank you for your concern, Samson," Robert replied, cheered to be at least one step away from the cause of his abstraction, "I do sometimes have thoughts that are too deep for words, for all my apparently light exterior!"

"Of course I realise," Samson, continued, "that the speech you are, it seems, inescapably going to have to make, is more than adequate cause for mental stress."

"Mental stress?" Dr Iris Bowker caught the words; she was a specialist in diseases of the heart and their palliation or cure, not a psychiatrist, and she had always regretted the fact. Unsurprisingly she related the problems of cardiac inadequacies to mental stress whenever feasible. "Unlike you to talk in so medical a manner, Samson."

"Ah, but he's talking about Robert, who's been so unusually quiet and distant these last few days" Muriel Thwaites was quick to point out. She was the same age as Robert and rather liked him; any clue to his state of mind was of interest to her. “Apparently he’s worried about a speech he has to make in the not-so-distant future.”

“But surely you’re well used to giving lectures, Robert?” Even Iris Bowker couldn’t make a speech by an academic a valid cause for dangerous levels of stress.

“This speech is not, however, a lecture, but a best man’s speech at a wedding.” Samson announced in tones that implied portent.

“Really? Whose wedding? Anybody we know?” Muriel Thwaites could not be accused of lack of interest in her fellows, especially if Robert happened to be one of them.

“Come, Robert, you should share your trouble. Somebody may be able to help.”

“Yes, Robert,” Iris Bowker had renewed hope of finding a really valid cause of stress.

Robert gave in, seeing that the prospective bridegroom in question was not present. “All right, Samson, you tell them. I can’t quite bring myself to own up to it.”

All the surrounding heads turned to Samson with fascinated interest. “It appears,” he pronounced “that Robert has been prevailed upon to be best man at the third wedding of Nigel Nethercott.”

Samson’s timing and delivery were exemplary and his pronouncement had all the desired impact. There was a chorus of exclamations: “Oh, Robert how *could* you!” “What on *earth* can you say?” “That really is a genuinely stressful situation!” Iris Bowker beamed satisfaction. “I think we should all try and help him.” Muriel turned kindly to Robert. “How about starting off by saying ‘Nigel should really be a Muslim; then he could have four wives all at once’.”

“Not unless he lived in somewhere like Dubai. Still, it would be a good opening,” Don Anderson, Politics, interposed.

"Excellent!" Professor Frances Walsingham, ex nun, entered the conversation with relish. "And he could go on to say the only problem would be that those countries have rather unsympathetic laws about adulterers; they stone them to death."

"Well at least that would preclude another wedding and save another best man from the torment of preparing a speech!" Samson's contribution had at least the virtue of logic. Even Robert couldn't resist joining in the laughter and feeling lightened in the general mood of hilarity. As he left the table Muriel Thwaites caught up with him and said "I really do feel for you, Robert, and if I think up any genuinely helpful speech fillers I'll let you know."

"Thank you, Muriel, I'll bear that in mind. The sooner I get down to writing the wretched thing and stop merely thinking about it the better."

"Yes," Muriel replied with a sigh, "we all know that syndrome."

Robert had barely returned to his room when the telephone rang. He let it ring a couple of times as his heart pounded because he thought it might be Cassandra. It was Samson, who said without preamble: "You realise, of course, Robert, that my lunchtime disclosures were merely to save you from impertinent and potentially embarrassing enquiries about the actual cause of your present behaviour."

"What behaviour?"

"Don't be ridiculous, Robert; even you yourself must be aware that you're quite unusually silent, distant and preoccupied, and that this has been noticed and talked about by everybody."

"I didn't know it was so obvious. I just haven't been worrying about other people."

"Clearly. Now that an explanation has been offered you may be able to go on with impunity for a little longer, and doubtless the real cause will eventually resolve itself one way or another. Personally I find it a matter of no great interest and you can rely on my discretion. Goodbye."

Robert spent some time pondering on the substance of Samson's unusual telephone call. He knew Samson to be an acute observer and adept at deducing information from his observations. So he must know something about Robert's feelings for Cassandra. On the one hand Robert was sufficiently elated to feel like singing 'I'm in love, I'm in love, I'm in love'; but on the other hand he considered the emotion a private one and so precious that he could not bear to expose it to possible teasing or ridicule. The Oxford Pot complicated matters as it overhung people's perception of Cassandra and her mother and laid their names open to ribald comments and lavatory humour, however much their actual physical presence in normal social contexts rendered these things unthinkable. He found himself agreeing with Cassandra that the sales in the Thursday market should be phased out as soon as possible.

***

By Friday morning Pete was almost used to eating muesli for breakfast. Melissa had taken pity on him so far as to buy bread called 'Whole and white', which proclaimed that it had 'the taste of white bread with the goodness of wholegrain' and 'no bits.' She tried to induce him to eat a grapefruit but his reaction on seeing its inside revealed when it was cut in half: "Cor it's all red! Looks like blood!" made her decide to delay persuasion until he was at least accustomed to seeing it eaten with relish by herself and Cassandra. Perhaps he could be started on the yellow variety.

Cassandra had intended to meet Robert at the theatre but he insisted on picking her up from Huntsfield. She spent the day wondering what to wear and deciding on something darker and a little less noticeable than her Tuesday garments, with one of her mother's less valuable necklaces. Pete found her a little more silent than usual but put it down to the interesting decision to buy a computer. Actually she was wondering whether it had ever occurred to Melissa to sell some of her jewellery now that they were near Oxford and within range of somebody to sell it to. Somehow she didn't like to suggest it. Besides, there might come a time when she would be rather pleased to wear it herself. She didn't dwell on the coming evening with Robert too anxiously. She was aware that he thought he was in love with her and though she liked him very much and enjoyed his company she considered that they really knew each other very slightly. Robert, on the other hand, spent the day in what might be called fervent anticipation. He was glad they were going to a play; there would be time to talk in the car before and after and the play itself would provide a topic if they needed one. And of course there was supper after the play. He'd booked a table at a nearby Chinese restaurant; it was always open late.

Cassandra was ready when he arrived at Huntsfield; he now knew how long it would take and managed not to arrive too early. There was no dearth of conversation; Cassandra told him about the need to buy a computer and he offered to help her get one as inexpensively as possible from the university computer centre; he could get it as if for himself and they could simply pay him for it. Cassandra laughed, "I'm sure that will appeal to my mother, she's got a good eye for a bargain!" Robert rather hoped it would be Cassandra he escorted to the computer centre and not her mother, but decided to deal with that situation when it arose.

Charley's Aunt was a great success. As they walked to the restaurant afterwards Cassandra was still laughing. "Oh Robert, I don't know when I've enjoyed a play so much! Of course it's ages since I've seen one, but it was so well produced and acted and so *funny!* No wonder my old philistine forbear enjoyed it too. Oh I *am* having a happy evening. A Chinese restaurant's just the right thing, too. There wasn't one for miles and miles in our part of Devon and I love Chinese food and they always give you a doggy-bag if you can't eat it all."

Robert found Cassandra's spontaneous enthusiasm completely appealing; for such an intelligent woman to be so artlessly appreciative was a most gratifying reward for his planning of the evening.

"It's very good of you to be so nice about everything," was his (he thought most inadequate) response.

"Oh, I've got a great capacity for enjoyment," Cassandra replied, "and living in poverty in the depths of Devon has enhanced it, if anything."

The Chinese restaurant did nothing to mar the happiness of the evening and they needed nothing stronger than china tea to keep it afloat. They'd had drinks in the interval at the theatre and Robert was so overcome by the responsibility of conveying Cassandra the ten or so miles back to Huntsfield that he firmly resisted the temptation to order wine for himself at the restaurant when Cassandra said she preferred tea and resisted all offers of alcohol. The food was delicious and they lingered over it long enough to dispose of it all and depart without a doggy-bag. They held hands all the way back to the car and would have felt like singing if they hadn't still been engaged in animated conversation. Robert found Cassandra's enjoyment infectious and was feeling more relaxed and, as he described it to himself when re-living the whole occasion later, elated and even childishly excited, than he ever remembered feeling as an adult.

They arrived back at Huntsfield and drove into the courtyard. They kissed with fervour and Robert found the fastenings on Cassandra's dress (which of course he had been covertly assessing during supper) and undid them.

"Oh no, Robert!" she demurred, though without pulling away from him.

"You don't really mean 'no', do you?"

"Well I ought to."

"Why?"

"Because I don't want to be tempted and I find you very tempting."

"Can't you be just a little bit tempted?"

"Oh dear!"

Robert decided that tempting was better than talking and combined a lingering kiss with a little more temptation to which Cassandra responded with a shudder of appreciation. She detached herself with an effort.

"Oh please Robert, don't make it difficult!"

"It's very difficult not to."

"I must go inside. It's too soon----we mustn't spoil it---"

Robert drew her to him very gently and kissed her again. "I understand" he said softly. "Don't worry. Next time. When can we go out again? I'd like to say tomorrow. Can we have lunch tomorrow?"

Cassandra considered lunch safer than dinner. "That would be nice," she said "but I do try to do some work on Saturday mornings. Would half past one be too late?"

"Can I pick you up at ten past? The place I have in mind can't be more than twenty minutes away."

Cassandra finally arrived at the door to the house, blew a kiss to Robert and went into the house feeling a great deal more disturbed, elated and emotionally out of control than she had been on leaving it a few hours before.

22

Pete came down to breakfast on Saturday morning brimming with the news that his father and several friends and relations were coming round to have a look at 'the jobs.' Cassandra decided to work until they came and then go round the house with them in case her mother got carried away by delusions of unnecessary grandeur. They'd agreed that the main entrance, the showers and the rooms to be prepared for guests were the first things to be done and that the cost of these should be discussed along with the details of decoration and so on. Pete insisted on helping her in the workshop although she told him it might look bad to his stepfather and uncle, who would think she was treating him unfairly.

"Don't worry, Miss, I'll go in the house when they comes" he replied cheerfully.

Cassandra tried to fix her mind on work and house improvements but found it difficult to prevent her thoughts from wandering to her evening with Robert and the coming lunch with him. She valued her peace of mind and generally fought to maintain it and managed to distance herself from emotional entanglements. She realised she was very much in danger now. She had never before had the experience of being with a man whose education and intellect matched her own, with whom she felt so much on the same wave-length. She would have to use the lunch and ensuing afternoon to explain, to tell him---. She was up to this point when the noise of an approaching vehicle was heard. Pete went into the house then came out again to show the first driver, his uncle, the way in.

"Why didn't you follow me Uncle Morris? "Pete asked him.

His uncle laughed "He's too slow for me!" was his answer.

Cassandra came out of the workshop and greeted the new arrival with her usual unaffected friendliness: "Hullo! I'm Cassandra Marjoribanks, thank you for coming to help us."

Pete's uncle said "Hullo—o!" with the intonation of a wolf whistle as he looked her up and down in a very obvious way. Cassandra drew back a couple of paces, giving him a dauntingly cold glance, which was not entirely lost even on such a specimen. Pete glared at him disapprovingly and by the time Melissa came out he managed to moderate his behaviour to an almost passable civility. He had been misled by Cassandra's clay-covered work clothes and friendly manner, but there was no mistaking the classiness of her mother. "Me uncle," said Pete dismissively, by way of introduction.

"Oh yes, Mr er?"

"Just call me Jason; I do electrics and put in showers and that."

"Oh good. Very useful. I'll show you where we want them and you can give us a rough estimate and perhaps some advice about the best kind to have. But we shall want to go to the builders' merchants to look at them for ourselves before we decide anything."

"Yes; right; course you will, Missus."

Melissa led the way to the first floor bathroom, indicated the intended position of the shower, then proceeded to the bathroom directly over it on the floor above. They discussed the merits of electric showers rather than the ones that worked off the hot water system; Jason took some measurements, noted that water supply and pressure shouldn't be a problem, and wished his brother-in-law would turn up and help him to feel less awed by this toffee-nosed lady.

Morris was in the kitchen with Pete and Cassandra when they came down.

"Have you finished in the bathrooms?" Cassandra asked. "I want to have a wash and change because I'm going out to lunch."

"Are you, darling?" Melissa queried "You didn't say so before."

"No, I'd forgotten," Cassandra replied untruthfully.

"I'll just take some measurements for the decorating," said Morris, "Pete can come up with me."

"I'll come and show you about the showers," Jason immediately volunteered. Being left with Melissa and Cassandra was more than he could cope with and he loped up the stairs after his relatives.

"Can we do the main entrance next and then I'll go and change?"

"It's only eleven o'clock, darling."

"Yes, but you know how it is; I can't seem to settle to anything else. Shall I just make them a cup of tea in the meantime?"

Melissa cast a knowing glance in her daughter's direction, realised that *Charley's Aunt* was not the only thing that had made an impact, decided to ask no direct questions until the time was a good deal more ripe, and said "Yes do; and some coffee for us."

Having swallowed her coffee in some haste Cassandra went to tell the men there was a cup of tea ready by way of shooing them out of the bathroom in case they were dawdling in there. They were; but they swiftly finished their measuring and discussions and went downstairs. Pete and his stepfather had a healthy respect for Cassandra, which they had somehow managed to impart to Jason without direct verbal communication. Cassandra ran a bath and wished the shower had been installed already; it would be so much quicker and easier. She decided that one of the items on what she and her mother called 'the loan list' ought to be clothes for her. Of course she might not need them once she had told Robert---. But she preferred not to think any further about that; maybe there'd be an opportunity over lunch, she must wait and see. Anyway, the sooner the better, before the combination of habit and involvement made it too painful.

Robert was exactly punctual and Cassandra, despite having tried and rejected a number of garments and finally decided on the first one tried and put it on again, had been ready for some twenty minutes. They drove towards London, but after some fifteen minutes turned into a road between two high stone walls and down to a gateway blocked by a barrier and defended by a porter in a kind of small, stone lodge, who asked who they were. Robert gave his name and said they'd booked in for lunch. The porter looked them up on a computer and the barrier swung upwards to let them pass. They wound down the drive towards a very stately, beautifully proportioned, stone house, passing a small chapel on a slight rise to their left. In the distance was a stone bridge over a wide stream and to their right the house itself, reposing in its Capability Brown grounds. Cassandra gasped at the perfection of it all. "Oh Robert," she exclaimed, "I've never seen anything like it!"

"But you live in a house not very much smaller, and the grounds could be equally grand."

"Well yes, I suppose so; but our house is brick, not stone, and it can't be nearly as old as this. And the grounds are rather rough in comparison. But is this really where we're going to have lunch?"

"It is indeed. We'll leave the car at this entrance and a porter will park it for us."

The magnificent door opened as if by magic and they were ushered in by a soberly dressed, dignified, middle-aged man who greeted them with the utmost politeness. Robert handed over the car keys and they were asked whether they would like their drinks in the morning-room, the drawing-room or the library. Robert chose the library. "They have wonderful book-cases with the original gold wire set in the doors," he told Cassandra, "I'm told they're the best example in the country." They followed their dignified guide into a fine hall, past a staircase with banisters composed of statues and went into the library. Cassandra sank into a sofa whose comfort belied its appearance of antiquity, looked all round her, taking in the marble chimney-piece, the bright fire, the vast windows, the views of autumn landscape, and gasped again. "Oh," she sighed contentedly, "it's like Cleopatra: it beggars all description."

Robert looked at her fondly; "You are the most wonderful person to take out," he said, and would have said more but that he was aware of a soberly dressed servant waiting to take their orders for drinks, while another, carrying menus, hovered in his wake.

"What would you like to drink? Have something special; have a white Russian!"

"Heavens!" Cassandra was amused "I know what a White Russian is, or was; and I suppose a good many of them were liquidised----oh, no, I mean liquidated, don't I---- during the Revolution, but I never imagined it was possible to drink one these days! Yes, I think I really must have one." Robert gave a nod to the servant to confirm the order for a white Russian and asked for a bottle of Provencal rosé to be served so that he could have a glass from it in the library and then take it to their table.

They had barely begun to look at the menu when the drinks arrived, accompanied by dishes of nuts and olives and the most elegant of *petits fours.* Cassandra found her strangely named drink utterly delicious and asked what it was made of. "I'll tell you when you've finished it," Robert teased.

"Are you afraid of putting me off? You needn't be; it's too sumptuous for me to leave undrunk, whatever's in it." Cassandra took a large, satisfying sip.

Their food orders were taken; Cassandra's drink was finished before they were summoned to their table. "Now tell me what was in it," she demanded.

"Well, vodka, kahlua and milk or cream, I rather think that was cream; oh and ice, of course."

"I don't know what kahlua is."

"It's a coffee liqueur."

"No wonder I feel so good. It must have been much more alcoholic than it tasted. I hope I can walk into the dining-room!"

"I'd willingly carry you, but it might cause comment."

The lunch was as successful, and almost as beautiful, as the setting. After coffee and hand-made *bon-bons* they decided to walk round the grounds as it was fine and dry. Cassandra took Robert's arm and they progressed happily over the stone bridge. Robert summoned the courage to say: "You know we could stay here."

"*Stay* here?"

"Yes; for a night---or two if you like."

"Oh, Robert!"

"You must know I love you."

"Already? You hardly know me."

"Yes, already; if you want to put it like that. I feel I know you; we're on the same wave-length. Time won't make any difference to that."

"You might not think so when I tell you."

"Tell me what?" Robert was unable to keep his anxiety entirely out of his voice.

"It's so strange. Barely a hundred years ago a girl like Hardy's Tess was terrified of telling her lover that not only was she not a virgin but that she'd had a baby; and of course when they were married and she did tell him the results were absolutely disastrous."

"And?" said Robert, with a blend of puzzlement and apprehension.

"And," Cassandra continued, "I'm almost terrified to tell you that I *am* a virgin and that I have no intention of being anything else until I'm married."

"Why?" Robert was nonplussed and in fact startled. He'd rapidly dismissed the notion, which had come into his head unbidden on Cassandra's reference to *Tess of the d'Urbervilles*, that there might be a child lurking in an orphanage somewhere or farmed out to foster-parents, but he'd been quite unprepared for this revelation.

"Because I've made a vow."

"Why did you make such a vow?"

"Because a mere resolution might have been too difficult to keep."

"Yes, I understand that; but---but what gave you the idea in the first place?"

"Perhaps as a protection from the married men who propositioned me---most of the potters were married, the ones who weren't gay, but really because I value and believe in the teachings of the Church, I think they're right. I couldn't live in sin and be deprived of holy communion."

"People don't necessarily live together because they go to bed together sometimes."

"Oh I know. But sex is very addictive, every girl knows that, or should. So if it doesn't work out well enough with the first man to progress to the moving-in-together stage she's not too unlikely to take on the next man largely for the sake of sex."

"But a lot of couples live together happily for a while and then get married when they think it'll work out."

"That may be true, but I've known a few who seem to fall out almost as soon as they're married and then get divorced. You might think living together first would prevent that from happening, but it doesn't seem to. And of course a divorced practising Catholic can't remarry unless they get an annulment; and that can take a long time if it's granted at all."

"It doesn't seem to have changed since the days of Henry VIII!"

"And look what happened to the girl who married *him* when his previous marriage hadn't been annulled!"

Robert laughed; "that's a terrible warning, but he didn't have her head chopped off until after his first wife had died. And things really have moved on since then."

"Just as well, or think what would have happened to poor Diana, never mind what her husband had done. And at least the double standard isn't as operative as it used to be."

"Surely though," Robert countered seriously, "this means that now it's not considered any worse for a woman to have sex outside marriage than it is for a man."

"That's true, but that's a social point of view since the invention of the pill and *almost* foolproof contraception made resulting pregnancy unlikely. The Catholic point of view never differentiated, however, and it's still the same: sex outside marriage is a mortal sin, for both sexes."

"So that's why you've forsworn it?"

"Mainly. But also I've seen how many women get stuck in unsuitable relationships, perhaps even more in France than here, with a man who doesn't want to commit himself, doesn't want children; and then, when the girl's in her forties he suddenly leaves her, leaves her with absolutely nothing, and then he goes and marries a younger woman and starts a family with her. So much for the liberation of women!"

"I can see you've thought about it very deeply."

"Yes I have; from every angle, and I always come to the same conclusion."

"I must admit," Robert said after a long pause "that I've never really thought about it at all. I'll have to, now."

"Well in the meantime," Cassandra spoke more lightly, "let's pick up the keys and go back to the car before we're tempted to ask for the room rates; though we might a shock if we did---it must be expensive; or do you know them already?"

Robert was distressed at the implication that he might have stayed there with somebody else, or even that he had planned everything in advance without asking her, and he found himself feeling very hot in the face and hoping his colour didn't show it. It did, but Cassandra was far too tactful to notice it overtly and inwardly considered that it was probably a sign of grace rather than guilt.

"No," he said with some emphasis, "no, indeed I don't; it's just that it occurred to me after we arrived when I saw how much you liked it and I thought that nothing's too good for you."

"Thank you, Robert, that's very kindly said."

The drive back to Huntsfield was almost silent; they were both too thoughtful for conversation. When they arrived Robert said: "I feel rather awed."

"I knew it would make a difference," Cassandra spoke a little sadly, "but I said you didn't really know me. I'll understand if you don't want to see me again."

"Oh please don't think that! I believe I admire you all the more; but I don't know how to treat you. 'I hold you as a thing enskied and sainted / By your renouncement'."

"Oh, Robert, I'm not a nun, you know! Here, give me a kiss and accept my heartfelt thanks for a wonderful, wonderful lunch in one of the most beautiful places in England----and don't get in touch with me again until you've had time to think a little." Cassandra slid lithely from the car and ran to the house; she paused briefly at the door and waved before disappearing inside.

23

That evening there were few people in to dinner at Chester College but Robert was slightly surprised to see Nigel among them. “Hullo Nigel, not out with your fiancée tonight?”

“No, she’s in London with her mother; they’re doing a couple of days’ shopping.”

“She still lives at home, does she? I mean not with you.”

“Oh no, she’s got her own flat; but of course I stay there sometimes.”

“Mmmm. Tell me, did you actually live with either of your previous wives before you were married to them?”

Nigel looked at Robert suspiciously. “Are you gathering information for your speech?”

“No, no, no, of course not. I’m just wondering about present customs, that’s all. I think I must be a little out of touch.”

“Well, with the first one we just went on holiday together once or twice; we were both in digs and didn’t have a place of our own at all; but with the second one we did actually live together for a year or more. I think we were pretty typical of the general trend.”

“Yes,” Robert observed, “I don’t know of any couples who didn’t go to bed together before they were married; do you?”

“I can’t think of any,” Nigel replied, “oh, except for a chap who married a Coptic Christian girl from Cairo, who lived with her parents and barely saw her fiancé out of their sight before the wedding. She was twenty-eight, too; but that’s different.”

“How did they meet?”

"On the internet. They'd been emailing each other for at least a year before she'd even send him a photo of herself."

"What does she look like?"

"Very beautiful, as a matter of fact."

"How's the marriage going?"

"They're the most devoted couple. There are three children now. Not that I've seen them for a while; I don't find people like that very interesting."

Robert looked questioningly at Nigel. "Don't you envy them?" he asked.

Nigel looked as blank as if he hadn't understood the question. "No" he answered, "do you?"

Robert considered; "I think I feel more admiration than envy" he said slowly.

"Yes, they've been lucky. After all, they didn't have a chance to find out beforehand if they were really suited to each other."

"Did living together before you married your second wife help you to find out that you weren't really suited to each other?"

"Well of course we thought we were at the time. I mean the bed part of it was fine and we considered that was most important."

"It's not really, though, is it?"

"When it stops being important that's when you start looking round."

"Looking round for somebody else, you mean."

"Really, Robert, you're being very analytical; it's not as simple as that and I'm sure nobody thinks these things out so objectively. They just happen."

"Of course you've never had any children, have you?"

"No, it never seemed to be a good idea at the time."

"I suppose you discussed it beforehand?"

"Before we got married, you mean? I don't think we did. We were too busy getting on with our own lives."

"What about now, with Effie?"

Nigel paused for a moment and seemed to be considering how to answer. Actually he was wondering why the thought had never occurred to him.

"I don't know," he eventually answered inconsequentially.

"You don't know whether you've *discussed* it?"

"No; I mean I don't know how she feels about it."

"Isn't it rather important?"

Nigel looked at Robert as if he'd made some strange revelation. "Perhaps it is," he said.

Robert walked back to his room slowly and almost failed to notice one of his pupils greeting him on the way. Once inside he telephoned Cassandra: "I want to see you," he said.

"I'm glad," she answered. "When?"

"Now. But I know that's not viable. Can I just come and talk to you later this afternoon? Then we'll decide what to do."

"All right, I'll probably be in the workshop,"

"I still want to take you to Hartwell House for a night."

"Oh Robert!"

"But we'll have separate rooms."

"That would be very expensive."

"I don't care."

"Well, we'll see."

"Yes. Soon."

Melissa regarded her daughter closely as she came away from the telephone. "You've been awfully quiet lately, darling."

"Mmmmm," said Cassandra.

"Yes," her mother replied. "That's what I mean. How's Robert?"

"I think he's all right."

"Doubtful, is it?"

"Not very."

"Do you really want him?"

"He's very intelligent and we're on the same wave-length ---in many ways."

"I shouldn't think you'd find his family quite the thing!"

"I don't suppose they'd think ours quite the thing either; a bankrupt disappearing father! And they might consider you a bit snooty,"

"Darling!" Melissa spoke reproachfully. "You know how charming and disarming I can be, even with ghastly people like that Fraser woman we met at the college dinner."

"Yes, but would you be?"

"Well perhaps not if I thought they were too impossible. After all, the Fraser woman's not going to be your mother-in-law."

"I don't believe they'd approve of the way we sell the Oxford Pot, either. I really don't think I can go on with the market stall now that we know people here."

"I do see your point. We'll discontinue it now that we've got enough money to do the rooms and bathrooms for the guests. We can surely find a less public outlet."

"Thank goodness for that! I'll tell Robert this evening,"

"Oh, you're seeing him this evening?"

"Yes he's coming round some time. I'll probably be in the workshop. Can he eat with us if it's a suitable time?"

"Well of course! Need you ask? Nobody comes to my house without being offered food and drink."

"Especially drink."

"Well, a drink does help to take the strain out of handling people."

"Handling?"

"Darling! *All* people need handling, especially male ones."

"You've certainly done very well at handling the North Oxford Marjoribankses!"

"Thank you darling. One does like to be appreciated. I just hope you can handle your Robert equally well."

"Mmmm. I hadn't thought of it quite like that."

"No, it's a little less deliberate at your age, but it's there. You're not your mother's daughter for nothing."

"Oh dear!"

"You may say 'oh dear' now, but you'll be thankful one of these days!"

Late in the afternoon Robert came into the workshop as Cassandra was throwing a pot. "That's a beautiful sight, " he said.

"What? The pot?"

"Well, you making the clay grow into a pot under your creating fingers. It looks magical."

Pete, from the other side of the workshop, watched Robert suspiciously for some minutes before turning back to his work with a loud sniff, which being interpreted meant: 'not good enough for Miss'.

Cassandra finished the pot, dexterously slipped the wire under it and cut it off the wheel-head. Robert followed her every move with admiration. Pete looked up from his bench and gave another sniff, unnoticed by Robert and Cassandra, who were more aware of each other than of anything else.

"That'll do for today," Cassandra said finally, "I'll go and change and you can talk to my mother; she'll no doubt offer you a drink! But have some elderflower if you think it's too early!"

"Well I think it is a bit---Though if your mother wants one----."

"Oh, don't worry, she'll have no qualms about having something stronger herself; after all, she hasn't got to drive anywhere." She turned to Pete and told him to stop working when his tea arrived, which it should do any minute.

"OK, Miss, thanks a lot. Take care," he added darkly, eyeing Robert with dislike.

Robert and Cassandra crossed the courtyard together.

"Do you really need to change?" Robert asked.

"Oh yes; I can't sit down to the table covered in clay. I won't be long."

"I haven't had a chance to talk to you."

"What do you want to talk to me about?"

"I'm not sure. Just to say I've been thinking a lot about what you told me---about how you feel---I can see it makes sense though it's still difficult. I want you to know I respect your reasoning even if I don't completely understand the religious background."

"That's not too surprising; you can't have practised any religion since you were a child."

"I'm not against it; I just never thought of it."

"My mother's only just begun to go to mass again; I doubt whether she thought much about it for years."

"But she sent you to a Catholic school."

"You can talk to her about it if you want to."

"I think I'd be embarrassed; non-practising Protestants don't talk about religion easily."

"Don't worry; I won't leave you with her for long." They opened the door of the house; Cassandra ran upstairs and Robert went into the kitchen. Predictably Melissa refused his offer of help and told him to sit down and have a drink. Robert decided to have one; despite the early hour he felt the need of it. He would have liked to ask Melissa why she'd decided to go to church again but had no idea how to begin. Fortunately his hostess was at no loss for words and chatted happily about the vagaries of workmen and the number of people who telephoned on Sunday mornings when she and Cassandra were at mass.

"Do Catholics go to church every Sunday?" asked Robert, seeing a breakthrough.

"Proper ones do. Of course it's a mortal sin to miss mass on a Sunday---without a very good excuse."

"What's a mortal sin?"

"Oh, you know---." Robert obviously didn't know, but Melissa was trying to think how to explain it. "Well," she managed eventually, "a really serious one; you can't take communion after committing a mortal sin until you've been absolved by a priest in confession."

Robert did know, more or less, what that meant; he'd read a certain amount about confession in Chaucer. "That seems a bit harsh," he ventured.

"Yes," Melissa replied musingly, "I used to think so, but the older I get the better I understand it. Missing mass is the surest way to start leaving the Church altogether. People can commit other mortal sins---even really bad ones like adultery, for example---but if they keep on going to mass they'll be so ashamed and distressed about their inability to receive communion that they're bound to go to confession sooner or later and they won't give up entirely and lapse from their Faith. The Church is for sinners as well as saints, you know. Our Lady's not called 'refuge of sinners' for nothing. But Cassandra can explain it better than I can; she seems to have a natural understanding of these things." At this juncture Cassandra herself appeared in time to catch the sound of her name. "Now, Mummy, what have you been saying about me?"

"Oh, just that you know more about mortal sin than I do."

"Well really! I hope that's not the case, even if only because you've lived a lot longer than I have, not to mention lapsing for years!"

"Oh dear! Yes I did phrase that badly. Of course I meant you know more about the Church's teaching on the subject. I've been trying to explain it to Robert."

"You explained it very well and I think I understand it now" Robert interposed.

"It can't be the commonest of subjects for drinks-before-dinner conversations" Cassandra laughed "but I'm very impressed at its being brought up at all. We'll be getting on to the Seven Deadly Sins next and their order of gravity and punishments in Hell for those who die unconfessed and unabsolved!"

"Well I do know about those" Robert was happy to emerge from the vale of ignorance "because it's impossible to read, let alone teach, medieval literature or even Shakespeare without a knowledge of them. But somehow I hadn't related them to present day situations."

"Well fortunately," said Melissa as she picked up the wine bottle, poured a drink for Cassandra, offered Robert 'a tiny top-up' and took a not very tiny one herself, "*fortunately,* there's nothing sinful about alcohol."

"In moderation" Cassandra added.

"Well of *course* in moderation, darling. One should do practically everything in moderation; excess is so *vulgar*, don't you think?"

Cassandra laughed and said "Undoubtedly" though not without a sideways look at her mother. Melissa continued the conversation with references to the work about to be done on the house and a few comments on Pete's friends and relations; Robert remembered his promise to help with the purchase and setting up of a computer and there was a happy aura of progress and euphoria by no means dispelled when Melissa served up a simple but elegant meal with distinctive flavours and not too many calories. Robert found it delicious and complimented her on its excellence.

"Thank you," she replied, "it's a joy to cook meals like this after the awful stuff I still have to produce for Pete, though we've succeeded in getting him to eat muesli for breakfast and we haven't given up hope of grapefruit and brown bread in due course."

Robert found himself reflecting that girls were supposed to become like their mothers and he wouldn't mind at all if Cassandra became like hers, though with a very slight reservation about the amount of alcohol consumption. But of course, he told himself, that's a generational thing. This idea didn't quite square with his own experience of family life where his parents drank little and infrequently. Somewhat ruefully he admitted to himself that class was at the bottom of it: respectable lower-middle-class people had other priorities and insufficient funds to spend on unnecessary and potentially dangerous luxuries such as wine without a very special occasion to warrant such expenditure. Besides, the consumption of alcohol in any form did little to betoken respectability; families where money was spent on drink rather than good warm clothing, nourishing food, solid furniture, and the support of children into the upper reaches of education could hardly be considered respectable.

All this passed through Robert's mind as he sat at the kitchen table with Melissa and Cassandra, joining in occasionally as they outlined their plans for the house and sought his opinion and made him feel comfortable and at home despite his reflections on his own background. Being an academic in Oxford had neutralised his perception of his own class, he had imperceptibly blended in with the life-style of the high table and the Senior Common Room. But it dawned on him suddenly that he ought to introduce Cassandra to his parents before he asked her to marry him; and at the same time he realised that he neither knew how to nor wanted to.

Sensing a change in atmosphere Melissa and Cassandra said simultaneously: “Coffee!” Cassandra got up to put the kettle on and asked Robert whether he’d like ‘real’ or decaffeinated or something else.

“What are you having?” he asked her.

“Oh, decaff I think, but Mummy has the real thing. We just use different cafetieres. Perhaps you’d better have real too as you have to keep awake and drive back to Oxford. I hope you don’t mind our staying in here; it’s a bit chilly in the drawing-room and we can at least sit in the relatively easy chairs here.”

“I like it in here,” said Robert sincerely, “and you’re right about the coffee. I mustn’t drink any more, either.”

“Oh they’re only *tiny* glasses,” said Melissa predictably.

“Really, Mummy! The combination of your belonging to the generation you do and living abroad for so long has a very bad effect on your regard for the law. I’m sure Robert doesn’t want to lose his licence, and think how ghastly it would be if either of us was unable to drive, living out here as we do.”

“But we’re not going to drive tonight, darling!”

“No, but I’m just trying to point out how important it is. Anyway, when we’ve finished our coffee I’m going to show Robert the main door and hallway and some of the other things we’ve been talking about so he’ll have time to absorb any wine in excess of two glasses before he goes.”

Coffee finished, Robert and Cassandra helped Melissa with the washing-up before going into the main hall.

"Heavens!" exclaimed Robert, "it's pretty imposing as it is. What do you need to do to it?"

"Open the front door for a start; there's no key for it, and we'll have to have extra ones made. Then we thought it should be painted to make it look more welcoming and less gloomy; but it's not a priority compared with the bedrooms and bathrooms."

Robert put his arm round Cassandra and kissed her. "Now that was a priority," he said. "I have enjoyed this evening."

"I thought it would be easier for you to get to know me better in home surroundings," Cassandra answered, "but have you really enjoyed it?"

"I really have; but I don't think I can reciprocate. I mean, you wouldn't get to know me better in my home surroundings: I don't feel I belong there any more. Besides, you live in such a grand house!"

"You should have seen me in my flat in Devon; nothing grand about that. Yet I was more at home in it than I am here, even though we really live in our kitchen-cum-everything room as you've seen this evening."

"I like it; homely domesticity's a very pleasant change after college life and I like your mother, too. Can I come and have supper with you again some time?"

"Well, perhaps if you're *very* well-behaved," Cassandra laughed "but Pete's friends and relations are starting work here on Monday and we'll have a lot of organising to do before that. By the way, we're discontinuing the market stall, greatly to my relief. We want to leave off while it's going well and hope people will be tempted to buy from here and from a couple of other outlets we've found. The sort of act we put on in the market is unsuitable now we've got to know people."

Robert was entirely in agreement with this but deemed it wiser not to say so directly.

"I can see how you feel about it," he ventured, "but I'm afraid a number of your admirers will be sadly disappointed."

"They're not the ones who buy things, on the whole; they only come for the show! We always thought it would be a nine days' wonder and one could say we've got through about eight of the days by now. Still, it has started us off with what one might call éclat!"

Robert agreed and remembered with gratitude that without such a beginning they might never have met.

"Do you think your alcohol count's low enough by now for you to drive back to Oxford?" Cassandra enquired.

"Are you sending me away?"

"Yes. Remember that things can be spoilt by 'overdoing and lack of measure' and I'd hate that to happen."

"So would I; but I don't feel there's any danger. It seems no time at all since I arrived here."

"That's true; but in fact," looking at her watch, "it's some five and a half hours and I'll have to do some work tomorrow."

"All right; I'll go quietly---- if unwillingly. You know I really want to stay with you. One day I will, somehow!"

They kissed again, and again. Then Robert went to say goodbye and thank-you to Melissa and Cassandra saw him to his car.

24

Melissa and Cassandra spent an exhausting Saturday moving their bedroom paraphernalia from the first floor to the second in order to make way for the work to be done to render the former suitable for paying guests. Cassandra had little in the way of clothes and a relatively small number of cosmetics though she did have pictures and works from other potters and religious artefacts to be arranged with precision and aesthetic exactness in their new setting. Melissa had rather more clothes and many more cosmetics, not to mention a surprising abundance of jewellery, which had once reposed in elegant cases but was now hidden among her clothes. It took some time to locate all the items and sort them out. Cassandra helped.

"Really, Mummy! I'd no idea you had so many valuable things. Half of these I've never even seen before."

"Oh, I'm sure you have, darling. It's not as if I've been hiding them, except from potential burglars, of course. But there haven't been many occasions for wearing them since I fled from France."

"Are you sure you didn't keep them from me in case I suggested selling them to pay the bills?"

"Now where in Devon could we have sold them?"

"I must admit I've no idea. But it surely wouldn't be too difficult in Oxford. They'd add up to enough for a new car; well, a nearly new one."

"Oh, darling, cars decrease in value and become worthless in time; 'but a diamond and sapphire bracelet lasts for ever'! Besides, you might be glad of them some time!"

"Oh, Mummy! Can you imagine me wearing something like that to an Oxford college lunch or dinner?"

"Ah!" Melissa said meaningfully, "so you do intend to become an Oxford don's wife."

Cassandra laughed. "I could just be keeping it in the back of my mind; not that he's asked me."

"He will, I've no doubt of that; but it's early days. He'll want to feel more sure of a favourable reply before he ventures."

"He doesn't seem to want me to meet his family: he says he doesn't belong there any more."

"That's probably true but not necessarily a good sign."

"Why not? I thought you'd be glad I wouldn't have to mix with his people."

"Families are important. I virtually cut myself off from mine and often regretted it bitterly. Children need grandparents and on your side they'd have only one and not an uncle or aunt or any cousins to make up for that deficiency."

"Oh dear. I'll have to give that some thought. But never mind it now; let's get all your things up to their new home and you can stash them away as carefully as ever."

It took them most of the day to render their second floor rooms as habitable as possible without trying to move the heavy furniture which was to await the muscle power of Pete's friends and relations to relegate it to other rooms even further up.

***

Robert Taylor was glad to see Samson Southey at College lunch on Saturday and put down his napkin in the place beside him to make sure they could sit together without anybody else sitting there while Robert was helping himself to soup. Soup was always the first course at lunches and was generally of a reasonable flavour, if rarely as hot as it should have been. As Robert, plus soup, sat down beside him Samson remarked that he presumed from this unwonted attention that Robert wanted to talk to him about something.

"How very perspicacious of you, Samson," Robert replied, "and entirely accurate. Ummm-----."

"I gather from your tone and manner that you are going to ask me to do you a favour."

"Only if it doesn't put you out in any way."

"Even my perspicacity, Robert, is unable to provide an answer to that as yet."

"Well, are you going to the service at the Oratory tomorrow?"

"I presume you mean the high mass at eleven o'clock. Do you want to come with me?"

"Well if that's the one----."

"The one attended by my Marjoribanks kinswomen? It is indeed."

"Really, Samson, you are amazing!"

"Merely logical, dear chap, merely logical."

"Well either way you make things easy for me and I'm grateful. Shall I drive you to the church tomorrow?"

"No, no. It's a pleasant walk and not far. Besides I often hear people complaining about the difficulty of parking anywhere near. I'll come in to breakfast so that we can go together from here. We should set off at half past ten to be in time to get a good seat where you can see everything---or possibly everybody---and make sure the necessary books haven't run out."

***

Robert was ready to set out for the Oratory at ten o'clock on Sunday morning but Samson insisted that it was far too early and that he must spend half an hour working in his room before they left college.

"You seem rather nervous, Robert", his companion remarked later as they were walking along together. "Is it due to the unaccustomed attendance at a place of worship or to the members of the congregation you expect to see there?"

"Both, probably," Robert admitted. It was pointless not to admit things to Samson; he was capable of deducing them anyway. "I can't remember ever going to a service in a Roman Catholic church before, though surely I must have been to the odd funeral. But that's different because half the congregation wouldn't be Catholics anyway."

"You told me you went to an Anglo-Catholic church in your extreme youth, however," Samson said soothingly, "so that should help you to feel at home. I expect you're more anxious about what that young woman's going to think when she sees you there."

"How do you know that, Samson? I can't believe you've been in the same situation yourself."

"Certainly not!" Samson replied with some feeling. "But I have read a great deal and one can't entirely avoid encountering scenes and descriptions of the tender passions even in the really great Russian novels, let alone the English and French classics. It is possible, even occasionally necessary, to enter into these things imaginatively. In fact it can enhance the ability to take a sound, objective view of such things if one is not biased by one's own experience."

"Dear Samson! Even the college porter Butler considers you to be what he calls 'a real scholar', and I'm inclined to think he's right."

"Really? How very surprising of him. But here we are already; early, of course. Good morning!" Samson greeted the men behind the book stand as they stood ready to hand out a mass sheet, a hymn book and a small mass book in

Latin and English. “Yes, Robert, take one of each of these. I’ve got a missal but I’ll use a mass book today so that I can show you what page we’re on; it can be quite hard to follow at first. Rather like computers, I often think, you have to know what *not* to look at. Now do you want to sit near the front where you have a good view of the sanctuary or near the back where you can see the other people? My kinswomen always sit at the back; I’m inclined to suspect the mother of the latter kind of motivation.”

“How about somewhere in the middle?” Robert suggested tentatively. “I don’t want to be conspicuous at all.”

“Very well; halfway back in the middle on the left. You’re tall enough to see what’s going on anyway.” Samson reached a suitable pew, genuflected and went in. Robert followed suit and blessed his Anglo-Catholic childhood for coming back to him to provide something of a sense of happy familiarity.

Melissa and Cassandra went into their usual pew, well back on the right, shortly after Samson and Robert had taken their places. They immediately knelt down to pray and Cassandra was still doing so when her mother was already sitting up and surveying the rest of the congregation. People were still coming in in large numbers and it was not always easy to see past them. It was, therefore, some little time before she caught sight of Robert sitting by Samson. She could hardly wait for Cassandra to sit up from her kneeling position before tapping her arm with the back of her hand.

“What’s the matter?” Cassandra murmured.

“Look over there, on the left!” her mother murmured back urgently.

“Oh, Samson Southey you mean.”

“No---yes, but look who’s with him!”

“Oh! Heavens!” Cassandra’s heart missed a beat and she felt herself getting breathless, “it’s Robert! What on earth’s he doing here?”
“That,” her mother replied “is not very difficult to guess!”
The entrance bell rang, the procession of altar servers in their black cassocks and spotless white surplices, deacons in their lustrous, heavily-brocaded dalmatics and the celebrant in his matching chasuble entered from the sacristy to the tune of the first hymn, processed to the back of the church and made their way down the central aisle to the sanctuary. Robert turned round to watch them and gave a loud gasp, partly at the unexpected splendour of the spectacle and largely because he saw Cassandra regarding him with a mixture of puzzlement and pleasure. They caught each other’s eye and smiled. Robert was tempted to wave but decided it would be out of place, even though he had just seen a small child waving excitedly to a probable grandmother. ‘He can’t be more excited than I am,’ Robert thought to himself, ‘this feels like the most exciting thing I’ve done in years.’ If possible he was even more excited when he heard the Kyrie and then the Gloria sung by the choir to the music of Haydn. As he listened, without paying great attention to the text so kindly pointed out by Samson, he reflected on the use of references to Catholicism and Catholic practices by the Romantics: in Christobel and The Eve of St Agnes with its ancient bedesman, references to the unfamiliar-in-England with its hint of dangerous glamour. He felt caught up in the excitement of it all as he watched the organised movements of the company round the altar, the swing of the censer, smelt the exotic odour of the incense----and felt all the while that Cassandra was not far away from him, was watching the same scene, was equally, indeed more, moved by the whole occasion. He

took a deep breath and let it out in a slow sigh of true satisfaction. At the end of mass Robert and Samson joined the slow shuffle of the crowded congregation as everybody made their way to the bottlenecks of the two exit doors.

"There really are vast numbers of people here," Robert observed, "and I'm not surprised. The whole thing's superb. I've never before seen such collection plates either: there were far more five and ten pound notes than coins. Ah!"

Robert saw Cassandra in the throng, but so far ahead it was impossible to reach her.

"Don't worry," Samson countered his exclamation and expression of anxiety, "they'll wait for us outside."

Robert gave Samson a glance of gratitude and reflected on the advantages of associating with a person of his intelligence, who continually saved one the trouble and possible embarrassment of cumbersome explanations. Moreover he was right of course, Melissa and Cassandra were waiting for them in the courtyard and the former greeted them immediately with an exclamation of pleasure at seeing them and an invitation to come and have a drink in the bar. They complied happily.

Seated at the last available table with their chosen drinks they noted that Sir Felix was not there and Samson informed them that he had to go to Blackfriars with his wife sometimes, greatly though he preferred the Oratory.

"I hope you enjoyed the mass and the music, Robert," said Cassandra.

"I can't tell you how much!" Robert replied. "The whole thing was a wonderful experience. I've never known anything like it. I'm grateful for the Anglo-Catholicism of my childhood that enabled me to understand it, or most of it, but its sum total was something outside my previous range. The number and variety of people in the congregation, for one thing; it made me think of Langland's 'field full of folk', though there were more different colours than there would have been in England in the 14th Century."

"Colours of clothes or of people?" Melissa asked.

"Well both, I suppose; only the rich and some of those in their service wore bright colours then, though the men would have been at least as colourful as the women. I really meant people, however; two black altar boys and numerous Oriental or Asian people too. I think it's wonderful: truly universal as it should be." Robert was grateful that nobody had asked him what he was doing there or why he had come. Melissa thought it too obvious for explanation and would have considered it vulgar and indiscreet as well as pointless to ask him, since he would hardly have said merely that he wanted to see Cassandra. Cassandra herself, having had time to recover from the first shock of seeing him and to reflect on possible reasons for his presence there, thought, indeed hoped, that his motivation was more complex and included a genuine desire to know and understand her better, and a realisation that some understanding of her faith was a necessary adjunct to this. She counted on his telling her about it when they were on their own. Meanwhile Samson was speaking learnedly about Haydn's masses and Robert showing his appreciation by asking intelligent questions, as became an interested and reasonably knowledgeable listener.

After a second round of drinks for the others and a cup of coffee for Cassandra they left the bar and went their separate ways, Samson and Robert to lunch in college and Melissa and Cassandra to drive home.

"Well," said Melissa indistinctly, lighting a cigarette as her daughter drove down the Banbury Road, "that was very illuminating---though I will say he showed a most convincing interest in the music and the service."

"Robert you mean, of course."

"Naturally."

"I'm sure his interest was perfectly genuine."

"Oh yes, *as it turned out!* But that was not his reason for going in the first place; it was simply a very fortunate bonus for him. He is intelligent, as you say. I wonder how you can contrive to meet his family before you get too involved."

"Do you really think I need to?"

"I'm afraid I do. It's obvious you're thinking about marrying him ---and that he's set on the idea of marrying you, and I know you're not the kind to marry without wanting children; so it's important for you to envisage having his parents as their grandparents. They might insist on making them say 'pardon' and 'toilet' and using 'serviettes'. Could you bear it?"

"I don't think such things are important."

"Hmph! I wonder. Or they might be deeply anti-Catholic and try to influence them against their faith; you must think *that's* important."

"Yes, I do. But could I find out all that about them at one meeting?"

"I'm sure *I* could."

"In that case you'd better go and meet them instead of me---or perhaps you could ask them to come and stay?"

"Now that is actually a very interesting idea. I think we should work on it."

"Oh *really* Mummy, I didn't mean it seriously."

"I did." Melissa tossed her cigarette out of the window as if to underline the point she was making. "They'd be very impressed at our house and we'd be able to see whether they'd be amiable and compliant or chippy and aggressive."

"*Mummy!* I do wish you'd stop spreading litter! And what if one of them were to be amiable and the other one chippy?"

"It would be for you to decide how you felt about that; and now I come to think of it, you are rather conformist yourself and you wouldn't find their middle classness half as tiresome as I would. I daresay they disapprove of spreading litter, too. Of course it would mainly depend on whether they *said* so or not; probably not, in our house. But doubtless they would in their own. Yes. You should have them here and then go and stay there. It should be very revealing. I daresay they disapprove of smoking, too."

Cassandra smiled in spite of herself. "I think I will have to meet them; otherwise you'll build up such a picture as to discourage me totally."

25

Monday morning arrived and with it Pete's stepfather, Morris Miners---aka 'me Uncle Morris'—-, his actual uncle, Kevin, 'electrics', and a couple of younger helpers. Morris got going on the preparation of the front hall for painting while Melissa demanded that 'Jason' take her to a couple of builders' merchants where she could look at showers and bathrooms. Jason was not greatly in favour of this expedition but was too much in awe of Melissa to demur. "If I decide to buy something and they have it in stock we can take it in your van and save delivery charges," she had said in a voice which brooked no argument. Kevin did not argue. They set off. Cassandra extracted Pete from the house, where he felt one up on his stepfather for the first time in his life and was thus rather liable to try and take charge. Fortunately he was not averse to staying in the workshop with 'Miss' when she said she needed him.

By the end of that day all the immediate projects were satisfactorily under way and Melissa decided that they could now invest in a computer, have it set up, begin advertising and fairly soon draw in some guests to help pay for the next stage. Cassandra was required to ring Robert and arrange the purchasing procedure. He was not in his room in college so she rang his mobile number and, as it was not switched on, left a message. Robert rang back later in the evening when they were sitting over their after-dinner coffee. He was distressed that he hadn't been able to speak to her before. "I was teaching a class in one of the college class-rooms from six o'clock till after seven, and then I dashed over to dinner somewhat late. Of course I couldn't have my mobile on in either place."

"Oh that's all right, there's no hurry. Was the class fun?"

"Not really. I'd much rather give a lecture or teach one or two people in a tutorial; I tend to find that the most boring people are the ones who do most of the talking in a class and it's rare for anybody to learn very much. The slower or shyer ones only get going towards the end by which time some of the others are eager to get away. But never mind that; I want to help you buy a computer, tomorrow if possible. Could you meet me in town and then perhaps we could go and have lunch somewhere?"

They duly arranged a meeting place and Cassandra eventually hung up the receiver feeling rather surprisingly excited. They'd never been to town together before. It seemed in some ways a more intimate kind of thing to do than going out to dinner or to a theatre. Cassandra wondered why.

"I don't suppose," Melissa ventured as her daughter sat down again, "that you want me to come and help choose the computer?"

"I never thought of it; why? Do you want to? I mean what about Pete's lunch?"

"His *dinner!* Oh yes of course I'll have to be here for that----unless I were to leave him something cold to have with his friends and relations."

"Well, they might need you, too. You know, to ask about paint or where to put the showers and so on."

Melissa smiled. "It's all right, darling; I wouldn't dream of coming really. I don't know the first thing about computers but you were looking so ---well--- so distant, for want of a better word, that I couldn't forbear a little probing to find out how you were feeling. Is it so exciting to be going shopping with Robert?"

"You are impossible, Mummy! But yes, since you make such a point of it; only it puzzles me, because I don't know why."
"Probably because it's the kind of thing engaged and married people do; one doesn't normally go shopping with a mere male acquaintance, even a boyfriend. It's rather special."
"Maybe; it's special to be buying a computer, anyway. I feel we're really getting somewhere, having one, though I'm a bit scared to think how we'll manage to use it. I hope Pete knows something about them. He must have done a bit of computer training at school."
"Heavens! Is that the sort of thing they do in schools now!"
"I believe so. I wish I'd done some. But actually I'm thinking that since I'm taking time off to go into Oxford it would be rather nice to go and look at some clothes while I'm there. I need a few more things to go out in and since we're not living quite such a hand to mouth existence as we were perhaps I can afford some."
"Now that really *is* a good idea. Go in early and get a good parking place and take your time."
Cassandra spent a very happy morning trying on a lot of clothes and buying a few, which she put into the car before meeting Robert. They were both at the computer centre slightly early and both equally pleased at synchronising their meeting. The choice and purchase of the laptop was largely Robert's doing and was achieved with speed and efficiency. They took it to the car and went to have lunch. Robert wondered briefly why he had not wanted to take Cassandra to lunch in college; she was too special, he told himself, he couldn't bear the idea of her being the subject of queries or comments from any of his colleagues, almost all of whom knew who she was. Unaware of this,

Cassandra was perfectly happy in a French restaurant in Little Clarendon Street with unnoticeable furniture and excellent food.

"You can't imagine how exciting I find all these restaurants after a little town in Devon where the only places one could go out and eat in were a couple of pubs. Not that I did go out to eat very often because potters don't, on the whole, and when my mother came to live with me we were rather on the breadline. Life's very different now."

"I'm glad of that," Robert replied happily, hoping he was providing some of the difference, "and I'm glad you like restaurants---and food."

They conversed fluently and cheerfully until Robert realised he was going to be late for his next class, paid the bill hastily and left Cassandra unwillingly but making a promise to come out to Huntsfield the following afternoon to set up the computer. Cassandra drove home smiling to herself in general contentment over her well-spent morning.

Her mother observed her with interest when she arrived, was glad to see she'd spent her time happily and expressed more enthusiasm for her new clothes than for the laptop and all that went with it.

"Robert's teaching the rest of today, on and off, but he's coming tomorrow to help us set it up," Cassandra told her eagerly.

Melissa sighed. "Oh well, sufficient unto the day---!"

"Whatever do you mean?"

"I'm not entirely sanguine about that machine. I fear I'm going to find it quite beyond me."

"Well I hope I'll be able to do the basics fairly soon; it's not as if I've never seen one, I just haven't used one myself."

"Of course Robert will have plenty of reasons to come out and help you with it!"

"I'm sure he'll be very helpful."

"Mmm. How do you feel about asking his parents to stay?"

" I don't see how I can. Even if he were to ask me to marry him I could hardly refuse to give an answer before I'd met his parents, could I?"

"I don't really see why not; and I don't suppose I can ask them either, unless I have a brutally frank talk with Robert and tell him how important I think background is, especially in the light of my own experience, and so on and so forth."

"Thank you; I can see you putting him off entirely and my ending up with nobody to help with the computer!"

"I wish I thought that was all you really cared about!"

Cassandra laughed a little consciously and said: "I'm afraid I can't really pretend it is. We do get on very well."

Melissa pursed her lips. "Early days," she murmured, "early days!"

Robert duly arrived the following afternoon and the computer was set up, wireless installed and Cassandra instructed in the art of sending emails. They then had supper in the kitchen as before. Melissa was, of course, anxious to know how her daughter had progressed. Robert said she was a very apt pupil and Cassandra said he was a very good teacher. Melissa said 'oh well of course they'd both say that' and had to be assured that they were speaking the honest truth.

"Yes, really," Cassandra assured her mother, "he's not the sort of teacher who wants to do it all himself and says 'there, you see' at the end of some swiftly executed manoeuvre; he made me sit down in front of the screen and do the clicking myself. Only I do find the mouse a bit wilful! It jumps about all over the screen and I can't always control it."

"They would call it a mouse," Melissa complained, "very off-putting."

"If you'd like to write out the advertisement for the Gazette," Robert volunteered, "I'll type it and send it by college messenger tomorrow. I've brought a copy with me so we can look at the terms and the word limits and so on. I honestly don't know much about it as I've never used it for advertising anything myself, but I do look at the advertisements idly from time to time. You could really compose a very tempting write-up of this place."

"Yes," Melissa mused: "Two very attractive women in dire need of cash willing to put up (with) paying guests in their somewhat dilapidated and rather inaccessible once stately home; breakfast provided, dinner at guests' own risk, French lessons and stern discipline extra."

"Mummy! Really! You are the absolute limit!"

"I'm sorry, darling; it's just that sometimes I find it difficult to take the whole thing seriously. I never thought I'd end up running a lodging house. A brothel might be more fun, and certainly a lot more lucrative. Still we are a bit off the beaten track and it could be difficult to advertise. Once upon a time it would have even been more socially acceptable, but people are more broad-minded about being in trade these days."

"Don't take any notice of her, Robert," Cassandra broke in, trying to keep her voice level and show none of the anger she felt, "she gets teasy like this sometimes. It's the same streak that was responsible for her advertising of the Oxford Pot. We're not meant to take her seriously."

"No, of course not. I didn't for a moment, though I must admit the deadpan voice with no change of tone at first made me wonder if I could be hearing aright. You really are very amusing, Mrs Marjoribanks!"

"Thank you, Robert dear; one does enjoy being appreciated, and I can't let this lodging house business get me down; but it is a little hard after the kind of life I was used to for nearly thirty years, well indeed far more than that if I count the time before I was married. So 'if I laugh at any mortal thing 'tis that I may not weep.'"

Robert had the tact not to express surprise at Melissa's ability to quote Shakespeare, but she underlined it by saying "My father was always quoting that. His generation did a lot of quoting; I suppose it gave them a sense of fellow feeling with contemporaries who'd had a similar sort of background."

"People still do quote," Cassandra averred, "but it's considered rather clichéd, especially if it's being 'cruel only to be kind' or remarking that 'brevity is the soul of wit'; we're probably more likely to bring in *bons mots* from the Pooh stories and say it's 'time for a little something' or call oneself---or somebody else---'a bear of very little brain'. But I suppose it amounts to the same thing: exclusion of those who don't understand or pick up the allusion."

"That's such an interesting observation!" Robert was impressed by Cassandra's perspicacity. "Exclusiveness is behind numerous developments in languages; it's even said that Castilian, the 'best' Spanish, pronounces s as th because there was a Castilian prince who lisped---like Violet Elizabeth Bott---and the courtiers all copied him and it caught on."

"And there we go again!" Cassandra exclaimed delightedly. "Readers of the William books are always thrilled to recognise another aficionado. Only the author, with her excellent ear for language, made that child's very nouveau riche mother call her 'Vi'let Elizabeth'. Do you love the William books, Robert?"

"Adore them. If ever I get a bit low and need cheering up I read either a William or a Jane Austen, depending on the degree of lowness and the amount of time I have for dealing with it."

"No! Really? That's just what I do. Isn't that amazing?"

Robert and Cassandra beamed at each other with mutual understanding glowing in their faces and Melissa was greatly tempted to interrupt with the observation that actually rather a large number of people, including Harold Macmillan, read Jane Austen with the same motive. Reactions to William Brown was less well documented and the books were not available to people of Macmillan's generation until they were past the age of normal introduction to such literature. Instead, however, of throwing cold water on the glowing young people she decided to delay imparting this information until she had Cassandra on her own; now she merely cast her eyes heavenwards and contemplated the possibility of inviting Robert's parents to stay before it was too late. She had rather hoped that her spoof advertisement with its talk of brothels would shock him into a worthy display of lower middle class primness and cause Cassandra to look at him in a different light. Seeing him and her daughter so patently wrapt up in each other, however, Melissa sighed quietly and took pen and paper to write a genuine advertisement for paying guests. She mentioned the age and beauty of the house and grounds before giving details of the rooms and bathrooms and rounded off by writing the telephone number and the word 'email'. She felt it would be too cruel to bring Robert and Cassandra down to earth by asking for the email address; Robert, she decided, could put it in when he typed the thing. She poured herself another cup of coffee and lit a cigarette. Robert and Cassandra didn't appear to notice. Melissa puffed appreciatively and thought a little ruefully that there were times when one felt somewhat isolated in being no longer part of a couple.

Her cigarette finished she got up to clear the table and deal with the dishes. Robert finally remembered his manners and jumped up to help, though of course Melissa murmured that there was no need. Robert replied that doing dishes was a pleasant change after college life and they proceeded harmoniously.

"I suppose your parents come to see you in Oxford sometimes, do they Robert?" Melissa ventured.

"Well, they came to my degree ceremonies," Robert responded, "but even the last one was a long time ago."

"Oh, I was just wondering where they stayed. I suppose we're too far out to be much use for that sort of thing. We really want long term people; but it might be a good idea to have some short stayers to practise on."

"They came up by train and stayed in Walton Street, actually. It's the nearest to my college---if you don't count the Randolph. But it's often hard to find accommodation over degree weekends, and most places put up their rates then, too. You might well be able to attract visiting parents and friends who come by car. They could use the park and ride into Oxford."

Melissa had hoped to lead into an invitation to Robert's parents, but she was conscious of Cassandra glaring at her from behind his back and decided reluctantly that the time was not propitious.

Robert took his leave and Cassandra went out to the car with him. The wind was cold so she accepted his invitation to sit in the passenger seat 'for a few minutes'. Cassandra's gratitude for all his help and the sense of bonding they had both felt in their discussion of favourite books lengthened the few minutes very considerably and overcame the barrier Robert had felt between them since Cassandra's revelations about her unfashionable attitude to sex before marriage. As she had told him on that occasion, she wasn't a nun!

More than an hour later Cassandra finally went inside, hoping her mother might have already gone to bed. 'Really,' she thought to herself, 'there were problems in living with one's mother at such an advanced age!'

The lights were on but there was no sign of Melissa. Cassandra crept up to her own room breathing consciously quietly, closed the door and wished she had an en suite bathroom. She found some wet wipes and wiped her face---not that there was much makeup left on it---rubbed in some quite unnecessary anti-aging cream, threw her clothes on the floor, got into bed smiling a happy smile and settled down to recollect emotion in something rather more robust than tranquillity.

26

The bedrooms were ready, the showers and new bathrooms completed, the hall was resplendent in fresh paint and its door had a key, several keys in fact, because there was an extra one for each prospective guest. Advertisements had already appeared in the University Accommodation Office and the Gazette and Cassandra had had one put into the parish newsletter, produced each week by the Oratory. Only the guests were lacking, until one morning Cassandra, sitting at the laptop, announced excitedly: "There are two emails about rooms! Look! One from America and one from Australia!" Melissa hurried to see what they had to say and Cassandra put the American one on the screen,

"Oh dear!" she exclaimed. "They begin with 'Hi!' What sort of people can they be?"

"Not your sort, I'm afraid, Mummy. But Americans are like that."

"Really? Even academic ones?"

"I'm afraid so. They think it's friendly."

"Oh gloom and despondency; I can just imagine. They'll be bouncing about being friendly all over the house. Do we have to have them?"

"You know we do, if they actually want to come and stay, and it seems as if they do, for a whole term and a week on each side. That's ten weeks."

Melissa sighed. "What about the Australians?" she asked unenthusiastically. Cassandra got it on the screen.

"Well they, that is he, just begins: 'I have seen your advertisement-----."

"That sounds relatively civilised; perhaps he's an Englishman in disguise."

"Mummy! You'll have to be a lot more tolerant and positive if we're to make a go of this; it's not going to be inviting people because you like them, you know."

"Even that's not fool-proof; one can have some quite nasty surprises with people one considered absolutely OSP before they came to stay, and of course I did sometimes have to put up with your father's business people. Oh don't worry, I'll be tact and discretion itself when they actually arrive!"

"Well at least you can go on using initials because they're unlikely to guess that OSP means 'our sort of people'. In fact we'll no doubt develop something of a code when they're here. We won't want anybody overhearing criticism."

No sooner had Cassandra replied to the Americans and the Australian than another email came through from somebody at the University of Durham, who wanted to spend two sabbatical terms reading at the Bodleian Library in Oxford but living away from the city itself 'as he already lived in a university town'.

"Now that," said Melissa when told about it, "sounds altogether more like the sort of guest we want. What's his name?"

"Forbes-Mowbray, Nicholas Forbes-Mowbray."

"Now I wonder," Melissa mused, "if he's related to the Forbes-Mowbrays my parents knew, an old recusant family."

"I daresay we'll find out if he comes. I'll send him our terms and particulars and see how he replies."

His reply was prompt and promising: He'd like to stay for a week almost immediately and then, most probably, for the following term. Melissa went into a frenzy of preparation; did out the dining-room; looked out and washed table-cloths; decided that nothing looked good enough. Cassandra was busy making enough pottery for her Christmas sale, assisted by the fact that Robert was caught up with entrance interviews for next year's candidates and too busy for any but the briefest encounters. Pete was immensely helpful and not at all sorry to see less of Robert, in whom he could see nothing worthy of 'Miss'. He didn't ask himself why. On one of his rare visits home his mother questioned him minutely about 'Miss's boyfriend' and ended with: "You don't like him, do you?" Pete's only answer was a sniff.

"What's wrong with him?"

"He's got a reelly old car!"

"It can't be as bad as that thing Miss and her mum've got."

"They can't help that!" Pete was immediately defensive on their behalf. "They've got too many other things to pay for."

Even Pete and Cassandra, however, busy though the workshop kept them, were on tenterhooks of expectation the day Nicholas Forbes-Mowbray was to arrive and were covertly looking out for him. As he drove up to the front door, however, they were unable to view his arrival from the workshop window and saw nothing of him until he had been formally admitted and taken to his room with his luggage and only finally directed to take his car round to the courtyard. Pete saw it first and gave a gasp of appreciation; it was a nearly new Alfa Romeo. Cassandra heard the gasp, saw Pete's patent appreciation and went to the window in time to see their new guest emerge from his vehicle. She also gave a gasp of appreciation though she had not actually noticed the car at all. It was Nicholas Forbes-Mowbray who took all her attention; he was slim, tall, at least six foot two, with thick, fair hair and strong, regular, ascetic features. Cassandra immediately recognised him as the kind of man she'd always admired and never actually encountered. Pete looked at her approvingly. "Beautiful, innit Miss?"

"It? What?" Cassandra regarded him bemused.

"The car, Miss. It's an Alfa Romeo!"

"Is it?"

"Course it is! Isn't that what yer lookin' at?"

"Oh! Yes, but I didn't know what it was called. I do wish we had a new car."

"Never mind, Miss; 'e looks like a good start and with any luck you'll soon get in enough to buy one."

Cassandra worked very hard for another hour and a half and then decided to go inside, have a shower in the en suite of an unoccupied guest room and get ready to help her mother prepare supper for the new guest. She went down to the kitchen to find Melissa in a jubilant mood, which was not solely due to the diminished contents of the wine bottle on the table.

"Oh, there you are, darling! Have you seen him? Isn't he *gorgeous*? I mean *tres comme il faut*!"

"Well yes, so far, but then I've only seen him through the window---and as your nanny used to say: 'handsome is as handsome does.'" Cassandra was unwilling to admit to her shock of admiration. "Was he pleasant when he arrived?"

"He was indeed; admired everything, commented on the beauty of the house and setting; thoroughly gentlemanly."

"Pete seems to approve of his car."

"So do I; good but not showy; nice discreet dark blue. Oh yes, he really is quite the thing. You'd better take in his dinner so you can get a better look at him."

"Oh all right, if you want me to." Cassandra spoke unenthusiastically although she'd already had that in mind herself. She preferred not to acknowledge her keenness to meet Nicholas Forbes-Mowbray, though of course it was only reasonable to be excited about their first guest.

"I told him we'd ring the gong when his dinner was ready. In the meantime you could take Pete's tea over and then check that I've set the dining-room table suitably. I must say I'm glad not to be doing this on my own. It's really good of you to stop work early and help me."

"Well, we are in this together."

"True; but you've been earning money all along and I haven't done anything yet."

Cassandra laughed. "You're being unusually modest, Mummy; you made dozens of pairs of pantalettes; not to mention engineering Sir Felix's generous loan. And the Oxford Pot was entirely your idea. I hate to admit it, but you do seem to be the brains of the outfit!"

"Darling! How kind you are! I can take any amount of appreciation, as long as it's directed at me."

"You'll have some more of it if that dinner tastes as good as it smells. You've always managed to dish up good meals, however poor we've been."

"Thank you, darling; I never waste a thing, as you know. Anything left over goes into the stock- pot and that adds flavour and variety to any dish it's used for. Let's just have one tiny celebratory drink and then I think I can dish up."

The gong was rung and the guest came down with commendable promptitude. Cassandra took in the first course. To her surprise Nicholas Forbes-Mowbray stood up when she entered the room.

"Oh, do sit down!" she exclaimed; "I'm only bringing in your dinner."

"But I can see you're the daughter of the house," he replied, "you're so like your mother."

"So we're often told; yes, I'm Cassandra Marjoribanks."

They shook hands and Nicholas sat down again.

"Cassandra!" he repeated. "That's interesting. Did you go to St Mary's Ascot?"

"Yes, I did."

"A cousin of mine was there; younger than I am; she used to talk about a Cassandra whom she admired greatly. There can't have been many Cassandras, so could it have been you?"

"Well I started there twelve years ago and stayed for seven years. What's your cousin's name?"

"Artemis Elwes."

"Now that's another unusual Christian name, Artemis, if either it or Cassandra can be considered Christian; they're both Classical Greek, aren't they?"

"They are indeed, and perhaps a strange choice for good Catholic families."

"I believe the nuns thought so, too. And I do remember Artemis; she was in the year below me, and a very pretty and amusing girl, too. What's she doing now?"

"She's in advertising and seems to be thriving on it. She gives us all advice about washing liquids and powders and the best makes to use. She's already an account director."

"Heavens! She must be talented. But I'm keeping you from your starter; it's a good thing it's cold."

"I wish you were eating with me. I'm used to dining at High Table with the other dons in my college in Durham. I'm not really accustomed to solitary splendour. Couldn't you bring your dinner in here? Oh---and your mother too, of course. I would appreciate company."

"Well," Cassandra spoke doubtfully, "I'll see what she says. But please do begin."

Melissa was delighted at their guest's courtesy to her daughter but pleaded the necessity of finishing the preparation and presentation of the main course to excuse her own attendance. She insisted, however, that Cassandra take her dinner into the dining-room immediately. Nicholas stood up again when Cassandra rejoined him and she sat down hastily, almost embarrassed by so much politeness. She decided to discourage it as delicately as possible.

"I'm not used to such beautiful manners," she told him, "I lived in darkest Devon among potters for a couple of years before we came here and we were all rather free and easy, I'm afraid."

"What were you doing there?"

"I'm a potter myself." Cassandra was thankful that Nicholas had been well away from Oxford at the time of the Oxford Pot demonstrations in the market. "I took it up after university."

"Oh, how interesting; which university?"

"London: Holloway. I read English and Latin." As she spoke Cassandra realised with a pang that Robert had never asked her what she had read or at which university; but then of course he had met her as a potter and for all her knowledge of literature, which merely surprised him, he clearly thought of her primarily as simply a potter. Nicholas noticed that her face clouded a little.

"You don't mind my asking?" he said anxiously.

"No indeed; I wish more people would realise that I've had a university education; it's true I kept rather quiet about it in Devon among other potters, but people can be dismissive in Oxford if one's doing something merely physical, as they see it. What about you? I gather you teach in Durham University, but what's your subject?"

"You'll think it's strange but in fact I read the Classical Tripos at Cambridge and then did a doctoral thesis on the classical influence on English literature in the 17th century and now I teach English; mainly 17th century of course."

"That really is interesting. Oxford's such an exciting place: one meets the kind of people one simply wouldn't come across anywhere else, well, not all over the place and in such numbers, anyway. How is it in Durham? Do University people very much hang together?"

"I'm afraid they do, rather. I can't imagine staying anywhere in Durham where the person bringing in the dinner had an academic education like yours! Is your mother similarly educated?"

"Well she did go to St Mary's Ascot but left before the Upper Sixth and did the social round as girls were expected to then. An academic education was considered to be a danger to one's marriage prospects!"

"Yes, it was the same thing in my family. My mother and my aunts all left school relatively early and nobody thought of their going to a university, whereas all my girl cousins stay at school as long as their brothers and consider university the norm. I know Artemis did an Oxford degree before she went into advertising."

"I'm not surprised; she always seemed very bright."

Melissa's head came round the dining-room door and she noted the on-going conversation with considerable satisfaction before interrupting it to say: "I hope you're both ready for your next course because it's ready for you!"

Nicholas leapt to his feet again and began to take his plate out, simultaneously offering to bring in the next course. Melissa and Cassandra both demurred but he insisted that he couldn't have ladies waiting on him and begged Melissa to join them in the dining-room. She finally agreed to come in for pudding and coffee. When she did so she brought in a bottle of dessert wine and took three rather beautiful glasses from the corner cupboard. Cassandra had no recollection of seeing that bottle or those glasses before and eyed them a little askance. Melissa took no notice apart from saying that they really must celebrate their first and most excellent guest and Nicholas returned the compliment by saying he could hardly believe his good fortune in finding such a house and such denizens of it. From there they progressed to families and mutual acquaintances and of course Melissa found that Nicholas was in fact related to the Forbes-Mowbrays her parents had known and that they were indeed an old recusant family.

"I suppose you were at Ampleforth, then?" Melissa ventured. "I seem to remember my mother saying they were an Ampleforth family."

"Quite right" responded Nicholas with satisfaction and they all rejoiced quietly and inwardly at being part of the same complex; part of the small select group of upper class English Catholics whose faith had been their defining feature for hundreds of years. Melissa, whose marriage had deprived her of this sense of belonging, felt it again and almost rejoiced at the defection and disappearance of her erring husband, for all the material hardship this had caused her. She decided anew to regularise her position with regard to the Church----when she had time. Meanwhile she continued the celebration with a 'tiny top up' all round and privately added to her general sense of satisfaction by reflecting that if things were to continue so promisingly it might not be necessary to meet Robert's family at all.

27

Robert Taylor's first sight of Nicholas was on the following Sunday when he came into the Oratory together with Melissa and Cassandra, having thoughtfully insisted on bringing them in his car as their own was rather less reliable. Robert was with Samson as before and the latter noted a frown of anxiety clouding his companion's face as he saw the trio sitting in the usual pew preferred by Melissa, well to the back of the church.

After mass Robert and Samson met the others, who were waiting for them outside, and they were joined by Sir Felix, too. Nicholas was duly introduced and they all repaired to the social club and its bar. Cassandra smiled welcomingly at Robert as he took a seat beside her at their table and said: "I didn't know you were coming this morning, Robert; I thought you'd still be too busy with admissions and interviewing and discussions." Robert said he thought they'd got through the worst and anyway it was time he took a morning off. Nicholas was immediately interested and asked about his subject. "Oh, English!" he rejoined when told. "I sympathise. It's my subject too and we do have vast numbers of hopeful applicants for entrance; you must have even more. I've been on sabbatical so I haven't been burdened with it for once, but of course I know what it's like." They discussed their relative positions amicably, Nicholas with real interest as to how things were done in Oxford and Robert with a show of interest which disguised his real objective in finding out more about Nicholas's position with regard to Cassandra and her mother. He had been told that their first guest was due to arrive but had hardly expected to see them on such friendly terms, so much as if the guest were a friend or relative rather than a source of income. Sir Felix took advantage of a slight lull in their conversation to ask Nicholas about his family.

"Forbes-Mowbray, did Melissa say? I'm sure my wife knows some Forbes-Mowbrays; an old Catholic family, isn't it?"

"It is, yes. You know, never recognised the Reformation, ancestors imprisoned in the Tower, priest holes in the house, all that sort of thing."

"How terribly exciting!" Cassandra turned to Nicholas with unfeigned interest and not a little admiration. "Hasn't our family anything like that to offer, Mummy?"

"Well yes, darling, some of the Egertons have, the Catholic branch, but you know I've had nothing to do with them----or they with me----since I was so silly as to marry a divorced Protestant, or should I just call him an atheist?"

"Ah! I see." Nicholas spoke as if this explained a great deal, but he was too well bred to comment or enquire further. Instead he turned to Samson and asked whether he was also a relative.

"Only a rather distant cousin, I'm afraid."

"Samson's a descendant of the poet Southey" Robert put in, feeling he could make up for his own deficiencies of lineage by mentioning his friend's claim to some recognisable family connection.

"Really?" Nicholas was immediately interested.

"Sadly, yes, though only lineal." Samson replied. "Not a matter for congratulation even in his lifetime; hardly a great poet, though from an old enough family, I suppose."

Robert found himself hoping nobody asked him about *his* family and wondered a little facetiously whether, if pressed, he might hint at some kindred and affinity with Samuel Taylor Coleridge, or possibly Samuel Coleridge-Taylor, though the latter was rather too near in date and had African blood, which Robert with his very Anglo-Saxon looks could hardly lay claim to. Fortunately Nicholas was involved in an interesting conversation with Samson about the merits of Southey's works, Melissa was eagerly describing the house improvements and the ways of workmen to Sir Felix and Cassandra was able to devote some attention to Robert. They had met less frequently during the last couple of weeks due to Robert's involvement with entrance and Cassandra's necessary helping in the house with the invasion of the workmen and the consequent upheaval, not to mention her preparations for Christmas pot sales. She found, too, that coping with emails and the vagaries of the laptop took up more time than she had imagined it would. She had not been sorry to see less of Robert since their lengthy session in his car. He was a danger, she told herself, and one she didn't really want or intend to succumb to. She was not even sure that she wanted to marry him. The pleased surprise he always showed when she exhibited any knowledge of literature or indeed, she told herself a little unfairly, anything but pottery, was not entirely unpleasing but could hardly be considered flattering. It was a pity he had first seen her as a seller of the Oxford Pot even though they were unlikely to have met otherwise. Her mind wandered unbidden into the very different response of Nicholas, who was, in addition, so much more akin to her family. She refused to let herself respond to the almost sub-conscious mental whisper 'and better-looking'. All this went through her mind as she listened to Robert talking about the sombre beauty of purple vestments and how they'd been associated with the coming of Christmas in his childhood when he'd attended the High Anglican church.

"Oh, not Easter?" Cassandra asked. "Lent lasts longer than Advent."

"I suppose Christmas is more significant to a child."

"Well that's reasonable; Easter eggs are much less exciting than a load of presents in stockings or under decorated trees."

"We had pillow-cases!"

"So did I; though I think it was called a stocking. Do you go home for Christmas?"

"Not always; sometimes I've been away and occasionally my parents have been away; but I think I will go home this time, if they'll have me. Though I don't expect a pillow-case!"

"Do you go home for Christmas, Nicholas?" Cassandra saw that Nicholas was not talking or listening to Samson at that moment and took the opportunity to speak to him. Nicholas responded with a glowing smile, which lit up his rather severely ascetic features as he spoke of vast family Christmases with siblings and cousins of all ages and games and presents and floors knee deep in bright wrapping-paper and huge open fires carefully protected with ancient fireguards.

"What a wonderful picture of warmth and happiness," said Cassandra with a sigh. "I do wish I'd belonged to a large family. I always found Christmas rather lonely. Oh well, I shall compensate by having a large family myself."

"Oh, really?" Robert spoke a little anxiously. "How large?"

"Well, four children at the very least," Cassandra replied enthusiastically. "Preferably five or six."

"There are six in mine," Nicholas volunteered, "and I can certainly recommend that kind of number. We've always got on extremely well and been very happy to see one another."

"That must be unusual!" Robert murmured.

"The number or the getting on well?" Nicholas asked.

"Well, both I suppose. But perhaps it really is a case of 'the more the merrier'. I've certainly known families of two or three siblings with very little love lost between them."
"We did have the odd fight as children, of course, especially the boys; but they never lasted long and there were no lingering ill-feelings. But then my mother used to tell us always to remember that the best thing we'd been given was each other."
Sir Felix heard this part of the conversation and agreed heartily. "Absolutely right! We've got six and a happier bunch would be hard to find. Though it is a bit unusual these days. One of ours came home from school one evening and asked: 'What's a sex-maniac?' Of course we tried to get to the bottom of this and find out why he wanted to know. He told us he'd been talking about his new little sister and mentioned that she was child number six and his form master had said: 'Are your parents Roman Catholics or sex-maniacs?' I wasn't too pleased about this and wrote to the head. The form-master was suspended, I'm glad to say."
"A good thing he was. What an appalling thing to say to a child---or to anybody else, come to that."
"It certainly is," Cassandra agreed. "Don't you think so, Robert?"
Robert had in fact been thinking it was a fairly normal reaction, if not quite the thing to say to a young pupil, but he was hardly willing to express such an opinion to the assembled company. He had been taken aback, not to say somewhat aghast, at Cassandra's desire for an equally large family. He could think of nothing to say other than "Oh, yes; dreadful!" He then added, to disguise the lameness of his answer, "What sort of school was it?"

"A very reputable prep school, actually," Sir Felix answered. "We sent them on to Catholic schools after that."

"A good idea. I went to Ampleforth, myself," Nicholas spoke approvingly. "Some people say Catholic schools put young people off the faith, but it didn't do that to me."

"Now here we are," Melissa broke in, "with two non-Catholics among us, talking tactlessly about our own opinions as if they were the only ones that mattered; no wonder people accuse us of being a 'Catholic Mafia'."

"I'm terribly sorry, I hadn't realised! I suppose this kind of service is often attended by non-Catholics in Oxford: the music's worth a visit in itself."

"That's very true," Samson was happy to admit, "It's less expensive than a concert and better than many of them, and personally I prefer a mass doing the work it was written for to a mere performance in a concert hall. Wouldn't you agree, Robert?"

"I don't pretend to be as knowledgeable about music as you are, Samson, but I find the combination of the music, the spectacle and the whole atmosphere of devotion a most moving and satisfying experience." Robert was genuinely sincere in making this statement but he also took comfort in Cassandra smiling at him with obvious approval and felt he had made up for his lukewarmness in disapproving of the anti-large-families schoolmaster. He did not, of course, appreciate the fact that part of Cassandra's approval was due to his having given so good a reason for attending mass; she'd been a little afraid that Nicholas might suspect he did so for her sake.

Melissa pleaded the necessity of getting home before too long as Cassandra could not afford to take even a whole Sunday away from the workshop at that time of year, and the group broke up. Robert and Samson walked back to their college.

"I like that Forbes-Mowbray," Samson remarked to his companion "but I don't suppose you do."

"Why? What do you mean? Why shouldn't I like him?" Robert spoke rather sharply. "Do you suppose I feel inferior because I'm not a Classicist?"

"That was not the supposition uppermost in my mind," Samson replied cryptically. Robert looked at Samson with some hostility but the latter was smiling serenely and showing no inclination to expand on his statement. Robert decided not to give him the satisfaction of interest in his opinion and they walked the rest of the way in silence.

Sir Felix went home to ask 'Midge' about the Forbes-Mowbray family and the other three drove back to Huntsfield very happily to the accompaniment of Nicholas's enthusiasm for the Oratory and the beauty of the mass and the music as well as the pleasantness of the company he'd met there. Melissa wondered at his remarkable facility for saying just the right thing; hoped that her daughter was equally impressed and hoped even more that they wouldn't be long getting home so that she could sit down to a cigarette and a glass of wine.

***

The week of Nicholas Forbes-Mowbray's stay sped by in what seemed a remarkably short time even though he lengthened it to eight nights instead of seven. He also asked whether he could come back a week earlier than he had originally intended. This of course was graciously agreed to, though Melissa managed admirably to express her agreement with an enthusiasm more muted than she felt. Cassandra, when informed of this, conveyed the impression that she was pleased because it was that much more money to come in and because it showed they were making a success of the venture.

"It would be difficult," her mother responded "not to make a success of looking after somebody as pleasant and appreciative as that young man. I can't imagine we'll always have it so easy. Have you heard from those colonials again?"

"The Americans and the Australian, you mean? No, but I haven't looked at the emails today. I'll do it now."

Melissa watched as her daughter clicked on Outlook Express and the already arrived emails appeared on the screen.

"I must learn how to do this," she murmured "I can't expect you to do it all the time."

"But you do all the cooking and shopping and most of the housework."

"True, but you might not always be here. Why does it say 'not responding'?"

Cassandra sighed. "Oh, it often does that. You just have to wait. There, you see. It tells us the firewall's not turned on."

"Good heavens! Why do we want a firewall?"

"It's part of the security system. It stops us being invaded by viruses and so on. There! I've clicked on it and now we can go ahead. Look! An email from the Americans: 'Hi Cass, we'd really like to come and stay with you but can we have some pictures of the house and rooms?"

Melissa groaned. "Oh dear! How absolutely dreadful! How dare they address you as 'Cass'? They must be the most frightful people. It sounds as if they don't trust our description of the house. Will you have to post some photographs to them?"

"No; I can scan them and send them by email. Well, that is, I should be able to but I can't remember how to do it. I'll have to ring Robert. Or maybe Pete can show me. He's still in the workshop making presents for his family."

Pete was summoned and appeared somewhat unwillingly because he was in his clay-stained work clothes but he was soon reassured as his usefulness outweighed such a minor consideration. He explained exactly what to do and offered to do it himself if 'Miss' ran into any problems.

"You really are an absolute treasure, Pete," Cassandra began, but realising that the little dog was responding to her name and clearly expecting some choice morsel to be produced for her, said "Oh lord, I mean a jewel, a-----well anyway, I'm deeply grateful; I couldn't manage without you."

Pete turned a lively shade of red and muttered "S'all right, Miss. Glad to help, like."

Melissa gave Treasure a soggy biscuit, poured herself a decidedly untiny top-up, sank into a chair and lit a cigarette. "I think I've decided," she said faintly through a puff of smoke, "to give up on emails. They really are far too complicated."

Pete went happily back to the workshop basking in his usefulness. He was not sorry to be the only male in the household even though he had approved of the owner of the Alfa-Romeo, whose name he hadn't tried to remember. He considered him very much a cut above Robert and possibly almost good enough for Miss; but it did occur to him that if Miss got married she might not want to be a potter any more, and then where would he be?

28

Cassandra's pot sale, already advertised by the judicious placing of posters, Oxford Mail and Times advertisements and the sending out of illustrated cards to customers and acquaintances in the surrounding area, attracted a good-sized attendance. Robert was in two minds about wanting his colleagues to go to it. He had put up a poster in a not very noticeable place in the College Lodge, but he was really hoping that memories of the Thursday market Oxford Pot stall would dim into disappearance and Cassandra cease to be associated with it. Unfortunately the Oxford Mail had picked up on the advertisement and run a small feature on it complete with a photograph of Melissa standing to the side of the stall and Cassandra serving behind it. As the sale was to take place in the home setting, however, he hoped the grandeur of the house and grounds would do something to compensate. He felt guilty that he was not recommending it enthusiastically to all and sundry and unhappy that he was too busy in college to go out and help physically to set it up. Fortunately the interviewing of Entrance candidates was an absorbing and in many ways fascinating task and as Robert was unused to having anything to distract him from it he was much less distracted by thoughts of Cassandra than he had been for some weeks. His antagonism towards Nicholas Forbes-Mowbray had not survived the latter's departure and he had, in fact, barely given him another thought

At lunch that day Robert heard Muriel Thwaites ask: "Are you going to your relative's pottery sale this weekend Samson?" Somehow Robert had forgotten that Samson had, as far as anybody knew, more claim to be associated with the Marjoribanks duo than he had. He looked up, surprised.

"I'd very much like to," Samson admitted, "but it's not the sort of place one can easily arrive at without a motor-car."

"Oh if that's all that's stopping you I'll take you; I want to go myself. I've still got some difficult Christmas presents to find."

Samson noted Robert's expression with some amusement and enquired: "I suppose you'll be going, won't you Robert?"

"Yes, certainly; and Nigel will too, no doubt, won't you Nigel?"

"What's that?" Nigel spoke as if he hadn't been listening. "Oh, the Huntsfield House pottery sale; yes, Effie said she wanted to go." He was keen to throw off any suspicion that he was going there to see Cassandra; he strongly suspected Robert of implying just that and deliberately drawing attention to him, which was indeed the case. The topic spread round the table and several more people expressed their intention of going, if only to see the house and the grounds.

"I didn't know you were interested in pottery, Muriel." Robert remarked to Dr Thwaites.

"It's something I've never thought much about; but I did see that stall in the market and their stuff's useful as well as ornamental and certainly original. I like to buy special presents for a few special people, but I seem to have been too busy to give any real thought to them up to now and pottery might solve the problem. But what's your interest in it?"

Robert was at a loss for an immediate answer but prevaricated by saying he was going home for Christmas and really had no idea what to take for his parents. "Besides," he added, "I know it's a long time ago but I did pottery at school with a particularly inspiring teacher and I came to know something about it: enough to appreciate good stuff when I see it, anyway."

After lunch Samson sat next to Robert in the common room and said to him quietly: "I would have asked you to take me to the pottery sale, Robert, but I imagine you might want to stay rather longer than I do so in fact I'd hardly thought of going. It's very kind of Muriel to offer transport."

Robert remembered Muriel's sympathetic offer to help with his speech and said she did seem to be a kind person.

"But not otherwise very noticeable," Samson spoke as if he were finishing Robert's sentence for him rather than voicing his own view, a subtlety which Robert failed to notice at all. He was too preoccupied in thinking about his colleagues in conjunction with Cassandra.

So it happened unsurprisingly that Nigel and Effie, Effie's parents and Samson and Muriel all arrived at Huntsfield at the same time. Nigel tried to introduce his fiancée and her father to Muriel but his efforts were drowned by her mother's claiming acquaintance with Samson as "That friend of Nigel's I met at his college and oh, yes, you were here one night too, you and Robert and a Sir and Lady Somebody. Don't you remember?" Samson conveyed with the utmost politeness that he had found these encounters quite unforgettable, to the happy satisfaction of Norah Fraser and the barely hidden amusement of Muriel Thwaites, who remembered Nigel's prospective mother-in-law extremely well and had no difficulty in recognising the identity of Effie and her father.

Following the newly made signs they went into the house by the front door and admired the impressive entrance hall and the flower arrangements placed in it by Melissa.

"Well!" Norah Fraser exclaimed. "I must say this looks a bit different from what I saw last time: that sort of shed with mud all over the floor! I must say this is really smart!"

"It's not *smart*, Mother, it's grand. Don't you know the difference?" Effie glared at her mother crossly and went on ahead with Nigel to the dining room of the house, where the pottery was displayed to full advantage. Pete's 'electrics' uncle had put in some extra power points and helped with the lighting and the result was verging on the spectacular. Robert was already there and making himself useful helping Cassandra wrap up the pots as they sold. Pete had been doing the same but as he was not best pleased at finding himself in such close company with Robert he soon decided to abandon that task and said condescendingly: "You got the hang of it now; I'll go an' help Missus" and he went into the kitchen to take a large tray full of mulled wine and bread pudding from Melissa in order to offer food and drink to the assembled viewers and buyers. Grateful to have that burden taken from her Melissa followed him into the dining room in time to hear Norah Fraser hailing Robert like a long-lost friend and in the same breath asking what*ever* he thought he was doing there wrapping up parcels. To spare him the possible embarrassment of replying Melissa took the plate of bread pudding and a glass of mulled wine and hastened to offer them to 'Mrs Fraser' whom she greeted with flattering recognition. "And this must be your daughter," she continued. “Yes, this is ---Effie”. Norah remembered just in time not to put ‘our’ in front of her daughter’s name.

“Do have some bread pudding,” Melissa offered immediately without waiting for the introduction to be acknowledged.

“Bread pudding!” Norah’s high-pitched exclamation made the other people in the room turn their heads in her direction. “Well I never! What a thing to have for visitors! My Nan used to make it; we never thought it was anything *smart*!”

“Be quiet, Mother!” said Effie. “ For all you know it’s really fashionable.”

“There are mince pies if you prefer them,” Melissa said kindly, “but I make the bread pudding myself from an old family recipe; it’s considered to go well with mulled wine.”

“Well I don’t mind trying some,” said Norah as if conferring a favour, “I expect the wine’ll wash it down.”

Samson and Muriel took pieces of bread pudding with gratefully expressed appreciation; Muriel saying: “what an enterprising pair you and your daughter are, reviving two excellent things from earlier times, first the bourdaloue from France and now the almost extinct English bread pudding, which is absolutely delicious. I’m full of admiration.” She turned from Melissa’s murmured thanks to Cassandra and expressed her wish to buy *two* bourdaloues, which she proceeded to choose. Robert wrapped them up for her. She looked at him a little quizzically but made no comment. He had heard her appreciative remarks to Melissa and was grateful for them.

“I’m so glad to see you here, Muriel,” he said. “I do remember you as one of the few people who knew what a bourdaloue is.”

"I've been meaning to buy one since I first heard about them, but it's taken the incentive of Christmas and this sale to make me do it. This interesting house is a bonus, too." She would have liked to add that she hadn't expected to see Robert playing such a part in it, but thought better of it and turned away to see what Samson was doing. He was deliberating over which of the large bowls to buy.

"They're all so beautiful," he sighed. "I can't decide. Which one do you like, Muriel?"

"That dark one, almost black, with the delicate swirl of greenish blue."

"I agree. There's a sense of fathomless depth about it as you look into it. But I think I'll have to keep it myself and buy another one as a present."

Muriel helped him choose another and he bought them both. As Robert wrapped them he murmured: "giving yourself away, aren't you Robert? Or is it no longer a secret to be guarded with discretion?"

"Not much longer, I hope." Robert knew it was useless to prevaricate with Samson. "After Christmas, perhaps."

Muriel heard Robert's answer though she had missed Samson's quiet question. She wondered what it meant, but felt, from the timbre of Robert's voice, that it was not something to be questioned by an onlooker. So she merely asked Samson if he were ready to go, saw to it that he was holding his purchases safely, and led the way to her car. As they drove back to Oxford she ventured to remark that Robert seemed very much at home in Huntsfield House.

"He *has* driven me out here before."

"He must have driven himself here quite often, too."

"That seems not unlikely."

"You're the one who's related to them, however, aren't you?"

"Yes, albeit somewhat distantly. I see them at Sunday mass in the Oratory, too."

"I didn't know you were a Catholic, Samson!"

"No, I'm not. I merely appreciate the Latin and the music."

"Does Robert ever go?"

"He has been with me, yes."

Muriel sighed. "Of course the daughter's very beautiful, isn't she?"

Samson sighed in his turn. 'Dear me,' he thought; 'I was beginning to suspect that that was how the land lay. How very tedious people are.' Aloud he said: "I believe that's the general opinion; but I do not consider myself to be a very accurate judge of female beauty. What's your own view?"

"Oh, well, women can't judge other women very accurately either. I think I find the mother more attractive. But perhaps it's just appreciation of how elegantly she's aged."

"I can understand that *very* well." Samson's answer had a slight edge to it. He had no desire to be made party to Muriel's feelings for Robert and hoped to close the conversation.

Muriel picked up the nuance of his answer and began to feel that she had given away a little too much so she veered on to a different aspect, saying: "seeing her beside a woman of similar age who is rather conspicuously *not* aging elegantly makes it all the more appreciable, of course."

"Ah, yes indeed, Nigel's fiancee's redoubtable mother! And what, come to that, do you think of the fiancée?"

"There again, a woman's probably a poor judge; but I'm afraid she seemed, well, rather coarse. I suppose she's very sexy, isn't she?"

"Of that I fear I'm probably as poor a judge as any woman. I've hardly heard her speak unless she's trying to moderate or suppress her mother's utterances, so I've no opinion of her mental capacity either; but at least she can't be quite as vulgar as her female parent."

They continued with their opinions of Nigel and his forthcoming nuptials and Samson was relieved to find Muriel conversing with amusement and considerable volubility. She was not sorry to get away from the topic of Robert and Cassandra either.

When the last of the viewers and buyers had departed Melissa, Cassandra and Robert sank into chairs in the kitchen and thankfully shared a bottle of wine and a good, ripe camembert. Pete had been invited to join them but had preferred to go to his room with a bottle of coke and a couple of jam doughnuts---a special treat in gratitude for his help.

"Would anybody like something more substantial to eat?" asked Melissa, hoping they wouldn't. Robert and Cassandra said definitely not; they'd got past it, and anyway the sight and smell of mince pies and bread pudding had been enough.

"You have been wonderfully helpful, Robert, I'm so grateful," Cassandra turned to him, smiling, "I couldn't have sold so many things if you hadn't wrapped them up as they were bought."

"I'm sure Pete could have done it just as well or indeed better, though he was kind enough to say I'd got the hang of it before he went to help with the food and drink!"

"And I really did need help there," Melissa chimed in, "the trays were surprisingly heavy and the drinkers surprisingly numerous. I'd never have believed so many people would come all the way out here. Pete really is wonderfully useful and helpful."

"I don't know whether I'm imagining it," said Robert musingly, "but I get the feeling that he doesn't like me."

Cassandra had an idea that this was quite true, especially as Pete had reacted rather differently with regard to Nicholas Forbes-Mowbray, but she hardly liked to say so. Fortunately her mother had an answer. "He's very protective of both of us, actually, and he probably resents another male in the offing. Those animal programmes one sees, you know, about lions and so on, often make me think men are just the same; so primitive!"

Robert and Cassandra laughed and agreed that there was probably some truth in such an idea. None of them quite realised that Robert might have found more favour if he'd had a better car.

Robert rose to go and Cassandra went with him; she felt he deserved more than a cursory goodbye, especially as he was to go home the following day and she wouldn't see him again before Christmas. Besides, she'd wrapped up for him a bowl he'd always admired and put a Christmas card inside it. It seemed a suitable and innocuous present, thoughtful without being too personal.

"Put your coat on if you're going outside," said Melissa, "the wind's bitterly cold."

"Yes and please do come out," said Robert, "I've got something for you."

Cassandra put on her coat, picked up the gift-wrapped bowl and they went out to the car.

"Do get in for a minute so we can say goodnight properly."

"Well, just a little minute, perhaps, but you'll have to be good; I don't think I've got time to go to confession again before Christmas."

"You surely haven't had to go to confession! I thought that was only for really bad sins."

"Passionate kissing's a mortal sin, according to the Church---outside marriage of course."

"I can't believe that!"

"I must admit I rather regard it as a counsel of perfection; but of course it doesn't help. Besides, one should avoid the occasion of sin, and I'm not exactly doing that by sitting in your car with you---though it really is awfully cold tonight!"

"All the more reason to---." Robert finished the sentence with action rather than words.

"Oh dear!" said Cassandra when she was able to speak, "you do make me melt. I'm glad I put your Christmas present on the back seat; it might have broken."

"Well I don't think this will." Robert reached over to the back seat and produced something squarish and slightly heavy. "This is for you."

"Ooh! Thank you, Robert; how exciting. I'll keep it till Christmas Day." She felt round the parcel tentatively, making out the shapes, she thought, of a book and a box. "But I must go in. My mother's tactful and doesn't say anything, but I have the feeling that she's timing me. It's---well, you know---a bit embarrassing."

"Just five minutes. I'm going to miss you. I wish I was staying here for Christmas. I don't think I want to go home."

"It'll be awfully quiet here; though we're going to a party at the Oxford Marjoribanks' on Boxing Day. I'll be thinking of you."

It did take a little more than five minutes, in fact rather more than fifteen, before the final farewells were said and Cassandra emerged from the car feeling really very fond of Robert despite being rather annoyed to think that she probably should go to confession again. As her best friend at school used to say: 'Before a great feast like Christmas or Easter one should be as shriven as shriven!'

'I must go and see her again,' Cassandra thought to herself. 'She can't easily come and see me now she's a nun.'

Inside again Cassandra found her mother wiping glasses and putting them back in their boxes.

"I'm glad we had the sense to hire these" was all she said.

"Oh, I didn't mean to leave you to do all this; I feel really guilty."

Melissa fought the temptation to say: 'Well as long as that's all you feel guilty about!' and instead merely murmured that with Pete coming into the room for breakfast they must set a good example. "Anyway," she continued, "I feel tired only physically, not mentally; everything went so well and people were so pleasant and appreciative. Even that Fraser woman managed to say she liked the bread pudding. Did she buy anything?"

"She did as a matter of fact, and greatly to my surprise. She bought the biggest and most expensive vase I had. As they went out I heard her say to Nigel flashy-sports-car: 'Well, it might not be the most beautiful piece but it's certainly the most expensive!' Her daughter bought quite a few things including several Oxford Pots. I fear some of her friends are going to have a lavatory-humour Christmas present."

"I know you're not entirely happy about being associated with the Oxford Pot, darling, but it has produced some good results, and they still sell very well. It's only mealy-mouthed middle-class people who are silly about them."

"And prurient lower-class people who make lavatorial and sexy jokes about them."

"Very true; and there are not many of those among our customers."

"I suppose you're right. That woman French don, the one who came with Samson Southey, bought two. She seems like a very nice person. I believe she was at that dinner we went to, but I don't remember noticing her."

"I know the one you mean. Yes. I wouldn't have noticed her tonight if she hadn't been with Samson. There are some women like that; nothing actually wrong with them, no vastly irregular features, neither too fat nor too thin, but utterly unnoticeable. It's very sad. I've seen genuinely ugly women do much better; I suppose at least they're memorable."

"Well I'm going to be genuinely ugly if I don't get some sleep. Come on, Mummy, you've done enough for one day. Let's go upstairs."

29

On Christmas Eve Pete set off on his moped to spend the next two days with his family. He showed no very marked enthusiasm for this expedition but expressed considerable anxiety lest Miss and Missus might not be safe without him. He left presents for them both and repeatedly adjured them to 'take care' with more meaningful solemnity than is usually accorded to the phrase.

"Dear Pete," Cassandra murmured after seeing him off, "I really think we're going to miss him, he's so helpful and protective."

Melissa finished stuffing the larger than usual duck, 'no point in having a turkey or a goose just for the two of us' and said: "What time do you think we should set off for mass?"

"Well, the church opens at 11.00, so no point in getting there any earlier. Let's allow an hour to be sure of a parking place, so just before 10.00, perhaps. That's hours away, so how about a rest and then a bite to eat? I don't want much. A mousetrap would be nice. I'll make them."

At seven Cassandra was putting out the cheese and bacon for the mousetraps when her mother came downstairs and flopped into a chair in the kitchen.

"Isn't it restful," she remarked gratefully, "with just the two of us? I know it's very quiet but we can do with that after the workmen and Nicholas and the pot sale. I'm afraid it may be rather a bore for you, though."

"I'm very happy to have it quiet. I don't want to sound tiresomely pious but the Midnight Mass is the point ---the high point---of Christmas for me; the rest just follows on from that. I'm glad to be able to work up to it peacefully."

Melissa smiled and nodded in silent agreement, then after a minute's thought said: "You're right, you know. I did take you to the Christmas Midnight Mass when you were too young to go by yourself and it always made me feel a kind of happiness and perhaps a longing, though I suppressed it in those days."

"I remember, and I liked to have you with me, though you hid the longing rather well."

"I was not the only lapsed Catholic there, either; it's amazing how many one sees in church at that service. But I suppose most of us dismiss it as nostalgia and anyway, with the complications we live with nowadays---divorces, remarriages---we'd have to turn our lives upside down to get back into the Church. I believe I'm lucky to have had mine turned upside down for me."

"But you still haven't been to see the Oratorians about unlapsing yourself!"

"I know. I really want to but something keeps holding me back. Good heavens! What's that?"

Cassandra had jumped at the sound too, but tried to sound calm: "the front door bell."

"Who on earth can it be at this time of night?"

"It's not really late. Perhaps it's children singing carols."

"Away out here? Nonsense; anyway I haven't heard any singing. I wish Pete were here."

"It's all right, I'll go."

"Put the chain on the door before you open it."

"It's on already."

There was another peal from the bell. Cassandra ran to the door saying "all right, coming!" but she none the less opened it cautiously the few centimetres the chain allowed and peered out into the darkness to see who was there. It was a dark, stooping shape, seemingly masculine but otherwise unidentifiable. It said nothing.

"Just a minute, I'll turn on the outside light."

Leaving the door on the chain she went to the switch on the wall, turned on the light and peered out again. It was a man and this time he spoke: "Cassandra!" he said. Melissa came into the hall in time to hear the voice.

"Great God in heaven!" she gasped. "It's Fergus!"

Cassandra found her hands trembling as she fumblingly detached the chain from the door and stepped back to let her father in. It was not surprising that she had failed to recognise him; he had aged very considerably since her last sight of him and grown a beard, grey and unkempt, which would have made anybody look old. His stooping posture and general air of weariness added to the impression of decrepitude and even Melissa was aghast at his aged appearance. The three of them stood in the hall in silence, the women too shocked to speak. After what seemed like many minutes Melissa found her voice: "You look dreadful!" she said.

Her husband looked at her and then at the floor; "I'm ill," he answered.

Cassandra began to recover a little. "I think we should all go and sit down," she said. Her mother turned and led the way into the kitchen and her father followed. Cassandra paused only to put the chain on the door again then went into the kitchen too. "Thank goodness I didn't put the mousetraps in the oven," she said, "they'd be burnt to charcoal by now."

Her father sat down heavily. "Mousetraps!" he said. "That's a cheering word to hear."

Cassandra dealt with them and began to make another. Melissa walked about the kitchen undecided what to do. "I think I'll open a bottle of wine," she said finally, and proceeded to do so. "We weren't going to have any because we're going to midnight mass, but the circumstances are rather exceptional. Would you like some, Cassandra?"

Cassandra looked at her watch. "Heavens," she exclaimed, "It's only a little after half past eight. It feels like midnight already. Yes, I'll have a glass; I've got till ten to absorb it."

Melissa poured out three glasses and passed one to her husband. "Do you still smoke, Fergus?"

"No," he answered, "I've got lung cancer so I've stopped smoking."

"That's a prime example of shutting the stable door after the horse is out!" his wife remarked.

"True," he agreed. "People do odd things when they're terminally ill."

"How do you know you're terminally ill?"

"I collapsed a couple of months ago and they took me to hospital, did tests and all that; told me I've got an inoperable cancer of the lung. So I thought I should come and see you before I died."

"How did you find us?"

"Not too difficult; you've been in the papers."

"I suppose you want to stay here?"

"I don't want to go out again tonight."

Cassandra interposed: "Have a mousetrap," and put one down in front of him.

"Thank you, my dear. I've dreamt about these sometimes: this superb combination of cheese and bacon on crisp toasted bread. Nothing like it!"

"When you've had that," said Melissa over her own mousetrap, "I'll take you up to a room you can have for tonight. We'll be going to midnight mass before very long."

"Since when have you been going to mass?"

"Since we've lived here. I've been intending to get back into the Church, thinking I was a widow; it's going to complicate things, your being still alive."
"I'm sorry, but take heart; I might not be alive for much longer."
"How long have they given you?"
"Months, and not many of those."
"Hmmm," said Melissa.
"I suppose you want to know where I've been."
"No, not really."
"So you lost interest when you knew I'd gone bankrupt."
"It was your failure to tell me that I minded; letting me go to the bank and make a fool of myself over the bounced cheques; not to mention disappearing and leaving me to cope with it all alone."
Cassandra realised that her parents had forgotten her presence and she was unwilling to remind them of it by moving away from the table. It was necessary, however, to take her own mousetrap out of the oven before it burnt. 'It's amazing we can eat anything,' she thought, 'but somehow reassuring to go on doing normal things. I think I'd better make a couple more of these. I'm sure my father's hungry and I know I am. I expect Mummy prefers to smoke and drink.' Cassandra ate her supper hungrily and then went on to use the last of the cheese and bacon on two more pieces of bread. Melissa poured out another glass of wine for everybody. There was a silence.
"When we've finished this I'll take you up to your room," she said. "Have you got any luggage?"
"I must have left it outside the door," her husband replied. "I'll go and bring it in."
"It's all right, I'll go," Cassandra got up as she spoke; she didn't trust her father to lock up properly. On the tiled floor outside the front door she found a battered suitcase,

not very large. She took it into the kitchen. Melissa looked at it disgustedly.

"What a scruffy looking thing," she remarked, "Where on earth did you get it?"

"I exchanged the leather one for it and got a meal in return. The leather one was too heavy, anyway, and had my initials on it and I wanted to be as unnoticeable as possible."

"Yes, I've no doubt," Melissa responded acidly. Cassandra put down another mousetrap and asked her mother if she'd like one.

"No thank you. I seem to have lost my appetite."

"Well, I haven't," said Fergus gratefully. Cassandra hadn't either but merely finished hers in silence. She felt, as she so often had in her childhood, a mere unnoticed onlooker, much less important to her parents than their animosity to each other, often undeclared though it was. With an effort she made herself speak: "I'll take him up to his room, Mummy; which one do you want him to have?"

"One of the guest rooms will do for tonight; there's nothing else ready. Besides--." Melissa decided not to express aloud her thought that she didn't want Fergus on the same floor as herself and Cassandra. Instead she turned to him and said: "You won't be able to stay there for long; but we'll talk about that tomorrow."

Cassandra led the way upstairs, carrying the battered case. Her father followed slowly and breathlessly and seemed relieved to reach the room. She showed him the bathroom. "Luxury!" he commented. "I'm glad to see you've fallen on your feet."

"It hasn't always been like this."

"How did you manage it?"

"A very kind loan; and we're taking paying guests. Will you be all right now? You can make yourself a cup of tea if you want to; there's a kettle and cups and so on."

"I see. Yes. Thank you. I think I'll just go to bed. I'm very tired. Thank you. Good night."

Cassandra returned the 'good night' and left the room, closing the door quietly. Downstairs again she slumped into a chair in the kitchen and found to her surprise that she was dripping tears. Her mother regarded her, stony-faced.

"He looks so awful!" said Cassandra, by way of explanation.

"Yes," replied Melissa, "you'd never think he'd been a really good-looking man. How *dare* he turn up tonight of all nights and ruin our Christmas?"

"We'll feel better when we've been to mass."

"Perhaps. Earlier this evening---it seems years ago---I was feeling really sorry that I haven't got myself back into the Church and can't receive the sacraments; but now I'm almost glad because I couldn't possibly take holy communion the way I'm feeling."

"I do understand," Cassandra was sympathetic. "I'll just clear up and then let's go and get ready and leave as soon as possible. We can always have a drink somewhere if we're too early. There'll be ample space between 11.00 and communion time for me to fulfil the fasting rule. Let's keep our minds on the celebration in church and be as happy as we can be."

They needn't have worried about being too early. By the time they'd got into Oxford through still busy traffic, parked the car some distance away from their usual Sunday place and walked to the church, the courtyard was full of people waiting to go in and more kept arriving all the time; they were more than halfway down the throng when eleven o'clock came and the doors were opened. It was an orderly crowd; there was no shoving, just a slow, shuffling movement forward as people adjusted to the bottle-neck of the church doors and made their way inside. The church was dimly lit but the gold leaf round the apse glimmered and shone with a promise of the glories to come. They sat down in their usual place. The church was warm and the lingering scent of incense was appreciable. The winter decorations of flowers and ivy gave out no scent but their beauty blended with the whole ambience. The atmosphere was one of happy expectancy. Cassandra finished her preliminary prayers and sat back in the pew feeling contented, rested and consoled. The organ began to play. Carols were sung until the time came for the mass to begin. Then came the procession of the altar servers and the clergy, the two deacons and the celebrant in glowing gold vestments while the music of a jubilant hymn pealed out from the organ. The congregation stood to welcome them. Cassandra was conscious of a wave of happiness, which seemed to engulf her and wash away the cares of the world. 'I can cope with anything when I have this,' she thought, 'it's so lasting, so constant, so unchangeable; the little happenings of day to day pale into insignificance in comparison.' She looked at her mother and was surprised to see that there were tears in her eyes. 'That's all to the good,' she thought, 'she needs to express emotion. She hides and represses it too often.'

The mass progressed in solemnity and splendour. The joy of the Christmas message was celebrated. At communion Melissa went up for a blessing and vowed that she would waste no more time before doing all that was necessary to be fully received into the Church again. 'Perhaps this was what I needed,' she thought; 'seeing Fergus again has actually made me more determined.'

As they drove home at almost 2 a.m. Melissa said happily: "You were quite right about our feeling much better, not just after but during mass. The bitterness has gone; nothing really matters so much any more. Fergus is merely a poor old man who is sick and in need of help; so perhaps Christmas Eve was the best time for him to come back after all. Of course," she added a little less happily, "I may not feel the same tomorrow, but I hope I do."

30

Christmas morning; Cassandra woke up half expecting to find a pillow-case full of presents at the end of her bed now that she was at home with both her parents. She laughed at herself, put on a dressing gown and went down to the kitchen to make some tea and take a cup to her mother. Melissa was deeply grateful when Cassandra came into her room with a tray. "Darling!" she exclaimed, "You shouldn't have carried all this up two flights of stairs! How very, very kind of you."

"Happy Christmas, Mummy; how are you feeling this morning?"

"Very well, so far; not unhappy at all. I hope it lasts!"

"So do I."

"Feel happy or hope it lasts?"

"Both. I've brought up the cake as well. Would you like a piece?"

"You know I think I would; though it must be the only time I'd ever eat such a thing at this hour of the morning."

"Oh, it's just like solid muesli, really, all that dried fruit and flaked almonds and so on. Anyway, it makes the day special." Cassandra cut into the cake and they had a good-sized slice each.

"Do you think I ought to take some down---you know---one floor? He seemed to eat all right." Cassandra felt unable to refer to their unexpectedly arrived visitor by any acceptable name. It seemed so long since they'd lived in France and he was so changed. She'd never called him 'Fergus' or even 'Daddy'; he'd preferred 'Pa'. To say 'my father' seemed over formal and even a little proprietary in speaking to her mother. "Oh dear," she continued, "I don't know what to call him."

"There's probably no need to call him anything for the moment; 'he' and 'him' are quite adequate, at least until Pete comes back. And he never did like Christmas cake, so don't bother with that. I suppose a cup of tea wouldn't be a bad idea. We'd better keep an eye on him if he's as ill as he says he is. It would be rather ghastly to discover he'd been dead for hours and hours. We might even be had up for wilful neglect or culpable negligence or whatever it's called."

Cassandra couldn't help smiling. "You are marvellous, Mummy, nothing really throws you for long. Are you still feeling as happy as you did when we came home last night?"

"I think I probably am, though I mustn't be too sanguine. These things take time. But since I've experienced a complete lack of bitterness and felt how wonderfully liberating it is I've every intention of maintaining it for as long as possible. Anger and bitterness only hurt the one who feels them and the past can't be changed. It's pointless to dwell on it. So yes, take him a cup of tea, the poor old thing. At least it's only one storey up from the kitchen."

Cassandra took the tray down to the kitchen and, having loaded a smaller one with a fresh pot of tea and a piece of bread and butter, as they had no biscuits--- 'I wish we did have some', she thought--- she took it up one flight of stairs to what she described to herself as 'the occupied room' and knocked at the door. A rather breathless voice said "Come in!" and she went in to see a thin figure in a stained vest sitting up against two pillows, the cushion from the chair and a rolled up bundle of clothes.

"Good morning; happy Christmas! I've brought you a cup of tea and some bread. I hope you slept well."

"Thank you; you shouldn't be waiting on me; I'm not used to it."

"Aren't you?" was all she could think of to say, and she immediately regretted it.

"Well, I've got out of the way of it lately. But I'm very grateful. When do I have to leave here?"

"Oh, not until we need the room for a guest, a paying guest. Oh dear! I mean we're having to take them to make ends meet." Cassandra stumbled over her words feeling that everything she said was loaded with potentially accusing meaning.

"Are you comfortable?" she asked, eyeing the pillow and cushion structure on the bed.

"Oh yes. I have to stay sitting up; not much breath you see. I'll get up and dressed soon. I'll even have a shower."

"Have you got any clean clothes to put on?"

"Clean clothes? Not really. I tried to wash them sometimes but they never seemed to look any cleaner."

"Well bring down any spare ones and I'll wash them for you. We've got a washing machine."

"I'm sorry not to have any pyjamas; I gave up on that luxury a while ago."

"Never mind; the shops will be open tomorrow and the sales are on."

She took one of the cups from the guest tray and poured some tea, handed it to him and put the plate of bread and butter on the bed. "This isn't breakfast, of course, we'll have something else downstairs later." She left the room, thinking how surprisingly true it is that doing kind things for people makes one feel kindly towards them.

Christmas Day progressed a great deal better than anybody had expected. A shower and hair wash improved Fergus's appearance a little and Melissa managed to remain happy. The extra large duck was adequate for the lunch and the Christmas pudding was no problem as Fergus had never liked it and took only just enough to be an excuse for helping himself to brandy butter. Melissa reflected that some things never change. The conversation was limited to the present and the future with plentiful descriptions of the work already done in the house and the eventual flats to be fitted and furnished on the top floor, so that the atmosphere was one of cheering achievement and confidence. And that, Melissa considered, really was a change. She had never before, she realised, at previous Christmases, felt so confidently in charge, so pleasantly optimistic. Rufus was aware of the change in her and was both surprised and relieved. He still felt great guilt over his bankruptcy, rather more than he felt over his abandonment of his wife, his unexplained disappearance; but he began to feel that the harm done to her was less than might have been expected.

Towards evening Pete rang to wish them a very happy Christmas; he was thanked for his thoughtful presents but not told about the new arrival. A little later the telephone rang again. Cassandra answered it. "Oh, Robert!" she gasped, as if surprised.

"Yes! Why? Didn't you expect to hear from me?"

"Of course, yes, can you ring in five minutes or a bit less? I need to go into the shed." Cassandra had been so overwhelmed by the events of the past twenty-four hours that Robert had, in fact, been less than uppermost in her mind; but now she wanted to tell him about everything and, even though her parents were in the dining room and she was in the kitchen she felt inhibited by their presence and the possibility of their coming in while she was talking to him. She hastily put on her coat, took the shed keys from their hook and ran across the courtyard. She was just in time to pick up the receiver when the telephone rang again.

"Robert?"

"Yes, what is it? What's the matter?" Robert's voice was anxious.

"Oh I'm sorry, Robert, I so want to talk to you and I couldn't in the house because my father's there."

"What?!!"

"Yes. Oh I hardly know where to start. It was last night."

"Last night? Christmas Eve?"

Cassandra made an effort to speak more calmly, but reliving the event as it had happened made her tremble as if with delayed shock. "Yes, I'll tell you; the doorbell rang------." She told the whole story of what had happened and had the comfort of Robert's concern and even of his offer to cut short his visit to his parents and come immediately to stay at Huntsfield if he could be of any help.

"Oh, that's so kind, Robert; but I couldn't let you cut short your time at home."

Robert did not quite say that it would be no great sacrifice but did make it clear that he'd much rather see Cassandra.

"I really appreciate that, Robert. But I think we'll have to settle down a little before we see anybody here. Tomorrow we'll go out and buy him some clothes; he's hardly got anything wearable, and then my mother and I are going to a party in Oxford in the evening, though I must admit I've only just remembered it. I know she'll want to go. It's at the Oxford Marjoribanks, you know, Sir Felix and Lady Marjorie. So we are all right really; we got over the worst when we were at Midnight Mass. It's just that I felt the shock again when I was telling you about it. Please don't worry."

Robert and Cassandra continued their conversation for some time while Melissa and Fergus, in the dining room, faced the now unfamiliar task of talking to each other with no third party present. They had heard Cassandra run down the corridor and open and close the back door.

"Is that Cassandra?" Fergus asked.

"Yes, I expect she's gone out to the shed."

"The *shed?*"

"It's really her workshop but we don't always dignify it with that title."

"Of course, she makes pottery, doesn't she?"

"I'm gratified that you remember; yes, she's been our mainstay and breadwinner since we've been here, and even before, in fact."

"Ah!" Fergus was unwilling to pursue that line of conversation any further. "Why has she gone to the shed?"

"No doubt to talk to her inamorato in private; it'll be him telephoning."

Melissa realised that her daughter would be detailing to Robert all the latest developments and have no wish to be overheard or interrupted, but forbore to say so.

"What's he like? Is he suitable? What does his father do?"

"I have absolutely no idea what his father does, or did; he's probably retired as the son is at least thirty-five. It's irrelevant to young people these days, anyway, *fortunately*!" Melissa couldn't resist putting a little stress on the final word. "The young man himself is an Oxford don."

"Hm. Not much money in that."

"Possibly not; but it has some prestige and it's steady and *safe*."

"I take your point."

"Do you? It strikes me you look at things exactly as you used to in spite of all that's happened."

"How else can I look at them?"

"Your views sound ridic---er, strange, coming from a, a---."

"A down-and-out?"

"Well, since you say it yourself, yes. I would have thought you'd place less importance on money as the be all and end all."

"My recent experiences have made me realise the importance of money more than ever."

"But it's so insecure, so vulnerable to transience."

"So is life; but that doesn't make it less important."

"Well at least you didn't think money was *more* important than life and commit suicide, like so many men who lost all their money.

"I thought of it briefly, but I didn't lose my money shamefully after defrauding other people."

"That at least is something to be thankful for. What are you going to do now?"

"Die; but not by my own hand. Can I stay here until I do?"

"I knew you'd come back to us when you found out that we were relatively well off."

"You should have kept yourselves out of the papers."

"We needed the publicity to enable us to sell Cassandra's pots. I hope you realise you'll be living on her earnings?"

"Isn't that what you've been doing?"

"Yes, at first, but I have contributed a lot of work. And I'll be doing the actual physical side of the paying guests business. Cassandra need only do the emails. But this is hardly off the ground as yet."

"You must find it difficult to have to work for your living."

"No I don't; I'm happier than I was in France. I was so merely your wife there, and I see now that I lived a very superficial sort of life. I'm much happier now, more in control, more able to be myself. I really feel fulfilled."

"So I've actually done you a good turn after all!"

"I believe you have, however unintentionally. But I'm going to divorce you and regularise my position with regard to the Church."

"What Church?"

"The Catholic Church, of course. Though having you turn up and live here may make things more difficult."

"I don't suppose I'll be here very long. There's surely no point in your starting divorce proceedings when you'll soon be a widow anyway. Divorce is very expensive."

Melissa sighed. "I suppose that's true; I'll have to find out about the options. It must be possible to get a Legal Aid divorce. I don't think it's quite decent to wait about impatiently for you to die."

"Thank you for your consideration! It's true that might make me feel even more uncomfortable than I do already."

"Do you? I can't say I'd noticed. But you've always been good at hiding your feelings, from me anyway. I had no idea there were any problems until the cheques bounced and you disappeared. You could have confided in me; that's what wives are for. But I don't want to think about the past. There's so much in the present and the future and that's what matters."

The door opened and Cassandra came in. "Anybody like a cup of tea?" she asked brightly, sensing that some tension might have been building up between her parents.

"Yes, please, darling. It's too soon to start drinking alcohol again. How's Robert?"

"I'm not sure that he's totally happy with his home visit. Do you know he went to Midnight Mass? He had to stand because he hadn't realised how crowded it would be and he was too late to get a seat. He said it wasn't quite up to the standard of the Oratory, but he did enjoy it. His family thought it was very odd of him. They've hardly been to church since they moved away from the Anglo-Catholic parish they lived in when he was a child. I think that's very odd of *them.*"

"It can be all too easy to get out of the way of it," Melissa sighed, "and then not realise how much one's missing."

"I'll make the tea and bring in some Christmas cake and mince pies. I'm getting hungry again."

"Don't bring anything for me," Fergus murmured. "I think I'll go and have a rest. I'm afraid I tire rather easily these days."

"Are you sure? I could bring some tea upstairs for you if you like."

"No, no; thank you all the same. I'll just go and lie down." He left the room and went up the stairs slowly, with a pause every few steps. Cassandra watched him a little anxiously. He did look very old and tired. She made the tea and went back to sit with her mother.

"How did you get on while I was out of the way?" she asked.

"It could have been worse but I do find myself becoming a little acerbic when I'm talking to him. I'm glad you came in when you did. I've moved so far away from him since he left. I must have been suppressing half of myself when I was living with him."

"How much older is he than you are?"

"Oh, more than fifteen years. *Not* a good idea. I hope you don't experience anything similar; not that I think it's at all likely."

"Robert must be at least ten years older than I am."

"Women are so much more equal to men these days; so much better educated than they used to be."

"That's true; but Robert always seems very surprised when I know anything. I find that rather annoying."

"Fergus used to tell me not to ask people questions at dinner parties; he said he found it most embarrassing that I didn't already know the answers. I wondered how else he expected me to show an interest in their work."

"It must make life very difficult to have somebody listening to what you say to other people and then criticising it. You must feel inhibited."

"You do indeed. I'm very much more my own self now."

"And a very successful self it is, too."

"Thank you, darling; that's just the kind of compliment I need."

"I mean it."

"How wonderful. I can't think how Fergus and I managed to have a daughter like you. Heavens! To think I once loved that man. I can hardly believe it now."

"Haven't you any feelings for him at all?"

"Only unpleasant ones, if I let myself go. Do you have any?"

"No, I don't think I do; I never seemed to see him very often. I just think of him as a poor sick old man. I can't even bring myself to call him 'Pa'. Still, I'll take him shopping for some clothes tomorrow. Oh lord!"

"What's the matter?"

"I'd forgotten about Sir Felix and Lady Marjorie's party again. I can't seem to keep it in my head. We'll have to go shopping in the morning. He'll be tired in the afternoon, anyway. We can leave him some supper in the kitchen, can't we?"

Melissa yawned. "I'm quite tired myself," she said. "Come to think of it we were very late last night and we haven't stopped all day, but I'm happy enough to doze in here by the fire. Then we can open the rest of the parcels under the tree."

"*Beside* the tree, more like! It's hardly big enough for anything to go under it! But I'm going to open my present from Robert now; I'm sure there's a book in it and I want to see what it is."

"I think I can stay awake long enough to watch you do that; I'd rather like to see it too."

Cassandra unwrapped the parcel and found two presents.

"Ooh look: a book and a box, and the book's rather nice: the poems of Catullus with Latin on one side and an English translation on the other. Now I appreciate that. It's a very thoughtful present, don't you agree?"

"Isn't Catullus the one who wrote the poem translated as:

'I do not love thee, Dr Fell,

'The reason why I cannot tell,

'But this I know and know full well,

'I do not love thee, Dr Fell.' I believe there's a story behind it but I can't remember what it is."

"I'm impressed at how much you do know."

"I'm dying to see what's in the box. Do open it."

"I'm worried in case it's something I won't like."

"Well there's only one way to find out."

Cassandra carefully detached the circles of clear plastic, which kept the lid on the box, opened it and found another box inside it. It was lined with velvet and inside was a plain, silver cross with an unusual chain of small, oval, interlocked rings and a fastening which could be placed in any one of them to adjust the length.

"Ohhhh!" she gasped. Melissa leaned over to a dangerous angle to see the cause of the exclamation. Cassandra held it up.

"It's really *very* beautiful," said her mother. "*Very* well chosen and in excellent taste. The only kind of jewellery acceptable from a man you're not actually engaged to."

"Oh dear! I didn't give him anything like this."

"It would hardly be a suitable present for a man!"

"You know what I mean."

"I have to admit it's much better than I would have expected."

"Oh dear!"

"What's the matter?"

"Robert really is so very nice."

"So that if you decide not to marry him you'll still find it very difficult to give him up."

"You are very clever sometimes, Mummy; you know things I've hardly admitted to knowing myself."

"I suppose it's one of the advantages of age. One's seen so many of other people's problems as well as one's own. But never mind, darling, 'sufficient unto the day---'."

"Yes, I know: 'is the evil thereof'. You explained it before."

"Just enjoy what you've got now. I'm going to close my eyes."

Cassandra waited till her mother seemed to be asleep and then, feeling it unnecessary to brave the chill of the shed again, went into the kitchen to ring Robert and thank him for his presents.

31

On Boxing Day Melissa and Cassandra woke up quite late and went down to the kitchen even later. There was no sign of Fergus.

"I suppose," said Melissa over her cup of coffee and the first cigarette of the day, "one of us had better go up and see if he's survived the night."

"He may just be waiting for a cup of tea," was Cassandra's tentative suggestion. "I'll go up and see, shall I?"

"That would be kind."

Cassandra went up to the first floor with some trepidation and knocked on the door of 'the occupied room'. She heard nothing. She knocked again, a little louder and listened with her ear to the door. There seemed to be a faint sound like 'mmmm?' with a questioning intonation. Summoning her courage she opened the door. The figure in the bed opened its eyes and stared at her. "Oh," it said.

"Are you all right?" she asked anxiously.

"Yes, I think so. Sorry; I'd forgotten where I was. I was dreaming. Is it late?"

"Well, not very. Do you want to come down to breakfast or would you like me to bring you some?"

"No, no; I'll come down." His eyes searched the room.

"There's a towelling robe in the bathroom, you can come down in that if you like, there's nobody else here."

"Yes, of course; just give me a few minutes."

Ten minutes went by and he hadn't come down.

"I suppose he's past hurrying," Melissa observed.

"I'm afraid I wakened him out of a deep sleep."

"Well, at least we know he's still with us."

The door opened and Fergus shuffled in. He was wearing bathroom slippers and seemed to be having some difficulty managing them. They kept coming away from his toes as if about to walk off without him. The bathrobe, an extra large one, swamped his shrunken figure and he looked more ill and more pathetic than in his own clothes, grubby and worn though they were. Cassandra settled him down and gave him coffee and fruit.

"Do you feel well enough to go and find some new clothes this morning?" she asked.

"Where can such things be *found*?" he said, less as a question than as an almost derisive comment. Cassandra decided not to notice his tone.

"Well," she countered, "There won't be any charity shops open today, but Matalan's open---I've telephoned them--- and it's almost as cheap as the north Oxford charities."

"*Charity* shops?" Fergus asked incredulously.

"They're better than the ones in France," Melissa assured him.

"I've never been to such a place in any country!"

"Never mind," said his wife "we'll take you to some as soon as they're open. It's an interesting experience."

"I can't believe you've ever bought anything from any of them."

"I haven't bought anything except food and other such necessities anywhere; but Cassandra's an expert and buys marvellous garments for next to nothing."

"I really don't think you ought to shop in such places."

"Why?"

"Well, it's decidedly infra dig."

"And how do you suppose we're going to clothe ourselves? It's all right for me, certainly, because I managed to salvage enough to bring to England with me;

but Cassandra's been a poor student and then a poor potter for quite a long time and has few things to fall back on. And who do you think is going to pay for your clothes today? I don't imagine you've got any money. How did you get here? Who paid for you?"

"I hitchhiked."

"Really! And that, I suppose, is not considered infra dig!"

"It's all right for a man. Anyway, I don't need any clothes."

"Judging from the filthy ragged things Cassandra brought down to wash I'm afraid you obviously do. You're not in charge here, kindly realise that. You may have had the upper hand in all our previous dealings, but not now."

Fergus was silent. Cassandra felt almost sorry for him.

"I expect," she said kindly, "it'll take some time to adjust to."

"What?" asked Fergus.

"The different situation. But do you feel strong enough to come out shopping or shall I take your size and go and do it myself?"

Fergus looked at her helplessly. He didn't, in fact, feel quite strong enough to go out but on the other hand he didn't feel strong enough to stay in the house with Melissa either.

"Oh, I'll come with you. I'll go and get dressed now."

"It's a good idea to go to Matalan," Melissa told her daughter. "You're not likely to run into anybody we know there. Do you know how much you've got left to spend on your card?"

"Not exactly, but it should be enough."

"Don't get more than one of everything; we'll make do with that."

"Of course; unless there are any 'buy one get one free' bargains; I'll look out for those."

***

In Matalan Fergus looked round bemused.

"What's that for?" he asked, as Cassandra pulled out a trolley.

"To put things in."

"What things?"

"The things we want to try or buy.

"We hardly need anything that size!"

"There aren't any smaller ones."

"Of course! They want to encourage people to fill them up."

"The men's department's here on the left."

"Good God! What dreadful looking stuff!"

Cassandra took no notice but steered the trolley to the underwear section and picked up a pack of five pairs of underpants for a very reasonable sum.

"Are these the right size?" she asked.

"I hardly know. I've lost a lot of weight. Your mother used to buy them for me. I never noticed the size."

Cassandra sighed and got out her mobile. "Mummy! No, don't worry, it's nothing drastic. He says you used to buy his underpants and he doesn't know what size he should have." "No, I can't tell whether they look generous; they're in a pack." "OK, I'll get 'medium'. It's easier to take them in than let them out."

Cassandra switched off the mobile and headed for the vests, then for the pyjamas.

"I don't need pyjamas," said Fergus flatly.

"Just one pair," Cassandra spoke persuasively, "look, these are on special offer."

"I've got used to wearing a vest and underpants."

“That won’t look very good if you have to go to hospital.”

“Bugger that!” said Fergus.

“You’d better go and sit in the car. You’re not being very cooperative.”

Fergus was actually feeling decidedly weary and more cantankerous than usual. The journey to Huntsfield House, despite the lorry driver’s kind insistence on taking him all the way there, had exhausted him and the ensuing emotional strain had added to his tiredness despite the physical comfort of the place. All his reserves of energy had been used up in getting there and he had little left to sustain him. He went gratefully to the car. Cassandra helped him in and went back to finish the shopping. She guessed the size of a pair of trousers by holding them against herself and decided on a couple of sweaters (‘buy one get one half price’) instead of a jacket. The jackets really were too awful anyway; they’d have a much better chance of finding something acceptable in a charity shop.

There was a long queue at the checkout and Cassandra was glad the ‘poor old man’ was no longer standing with her. She totted up the total of her purchases and it was surprisingly reasonable; there’d certainly be enough on her card to cover it.

By the time she got back to the car Fergus was asleep. Clearly, he was not going to be able to go out very much; it was as well that the clothes she’d bought him were very suitable for indoors. ‘He must be in a worse state than he seemed yesterday,’ she thought. Fergus barely woke when she got into the car and started it and he slept all the way home. When they arrived there Cassandra helped him up the stairs, giving him time to pause for breath every few steps. At his bedroom door he stopped and turned to her. “Thank you,” he said, “you really are a very kind girl.”

Cassandra went downstairs to show her mother what she'd bought and tell her that 'the old man' was clearly not at all well and could not be expected to go out very much.

"That's all to the good," was Melissa's response; "I'd hate to have to take him anywhere with us!"

"We're going to have to explain him to Pete tomorrow," Cassandra suddenly remembered.

"That shouldn't be too difficult; though Pete may well be more used to disappearing fathers than returning ones, I think he'll take it in his stride. But *much* more important, what do you think I should wear to the party?"

"Let's go and look in your wardrobe and decide on something."

"What a good idea! I simply can't think of *anything* at the moment."

"Perhaps I should have got you something from Matalan this morning!"

"*Darling!* We may be poor but there is a limit."

"Well perhaps TKMax. They have designer clothes at greatly reduced prices."

"Thank you, darling, but I think I can make the things I brought from France last a little bit longer; the mention of those places gives me some incentive to do so. Honestly, I'd rather go to Oxfam."

They went to Melissa's room and drew out several things from her wardrobe.

"There's always the safe 'little black dress', but it's not very Christmassy, is it?"

"Couldn't you lighten it with a coloured stole or pashmina?"

"Now that is a good idea. I don't know what other women will be wearing and if the stole's too much I can always slip it off or just drape it casually over one arm.

Thank you, darling; you're such a help. What are you going to put on yourself?"

"Oh, one of the new skirts I bought the other day; I've got a top to go with it. I somehow don't think it'll be a party for many of my age group, anyway."

"The Marjoribanks children may be there and I suppose they're young grown-ups like you."

"I don't really feel it matters very much, but I can always talk about my pots!"

Melissa smiled. "Of course there's nothing ulterior about *that,* is there! One thing we must agree *not* to do, however, is say anything about the return of Fergus. That's definitely a topic for a later and more private occasion."

"Heavens yes! I couldn't bear to mention it. Shall I say you're a widow if anybody asks?"

"I don't suppose for a minute they will, but we must both agree on the same story just in case. Yes, I think widowhood is the best explanation of my apparently husbandless state. I can't imagine Sir Felix and Lady M. will give us away."

Fergus was still asleep at lunch time and they decided to keep his lunch for when he woke up, as well as leaving him something for later. When he finally came down at about 4.30 he expressed considerable gratitude, mainly directed to Cassandra but without being too specific. She made him a pot of tea and then went upstairs to dress.

Melissa and Cassandra finally set off after expressing admiration of each other's clothes and establishing an atmosphere of cheerful confidence. They both felt relieved to be going away from the house and Fergus.

"It seems like years since Christmas Eve," Melissa sighed as they drove out of the courtyard. "I'm really happy to be going out and meeting some other people."

"Well at least I went to Matalan today."

"Yes, but you had him with you, so that wasn't much of a break."

"He was asleep a good deal of the time."

"Not much help. One keeps wondering whether he'll wake up."

"I suppose it would be merciful if he didn't."

" To us or to him?".

"Both, really."

"Yes, true. But let's try to forget him for a few hours and concentrate on enjoying the party."

They arrived at the house feeling less stressed than when they had set out. Lady Marjorie greeted them with great friendliness and introduced them to a number of people, including Sir Felix's brother Jasper, who immediately showed every sign of wanting to 'look after' Melissa.

"Have you been acquainted with our family history?" Melissa asked him a little suspiciously.

"Only heard that you're kinsfolk and live in that great pile of Agatha Egerton's."

Relieved, Melissa murmured "But I don't know anything about you; tell me about yourself."

Jasper Marjoribanks gave a sigh. "Divorcing, I'm afraid; we managed to stay together for twenty-five years but we've come unstuck now."

"Oh dear! One simply doesn't know the right reply to that information," said Melissa sympathetically. "I once tried 'I'm very sorry' only to be told fiercely; 'well *I'm* not!' Can you give me any advice on how to respond?"

"How good of you to ask. So much kinder than a recoil of disapproval or a silence going along with an I-don't-want-to-hear-about-it expression. Then there's the prurient kind of 'Ah! Got somebody new, have you?' when they *do* want to hear about it and tell anybody else who's remotely interested into the bargain."

"I don't think I come into either of those categories," replied Melissa, smiling kindly.

"Of course you don't, so I'll tell you: it's my wife who's got somebody new, another woman! It's been a terrible shock."

"I can well understand that! Is it worse than another man would have been?"

"I think so; it makes me feel as if I've never really known her. And maybe it's my fault; I must have put her off men."

"Oh, I can't believe that's the case. It may be a sudden change of personality, what the French call 'le demon de midi'.

At that point a man of similar age came up to them and asked Jasper to introduce him: "Come on, old chap, can't have you monopolising the most interesting-looking woman in the room all evening!"

Melissa glanced at the speaker coldly, a fact that was not missed by Jasper, who nevertheless did the introduction with apparently good grace. "Mortimer Riley," he murmured, "Melissa Marjoribanks."

"Oh indeed! A relative then! All the more reason to interrupt your tete a tete."

"How do you do!" Melissa responded as distantly as possible. She did not appreciate Mortimer Riley's line in heavy-handed compliment. He appeared undaunted and went on talking volubly, addressing himself to Melissa rather than Jasper. "So how are you related? Closely?"

"Rather distantly, actually," Melissa stepped back a little as she spoke, "and only by marriage."

"Ah! Is your husband here?"

"My husband," she replied, "departed this life some time ago."

Jasper could hardly repress a smile on hearing this. Despite his disclaiming any knowledge of the situation behind Melissa and Cassandra he had, of course, been informed of the whole story as far as his brother knew it. 'Clever of her!' he thought. 'That phrase could well mean *he's out of my life* just as well as *he's dead.'* Seeing that Mortimer Riley was determined to go on talking to Melissa and ignoring him, he decided that the best method of rescuing her was to bring up two or three other people and introduce them to her.

Cassandra, meanwhile, was kept very well occupied by the older Marjoribanks boys, one of whom was her own age and two others a little older. She still managed, however, to keep an eye on her mother and see that she was something of a focal point and in the happy position of being able to stay where she was and have plenty of people come to meet her and talk to her. Mortimer Riley stayed at her side for some time before he gave up the unequal struggle and moved on to somebody else. From there, however, he caught sight of Cassandra and, instantly recognising her as at least a close relative of Melissa's, loped over to speak to her, leaving the unfortunate woman he'd been talking to in mid sentence. He broke into the conversation Cassandra was enjoying with the eldest Marjoribanks son, Stephen, saying: "You must be a close relative of Melissa Marjoribanks, you're so like her."

Stephen, seeing her somewhat taken aback at this sudden approach, answered for her: "That's hardly surprising as they're mother and daughter."

"I thought as much!" rejoined Mortimer triumphantly. "My name's Mortimer."

"How do you do, Mr Mortimer," Cassandra spoke as coldly as her mother had done and added the 'Mr' as a touch of off-putting formality.

"Oh, not *Mr* Mortimer, my dear, the surname's Riley; but you don't need to use it."

"I always prefer to be respectful to older people," said Cassandra politely.

"Here! Not so much of the older, if you don't mind!"

"I wouldn't presume to suggest how much older," Cassandra said with deliberate misunderstanding, "but clearly not of the same generation as Stephen and myself, Mr Riley. I've lived in France a great deal and there I would certainly address you as 'Monsieur.' I regard 'Mr' plus surname as the English equivalent."

Mortimer Riley stared at her, opened his mouth, closed it again and remained at a loss for words. Cassandra's casual, almost bohemian, way of dressing made her formality of manner all the more telling.

Stephen gave a cough to hide an incipient chortle and decided to take his tone from Cassandra and make Mortimer Riley aware of his age by the same tongue in cheek method of polite distancing.

"Is Mrs Riley here this evening?" he asked blandly, knowing very well that she was.

"Oh, er, yes indeed. She---um---enjoys talking to people."

"You must both know a lot of the people here tonight."

"Yes, yes, of course we do; we're neighbours after all." He made another attempt at chatting up Cassandra. "That's why it's so refreshing to see a new face." He looked at her with what he hoped was a smile of appreciative admiration.

"Most of the faces here are new to me; and Stephen is going to introduce me to his sisters, so you must excuse us," Cassandra smiled a smile of the utmost politeness and Stephen immediately took the hint and led her to the door so that they could escape from the room as if in search of his female siblings, who were, in fact, helping in the kitchen. Once outside the drawing-room they both began to laugh and congratulate each other on their dealings with the 'chatter-up'. Lady Marjorie came upon them and asked the cause of their amusement.

"Oh yes," she agreed, "Mortimer Riley's notorious. But it's often a good idea to have a lecher at a party, it keeps some of the women happy, especially if their husbands are similarly inclined or getting drunk. But I'm afraid, Cassandra, that you and your mother are likely to make it difficult for most other women to compete! By the way, I hope you'll both stay on and meet our family properly after the other guests have gone."

"I'd love to," Cassandra answered appreciatively; "I'll tell my mother, shall I? But we do have a complication---maybe we can tell you about it---it might be difficult."

"Don't worry, I'll go and ask your mother myself, if I can manage a quiet word away from her admirers!"

Stephen and Cassandra went into the kitchen, where they found his two sisters, and a happy conversation ensued. Lady Marjorie went to detach Melissa from a group of admiring men and rather more critical women and did so without too much difficulty by saying: "You must come and meet our daughters." As they went towards the kitchen and the invitation to stay on was extended Melissa demurred, saying they didn't want to impose on a family party.

"But you *are* family!" Lady Marjorie objected, "And it's so difficult to get all the children home together these days. We'd love you both to stay and meet them properly, do believe me."

"I'd very much like to, certainly, and I think perhaps we can; thank you. What does Cassandra think?"

"She did mention that there was a complication."

"Yes. We might be able to tell you about it when there's only family present. I think we should. I do appreciate your asking us."

So it was agreed and the party in the drawing-room began to break up as people had already been there at least half an hour beyond the specified time. Melissa joined her daughter and the others in the kitchen. She had already refused two invitations to go out to dinner from men whose marital status was doubtful but whose wives were, if in existence, apparently not present. Melissa found herself regretting that Englishmen of her generation almost never wore wedding rings.

At last all the other guests were gone and all the family were gathered in the large kitchen and sitting round the table with another drink and the remains of the finger food. Cassandra had been on elderflower most of the evening but Melissa was enjoying something stronger. All the six Marjoribanks children were identified for her benefit and remained long enough to give a polite account of themselves before they sloped off to another room to pursue their own amusements. Only Stephen and Cassandra stayed in the kitchen. Jasper Marjoribanks was sitting next to Melissa and receiving her thanks for looking after her so kindly. He had certainly seen to it that she had plenty to eat and drink and had met almost every other guest at the party. She turned to thank her host and hostess, too, not only for a particularly enjoyable party but also for the opportunity to meet their children and to join such a family gathering.

"This is almost the best part," she averred. "And I'm so grateful for a chance to tell you what's happened."

She was urged with obvious interest to tell them at once.

"It's so bizarre," she replied, "You'll hardly believe it. Fergus has appeared."

"Fergus? Your husband? Where?" Sir Felix and Lady Marjorie exclaimed almost in unison.

"At our house. On Christmas Eve."

"Only then?"

"Yes. But it seems ages ago."

"Oh you should have brought him tonight!"

"He's not up to it, I'm afraid. He looks absolutely terrible and he's terminally ill."

"How did he get to you?"

"He hitch-hiked; a kindly lorry-driver brought him all the way."

"That really was kind," said Jasper. "He must have looked very ill."

"He really does," said Cassandra, "and he really is. I think he's exhausted himself getting to us. I took him out to get him some new clothes this morning---heavens it seems like a week ago---and he slept all the way back and then went straight upstairs to rest and only came down in the late afternoon."

"You bought him new clothes?" asked Sir Felix incredulously.

"Yes. He looked as if he'd been sleeping rough, or very nearly. He told us he'd tried to wash his clothes sometimes but they hadn't looked any cleaner for the attempt."

"How dreadful!" Sir Felix was horrified at the idea. Lady Marjorie, however, merely said "Oh yes, some of our rough sleepers do that. There's one who spends hours in the women's lavatory at church drying his socks on the hand drier. He says it's better than the one in the men's loo."

The laughter that greeted this matter-of-fact statement lowered the tension of the atmosphere and made the revelations seem more normal and less reprehensible. Melissa turned to her hostess gratefully.

"You really are a tonic," she told her; "you make it all seem less awful."

"Still," Lady Marjorie spoke sympathetically, "it must have been a frightful shock."

"I'm afraid so; and I find it very difficult to be as kind to him as I probably ought to be. Cassandra manages much better. But then of course she's not going to divorce him and get an annulment."

"Do you need to do that if he's terminally ill?"

"I feel I must. I so want to be back in the Church; I want to be able to go to confession and communion. It doesn't seem right to wait impatiently for him to die. I've told him that. I'll still look after him, of course. I won't turn him out."

"As a matter of fact," said Lady Marjorie slowly, "I've actually asked one of the Blackfriars about your sort of situation, only in a general and hypothetical way, of course, and without knowing about your husband's return, but it seems things are greatly relaxed now and there's no problem about the return of a lapsed Catholic, especially if those married outside the church are no longer living as man and wife; simply going to confession and explaining the situation to a priest should be adequate.

So you won't need to go through a divorce, or wait for Fergus to die!"

Instead of replying Melissa began searching in her ornate and minuscule evening bag. Lady Marjorie looked on anxiously, fearing that her consulting a Blackfriar had caused offence.

"Cassandra!" exclaimed her mother. "Have you got a tissue? I'm going to cry!"

A tissue was immediately handed over and Melissa snuffled into it and dabbed her eyes and finally managed to say: "You're so kind! I don't know what to say. You've saved me so much ---given me courage---confidence---I'll go to confession tomorrow. Cassandra, keep me up to it!"

"I'll take you myself," said her daughter in a slightly choked voice.

Lady Marjorie got up and put the kettle on.

"I think what we all need now," she said, "is a nice, hot cup of tea."

"That would be marvellous," said Melissa with heartfelt gratitude, "and then we must go; I can't help worrying about Fergus. Though we did leave him with plenty of food."

32

In the morning Melissa was up and dressed before dawn. Cassandra came down in a dressing-gown as Pete was not expected until later.

"Good heavens!" she gasped, seeing her mother. "Here you are all up and dressed, and in black!"

"Yes; I thought it looked penitential. I haven't anything purple."

"I have; but I don't suppose you'd want to wear it."

"I'm quite happy like this. Can we get there at 9.45 at the latest?"

"I'm sure we can. I'll leave a note for Pete. He's got a key to the house and he knows where we keep the shed key. Do you think he's likely to run across 'him upstairs'?"

"Should we leave *him* a note too?"

"It's not a bad idea. Tell him to make a cup of tea in his room and say we'll give him breakfast when we come back."

"He probably won't wake up in time to see it."

"Perhaps he won't wake up at all. I'd better just open the door a crack and see if he's breathing."

"No, don't. If he's not I'll have to put off going to the Oratory and I'm determined not to."

"Well if you really mean it I'll just put the note under the door."

They set off in very good time, even though the car needed some persuading before it would start, and arrived at the church with at least ten minutes to spare. They went into a pew beside the confessionals and Melissa picked up one of the nearby guides to making a confession.

"These are an excellent idea," she whispered to Cassandra, "and reassuring, too. If they need to provide them it means I can't be the only one who's out of practice!"

A priest went into the confessional and turned on the green 'enter' light.

"Here I go!" said Melissa and went in. The green light turned red and said 'wait' and Cassandra knelt in the pew outside and prayed and waited.

It seemed like a long while. At last Melissa emerged, knelt in the pew, made the sign of the cross and dripped tears. When she sat back in her seat her daughter regarded her anxiously.

"Was it all right?" she asked in a whisper.

Her mother turned towards her looking radiant. "Marvellous!" she said. "He was so kind, helpful, reassuring. How can they be so young and so wise? Such a weight has been lifted from me I feel as if I could fly. We can stay for mass, can't we? To be able to receive communion after all these years!"

"Of course we can. It's time already: there's the bell."

The priest and the server came in from the vestry; the congregation stood up and the mass began.

After mass they didn't stay for the rosary but went to the car and drove home. Melissa sighed contentedly and said: "I'm sure I can face anything now, even Fergus. I feel a little guilty not letting you check on him, but somehow I'm sure he's all right. I must tell him I don't need to divorce him. That'll save a lot of trouble and expense."

"Does it make you feel less angry with him?"

"It certainly does. In fact his coming back seems to be what spurred me into action and got me to confession; that and Lady Marjorie. I'm going to write to her and express my gratitude. And thank you for coming with me this morning."

"I really wanted to; I'm so happy for you---but I also wanted to make sure you didn't turn tail at the last minute!"

"Darling! As if I would have! I was quite determined from the moment I woke up. But I'll change out of my black when I get home."

When they drove into the courtyard they were greeted by Pete, who looked very worried.

"Oh dear" said Cassandra, "I fear he's run into the occupant!" She got out of the car saying: "Pete! How nice to see you. How was your Christmas? Are you all right?"

"Thank you, Miss, yes Miss, but there's somebody in the house."

"It's quite all right; please don't be anxious, we'll explain. Have you seen him?"

"Well he come into the kitchen when I was taking down the shed key an' 'e said 'who are you and what are you doing with that key?' I told him I works here and lives here and for that matter what was *he* doing in the house? Mind you I could see he'd been staying because he had a dressing-gown on. Didn't look like he was wearing any pyjamas, though." Pete gave a sniff of disgust. In his family pyjamas were something of a status symbol and people who didn't wear them were regarded as 'rough'.

"Come in and sit down, Pete, and we'll tell you all about it," said Cassandra sympathetically. Her mother, still on cloud nine, had gone inside. They went into the kitchen, where Melissa was humming a hymn tune and putting on the kettle.

"Anybody for tea or coffee?" she asked happily. Pete opted for tea 'strong with milk and sugar' and Cassandra for herbal.

"Now Pete," she said, "I'm sure I've mentioned to you before that my father had disappeared?"

"Oh, yes, Miss. My dad done that 'n all. Mum says they usually always do; don't want to pay the maintenance, you see. Cor! That's never him turned up again?"

"Yes, I'm afraid it is! You've got it in one."

"Wow! He looks too old to be your dad."

"My mother's his second wife; he's much older than she is."

"Yeah, well; I can see that right enough."

Melissa gave him a happy smile of appreciation.

Greatly relieved at Pete's matter-of-fact acceptance of the situation, Cassandra prepared another cup of tea to take upstairs to her father. "I'll tell him to come down and have something to eat---when he's dressed."

***

Towards evening the telephone rang; it was Jasper Marjoribanks for Melissa. After the usual civilities about getting home safely and health and well-being he invited her to have dinner with him the following evening. She accepted. When Cassandra entered the room some minutes later she saw her mother still sitting over the telephone and looking uncharacteristically pensive.

"What's the matter?" she asked, "Have you had a thought-provoking telephone call?"

"I suppose you could call it that," Melissa answered vaguely. Then, feeling that an explanation might be in order, she added "Jasper's invited me to have dinner with him tomorrow."

"Jasper?"

"Yes, you know, Jasper Marjoribanks, Felix's brother."

"Heavens! Isn't he married?"

"Divorcing. Didn't I tell you? His wife's gone off with another woman."

"Good grief, how awful! Are you going?"

"Well yes, I rather like him. He was very kind to me last night and saw to it that I wasn't bothered too much by tiresome people and generally looked after me with great thoughtfulness and consideration."

"Where are you meeting him?"

"He's coming here at about six because I said I'd show him the house; he hasn't seen it for years, and we'll have a small drink here and then go out. He didn't say where."

Before Cassandra could comment the telephone rang again. Melissa answered it and had a brief exchange of friendly words with the caller before handing the receiver to her daughter, saying, "It's Stephen Marjoribanks, for you."

"Hullo Stephen, how nice of you to ring."

"Cassandra, could I possibly come and see you tomorrow? I have to go back to London the next day and I'd love to see your house. I'm told I've been there before but I was much too young to remember. Perhaps we could go out and have a bite of supper somewhere afterwards?"

"That sounds like a very pleasant idea, thank you. What time will you be here?"

"Is five o'clock too early?"

"No, I don't think so, not if I'm to show you the house---it's quite a size!"

"Excellent! I'll see you at five, then."

"Well!" said Melissa as her daughter put the receiver down, "At least it's all in the family!" Simultaneously they both began to laugh.

"You could do a lot worse, you know darling," said Melissa, "he's the eldest son of a baronet."

"Really Mummy, you are being ridiculous! He only wants to see the house."

"Of course, darling; how could one possibly suppose he had any other motive!"

They both began to laugh again and were still laughing when Fergus came in and looked at them suspiciously.

"What are you laughing at?" he asked.

"Oh, just that we've both been asked out to dinner," Melissa answered.

"Another party?"

"No, just private invitations from people we met last night."

"Who?"

"Felix Marjoribanks' brother and son respectively. They're keen to see the house."

"Oh yes! So *you're* going out with the brother, I suppose. Can't you wait till I'm dead?"

"No, Fergus, I can not wait; considering that I haven't been out to dinner since your disappearance I think I've waited quite long enough."

"It doesn't sound as if you're wasting any time taking up with somebody new."

"I have no intention of 'taking up with'---as you so elegantly put it---another divorced, non-Catholic Marjoribanks. The first one has been quite enough for one life-time."

"You'll have a job to find anybody who isn't divorced, at your age."

"There are such things as widowers, but as I value my freedom and am not in fact looking to find anybody at all, that is quite beside the point. And if you're going to be so uncivil I suggest you stay in your room while Cassandra and I are showing our respective relatives over the house."

"Certainly I will; I've no desire to meet either of them."

Cassandra felt rather sorry for him and tried to soften the situation. "You might like to meet Stephen," she said. "He's just a bit older than I am and he works in London. I don't suppose he'll be here again. He's coming at five and

I'll take him all over the house, though not into your room, if you'd rather I didn't."

Fergus looked at her closely, distrusting her kindness at first, but then remembering cups of tea and shopping for clothes and other little attentions.

"Thank you," he said finally, "I appreciate your consideration, but I don't think I want to meet anybody, especially family. I'll stay in my room."

There was a jangling ring from the courtyard door bell.

"I'll go," said Cassandra. A minute later she was heard to say, in tones of surprise: "Robert!"

Fergus looked at Melissa anxiously and asked "Is that her young man?"

"Yes, I'm afraid so. Oh dear."

"Why 'oh dear'? Don't you want him to see me?"

"That's not what I was thinking of, actually, and you can hardly escape now, anyway. Yes, I think he should see you."

Robert and Cassandra came into the room. Cassandra glanced at her father, thankful that he was wearing his new clothes---he had refused to let her throw out the old ones.

"This is my father, Robert; er---," she hesitated, not sure how to address her father, and simply continued "Robert Taylor."

Fergus rose to shake hands with Robert as they exchanged 'how-do-you-dos'. Robert began to apologise for his intrusion saying he'd been on his way back to college and couldn't resist the temptation to come and see how they were. Melissa reflected that he must have been coming back from the south by an unfamiliar route, and that it was a good thing he hadn't decided to appear unexpectedly the following evening. Nevertheless showed no sign of these thoughts as she welcomed him and invited him to stay for supper.

"Oh, no, no, I don't want to put you out, I know I should have rung first but the car just seemed to find its way here!"

"We really would like you to stay for supper, Robert," Cassandra eagerly seconded her mother's invitation, thinking that she must keep the next evening free for Stephen. Not that there was anything wrong with her going out for supper with a cousin (however distant) but it would certainly be easier to manage if Robert was not there. "We seem not to have seen you for ages."

Robert was, of course, unable to resist this appeal and Melissa decided it was time to lubricate the occasion with a drink. The presence of Fergus seemed to create an unfamiliar awkwardness, which needed careful handling. Melissa disappeared for a short time and came back bearing a rather dusty bottle of wine. Cassandra realised suddenly that her mother had in fact been drinking less in the last couple of days and that she unusually had had no bottle of wine immediately at hand. Fergus looked at the dusty bottle with interest, then rose to pick it up and examine it.

"Good heavens!" he exclaimed. "Where did you get this? It's extremely special; look at the date!"

"Oh is it? I didn't realise."

"Yes, Mummy," Cassandra was aware for the first time that she'd never questioned the provenance of the wine supply which had sustained them since their occupation of Huntsfield. "Where has all the wine we've been drinking come from? I've never thought about it before but you surely didn't buy it at a supermarket."

Melissa's usual equanimity seemed to desert her as she encountered three pairs of interestedly enquiring eyes. "Um---," she said.

Cassandra felt a pang of anxiety as she perceived the aura of guilt conveyed by her mother. But it was too late for the question to be left unanswered. “Um what?” she demanded.

“From the cellar,” Melissa answered at last.

“What cellar? You’ve never mentioned it.”

“I didn’t think you’d be interested.

“Well of course I am. How did you know about it?”

“I found the key quite early on and looked about to find out what it opened. I needed something interesting to do while you were working or out. I guessed a house like this must have a cellar, and I didn’t suppose Cousin Agatha knew a lot about it. The men of her generation used to keep their cellars to themselves. So let’s just be thankful and enjoy it.”

“There must be some really valuable stuff down there,” said Fergus, “you could sell it.”

“I was afraid that might be the case,” said Melissa gloomily.

Cassandra couldn’t help laughing. “I suppose that’s why you kept so quiet about it.”

“Well, darling, whatever the reason, it is still Christmas and I’m not going to put this bottle back. Perhaps you’d like to open it, Fergus?”

Smiling in spite of himself at this previously unperceived aspect of his wife’s character, Fergus complied. Cassandra fetched appropriate glasses and handed the first filled one to Robert, who had been too interested a spectator at this family scene to feel at all embarrassed by it. He found it most refreshingly different from his own parents’ household.

It only took one glass to animate the conversation, which mainly turned on the price of such vintage wine. Fergus, his commercial instincts aroused, became more animated than he had ever appeared since his arrival and Robert, with some experience of wine tastings and some understanding of college cellars, was well able to join in. Melissa regarded them benignly and reflected that there was nothing like drink to get men going, one way or another; except of course that so many of them spoilt it by going too far. 'No idea of moderation,' she said to herself, 'that's one of the main problems with men.' Aloud she asked brightly: "Now who's for a tiny top-up?"

The evening progressed in the same spirit; Robert got on extremely well with Fergus and both Melissa and Cassandra found it easier to accept his presence as a normality than they had since his sudden arrival. Cassandra even managed to address him as 'Pa', having once done it without thinking. She realised this with a sigh of relief as if she'd overcome a considerable hurdle.

Somehow, in a short time and with little obvious effort, Melissa managed to produce a meal: soup, pate and toast, baked potatoes (from the microwave) stuffed with smoked fish and horseradish, buttered beans. Another bottle of wine had to be opened to go with it. Cassandra was about to demur and Fergus showed some anxiety over it, his commercial instincts vying with his appreciation; Melissa, however, mercifully remembered that under the terms of Cousin Agatha's will nothing belonging to the house could be sold. Fergus thought this could probably be circumvented as regarded wine, at least with the help of a clever lawyer, but in the meantime it was perhaps wise to enjoy just one more bottle! Robert drank very sparingly, mindful of his drive to Oxford, but he was in no hurry to go. Finally he went to his car, and Cassandra with him. She had appreciated his company and she told him how much his presence had eased the situation.

Left in the kitchen Melissa and Fergus felt a little more comfortable with each other.

"You're looking better, Fergus."

"Sorry!"

"Don't be ridiculous; I'm glad you're looking better."

"That's very magnanimous of you".

"I know! But it's been a very pleasant evening, hasn't it?"

"The pleasantest I've had for a long time; that young man is really unusually nice."

"Cassandra certainly seems to think so."

"Don't you?"

"I'm not sure that he's quite husband material. I doubt whether his family will pass muster---but then who am I to judge?"

"Having chosen so badly yourself, you mean?"

"Well, Fergus, I didn't actually say so; you may not believe it but in fact I'm trying to be kind to you. I fear it may take some time to achieve but I am improving, and of course you know that I will look after you, I won't turn you out. You mustn't expect too much all at once. After you left I realised that feelings of frustration and disappointment I'd been suppressing for years were welling up to the surface; they still want to come out."

"Why did you suppress them all that time?"

"I'd been so stubborn about insisting on marrying you in defiance of my family; I suppose I couldn't bear to be proved wrong. The fact that so much of it was my own fault didn't make things any better at all!"

"I can see you've thought about it a good deal."

"Yes; you've given me time to do that."

"I hope you're grateful!"

"Don't be silly, Fergus, gratitude doesn't come into it. Your going away had nothing to do with consideration for me or for anybody but yourself. I've merely made the best of the situation and a lot of good has come of it. It's Fate and Free Will: Fate is what happens to people without their being able to prevent it; Free Will is what activates how they cope with it. I may be grateful to Fate, but I'm not grateful to you."

"I didn't know you were capable of such philosophical reasoning."

"No, that's part of the trouble. Women of my generation were not supposed to be clever, but I've been living with an intelligent, well-educated daughter and I've not been suppressed by a husband much older than myself, who regarded me as a 'mere woman' with no brains. I've learnt a lot."

Fergus was silent; he had to admit to himself that he'd never considered a clever brain to be a desirable quality in a wife and had certainly never regarded Melissa as the possessor of such an attribute.

Cassandra came into the kitchen and looked a little anxiously from one parent to the other; Melissa, she thought, looked rather triumphant and Fergus rather crushed. She hoped they hadn't been having a row; everything had seemed to be going so much more smoothly and amicably while Robert was there. She decided to bring him back, at least verbally.

"Robert really enjoyed this evening," she said.

Fergus immediately looked more cheerful. "So did I," he said. "He's a very pleasant chap."

"Yes, he is, isn't he? I'm glad you had another man to talk to. You really should meet Jasper and Stephen tomorrow---well, Stephen, anyway---it would do you good."

"Well, perhaps; I'll see how I feel. But I can't imagine your mother wants her 'date' to meet *me*! It might make him feel awkward, taking her out from under her husband's nose."

"Thank you, Fergus, that's very perceptive of you, even if you are speaking as if I were not here," Melissa chimed in. "But now I think it's time we all went to bed; we've had an excellent evening and we don't want it spoilt."

33

Robert telephoned Cassandra the following morning. "I don't suppose I'm allowed to come and see you and/or take you out this evening?" he said in a hopeful tone, which belied the negative.

"Oh, Robert, it's sweet of you to ask but I'm afraid not; we've got some relatives coming. They're Marjoribankses and only in Oxford briefly; they want to see the house."

"Oh; well, tomorrow then."

"Yes, tomorrow's fine. It would be nice to go out; that's if it's all right with my mother. We don't like to leave my father alone for too long; he is quite ill, you see."

"Can he go out too?"

"No; he's not really up to it; I told you what it was like when I took him to Matalan."

"Yes, you did; but I thought he seemed surprisingly well last night."

"He did, actually, better than we've seen him since he came back. That was because he enjoyed your company so much. I just hope he doesn't feel extra weary today to make up for it."

"I'm glad he enjoyed my company, anyway; I found him very nice to talk to."

"I told you in the car last night."

"I'm afraid I wasn't concentrating on conversation when we were in the car!"

Cassandra laughed. "No," she agreed, "You did make that clear!"

"I didn't think you minded."

"I must admit I didn't."

"I hope you don't mind now."

"Nothing like as much as I ought to."

"Will you go to confession again?"

"I'll tell you tomorrow."

At the end of their conversation Cassandra sat pensively for a few minutes and then reached for one of her mother's cigarettes and lit it. She had almost entirely given up smoking because she never smoked in the workshop or in Pete's company and she had stopped rolling her own, but, as she said to herself, there were times when nothing but a cigarette would do. Her mother came in and noticed the smoke but simply took and lit a cigarette herself. After a couple of companionable puffs she asked: "Is everything all right?"

"Life's complicated," Melissa answered. "Especially here. Devon was never like this."

"There were not so many people there."

"Well, not so many we needed to react with. When is Nicholas coming back?"

"Heavens! I'd almost forgotten. In a couple of days, well, at the beginning of next week."

"I wonder what he'll make of Pa?"

"Whatever he thinks about him I'm sure he'll say exactly the right thing."

"He's really very thoughtful and considerate."

"Have you heard from the Australian and the Americans?"

"Oh dear, it's a couple of days since I last did the emails." She stubbed out her cigarette. "I'll do them now."

There were messages from both hemispheres.

"Oh heavens, they all want to come and stay. What are we going to do about Pa? We'll be needing that guest room."

"He'll have to move. I warned him that might happen."

"I don't think we can have him on the second floor, he finds the stairs difficult even on the first."

"How about finding him a room down here? It would be a kindness, actually."

"There are certainly rooms we're not using, except for storage and we could probably deal with that. But what about a bathroom?"

"Have we got enough money left to have another shower put in?"

"I'm sure we have, especially as we'll be getting more in from the guests."

"I'll tell Pete and we can get hold of his friends and relations again."

Pete was delighted to be useful and set about telephoning relevant relatives, who promised to 'have a look at the job' over the weekend. Cassandra remembered that Stephen was coming at five and went to change into going-out clothes. Melissa did the same so that she could be ready to see Stephen as well as Jasper, though she also needed to prepare Pete's tea.

Very shortly after five Stephen drove into the courtyard. His car was low and sporty and not very new. Pete was not very impressed by it. He was inclined to sniff at Stephen as well but reflected that there was safety in numbers, though that was not quite how he would have expressed it. He thought it a bit strange that Miss didn't settle for going out with just one person, but if that one person was Robert Taylor he was not in favour of it.

Cassandra came out to meet Stephen and welcome him to the house. "You must come and see the main front hall first; we've had it done up so the new guests can use it, we want them to be impressed!"

"I'm sure they are," replied Stephen on seeing it, "but I have actually come to see you as well, you know."

"I'm glad to see you, too, Stephen. I don't know any of my close cousins as my mother hasn't seen her family for years; I find it wonderful to have a cousin of nearly my own age, a male one, too; I went to an all girls' school and a male relative, even a rather distant one, is a real asset."

"It's really sad not to know your relatives; we've always seen our cousins often and had a lot of fun times together. Never mind, you can join in with us now."

"I do appreciate that. Now tell me more about yourself; I'm afraid you only heard about us on Boxing Day, we were so selfishly telling you all about our problems."

"We wanted to know; it was interesting. Don't worry."

Between looking at rooms and bathrooms and exclaiming over the size and scope of the house and the amount of furniture in it Stephen managed to tell her about his Oxford degree in PPE and his job in a London banking firm. Cassandra was impressed by the degree as she herself found things like politics, philosophy and economics decidedly beyond her range of ability, not to mention her range of interest---but she was careful *not* to mention that! Getting on to a less puzzling subject than economics and banking she asked: "Where do you live in London?"

"In a funny little Victorian terrace house in Clapham, with some other chaps from school."

"That must be a lot of fun."

"It's great. All the company you have at school and in college---and no essays to write!"

"You must have to work hard, though, don't you?"

"Yes, but it's work you've chosen to do because you like it, and you get paid for it, too! But let's go out now; I've had a very good look over the house and I can see its potential, but also that it's a bit of a liability. You and your mother are very brave to have taken it on."

Cassandra laughed, "If you'd seen the alternative you might not think so, but thank you for the compliment."

They went downstairs to the kitchen to say goodbye to Melissa and found that Jasper was already there with her. He and Stephen greeted each other with some surprise and a certain amount of amusement, especially as they both said simultaneously: “I was awfully keen to see the house!”

“Well,” Stephen continued, “I’ve seen it now so we’re going out for a bite to eat.”

“Oh indeed!” Jasper laughed again. “Tell us where you’re going so we can avoid you!”

“I’d thought of The Bear at Woodstock.”

“How naff! We’re going to Hartwell House.”

“Oh yes; very suitable for older people,” said Stephen sympathetically.

Cassandra had difficulty in suppressing a smile and found herself wondering if Stephen would consider Robert an ‘older person’. Aloud she said: “I’ve never been to The Bear, though of course I’ve seen it from outside. I’ve been told it’s ‘very smart’; hardly a pub!”

“Well no,” Stephen admitted, “I agree it’s a bit ‘business account’, but it’s a beautiful old building and they haven’t spoilt the inside of it too much, it’s still worth seeing. *And* they still serve beer.”

“I don’t think they serve real ale, do they?”

“So you know about real ale?”

“I have been a student!”

“Well we’ll go to a real ale pub first and on to The Bear after that. OK?”

“Perfect.”

On the way out they encountered Pete coming over for his tea. Cassandra introduced her “cousin Stephen Marjoribanks.” The slight frown and incipient sniff, which had been clouding Pete’s features, relaxed into a smile as he shook hands with Stephen and looked genuinely ‘pleased to meet him’.

"Now Miss, if you and Missus is both going out," (Pete didn't miss a lot) "you mustn't worry about the old---um---your father. I'll keep an eye on him."

"That's really kind of you, Pete, thank you so much. We'd feel a bit anxious otherwise."

Stephen and Cassandra went and sank into the not very new sports car (it was rather low) and set off to find a real ale pub.

Once Pete's tea had been dealt with and he had reiterated his offer to look after 'him upstairs', Jasper and Melissa also set off, but in a sleek Mercedes, which met entirely with Pete's approval.

"I hope you'll like Hartwell House," Jasper ventured, "it's a bit more than twenty miles away, but definitely worth the mileage, in my opinion."

"I know I shall, Jasper. Cassandra raves about it and I've never been there myself."

"Oh, she's been there, has she?"

"Yes, more than once, I think. I saw her trying not to smile when Stephen remarked on its suitability for older people! She said it was the loveliest place she'd ever been to. You can't think how pleased I am to be going there."

"I think it might even come up to expectation. But I don't know what a girl with Cassandra's good taste will think of The Bear!"

"I'll look forward to hearing about it tomorrow."

"You and your daughter are very close, then?"

"We have been since I came back to England. Before that she was at boarding school a great deal and then at university, and I had a very busy social life abroad. Of course we went shopping together and that sort of thing, but she was quiet and studious and read a lot and I probably didn't engage with her as much as I should have. How about you and your children?"

"We've got three, two boys and a girl; none of them married. We haven't seen a lot of them since they grew up and moved into student digs, and I feel they've been deliberately keeping away since Myrna left. They just don't want to be involved."

"*Myrna*?"

"Yes, I'm afraid so. Awful name. I should have been warned. Her second name's Fiona and I tried calling her that early on, but she preferred Myrna."

'That,' said Melissa to herself, 'says it all.' But aloud she murmured "You mustn't blame yourself; young love can be very ungovernable. My own marriage was an appalling mistake, but I fought against acknowledging it until Fergus disappeared; the realisation's been surfacing ever since. I have to keep myself from pouring vituperations on Fergus now he's back. I don't think I could contain myself even as imperfectly as I do if he weren't so ill."

"My case is different; I thought we were jogging along happily enough until Myrna took off. I was busy, involved in my work, keen on my golf. I should have been more sensitive."

"You may consider yourself insensitive but you clearly realise how grateful *I* am to be with somebody of my own age and, if I may say so, kind."

"Well, if it's anything like as grateful as I am, I certainly do. You're the most understanding and sympathetic woman I've met in years."

They arrived at Hartwell House in a happy mood of mutual appreciation, which Melissa had already contributed to by outlining Jasper's unusually sensitive and thoughtful treatment of her at the party, and then enhanced by her very expressive admiration of the house and its ambience.

Stephen and Cassandra arrived at The Bear after enjoying a pint of Hook Norton at a very real pub. Cassandra had been happy there and not much looked forward to going on to the large, well known hotel. But she liked it better than she had expected. The lounge bar on the right of the main door was very genuine looking and a generous wood fire was burning in the grate. Stephen told her, *sotto voce,* that if she went upstairs to the loo she could nosey about and see some more of the building. She did as he advised and found it to be attractively decorated and well furnished.

Back in the lounge they gave their orders and relaxed with some wine.

"I'm so glad my mother's going out," said Cassandra, "she's really excited about it. I'm afraid I hadn't thought how much she must have missed it. She came out with me and the other potters in Devon occasionally, but it was only for a drink, and here she's been to your parents' house but never to a restaurant."

"Well," replied Stephen, "you don't expect older people to want to go out much. My mother hardly ever does, except to do good works and that sort of thing."

"Your mother's a wonderfully good woman, and very kind and sympathetic as well; my mother admires her greatly, although she's very different herself."

"There's something very attractive about your mother, and at least she can't be as hard to live up to as mine."

"That's certainly true! Not that I'd thought about it before. But tell me about your friends in London."

They were interrupted by a request to go to their table, where the conversation continued.

"You were telling me about your friends in London," Cassandra urged.

"One's an artist---very successful already and always looks very scruffy, one's in the same line as I am and one's got his own business; he flies about all over the world going to conferences."

"With very moneyed people, I suppose."

"Oh yes. He had a funny experience recently. A very rich woman who owns one of the biggest ranches in the States took a great fancy to him. She insisted that he sit beside her on the top table and ousted a rich Australian banker who was sitting there, saying 'I'm sorry, buddy, but you can't sit here now because Snuggle-bunny's got to sit beside me!'"

"Snuggle-bunny!"

"Yes, that's what she kept calling him. And do you know, she was over seventy! He told her 'You're older than my mother!' 'That doesn't matter, honey,' she said 'think nothing of it. I promise you I'm still really something in the sack. You'll see.' Poor chap he was quite horrified; he's got a fiancée he adores. But he got out of it all right, or said he did. Of course we all call him Snuggle-bunny now."

Cassandra, rather light-headed with the effects of a pint of beer and several glasses of wine, could hardly stop laughing at this. Stephen, who hadn't intended the evening to take on such a familial, almost fraternal, aspect as it had seemed to be developing, began to take heart. After all, Cassandra was only a very distant cousin.

Suddenly a strident voice broke into their *tête a tete.* "Well!" it said, " I must say you seem to be enjoying yourself!"

Aghast, Cassandra looked round to see the person whose voice she had immediately recognised.

"Er, Mrs Fraser, isn't it?"

"That's right. I was at your pot sale; you must remember, I bought the most expensive thing you had."

"I hope you're happy with it."

"I haven't got it out of the car yet; can't decide where to put it. But you're having a nice time, aren't you? Not the same young man who was helping wrap up the pots, is it? That friend of Nigel's, I mean."

"Oh, er, this is my cousin, Stephen Marjoribanks, Mrs Fraser."

"How do you do," said Stephen, standing up politely and giving a slight bow.

Norah Fraser eyed him with approval. "Charmed, I'm sure," she responded, though slightly disappointed at the word 'cousin'. She'd had thoughts of imparting interesting information to her prospective son-in-law about the fickleness of his best man's girlfriend, along with hints as to giving him a warning.

"Nice place, this, isn't it? I can see you've got good taste, Stephen. Me and Raymond often have dinner here; it's really smart. They have high-class business conferences here too, you know."

"Now, now Norah, leave these young people to have their evening on their own." Norah's husband greeted Cassandra briefly but was immediately interrupted by his wife's breaking in with "Oh it's all right, Ray, it's only her cousin." 'Ray' stayed only to be introduced and then, mercifully, propelled his wife away and placed her at their own table.

Cassandra glanced at Stephen and rolled her eyes heavenward.

"Who on *earth*---? Well, obviously a customer, but---!"

Cassandra couldn't suppress a giggle as she outlined the history of her acquaintance with Norah Fraser. Stephen almost guffawed at the delineation of earlier encounters and had to wipe tears of laughter from his eyes as he said: "What a marvellous person to know! You'll be able to dine out on her for years to come. Except that people will think you're exaggerating. But tell me about the colleague who's got to be best man at her daughter's wedding. Is he a friend of yours?"

"Yes; we met him through our kinsman Samson Southey; who must be distantly related to you as well. But tell me about yourself; you must have a girlfriend, surely?"

"We're rather on and off these days. She's very nice, very Catholic, very suitable, but I don't feel ready to settle down and get married yet. I'm not even twenty-eight, quite."

"And she does want to get married?"

"Yes. She's the same age as I am; it's different for girls."

Cassandra laughed. "That's what my apprentice Pete says; he doesn't want any children yet, unlike his cousin who's sixteen, as he is, and has a one-year-old child!"

"What does he say?"

"Just what you said: 'it's different for girls'."

"Oh lord! I'm eleven years older than he is---and saying much the same thing. That makes me feel rather bad. But what about you and the 'young man' who wrapped up the pots at your sale? He must be a good friend!"

"He is, actually; but I don't think I want to get married yet, either."

"And he does?"

"Well he's certainly showing signs of it; but then he's quite old: he must be at least thirty-five."

"Lord above! That really is old. He must be all of ten years older than you."

"Just about. But he really is very nice and quite attractive."

"Well maybe he's still all right now; but think about when you're our parents' age; you'll be pushing him round in a wheelchair."

Cassandra had to laugh at this picture of Robert and protest that things didn't always work out that way. "I might have some crippling disease and he'd have to push me round."

"He mightn't be strong enough to do it by then. Now *I* wouldn't mind pushing you round in a wheelchair!"

"Thank you, Stephen, that's a very kind, cousinly thing to say."

"It wasn't meant to be cousinly!"

"Stephen dear, I need a cousin, preferably a brotherly one, far more than I need a boyfriend. You come from a big family, with siblings of both sexes, and of course you've never felt that kind of need, but I always have and still do. Please let me join in your family without any complications."

"It's rather a second best!"

"Not to me it isn't. But now let's be practical; I don't think you can drive from here because we've both had too much to drink. We'll have to get a taxi."

Unnoticed by Cassandra and Stephen, who had by now forgotten their existence, the Frasers were hovering in their vicinity and had obviously overheard part of their conversation. Norah Fraser pounced: " Now don't you worry about that," she exclaimed, "Raymond'll drive you home. He never drinks much; it doesn't go with his medication. You'll drive them, won't you Ray?"

"Yes, yes of course. Do you live in Oxford, Stephen?"

Cassandra tried to insist that they would take a taxi and Stephen tried to insist that he was perfectly well able to drive, but Norah Fraser's strident insistence was audible all over the restaurant and Cassandra signalled to Stephen that they had better give in to save further embarrassment. She was very loath to be beholden to the Frasers but even more unwilling to have Stephen drive back to Oxford, so she thanked 'Ray' with every appearance of polite gratitude and promised to join them as soon as the bill was paid.

34

Cassandra came down to an early breakfast before Pete was likely to be up and found her mother already in the kitchen.

"Heavens, Mummy, you are early! I thought you'd be tired."

"I'm not tired at all, darling; I feel stimulated and full of life. There's nothing more tiring than boredom and I had a very lively and unboring evening."

"Oh I am glad; I was dying to know how you got on."

"Well I got on very well with Jasper, if that's what you mean; we thoroughly enjoyed each other's company and I agree with you that the hotel is truly special. The rooms are beautiful, the service excellent and unobtrusive and the food delicious. But how did you get on with Stephen?"

"He's very nice and good company but he does seem very young. He really wanted to drive home despite being way beyond the 'two small glasses' limit."

"I know your generation considers that a cardinal sin, especially in England."

"I wouldn't mind betting Jasper was over the limit."

"Darling! I would have considered it very rude to notice! But I gather you somehow managed to stop poor Stephen driving. Did you drive his car yourself?"

"Certainly not; I was over the limit too. It was actually quite funny in a way. You know we went to The Bear?"

"I gathered."

"Well who do you think was there?"

"Not---not that Fraser woman?"

"Yes; with her husband. They insisted on driving us."

"How ghastly! In their Jaguar?"

"The very same, but it was certainly smooth and comfortable. I was rather annoyed with Stephen for making it necessary to be beholden to them, but it might have been difficult to get a taxi and he was euphoric enough to have wanted to insist on driving. I didn't have enough money on me to take a taxi for myself."

"He didn't suggest staying the night in the hotel? People your age might well consider that a lighter sin, if a sin at all!"

"I think he's been convinced that our relationship can be upgraded from cousinly to fraternal, but nothing more."

"Hmmm! Possibly; but not probably. How did you enjoy your drive home?"

"We didn't have to say much. We heard the price and value of the Jaguar and the house they're living in at the moment. By that time we were here. But I don't know what it was like for Stephen from here to Oxford"

" He was probably questioned about his parentage and background and the make of his car."

"He may come in today; he'll have to fetch his car from The Bear, so he can tell us. Are you going to see Jasper again?"

"I rather think so."

"Soon?"

"We'll see."

With that Cassandra had to be content; her mother was clearly not going to divulge any more information.

While they were having breakfast Fergus came in, looking tired and grey but decently dressed. His breathing was rather laboured. Cassandra looked at him a little anxiously.

"You're very early this morning, Pa. Are you all right?"

"Hardly, but still alive. Dressing tires me and I didn't sleep at all well."

"Sit down and I'll get you some breakfast."

Fergus sat down heavily. "Good morning, Melissa," he said with a slightly sarcastic formality. "How did you enjoy your outing last night?"

"Immensely, thank you Fergus," his wife replied in a similar tone.

"It must have been quite a change for you!"

"Going out or enjoying myself?"

"Both."

" I haven't led quite such a dull life since we've been here as that implies. But we did go to a very special place and we did find each other's company pleasant and stimulating."

"That must indeed have been a change!"

"I know a number of people of whom I could say the same."

"But surely not in such intimate circumstances."

"Fergus, if you are so ridiculous as to be jealous I shall avoid you altogether. It's not impossible in a house the size of this one."

"You should be flattered. Plenty of women would be delighted to have a jealous husband."

"You're only jealous because you can't retaliate by taking somebody out yourself! You never used to be."

Fergus breathed wheezily and coughed a harsh, dry cough.

Cassandra looked from one of her parents to the other and said: "Now, now, you two, if you can't speak pleasantly don't speak at all. Pete'll be here in a minute and we don't want a bad atmosphere."

Fergus and Melissa stared at her in amazement. She had never intervened in this way before. Her relationship with Melissa had altered during the time since they had been living together, part of it spent in Cassandra's own flat, and she had gradually gained some ascendancy over her mother, which she had never had when at home with both her parents in France. Her calm reproof had its effect: it shocked them both into silence.

***

That evening Robert arrived at Huntsfield House at about six and he had barely sat down and accepted a drink of elderflower when the doorbell rang. Cassandra opened the door to find Stephen, bearing a bunch of flowers.

"Oh Stephen, come in. I thought we might see you; you must have been to fetch your car."

"Yes, my brother drove me out, but he's gone straight back to Oxford. I'd love to come in for a minute but I'm going back to London tonight so I can't be long."

Cassandra led the way to the kitchen where Robert was sitting. "This is my cousin Stephen Marjoribanks, Robert; Stephen this is Robert Taylor."

"Hi!" said Stephen and Robert changed his incipient 'how do you do' into something vaguely similar. They eyed each other with a curiosity that was scarcely concealed by politeness.

"Are you related to Sir Felix Marjoribanks?" asked Robert.

"Yes, he's my father; why, do you know him?"

"We've met a couple of times, here and at The Oratory."

"Yes, he's a great Oratory fan; I prefer Blackfriars myself---when I go."

Robert felt a wave of relief. A Catholic who preferred anything to the Oratory and didn't always go to mass anyway would be unlikely to appeal to Cassandra.

Stephen held out the flowers to Cassandra. "For you," he said, "to make up for last night."

Robert felt anxious again and almost asked what had happened last night. Cassandra noticed his expression and was tempted to elaborate without an explicit explanation.

"Oh Stephen," she exclaimed, "you really needn't have; it wasn't as bad as all that."

Robert swallowed. Stephen replied: "Quite bad enough. You were absolutely right not to let me drive and I should have got a taxi and not subjected you to being ferried by those frightful people."

Cassandra finally turned to explain to Robert: "We were at The Bear at Woodstock; we'd both drunk too much to be able to drive and we were almost forcibly carried off by---you can probably guess who!"

"No!" said Robert. "I mean yes I can; The Bear immediately makes me think of one particular person: Norah Fraser!"

"Do you know them, then?" said Stephen in surprise.

"Robert knows them because a colleague of his is engaged to their daughter and he has to be best man at the wedding."

"Yes," said Robert, "it's the bane of my existence at the moment. To make it worse, it's the chap's third marriage!"

"How ghastly! I really feel for you. Is the girl very beautiful or are the parents very loaded?"

"As far as we can see the main attraction must lie with the parents; but we don't really know."

"He must be quite old to have been married twice already."

"He's a year or two older than I am."

"Oh well, I suppose he's lucky to get anybody at that age."

Robert looked aghast and Cassandra burst out laughing. "Really, Stephen," she gasped between laughs, "you are quite incredibly agist, you know."

"Oh dear! Am I really? It hadn't occurred to me. I do apologise."

"Never mind. Have a drink before you go."

"Well just one very small one as I'm driving."

"I can really recommend the elderflower," said Robert.

"Is that what you're drinking?"

"It is."

"Oh. Well all right, I'll try some of that then."

Melissa came in and greeted both the men cordially. "Aren't you going to have a drink, Stephen?"

"Thank you; I'm just about to have some elderflower," Stephen replied righteously. "I'm told it's very nice."

"It's very boring," said Melissa, "but of course you young people make up for that in other ways."

"Mummy, please! Don't encourage Stephen to drink and drive; he has to get to London tonight."

"Darling! Would I do anything of the sort?"

"Hmmm!" said Cassandra.

Stephen swallowed his elderflower with a very good grace and pronounced it delicious. He then made his farewells with something of a flourish and Cassandra saw him off.

On her return Robert asked: "Am I allowed to ask you out to dinner this evening?"

"Well of course you are and thank you. But could I ask to be allowed to stay in and have you eat with us here? You're so good at talking to my father and he was greatly cheered by your company last time."

"I suppose that's what I'm good for at my advanced age!"

"Oh Robert! Don't take any notice of Stephen. He's actually older than I am but he does seem such a child. Still, we'll go out if you really want to---as long as it's not to The Bear!"

"No; perhaps you're right. I should have mentioned it earlier. And I do enjoy having dinner with you here. Your mother's cooking's better than most restaurants."

"Thank you Robert," Melissa called from the background. "But I don't pretend to the finesse of Hartwell House. I was taken there myself last night and it really is something special."

Robert felt vaguely guilty that he'd enjoyed meals cooked by Melissa but never given a thought to taking her anywhere himself.

"Perhaps we could all go there one evening," he said. "Would Fergus be able to manage it?"

"I don't really think so," Melissa answered, "and besides, he hasn't got a jacket as yet. All the charity shops are closed until after New Year. But don't worry about me, Robert, I think I might be invited again before too awfully long."

"My mother has an admirer, Robert."

"Well that doesn't surprise me in the least. I'm sure she made a number of conquests when she came to dinner in college. I'm surprised she hasn't been out with some of them."

"Thank you again, Robert; but I'm not in the way of husband stealing. One should never go out with a married man unless one's married oneself, and I didn't think I was at that time."

"Mummy! What are you saying? That it's all right to go out with a married man if one's also married?"

"Well, only *relatively* all right, darling. At least it allows for retaliation. And there's *much* less likelihood of breaking up marriages, at least among civilized people in Europe. I don't count Americans, of course."

"Why not Americans?"

"Oh they think people should get a divorce if they so much as *want* to be unfaithful. They're so puritanical."

Robert laughed. "So your present admirer's not married?"

"Not exactly; he's in the middle of divorce proceedings. But that's because his wife's gone off with another woman, so one really feels he's never been properly married at all. It ought to be grounds for annulment."

"What about Fergus?"

"Well I'd be divorcing him if he weren't dying."

"What does he think about the admirer?"

"He hasn't met him."

"Mummy! You know what Robert means; how does Pa feel about your going out with somebody? But perhaps you'd better not ask, Robert, because as a matter of fact he's quite jealous."

"Poor chap, I'm not surprised."

The door opened and Fergus came in. There was a silence as everybody hoped he hadn't heard anything.

"Robert!" said Fergus, "nobody told me you were here. But then nobody tells me anything. I'm pleased to see you, anyway."

"And I you," said Robert sincerely as they shook hands.

Fergus sat down next to the welcome guest and appeared stimulated by his company as they conversed and had a drink and some pre-supper nibbles. Robert noticed, however, that the older man's breath was becoming laboured and his cough more frequent, and he tried to make things easier for him by bearing the brunt of the conversation himself, even though Fergus clearly enjoyed talking and was trying to hide, or at least minimize, his difficulties.

The dinner was excellent as usual and Melissa was duly complimented and airily appreciative. Only Cassandra felt a little left out as her father was monopolizing Robert and giving them no opportunity to talk to each other. As coffee was being drunk, however, together with a dessert wine described by Melissa as 'something a tiny bit special---after all it is still Christmas', Fergus was seized by a more prolonged fit of coughing, which left him breathless and exhausted.

"Oh Pa! I wish we had the room down here ready for you," said Cassandra, concerned. "Would you like me to help you upstairs?"

Fergus, unable to speak, shook his head vehemently.

Melissa topped up his glass and said, as a command rather than an offer, "Have another drink, Fergus."

This injunction was promptly obeyed and Fergus did in fact look a little better for it. Robert then continued their conversation as if uninterrupted and something like cheerfulness was restored. It was clear, however, that Fergus's strength was flagging. Robert hesitated as to the next move; he didn't want to leave as he had hardly spoken to Cassandra, but he feared Fergus might force himself to stay up until he did. Eventually he said: "Can I come upstairs with you? I've never seen your room." This offer was accepted most gratefully and Fergus was not unhappy to be climbing the stairs with comparative ease as he leant heavily on the arm of a tall man.

In the kitchen Melissa and Cassandra looked at each other apprehensively.

"We ought to do something," said Cassandra.

"What?" was her mother's reply.

"Take him to a doctor and see about providing him with oxygen."

"We ought to have a doctor, anyway; we've never bothered about one since we've been here."

"Robert must know of one in Oxford."

"Wouldn't Kidlington or Woodstock be better?"

"Yes, if they have such things. We can find out tomorrow."

Melissa decided that a tiny top up was in order and lit a cigarette to aid its consumption.

"I've really been remarkably restrained this evening, haven't I?" she asked---or, rather, stated.

"How do you mean?"

"This is my first cigarette this evening, out of consideration for those men; well, mainly Fergus, of course. I don't want to be accused of making him cough."

"You've been positively saintly!"

"Thank you darling; what with that and Robert's kind appreciation of my cooking I shall feel quite set up for the next week, well, couple of days anyway. After that I might get some more ego boost from Jasper, if I'm frightfully lucky."

Robert came back into the kitchen.

"How's Pa now?" asked Cassandra, as Melissa chimed in with: "We've been discussing doctors and oxygen."

"That sounds like a very wise idea," said Robert, by way of answering them both.

"We don't know any doctors but we thought we'd try for a practice in Kidlington or Woodstock. We'll talk to Pete and try to hurry the downstairs room and bathroom, too."

"Yes," Melissa added dispassionately, "it may be too late but we could do with something suitable for a disabled guest, anyway. I believe it's absolutely *de rigueur* these days."

"Don't take any notice of Mummy," Cassandra saw the shadow of shock pass over Robert's face, "she's not as heartless as she makes out. She didn't smoke a single cigarette until Fergus had gone upstairs. Now that's a real sacrifice!"

"Thank you, darling. It's kind of you to salvage my reputation but I didn't want to spoil people's appetite for my carefully prepared dinner, either." Melissa exhaled an elegant spiral of smoke, stubbed out her cigarette and said: " It doesn't matter now we've eaten it."

35

In the morning before breakfast Cassandra looked in the local directory and found a medical practice in Woodstock; she telephoned and made an appointment as soon as it was open. Melissa came downstairs to be informed of this *fait accompli*.

"Thank you so much, darling; I don't know why but I was rather dreading doing that. Still I think I must take him as I can't escape the fact that I'm legally his wife. What time is it for?"

"Eleven thirty."

"That's excellent. I'll get him up just after nine."

"If you have time and he's not too exhausted you might look into the charity shop in Woodstock if it's open; it's awfully good and they have a lot of men's clothes, suits and so on. It's very small and compact and not tiring like a big town shop. It would be better than my trying to find something without him."

Melissa duly woke her husband and told him the news of the appointment. She didn't deem it necessary to mention the charity shop; there was no point in putting him off the whole expedition. He was not overjoyed but submitted with a reasonably good grace, got himself dressed and had his breakfast without delay and was ready to be waved off by Cassandra and driven by Melissa in good time.

Some two hours later Cassandra was just beginning to be a little anxious when the car swept into the courtyard. It was not the sweeping sort of car as a rule, but the way Melissa drove made it seem like one. She got out looking jubilant and then unloaded Fergus and some large parcels.

Cassandra poked her head out of the workshop door and asked: “How did you get on?”

“I’ll tell you all about it over lunch; I must put it on now.”

“Missus looks very happy,” commented Pete, who’d been watching with interest. “Do you think that means he’s better or worse?”

“Probably only that she’s done some useful shopping, I’m afraid,” Cassandra answered. “Come to think of it she hasn’t really done any but food and household and essential shopping since she’s been back in England; it must have been very hard for her. She’s always liked buying clothes.”

“She liked buying the bathroom things with me uncle. He said she did.”

They went back to work until Melissa called them for their lunch and dinner respectively; the food for each of them was much the same as Pete was beginning to get used to some subtly introduced vegetables other than chips and some lean meat. He took his meal back to the shed as usual. Cassandra went across to the kitchen.

“Now,” said Melissa when they were all seated, “I must tell you how well everything went. The charity shop actually was open; just one woman in there and she said it was better than having people dumping their unwanted Christmas presents outside and there were quite a few tourists about as well. They had some awfully good stuff and I’ve bought Fergus a suit *and* a jacket. And do you know, a really nice little suit for myself. It’s only Jaeger but really quite *chic* and extremely reasonable. I can see why you like these places so much.”

“Yes but what about the doctor?”

“Oh, just as expected really. They’re ordering the oxygen and making a hospital appointment. It should be sorted by next week. Now Fergus, you go and have a rest after lunch and then I'll come up and talk to you; there are things we must discuss and decide on."

Fergus was certainly looking tired but not too unhappy. He admitted to having liked Woodstock "and I must say," he continued, "the clothes in the charity shop were certainly an improvement on that place you took me to, Cassandra, Rataplan was it? The suit's a good make and very decent quality."

Sufficiently cheered to combat his weariness and eat a reasonable lunch, plus a glass of wine, Fergus went up to his room to lie down immediately afterwards. Melissa poured herself a tiny top up and thankfully lit a cigarette.

"As soon as I've had this, darling," she said to her daughter, "I'll show you the clothes."

"Good! I must say I admire the way you've handled things, Mummy, keeping the doctor and the hospital in the background and concentrating on more positive and optimistic things; Pa seems quite cheered and happy."

"Thank you, darling; it does seem to have worked out rather well." Melissa thought it unnecessary to admit that her motivation had been, perhaps, instinctive rather than calculated! She had, in fact, almost forgotten the original purpose of the expedition to Woodstock in the excitement engendered by some successful shopping. She had not, however, forgotten the discussion she was intending to have with Fergus that afternoon on a topic Cassandra might consider less optimistic.

Having given Fergus a good two hours to rest, therefore, she took up a tray of tea things, a pen, a large pad and the determined air of somebody who means business. As her husband sipped his tea gratefully she began: "Now Fergus; we're getting things organised and being realistic and we all know you can't be here with us a great deal longer."

“Where am I going?” Fergus was always apprehensive about his acceptance in Melissa’s house, despite her assurance that she wouldn’t turn him out.

“Well if you’re very lucky I suppose it could be Purgatory, but I don’t presume to be the judge of that.”

Fergus laughed until he coughed and spilt his tea and laughed and coughed again.

“I thought you meant I couldn’t be in this house.”

“Well of course you may be in a hospital in transit, as it were, but that was not what I was thinking about.”

“You’re thinking about the ultimate destination of my immortal soul, I suppose!”

“No, Fergus, I am not. That is quite beyond my powers of organisation. I am thinking, since you force me to spell it out, of your body.”

“Ah!”

“What do you want done with it?”

“I hadn’t thought about it. Buried, I suppose,”

“Buried? In consecrated ground? Aren’t you still an atheist?”

“I’m more of an agnostic; not that the distinction has been uppermost in my mind, exactly.”

“You certainly used to talk like an atheist, and a scoffing one at that.”

“A bright young university woman at a dinner party once asked me if I had any religion and I said I was a pagan. That was a mistake; she showed immense interest in finding out which pagan deities I was particularly inclined to. I had a job to remember the names of any of them. I could only think of Cupid. She looked rather puzzled and asked whether it was the aspect of cupidity or the erotic which appealed to me. I told her that at my age cupidity was perhaps uppermost. ‘Ah, yes,’ she said. ‘Mammon. The most popular object of worship in the world, though not always so honestly admitted to be. Though I daresay Eros comes a fairly close second.' I'm afraid she was rather disappointed. She was probably hoping for something like the ancient Druids' objects of worship. Or maybe she just put me down as an ignoramus who was using the word 'pagan' to mean 'unbeliever'."

"That was in fact the truth of the matter, wasn't it?"

"I'm afraid it was."

"So you really want to be buried rather than cremated?"

"You Catholics don't like cremation, do you?"

"Some do, now, but the Oratorians prefer the older Catholic practice of burial."

"Why?"

"Because some of the bodies of saints have remained uncorrupt."

"What nonsense!"

"Scoff if you like; but why do you want to be buried, anyway? You can hardly be anticipating sanctity. You don't even believe in it."

"I don't know what I believe in."

"Do you want to talk to somebody about it?"

"I'd like to talk to Robert. We just touched on the subject last night when he said he goes to the Oratory."

"What did he say?"

Fergus gave another rasping laugh that turned into a cough. "Oh only that being a believer you can't lose. If it's true then you're going to be happy forever and if it's not true you'll never be aware of the fact but you will have had a pleasant life with a lot of nice, well-intentioned, like-minded people and plenty of support and comfort. But that can't be the whole story; there must be a down side to it. It was just in passing. I'd like to talk to him some more about it. He's a very sensible chap as well as being intelligent."

"Well, this is a turn-up for the books! I'll tell Cassandra to get hold of Robert. I don't think we can do anything more until you make up your mind what you believe and whether you want a Christian service. But I'll tell you one thing: it's either to be properly Christian or not religious at all; I hate those pseudo-religious services with horribly unsuitable hymns and sentimental readings from ghastly so-called poems and untrue eulogies about the deceased."

"There is something to be said for sitting on the fence!"

"Well of course it is your funeral, in the quite literal sense of the phrase."

"True, but I don't suppose it'll be very well attended; we can hardly expect any of our erstwhile French friends to come!"

"It's interesting, when you think of it. If you hadn't gone bankrupt and we'd still been in France I suppose we would simply have had a standard C.of E. funeral like all the other ex-pats, with a big catered reception after it, and you would never have thought of talking to Robert or anybody else."

"You wouldn't have been talking about Purgatory, either."

"No, I fear not. I've changed since I've been away from you; perhaps I'm more myself than I'd been for many years."

"Are you saying that I repressed you?"

"You and the whole milieu we were living in. But now I've got my own house and my own life---and my own religion."

Fergus gave a large sigh and began to cough again.

"Can you ask Robert to come this evening?" he said.

Melissa propped him up on his pillows and went to tell Cassandra of this astonishing development. She couldn't wait until dinner time so went into the shed, regardless of the presence of Pete.

"Is Robert coming this evening?" she asked her daughter.

"Yes, he wants to go out to dinner; why?"

Pete gave a loud sniff, but it was not acknowledged by the others.

"Fergus wants to talk to him."

"He talked to him last night."

"He wants to talk to him about religion."

"What?!!"

"I know it's astonishing but apparently Robert said something about it which captured his interest."

"I would hardly have thought of Robert as an authority on the subject."

"That's probably what appeals to Fergus; he thinks of him as a man after his own heart."

"Well! I'll telephone him now and see what he says."

Cassandra felt a little more inhibited by Pete's presence than her mother did and decided to wipe the worst of the clay off her hands and go into the house.

"Have you rung him already?" her mother asked as she went in.

"No, I could see Pete's ears flapping and he does tend to sniff disapprovingly when I'm talking to Robert. I'll ring from here……. Hullo, Robert! Yes I'm quite all right; it's my father, he wants to talk to you. Can you come early? Well about religion, apparently. You evidently said something last night, which impressed him deeply. No I know you don't know anything about it, Mamma says that's why he trusts you. Oh that is good of you. See you soon then." She turned to her mother. "He's coming as soon as he can get away."

***

Robert arrived a little more than an hour later, looking decidedly worried. Cassandra heard the car from the shed and went out to meet him.

"I really don't know about this at all," he said anxiously.

"It's more than we can fathom, too. Pa must tell you what you said that made him think of it."

"I hope we'll be able to go out afterwards."

"Well it's early now and he gets tired if he talks for too long. Do go and start and we'll see what happens."

Robert went in, spoke briefly to Melissa and then climbed the stairs to Fergus's room. He was greeted with gratitude and as much enthusiasm as could be managed between coughs.

"I'm so glad to see you. You've made me think."

"I can't imagine how!"

"You described a no-lose situation. Now to a failed business man like me that has a lot of appeal."

"You must have been a successful business man for a great deal longer than you were a failed one."

"That's true; but it's how you end up that matters. Look at me now: dependent on my young daughter for my clothes and food. She's the only one getting in any money at the moment. I'm a prime example of the insecurity of money. But it's the ending up that I'm concerned with."

"How can I help?"

"You said yesterday that believers are in a no-lose situation; I want to be enough of a believer to achieve that myself. If there is a heaven then it's wonderful; if there's nothing then I'll never know about it, so I won't even be disappointed. It's a better bet than taking a ticket in the lottery."

"So what do you want to do about it?"

"That's where I want your advice."

"But I'm almost as unsure as you are. I've only recently thought about it at all."

"Inspired by Cassandra, no doubt. Your inspiration's due to love; mine's more pressing, being due to imminent death. But they're basically similar and self-centred. We've turned from being negative, or at least unthinking, agnostics to being positive ones. What can be done about it? What are you going to do?"

"If I marry Cassandra I'll become a Catholic. I might become one anyway. I'll start taking instruction and spend time working on it and thinking about it."

"I haven't time for that. Do you suppose they do a crash course?"

"I don't see why not but I've really no idea."

"Do you think you could find out for me?"

"Why don't you ask Cassandra?"

"It goes against the grain. She's too young and she's too pious. I'll never catch up with her degree of faith and I'm all too dependent on her already."

"Do you mind if I tell her about it? At least she could suggest somebody for me to go and see."

"That's it! Do that! Tell her *you* want to see somebody---then you can ask him about me!"

"I hadn't really thought of doing anything just yet."

"Please! Don't put it off. You'll never get round to it at all if you do that and I can't afford to wait. Couldn't you arrange for us to go together?"

"You're forcing my hand!"

"Perhaps that's what it needs."

Robert was silent. He felt the urgency of the older man's plea. He also felt the truth of his accusation.

"You may be right," he admitted at length, "I am rather given to procrastination. I haven't even asked Cassandra to marry me yet. By the way, I hope you don't object?"

"To your marrying her? Of course not; couldn't be more pleased; though nobody would take any notice if I wasn't. Good of you to mention it, however." Fergus barely finished his sentence before breaking into a fit of coughing, which left him looking weak and exhausted. He turned to Robert and said faintly: "You see what I mean!"

"Oh I'm sorry!" Robert replied. "I've made you talk for too long. I'll do as you say on the one condition that I can tell Cassandra about it. She knows why you're talking to me anyway. I can't go all mysterious and refuse to say anything."

"All right; I suppose it's inevitable. I can't ask for more."

Robert left him and went downstairs slowly, he was feeling quite drained himself. Such a conversation was not in the everyday run of things. He went into the kitchen hoping not to be asked any immediate questions. Melissa was there, humming to herself as she prepared some vegetables. She turned as he came in, took a quick look at him, said: "Robert, you need a drink!" and poured him one immediately. He didn't demur.

"That's right!" she continued approvingly, "and don't worry. You don't have to say anything. I can see you've had a difficult time and I'm sorry you've been let in for it. You can talk about it if and when you want to. Cassandra's upstairs getting showered and dressed. Just relax and look forward to a happy evening out."

"Thank you. You're very kind and understanding. I don't know why I feel so exhausted."

"The sick and dying can be very demanding and it goes against one's conscience to refuse them anything. The insistent reminder of one's own mortality isn't exactly stimulating, either.

Chapter 36

Robert and Cassandra went to the 'upmarket pub' where they'd been once before and eaten samphire. They wanted somewhere simple but good and not too far away. Robert told Cassandra the purport of his discussion with her father and how inadequate it made him feel.

"He wants to have *me* go and talk to a priest at the Oratory and ask him whether there's a crash course for people who are dying. I don't know anything about it."

"I think the usual thing might be to ask the parish priest to do it or to recommend somebody. There must be one who's in charge of instructing converts. Shall we ask Sir Felix? He knows them all well. I'll ring him tomorrow if you like and then perhaps we could both go and see him, or both go to the Oratory. Would that make you feel better?"

"It certainly would. How thoughtful you are. I couldn't have faced it on my own."

The evening passed quietly; Robert was happy to see that Cassandra was wearing the cross he'd given her for Christmas, but she was a little unhappy to know that her father was causing him problems and anxiety.

"Don't be sad," he reassured her, "you're actually opening up my life in many ways. Both your parents belong to a section of society that I've never really encountered before and you yourself are so different from anybody I've ever known; I feel I'm learning from you all the time, even though I'm so much older than you are."

"Not so *very* much, Robert," Cassandra said smiling; "you really mustn't let Stephen get to you."

"It was a shock to realise how ancient he considered me," Robert admitted; " I wonder if that's how my undergraduates feel about me too."

"I rather hope they do, especially the female ones, otherwise they might be getting much too friendly!"

Robert laughed. “Not much fear of that, I assure you; they’ve all got boyfriends much nearer their own age; oh, except for the odd one or two who’ve got girlfriends.”

“Do they make it obvious?”

“There’s one at the moment who usually sports a large badge with a rainbow and the word ‘GAY’ on it. Mousy little thing she is, too. She reads her essays so quietly I can hardly hear what she’s saying. I’m afraid she annoys me rather.”

“I’m not surprised. What’s her girlfriend like?”

“Quite the opposite; big and dark-haired and hefty. They make a strange pair.”

Conversation ranged over the vagaries of human nature; there was never any dearth of subject matter. The evening ended with Robert feeling happier and less weary than he would have considered possible when they started out, but Cassandra left him in the car after a brief goodnight and promised to contact him the next day as soon as she’d spoken to Sir Felix.

***

In the morning Cassandra went early into the shed to telephone from there, where she couldn’t conceivably be overheard by her father, unlikely though he was to be up at that hour. Sir Felix proved most helpful and even offered to invite the parish priest round to his house as Fergus would perhaps be more comfortable there. Cassandra thought this might be a little complicated as Robert was to be there too, but promised to consult the priest about it and let Sir Felix know.

Eventually a meeting was arranged at the Oratory House for 6 pm the following day so that Cassandra could go to mass while Robert and her father talked to the priest. Fergus was informed and seemed almost excited about it.

He was not displeased to be going out, and quite glad of the opportunity to wear his new jacket.

"I'll be all right if I rest in the early afternoon," he said, as Melissa expressed some anxiety about the time of day.

Allowing over an hour to get there Cassandra arrived well before six and met Robert in the courtyard of the Oratory. She was grateful to see him and her father go into the house together, to go to the church to mass herself and leave them to it.

Father D., the parish priest, greeted them kindly. He had, unbeknown to Cassandra, been telephoned by Sir Felix and given some outline of the situation as concerned Fergus. He had not, of course, heard anything about Robert, though he recognised him from several Sundays in the club room after mass. He took them into a pleasantly warm room furnished with several armchairs, sat down and asked how he could help.

"Well," Fergus announced, "I'm dying."

"Of course we're all doing that," Fr D. responded, "only some faster than others. I gather you're in the fast track."

Somewhat deflated by this matter-of-fact attitude, Fergus elaborated, saying: "Yes, lung cancer; I haven't got long."

"Are you a Catholic?"

"No, I'm not. Brought up C. of E. but really nothing for years now."

"Why have you come to see me?"

"My friend here," he indicated Robert, " said something that made me think: that you can't lose if you've got religion because if it's not true you'll never know about it and if it is you're in clover." Fergus felt a little embarrassed at saying this to a strange young priest and his expression was clumsy.

Fr D. turned to Robert: “You are a Catholic, are you?” he asked.

“No, I’m afraid not.”

“Oh, I thought I’d seen you here.”

“Yes, I’ve been coming recently with a friend of mine; he likes the music.”

Fr D. smiled. “Oh good,” he said, “we do rather pride ourselves on our music.”

“He’s in love with my daughter,” Fergus broke in, feeling that the conversation was in danger of going off the point, “and she’s very devout. Her mother had her brought up a Catholic. He won’t stand a chance if he doesn’t show an interest. He’s a sensible chap.” Robert felt himself to be in danger of blushing, which he was not aware of having done for a great many years.

“I, er um well, it’s not only that; I’m really interested myself, but I didn’t feel, I haven’t felt, quite ready to ask for instruction; I’m just an escort.”

“So *you* want to receive instruction?” the priest asked Fergus. “Do you feel drawn to the faith?”

“I don’t know that I’d quite put it like that, Father, but I look at it this way. Suppose I buy a lottery ticket; I don’t actually believe I’ll win but I believe it’s possible. It’s the same with religion; I don’t actually believe it’s true, but I believe it’s possible. Is that good enough?”

Fr D. looked a little nonplussed. “It is a somewhat unusual approach,” he ventured. “Are you sure you want to become a Catholic? Could you not be content with rejoining the Anglican Church? They might be a little less, well, shall we say less demanding? We really do require that you believe the articles of the creed---do you remember the creed? It starts ‘I believe---‘.”

“I’m not sure that I do,” Fergus answered, “well not what it says, anyway. Could you give me a sort of crash course and I'll see what I can make of it? I thought I might as well be a Catholic; my wife and daughter are Catholic and it'll be easier for them to bury me from their church and I quite want to be buried and have a sort of family lot of graves, all together. I can't think why."

Fr D. sighed, "Perhaps it's a sign of grace," he ventured, a little doubtfully. He decided to ask for the help of his colleagues on this one, perhaps even the Provost. Fergus Marjoribanks was not a kind of prospective convert he'd ever met with before. It would have been easier if he'd waited until he was actually on his deathbed, *in extremis,* barely able to speak, and then they could give him the benefit of the doubt and the last rites. As long as he died pretty soon after that a Catholic burial could follow 'as the night the day'; but he clearly hadn't yet reached that stage and it really was necessary for him to show some rather more definite signs of having the faith. Fr D. sighed again.

"I don't mean to be difficult, Father; at least I'm a *positive* agnostic. For me that's progress."

"Perhaps we can build on that and help you to progress a little further."

"I'll give it a try. How do I start?"

"I'll give you something to read." Fr D. looked round the room in search of inspiration. His eye lighted on a very small booklet. "Ah! Here we are! The penny catechism; not so much used now but I consider it unsurpassable. It's gone up to 50p, however, I'm afraid."

"I didn't think to bring any money. Have you got 50p, Robert?"

Robert handed over a pound coin. "I'll have one myself as well," he said. "It seems like a good beginning."

"Can I come again when I've read it?" asked Fergus.

"Certainly. Let me know when you're ready and we'll meet again."

Robert and Fergus expressed their thanks and Fr D. showed them out, hoping that the relief he felt was not actually visible.

They went across the courtyard and into the church. The last communicants were just returning from the altar, Cassandra among them. Fergus and Robert sat down in one of the furthest pews near the entrance door. Robert knelt down and said a prayer. Fergus had made him realise that he was not, in fact, an agnostic. He did believe in the truth of Christianity, it had just not occurred to him to do anything about it until he had met Cassandra. He prayed for her, for her father, for his own parents, and was still on his knees when she came up to them after the mass had finished. She sat down by her father and took his hand.

"You look rather pleased with yourself, Pa," she whispered. "Did it go well?"

"I think so," Fergus replied happily. "The priest seemed quite impressed."

Robert finished his prayer and sat up to meet Cassandra's smile of approval for him and amusement at her father. She determined to have Robert give her some details of the encounter if he would. She need not have worried, however, Fergus was so pleased with himself and had so much enjoyed being the centre of attention that he began to talk about it as soon as they were outside the church. Robert said goodbye and elected to walk back to college and Cassandra drove home to the accompaniment of her father's almost verbatim account of the proceedings.

Over dinner that evening he repeated a good deal of it for Melissa's benefit. She was considerably less sanguine than he was about the likelihood of his becoming a Catholic but heard him with considerable patience until he suddenly announced that he'd had a bright idea., and explained the purport of it.

"If I become a Catholic in good time we could get married again, properly in the church, couldn't we?"

"Really Fergus! Has your wife died?"

"My wife?"

"Your first wife, if you insist on regarding me as your second."

"Died? Not that I know of. Why?"

"Because the Church won't allow it if she's still alive. Surely you knew that!"

"I'd forgotten. But I didn't marry *her* in a Catholic church!"

"There's no point in going into all that; I wouldn't marry you again anyway, not even if your wife was as dead as a doornail! Which reminds me: I'm going out to dinner tomorrow, Cassandra, so could you possibly see to Pete's 'tea' and your and your father's supper?"

"Yes, of course; I hope you're going somewhere nice."

"Undoubtedly! Though I don't know where as yet."

"You know who with, I'm sure." Fergus spoke in grumpy tones.

"Yes, thank you Fergus, I'm not in the habit of going out on blind dates."

"You shouldn't be in the habit of going out on dates at all. Can't you wait till I'm dead?"

"No, Fergus, I'm afraid not. And if you've got any sense you'll realise that if I had to wait till then I might be considerably more reluctant to put up with you alive! Now why don't you just go to bed and count your blessings. You're being exceedingly tiresome and I really don't want to talk to you any more. Besides, I want a cigarette and I've put off having one out of deference for your cough."

"There's no need for that. I cough anyway."

"Possibly, but I'm not willing to suffer a guilty conscience over it. Nobody can say I don't look after you properly, not even you! And it's hardly fair of you to grudge me an occasional outing."

"Hmph," said Fergus.

"Come on Pa," Cassandra gave him an arm and helped him up, "you've done a lot today and you mustn't overtire yourself. I'm going upstairs now, come with me." She really meant 'lean on me' but didn't quite like to say so.

"I wish Robert was here," grumbled Fergus, "it's always nicer when Robert's here."

"Never mind; I'll ask him to come again tomorrow when Mummy's out."

36

Robert helped Cassandra prepare Pete's tea and supper for themselves and Fergus, who seemed greatly cheered by his presence. Cassandra rather suspected that Melissa's absence affected him less adversely than might have been expected, too. For all his disgruntled attitude to her 'dates' he was actually more than a little afraid of her and seemed to relax significantly when she was not present. After supper and a discussion about the merits of the penny ("fifty penny" said Fergus crossly) catechism, Robert helped the older man upstairs as before.

"Well," he gasped breathlessly as they reached his bedroom, "I like that bit at the beginning where it says God made us to 'know him, love him and serve him in this world and to be happy with him forever in the next', it's a very pleasant idea; too late for me to do any serving, of course, but at least I'm giving *you* plenty of opportunity!"

"I admit it's a new experience for me," Robert admitted honestly, making no pretence of misunderstanding, "though I hadn't thought of it in that light."

"It's a valid way to look at it, however," Fergus averred. "You're doing a lot of good looking after a tiresome old man and cheering his last days, even if you are doing it more for Cassandra's sake than mine or the Lord's. I'll be all right now; you go down and join your beloved and make the most of having the place to yourselves."

As Robert helped Cassandra with the dishes he said suddenly "If we were married would we be able to live in one of the flats at the top? I don't suppose you'd want to leave here, would you?"

"Really, Robert! Is this a proposal of marriage?"

"It must be! I'm too scared to ask you directly in case you say no."
"So you're making an offer for my accommodation? Not that it's ready yet."
"I could help you get it ready if you agree."
"So you add DIY to your other talents?"
"Well, not quite on that scale. I really meant financially. I'd feel better if I paid to have it done. It's not *just* the accommodation I'm after!"
"Tactful of you to say so!" Cassandra laughed. "Not that you've made that a hundred per cent clear as yet!"
"Would you like me to go down on one knee?"
"Clasping a tea-towel in front of the kitchen sink? Surely kitchen sink drama's a bit passé! Can't we find somewhere more in line with contemporary taste?"
"I don't think I know much about contemporary taste. I always thought of somewhere like Hartwell House when rehearsing it in my mind. I didn't mean it to come out in the kitchen the way it has."
"It could be called beginning the way you mean to go on! Modern marriage has rather a lot to do with kitchens."
Robert threw the tea-towel over the back of a chair and took Cassandra in his arms and kissed her lovingly. "You won't say no, will you?"
She kissed him fondly but disengaged herself and looked at him seriously. "No," she answered, "I won't say no, but like the flats I'm not quite ready yet, so I won't say yes either. There have been such upheavals in my life in the past year I don't feel I'm on an even keel. I could be tempted to marry you for the sake of stability and I don't think that would be right. It could even be considered an ulterior motive."
"Don't you love me?"
"I often think I do."

" Only often?"

"That's better than 'sometimes'!"

"Couldn't you manage 'always'?"

"That's what I'm not completely sure of. 'Always' and 'forever' are very big words and very important ones. They need a great deal of thinking about."

"I don't have any problems with them when I think about you."

"Thank you Robert, I appreciate what you're saying, but you're at a steadier time of life than I am and more sure of yourself and your goals. I still have to assess mine and so far I haven't been able to think about 'always' and 'forever'.

"Will you think about them now?"

"Yes, I promise I will."

"I suppose I'll have to be content with that, for the present. But I'm going to keep on asking."

"Are you going to try and wear me down?"

"I'm going to try anything, within reason!"

Cassandra laughed and they continued to talk happily and without reserve until an opening door and animated voices announced the return of Melissa and Jasper.

"Well," said Cassandra as they came into the kitchen, "it sounds as if you two have had a very happy evening."

"We have indeed!" Melissa answered gaily, "We've had a most stimulating and pleasurable evening!"

"Dear Melissa," Jasper chimed in, "you're a wonderful companion; so appreciative and responsive!"

Robert and Cassandra exchanged a swift glance, which each of them understood to mean 'they've obviously had too much to drink but they're clearly more interested in talking to each other than to us so we'd better leave them to it!' Robert put on his coat and he and Cassandra went out to his car. Once inside it they both burst out laughing.

The spectacle of a couple of people they considered 'elderly' behaving in such a youthfully excited way struck them as exceedingly funny.

"Oh dear," gasped Cassandra as she wiped the tears of laughter from her eyes, "I'll have to go in and creep up the stairs and avoid the kitchen altogether."

"Well don't go in yet."

"I'd just as soon not, to be honest. But I wonder how long Jasper's going to stay? I can't believe he's in any fit state to drive home; he lives in London!"

"Perhaps he'll stay the night!" Robert suggested. They both burst out laughing again.

Some considerable time later Jasper had not emerged from the house and Cassandra had not emerged from the car. Finally she said she really must go in, despite Robert's plea for her to stay a little longer.

"No, Robert, stop tempting me. At my age I really can't make the excuse that my mother's setting me a bad example!" They laughed again and the evening ended as happily as any they'd spent. Robert drove back to Oxford feeling elated and very hopeful that Cassandra would resolve her problems with 'always' and 'forever' in the near and not the distant future.

***

Early in the morning, before anybody else was up, Cassandra crept into the shed and rang Robert.

"I hope I didn't wake you," she murmured apologetically in response to his sleepy answer.

"Cassandra!" he exclaimed, wide awake at once, "Are you all right? What's the matter?"

"Oh Robert, I'm so sorry, it's just that I wanted so much to speak to you!"

"Well, don't be sorry about that! I'm delighted. But tell me why. I'm not conceited enough to believe it's merely for my own sake!"

"In a way it is, because of what we were saying last night and I wanted to go on talking about it. Jasper did stay the night here, I could hear him snoring."

"Which room was the snoring coming from? The other spare room on the first floor?"

"No, that's just it; it was coming from *my mother's* room!"

"Are you sure it wasn't your mother snoring?"

"No---I mean yes, I am sure. I don't think she ever snores and it sounded very deep and masculine."

"Do you mind?"

"I'm not sure. I---well---how would you feel if it were *your* mother?"

"I simply can't imagine it."

"I suppose your mother's very respectable."

"I'm afraid rather boringly so. But yes, I'm pretty sure I would find it funny, all the more because of that."

"It doesn't seem as funny as it did last night. But it's still *quite* funny. I don't know what I'll say at breakfast."

"Nothing might be the most advisable. But do tell me about it, whatever it is."

"I think I find it rather embarrassing; but it won't be so bad if I know I can tell you."

"Thank you. Don't worry about it. Just think about us instead."

The conversation degenerated into the well-worn tracks of love language and Cassandra finally went back into the house feeling comforted.

Her mother was not down at the usual time so Cassandra saw to Pete's breakfast and her own.

"Missus not coming to breakfast today, then?" Pete asked innocently.

"Well, not so far, Pete. I suppose she'll be down soon. There's no real need for her to get up early."

"Out last night, wasn't she?"

"Yes, that's true. I suppose she's tired. She doesn't go out very often."

"Don't see why not; nice-looking lady like her. She works hard, too."

"You're quite right, Pete, she does work hard and she deserves to have a good time once in a while."

Melissa opened the kitchen door in time to hear the last remark and had no hesitation in applying it to herself. "Thank you darling, I'm glad to hear I deserve something good. At the moment a good cup of coffee is what I could do with. Jasper's having a shower; I wanted him out of my room so that I could get dressed. I slept in the second guest room because Jasper told me he snores dreadfully and I didn't want him waking Fergus, so I let him have my room. I just swapped the pillows over. You'll be glad to hear I wouldn't let him drive to London; he must have been a long way over the limit. Not that he showed much enthusiasm for driving, actually. And what's the use of a big house like this if we can't put people up?"

Cassandra handed her mother a cup of the coffee she'd already made and asked: "Does Jasper have coffee or tea?"

"I've no idea. We'll have to ask when he comes down; but make some more coffee anyway, I need plenty. I'm not used to late nights these days." Melissa lit a cigarette to go with her coffee and after a couple of satisfying inhalations continued with "I'll see to the rest of the breakfast if you've had yours. I know you've got work to do."

Thus dismissed, Cassandra simply filled and turned on the coffee maker and went into the workshop. She was dying to ring Robert but as Pete followed her into the shed and her mother was still in the kitchen and there was no other extension in the house she couldn't do so. 'Perhaps I should have a mobile', she said to herself, 'then I could ring from my room in private.'

Her reverie was interrupted by Pete asking: "What's he like, then?"

"I'm sorry Pete? What did you say?"

"Your mum's boyfriend, what's he like?"

"Oh, er," Cassandra thought of disclaiming the description of Jasper, decided it might be making too subtle a point and gave up the idea. "He seems very pleasant and he certainly appreciates my mother. But I hardly know him really."

"I remember when my mum started going out with me Uncle Morris; I didn't think I liked him much at first but he did seem to make mum feel good. She wasn't so snappy with me, either. And he used to give me things."

Cassandra laughed. "Well that all seems to have worked out for the best, Pete, but I can't imagine Jasper Marjoribanks giving *me* anything! My mother might not like it if he did!"

"Oh, he's got the same name, has he? Where's he come from?"

"He's actually a distant relative of my father's. He lives in London. That's almost all I know about him."

"Does your pa know him?"

"No, I don't think he does."

Pete chuckled. "I bet he's not too pleased about him. They never are."

"I believe you're quite right about that, Pete."

"Yeah; I heard me dad was just the same; funny when they're like that, even when it's them what's gone off."

With this wise observation Pete retreated, whistling, to his own work bench.

At coffee time Cassandra hoped the kitchen might be empty enough for her to ring Robert and went across accordingly. Her mother was there and so was Jasper. Cassandra greeted him politely and without, she hoped, showing her surprise.

"Oh darling," her mother said immediately, "I'm so glad you've come over, can you see to Pete's dinner and the lunch? Jasper and I want to go out. I took your father's breakfast up to him and I think he's just getting up now. We'll be going very soon as it's a nice, bright day and we thought we'd tour round the countryside a little and then eat at anywhere attractive that we come across. You don't mind, do you?"

"Of course not. You've been doing the meals all the time. You ought to have a day off. Is there anything else you want done?"

"I don't think so; I can catch up with any extras tomorrow. I've made the coffee so do have some and take Pete his coke. Shall we go now, Jasper?"

"I'm ready whenever you are, dear Melissa" was Jasper's gallant reply, which sounded to Cassandra's ear to contain just a hint of *double entendre.* Cassandra was not, however, at all displeased at the opportunity at last given her to telephone Robert. As soon as they were out of the door she reached for the receiver and dialled his number, only to hear a distant "excuse me a moment" before his voice said "Hullo?"

"Oh! You're in a tutorial!"

"Yes. Can I ring you back?"

"What time?"

"I'm teaching till one."

"Say two o'clock. I'll make sure I'm in here---in the kitchen."

"OK, till then, bye."

Cassandra was well occupied not only with the preparation of Pete's dinner and her and her father's rather different lunch but also with the latter's queries and observations about her mother's whereabouts.

"Your mother's gone out again, I gather."

"Yes. She'll be out for lunch."

"Still with that same chap, Jasper isn't it?"

"Yes. I'm glad. She can do with a break."

"She brought my breakfast up to my room this morning."

"Yes, I know."

"Guilty conscience I expect."

"Now, Pa; why should she have a guilty conscience?"

"Well, that chap must have stayed the night."

"Yes, he did, but not in the same room."

"Hmph! That's a likely story!"

"Now, Pa! That's not a very kind thing to say. If you want to become a Catholic you'll have to learn to be more charitable."

"I don't see why I should be charitable about my wife's fancy man!"

"If you mean Jasper, I'm afraid he's rather plain."

"That makes it worse. I don't know what she sees in him."

"Oh dear! I'm glad you're saying this to me and not to her. She'd be very angry, you know."

"Yes, I do know."

"Now as she'd probably say to you, eat your lunch and count your blessings!"

The lunch was in fact very good, and Fergus had no difficulty in eating it, though he found his blessings less appetising to count. He decided to keep out of Melissa's way when it was possible and his mouth shut when it was not.

"Robert's coming this evening," said Cassandra, by way of changing the subject if not of giving Fergus a blessing to count.

"Well that's a mercy, anyway," he responded. "But then I suppose you'll be wanting to go out with him."

"We haven't decided yet. But anyway, you'll have time to talk to him beforehand if we do.

At two o'clock the telephone rang and Cassandra was on her own in the kitchen to answer it. Her father had gone upstairs to lie down again. She had taken the precaution of unplugging the shed telephone so that Pete would not be tempted to pick up the receiver in there. It was not that she didn't trust him, but one never knew.

"I'm on my way over from lunch," said Robert, "how are things now?"

"I'm glad I can speak to you at last. I think you're right about my needing a mobile."

"Of course you do." Robert was too tactful to say 'I'll get you one' but he decided to do so immediately.

"My mother came down quite late and talked rather rapidly about giving her room to Jasper so that he wouldn't wake Fergus with his snoring."

"How did she know he snores?" said Robert, and immediately wished he hadn't.

"She says he told her."

"Well that's perfectly possible.

"Well I suppose so. It did go on a bit like a planned speech."

"You thought 'the lady did protest too much'? (Not that that's really what it means in the context---but I must remember I'm not teaching!)"

"It didn't sound quite normal."

"But she'd naturally want to explain. She might have been worried that you wouldn't believe her. It's not a familiar situation after all, is it?"

"No, I suppose it would be a little awkward however true it is."

"Where's your mother now?"

"They went out to drive round the beautiful countryside and light on somewhere for lunch."

"Well I'm glad. Your mother's been at home seeing to things very often while we've been out. Do you think we could go out this evening?"

"It might depend on what my mother's doing!"

"Well I'll come and see you anyway and we can decide then."

When Robert switched off his telephone he remained so deep in thought that he almost missed his own room. Once in it, however, he sat down and continued to ponder. He had a glimmer of understanding of Cassandra's anxiety but could hardly consider the matter as significant as she did. His own view was that Jasper had probably gone to sleep in Melissa's room and, rather than try to wake him and take him downstairs she had crept down to the guest room herself. She was not a stupid woman. Robert found himself laughing at the imagined (and perhaps true) situation and resolved to say as little as possible about it to Cassandra but to go out immediately and buy her a mobile phone.

37

Jasper and Melissa returned to Huntsfield at about half past five and Robert arrived a very short time later. He knew Cassandra would still be in the workshop and went in there, duly rewarded with a loud sniff from Pete and a happy smile and a warm, if physically distant, outstretching of clay-covered hands from Cassandra.

"Shall I go into the kitchen?" He was dying to give her the newly purchased mobile phone but decided the shed was not the best place for the presentation!

"Yes, do. I think my mother and Jasper are in there but I'll come in as soon as I've washed the worst off and then go and change. Actually, would you mind awfully going up to see my father? He was a bit upset at lunchtime; you know, about my mother and Jasper, and my telling him you were coming was the only thing that cheered him up."

Robert went up willingly enough. Fergus was immensely pleased to convey his gloom to a sympathetic ear.

"Glad there's a rational person here," he grumbled, his tone registering anything but gladness. "I don't feel like going downstairs when Melissa and her fancy man are there. She's behaving like a twenties flapper."

"She hasn't gone out much since they've been here," said Robert soothingly, "and she does work hard. Don't grudge her a break."

"Hmph!" said Fergus. "Anyway, don't let's talk about her. How about going back to the Oratory some time? I want to speak to that priest again. I've read the book through."

Robert agreed and they fell to discussing life in general and death in particular without covering any new ground.

Cassandra was heard on the stairs, going up to shower and change. Robert felt impatient to see her and he rather lost track of Fergus's conversation until the latter mentioned that a guest was arriving the following day---"chap who was here before Christmas, apparently, quite a well-known family, double-barrelled name."

"Oh? I didn't know; I expect Melissa's been too preoccupied to think about it." He didn't mention that Cassandra probably had, too.

"You can say that again," was Fergus's reply.

"There'll be a lot for her to do, looking after a guest. Cassandra too, I expect." Robert felt suddenly queasy and even more anxious to see Cassandra.

"You'll be wanting to get away and take her out; I'm selfish to be keeping you up here. We'll go downstairs, even if that Jasper's still there. I can face it if you're here."

Jasper, however, was not there. Melissa informed them that he'd just gone and Robert and Cassandra were free to go out if they wanted to.

"I want to be sure the room's ready for Nicholas to come into tomorrow."

"Oh dear!" Cassandra felt guilty. "That's going to be a lot of work. I feel I should be helping."

"Nonsense, I've only got to change the bed, and that's very easily done. Your father can do with something easy to eat and Pete's food's no trouble. I don't want much myself, having had a very good lunch."

"Where did you go?"

"To the Swan at Tetsworth; very interesting, it's a very old house with a pub restaurant on the ground floor and the rest of it a vast, rambling antiques centre. Not that we need any more antiques, but it's always fascinating to see what things cost these days. Made me wish we could sell some of our surplus."

Fergus gave a cough and said, with some difficulty, "Well I'm glad to hear you were doing something moderately useful!"

"Now Fergus!" Melissa spoke firmly. "I did something very useful when I took you to the doctor and the charity shop, not to mention the fact that I do the shopping and the cooking. So be quiet."

"We'll soon have your room downstairs ready, Pa," Cassandra deftly added range to the subject of usefulness and soothed the situation. Robert appreciated her tact and even her father managed to say: "You're very kind."

Cassandra felt torn between her genuine wish to go out with Robert and her feeling that it was incumbent upon her to help her mother with the housekeeping and keep the peace between her parents. She looked helplessly at Robert, who saw her dilemma and decided (for her sake, he told himself) to take her out immediately.

They went to their favourite 'samphire pub' and with the pre-dinner drinks Robert at last managed to produce the mobile phone.

"I particularly wanted to go out so that I could give you this," he said. "You can ring me in private any time now without worrying about somebody else picking up an extension."

"Oh, Robert, you think of everything. You're so kind. But I must pay for it."

"Don't spoil my present! I've been dying to give it to you."

"But surely I have to pay to make it work?"

"I've had some money put in, it's pay as you talk."

A good deal of the evening was spent on the mysteries of the mobile and the main features of its use. Cassandra made no attempt to diminish her excitement and appreciation and Robert might be excused for feeling that she really did love him more than a little. 'We do have happy times together,' he thought, 'surely there's something special in our relationship.' She returned his smile affectionately and they drove back to Huntsfield in contented companionship. Cassandra stayed in the car for quite a long time before going inside.

Nicholas Forbes-Mowbray duly arrived the following afternoon. Pete heard his car and rushed to the window to look at it.

"Here he is, Miss!" he sang out triumphantly. "He keeps that car lovely, not a mark on it. Beautiful, innit?"

Cassandra had intended not to notice the arrival, but of course she had to look at the car. Nicholas rose out of it in one graceful movement. Cassandra's mental picture of him had faded a little since he'd been away and she was almost shocked by the perfection of his looks.

"Amazing!" she murmured. 'Just as well I wasn't holding a pot,' she thought to herself, 'I might have dropped it---like Cenerentola when she first saw the prince. Except of course that it isn't the first time I've seen Nicholas.' She went on with her work automatically, as if programmed to do it while her mind was absent.

As soon as possible she told Pete she was finishing early in order to help her mother organise the dinner and the table setting for their guest. She showered and dressed in rather dark, understated clothes. Melissa was already in the kitchen preparing a dinner just a little more special than usual. She looked slightly anxious.

"Let me help, Mummy, you look a bit worried."

"It's not the dinner, it's Fergus."

"Is he worse?"

"Not that I'm aware of. Does Nicholas know about him?"

"He can't know he's here; he arrived after Nicholas left."

"I meant know about his having disappeared. How are we going to explain why he wasn't here before? Really it's too tiresome; we always seem to have something to hide. If it's not Treasure it's your father!"

"Really, Mummy, you do say some awful things."

"You know very well what I mean."

"I don't think we need offer any explanation. Nicholas is far too well bred to ask questions. Besides, Pa won't be eating in the dining-room, will he?"

"That's going to seem odd in itself. I'd really prefer to keep him hidden, but I don't suppose it's possible."

"Shall we just give up on that and all eat in the dining-room? Can you manage it? I'll go up and ask Pa how he feels about it if you like."

Melissa gave a large sigh, said nothing for a few moments and finally agreed that that might be the best plan of action. Cassandra went up the stairs rather slowly, wondering what her father's reaction might be, fearing that he would monopolise Nicholas if he came to dinner or that he would argue audibly with Melissa in the kitchen if he did not. She tapped on his door and went in to find him reading the 'penny' catechism.

"I'm glad to see you so well occupied, Pa."

"Yes, I want to see that priest again, tell him I'll go along with all this. It'll make it easier for you and your mother to bury me."

"Very good of you, Pa, but to concentrate on more immediate matters, would you like to have dinner in the dining-room with the guest?"

"Oh, the double-barrelled chap? Pity it's not Robert, but yes, I think I can cope with it. I'll tidy myself up a bit." Fergus looked positively cheerful at the prospect of having another man to talk to, tossed the catechism on to a chair and got off his bed with something like alacrity. Cassandra went down to inform Melissa and set the table for four.

Nicholas Forbes-Mowbray came down in very good time and professed himself delighted to see Cassandra again. She responded suitably, if with less obvious enthusiasm than she felt, and said how much she was looking forward to hearing about his enviable family Christmas.

Nicholas laughed. "I promise I won't go into too much detail, there are so many siblings and cousins and in-laws it can sound very complicated. But I see there are four of us for dinner. Are there some new guests?

"No, not guests yet, it's only me, as before, and my mother and father." Seeing Nicholas look a little puzzled and clearly at a loss for what to say she added: "my father came here for Christmas and he's actually very ill and needs looking after, so we're keeping him with us. He had been living in France."

Before Nicholas had time to reply Fergus himself came into the room; Cassandra performed the introductions and then hastened to the kitchen to tell Melissa of the trimmed version she had given Nicholas of her father's arrival and continued presence. Melissa approved entirely and only hoped Fergus could be trusted not to say too much.

"Let's take the dinner in quickly and hope to steer the conversation in the right direction."

As Cassandra had feared, Fergus was inclined to monopolise their guest and by the time they were all settled at the table had already informed him that he had terminal lung cancer. Nicholas was of course adept at saying all the right things and the conversation led painlessly into apologies for any noise and disruption the work on the new ground floor bathroom might cause. Nicholas professed interest and commented, albeit delicately, on Fergus's good fortune in having such excellent care taken of him.

38

There were not a large number of dons having dinner in Chester College but Robert Taylor was one of them.

"You're in to dinner more often than usual these days, Robert," Muriel Thwaites mentioned as if by way of conversation. "Not that it isn't very pleasant to have your company."

"Thank you, Muriel; I'm glad somebody thinks so." Robert's response was gloomily grateful.

"Oh dear! I hope things aren't as bad as that sounds."

Robert made an effort to smile but it was not very successful. Muriel, quick and perceptive, especially perhaps where Robert was concerned, had a shrewd idea as to the reason behind his less frequent absences from college meals and his lack of cheer. She turned to Samson Southey.

"How are your stately home pottery relatives these days, Samson? I hope you're going to bring them to a guest night again this term."

"They're frightfully busy at the moment; we saw them on Sunday but couldn't so much as persuade them to come to the club room after mass. They're clearing a room on the ground floor to turn into a bedroom and having the room next to it made into a special bathroom for disabled people. Also they've got a guest staying and a couple of others expected. The guest was with them, in fact, but they'd come separately because he had to go on to lunch somewhere. I was sorry not to see more of him; he's both pleasant and interesting. I shall probably bring him in to a guest night."

"There's a treat in store for you, Muriel," Robert broke in with a hint of sarcasm in his voice, "he's extremely good-looking, too."
"Oh, were you there as well, Robert? I'd forgotten you went to the Oratory."
"Yes. I believe I'd feel deprived now if I didn't go. It's quite a high point of the week."
"Perhaps I should come and sample it some time. It's at 11.00, isn't it?"
Before Robert could summon up a suitable reply Samson Southey answered her: "Yes indeed, Muriel, perhaps you should; who knows what might come of it."
Muriel coloured slightly and looked searchingly at him. She had less direct experience of Samson's perspicacity than Robert but was aware of his formidable intelligence and his ability to penetrate the motivation of others. He was, however, looking as blandly uninterested as ever and nothing could be read from his expression.
Back in his room after dinner Robert felt wretched and unable to settle to anything. He switched on his mobile to see if there was any message from Cassandra. In measured tones the machine announced: "You have no new messages." He dialled Cassandra's mobile number, only to be informed by the same impassive voice: "I'm sorry but the person you have called is not available; please leave your message after the tone."
"Cassandra," he said in unintentionally pleading tones, "are you all right? Please ring me." He disconnected the call but left his phone switched on. A minute later his college telephone rang. He seized it eagerly, expecting it to be Cassandra.
"Hullo Ca---"
"Hullo Robert, it's Muriel."
"*Muriel?*"

"Yes. I didn't think you looked well at dinner. Are you all right?"

The words he'd just used in his message to Cassandra struck a chord.

"Why, how kind of you to ask. I don't know. I feel restless, aimless. But not ill."

"Would you like to come and have a drink?"

"Where?"

"In my room."

Robert really wanted to say 'I don't know', but felt that to be hardly a polite response. He hesitated, decided he couldn't possibly see Cassandra that evening anyway, despaired of concentrating on anything else, and finally said in what he felt to be a feebly expressed, dully non-committal response: "Thank you; that would be very nice. Um, when?"

"Now."

"Shall I bring a bottle?"

"No, certainly not. I've got plenty." Muriel did keep a stock of various kinds of drink. She was a follower of the old Oxford tradition of giving her pupils sherry if they were lucky enough to have tutorials at 12.00 noon or at 6.00 o'clock. This was by now a largely discontinued practice but it had been not uncommon in Muriel's own undergraduate days and she thought it an excellent one. She'd even been known to give out alcohol at 9.00 in the morning to pupils showing signs of distress of any sort. She thought of mentioning this to Robert with some hope of leading into the origins of the distress he was obviously in. She would not, however, mention that she had already swallowed a couple of quick nips herself to summon up the courage to ring him at all.

Robert knocked at the door.

"Come in!" Muriel used her most dulcet tones.

Robert entered, closed the door behind him and held up a bottle of port wine.

"I know you said not to but this was given to me and I can't drink it by myself." He didn't divulge that he'd decided against taking it to Huntsfield because it was much inferior to the hoards in Melissa's cellar, and also very dangerous to drink before driving, especially as he liked it.

"Thank you Robert, but shall we start with red wine and go on to the port as it's tempting but not good in quantities; it does give the most awful hangovers, and I daresay we've both got to teach tomorrow."

"Good idea!" Robert reflected that Muriel was showing more *nous* than he might have expected in a quiet woman don. She even had the red wine open to breathe a bit. In spite of himself he felt a little cheered.

Muriel poured the wine, hoping her guest didn't notice that the bottle was not quite full, and began the conversation by asking if he ever gave drinks to his pupils. Robert said he didn't, but admitted that it might be a good idea.

"What do you do if they get upset?" Muriel asked.

"Upset?" Robert was puzzled.

"Yes. Don't they ever get upset and start crying? Usually about something quite unrelated to their work."

"I have occasionally had that happen with a female pupil, now I think of it; I'm afraid I had no idea what to do; I found it very embarrassing."

"Oh well, if it happens again give them something strong to drink. It obviates the embarrassment if nothing else."

"I'll remember that, thank you; very good advice. Do you think they're more likely to burst into tears with women tutors than with men?"

"An interesting question; but I don't think we can find the answer without doing a count with a balanced group of our colleagues. Of course there are one or two who might reduce a pupil to tears by sheer nastiness."

"Do you really think so? I can't imagine it."

"Well I'm sure you're not that kind of tutor, Robert. But what about male pupils? I don't suppose they ever start crying."

"No, but I have had them confide in me about problems; usually to do with girl friends. I don't think I've been able to help them very much."

"They probably want a sympathetic ear rather than actual help. You know, 'a trouble shared is half repaired.' How would you feel about it yourself?"

"About what?"

"About sharing a trouble."

"I don't know who I'd share it with."

"A friend, I suppose; people our sort of age don't usually have tutors or any other older and supposedly wiser people to consult."

"Do you think I seem old?"

"Of course not, you must be the same age as I am, we came up in the same year."

"Did we? I didn't realise."

Muriel forbore to remind him that this fact had been mentioned on more than one occasion; clearly it had been of no significance to Robert and he had forgotten it.

"But of course," Muriel continued, as she replenished their glasses, "we must seem old to undergraduates if only by virtue of our position in relation to them. They can expect us to be their mentors but we have to rely on friends, or maybe siblings if we're lucky enough to have the right kind."

Robert sighed; "I don't think mine are," he said sadly. "What about you?"

"I haven't any."

"Oh, you're an only child; so is Cassandra."

"Cassandra?" Muriel's tone was intended to disguise the fact that this was precisely what she had been leading up to. "Oh of course; Samson's distant relative, the beautiful young woman potter."

Robert's glass was already empty so Muriel filled it up again. Having mentioned Cassandra's name (and already drunk two glasses of wine) he felt less inhibited.

"Yes, thank you," he murmured appreciatively, though whether the appreciation was of the refilled glass or the compliment to Cassandra was not entirely clear. "She is beautiful, isn't she." It was not a question.

"You're very fond of her." Muriel's answer was also a statement.

"Yes, I'm afraid so."

"Why afraid?"

"She's not equally fond of me."

"Is she much younger than you are?"

"About eight years.

"That's hardly a vast difference."

"Her cousin Stephen Marjoribanks seemed to think it is, though she did laugh at his 'ageism' as she called it."

"Well that's encouraging."

"I think she was just being kind."

"And how old is the 'very good-looking' guest who's staying there?"

Robert finished his third glass of wine. "I don't know, but he must be younger than I am."

Muriel was torn between empathising with Robert and hoping the guest would charm Cassandra away. Robert was too immersed in his own feelings to remark on Muriel's intelligent perception or to perceive that she was anticipating the possible provision of a shoulder to cry on: hers.

"Well don't despair, Robert, it must be early days."

"She seems to be too busy to see me. It wasn't like that before."

Muriel removed his empty glass and handed him a glass of port.

Making an effort to appear sober and sensible Robert demurred and then murmured the usual "Well, only one, then," as he took the port.

"How long have you been---um---fond of her?"

"It must be since the first time I went to the pottery; Samson asked me to take him. Nigel was already there and had just invited her out to lunch. She gave him very short shrift and he was desperately embarrassed to have it witnessed by colleagues."

"Really he is the end! *And* he's supposed to be engaged."

"Yes; even Samson felt protective and saw to it that Cassandra was warned. Not that it was necessary; she wouldn't be interested in a Nigel."

"But she is interested in you."

"I thought she was. She said she often thought she---cared for me."

"That's better than 'sometimes'."

"How amazing you are, Muriel! That's exactly what *she* said. You really are very perceptive, and---and sympathetic. No, no, I won't have another glass of port. I must have had too much already; I'm not usually so garrulous. But it's been a great help to talk to you."

Muriel decided she'd probably done enough for one evening and made no attempt to hinder his departure. She cleared the glasses and made up her mind to go to the Oratory on the following Sunday if only to see if she could perceive any attachment between Cassandra and the 'good-looking guest', whose name she had not yet heard. She could even pray for one to develop! She went to bed feeling almost hopeful.

Robert, on the other hand, felt that he'd behaved uncharacteristically, drunk too much too fast, departed from his usual reticence and given too much away. He was not sure whether he was grateful to Muriel for being so sympathetic or annoyed with her for getting him to reveal so much. Pondering indecisively, and not very coherently, he went to sleep.

***

Samson Southey, having had a short, pleasant walk from his house in Jericho, was in the college hall enjoying his breakfast. Robert came in somewhat later, but as he toyed with his food and ate little of it he finished at the same time as Samson and they walked from hall to their rooms together.

"If I may say so, Robert," Samson remarked, "you're looking a little hung over. Rather than accuse you of drinking alone I deduce that you were imbibing with Muriel Thwaites."

"How on earth---?"

"You were looking a little vulnerable at dinner last night; Muriel is a kind soul and I'm sure she has your interests at heart."

"Well---you're quite right of course, at least about the imbibing."

"And not about the interests?"

"That had never occurred to me."

"Which could ascribed to modesty; but to put it less charitably, Robert, you do at times appear to be quite lamentably lacking in perspicacity."

"It's true I haven't your ability, Samson," Robert admitted, more aware of his own deficiencies than of the main import of Samson's statement.

39

Nicholas Forbes-Mowbray was enjoying an excellent breakfast of muesli, fruit, boiled eggs and home made bread as he read The Times. Cassandra went in to see if he needed any more coffee.

"Only if you'll sit down and have some with me," he smiled.

Cassandra smiled back happily, took the empty cafetiere and soon returned with a full one and a cup for herself.

"Thank you," said Nicholas, "both for the coffee and the company. I shan't be here for dinner this evening; I'm going to a concert of baroque music in one of the colleges. Would you like to come with me? It's at eight o'clock so we could have a 'light bite' somewhere at about six."

Cassandra was delighted and accepted with real appreciation. Nicholas had been so uniformly polite and charming to her and to her parents that she had all but despaired of ever receiving any special treatment.

"I'm grateful," she told him, "not only for the invitation but for your crediting me with the ability to appreciate baroque music."

"Anybody who goes to the high mass at the Oratory must surely appreciate music of that period and even earlier; and besides, I've heard it issuing from your room early in the mornings."

"Oh dear! I hope I haven't disturbed you. I didn't realise it could be heard from the next floor."

"Only from the foot of the stairs, and I have climbed a few to listen more closely. I'm very happy to hear it. In most places there'd be nothing but pop music."

"Pete listens to pop music of course, but he's good about using his earphones and not disturbing us. I admit I like to get up to good music; it seems to start the day on the right note, one might say quite literally. But I can hardly use earphones when I'm washing and dressing."

Nicholas agreed; the coffee was finished; he helped Cassandra take the breakfast things into the kitchen, said "is it too early if we leave just after five?" and went upstairs on being assured that it wasn't.

When Melissa came down from doing the bedrooms and bathrooms her daughter was happily humming an air from The Magic Flute.

"I'm glad to see you so radiantly cheerful, darling. Can I guess the cause?"

"I doubt it, but you don't need to. Nicholas won't be here for dinner this evening because he's going to a baroque concert in Oxford *and he's asked me to go with him!"*

"And of course you refused because you thought Robert might not like you to accept!"

Cassandra knew her mother was not serious but laughed a little guiltily all the same.

"I do feel a little guilty about Robert, but mainly because I know Pa wants to see him."

"And what am I to tell him if he rings up?"

"Oh, he won't. He rings me on my mobile and leaves a message if it's switched off."

"There's a great deal to be said for those machines. How very useful they must be to lovers; especially illicit ones!"

"Yes; no need for a go-between carrying secret correspondence; though I believe other people can tap into them somehow."

"Oh, I suppose that only happens to famous people, and anyway, you and Robert are hardly illicit lovers." Melissa was on the point of saying 'hardly lovers, in fact,' but decided it might lead her daughter to expostulate and have Robert rather more in mind than was necessary or desirable. So instead she continued with mundane queries about what time she and Nicholas would be going out.

Unsurprisingly, Cassandra was dressed and ready to go out well before five o'clock, but she stayed in her room rather than come down and make this too obvious. Somewhat unwillingly she checked her mobile for messages; there were two from Robert, both similarly saying: 'I know you're very busy; can I come and help? I won't stay to supper if it's too much for your mother; I could always talk to your father if you want me to. Perhaps we could go out after that?' Rather than 'ring the person who left this message' Cassandra switched off the phone. It was nearly five o'clock, anyway, she told herself and she didn't want to start an altercation with Robert or tell him the truth ---or the opposite---about what she was doing that evening. She'd ring him tomorrow about going to the Oratory with her father again and they could meet there. Relieved, she put the phone in her handbag and went downstairs. Nicholas appeared a very few minutes later and they set off.

Cassandra sat back in the front passenger seat and remarked how comfortable it was and how pleasant to know it was not likely to belch black smoke or break down.

"Yes," Nicholas replied, "I'm afraid I care a little too much for creature comforts."

"Why afraid?"

"Material things shouldn't be important."

"Surely, as long as they're not too important for their own sake, they merely make life more comfortable and give one more time and energy to devote to more important things."

"That's a very sensible viewpoint, but I feel I can confide in you---can I?"

"Of course, if you'd like to." Cassandra was not sure whether to feel flattered or apprehensive.

"I'm here in Oxford partly because I want time to think, to consider."

"Yes?"

"To try and decide whether to enter a religious order, and if so, what order. Mainly the latter, really, as I do mean to try my vocation somewhere."

Cassandra realised that an interested and sympathetic response was expected of her and did her best to make one.

"You were at a Benedictine school, weren't you?"

"Yes and I love the Benedictines with their generous views on hospitality and their gentleness. But their teaching is largely confined to schools, especially in this country, and both the Jesuits and the Dominicans do a good deal of high level teaching, especially in Oxford."

"You're not considering the Oratorians, then?"

Nicholas smiled: "I certainly appreciate their music and their outgoing attitude, but I think I need more demanding rules. I'm too self-indulgent by nature."

"I find that hard to believe."

Nicholas sighed. "No," he said, "it's true. When I was talking to you about our family Christmas I felt how much I appreciated it all and how sadly I'd miss it."

"Wouldn't you be able to go home for Christmas?"

"Well not for Christmas Day itself, I think; it's such a busy time in churches. And I'd never belong in the same way as a father with his own children adding to the numbers of grandchildren and cousins. But I mustn't linger on that note. It's probably the consideration most likely to deter me. And anyway, I'm using you as a captive audience and talking about myself far too much. But for what it's worth I haven't felt able to talk to anybody else in such a way; you're so *sympatique* and yet not emotionally involved as a member of my family would be."

Cassandra paused for the right words to present themselves.

"Thank you, Nicholas," she said finally. " I value your confiding in me. Please believe that you can do so any time you like. As it happens, my best friend at school became a nun, and she used to talk to me about her vocation at times."

Nicholas was immediately interested and plied her with questions about the kind of convent and its location and the age at which her friend had joined it. Cassandra said it was Benedictine and that her friend had been about twenty-three or four, having finished her degree. "Not that I saw so much of her then because she was at Cambridge and I was at Holloway. But we did keep in touch to a certain extent, and I always send her a Christmas card. I'd like to do more but I don't think she's allowed to carry on an active correspondence, though I believe I could go and see her; but of course Devon was too far away and we've been so busy here."

They arrived in Oxford; found, with some difficulty, a parking place, for which they fed an exorbitant number of coins into a machine, and went to have a small meal at a restaurant very near the college where the concert was to take place. The course of the evening was not exactly running as anticipated by Cassandra but she felt that questions about baroque music and an appreciative ear given to Nicholas's knowledgeable words about it made a very suitable accompaniment to their meal.

"I suppose," she remarked, "it wouldn't be very easy to go to concerts like this from Ampleforth."

"No, I'm afraid not; even if it were permissible. I must admit I'd dearly love to live in or near Oxford, as I'm doing now, in fact. I think you're ideally situated at Huntsfield. You must be very happy there."

"It has its disadvantages, but in general yes, I think we are. It's certainly more comfortable than the flat above the grocer's shop in deepest Devon. But don't you like living in Durham?"

"I do on the whole, especially in term time. But I do feel drawn to Oxford."

They progressed pleasantly from the restaurant to the college ante-chapel and took their seats. The players---flute, oboe, violin, viola, cello and harpsichord---were a little late starting but their playing and their programme were superb: Telemann, Bach J.S., J.C. and C.P.E., Mozart and Telemann again. Cassandra felt almost happy, though she did reflect that Robert had never offered to take her to such a musical feast---or indeed to a concert of any kind---and felt aggrieved that he regarded her as an ignorant artisan with little intellect. She determined to tell him so.

As they walked back to the car Cassandra expressed her heartfelt thanks to Nicholas and her immense appreciation of the evening.

"Do you play a musical instrument yourself?" Nicholas enquired.

"Not unless you count CDs," Cassandra smiled. "I did play the piano at school, in fact I passed Grade 7, but I was never very good and of course I haven't played a note since even before I went to Devon. My friend who went into the convent used to play the flute most beautifully; do you think she'll be allowed to play now?"

"I'm not sure. I suppose it depends on Reverend Mother. It would seem a sad waste if she can't. She sounds a most interesting girl; but then I'm sure you would have an interesting best friend."

"Thank you, Nicholas. I wish I'd kept up with her more actively after we left school, but you know what student life's like. Strangely, though, I think I actually miss her now. I've never made another friend who had such depth and such real goodness. I'd appreciate her even more now that I'm older."

"I expect she was unusually mature and thoughtful for her age."

"She was, I suppose, but more than that; I don't know why I'm thinking so much about her suddenly."

"Perhaps she's thinking about you."

"Do you believe in telepathy?"

"Certainly I do. It happens so often that one's talking or thinking about somebody and then they ring up or write a letter, or these days send an email! I can't believe it's never anything but mere coincidence."

"I think there could be another reason."

"Yes?"

"You remind me of her. I hadn't realised before; it must have been subconscious."

Nicholas smiled. "I don't think I can cope with such commendation!"

"Perhaps it's to do with your wanting to join a religious order, though of course I didn't know about it until tonight. That must take a certain kind of person."

"Most orders contain vastly different kinds of people."

"But at least they all have one thing in common."

They reached the car and started on the journey back to Huntsfield.

"I'm so grateful to you for listening to me," Nicholas said as they drove into the long, straight road that led north out of Oxford. "I don't want other people to know about my intentions yet; I know some will try to talk me out of it and others will start to treat me differently, as if I'm not a normal human being, or not the person they thought they knew. But you haven't known me for long enough to have that problem. You're the ideal confidante."

"I'm very glad; in fact I feel honoured. And you can be sure I won't betray your confidence."

Cassandra reflected that she might have expected to feel devastated by Nicholas's revelations, but in fact she felt that she esteemed him even more than before and his confiding in her gave her a new and very pleasing sense of being special.

Melissa was still up and sitting on her own in the kitchen when they got back. She offered them a drink, of course, but Nicholas declined, saying he needed an early night. When he'd gone upstairs Cassandra flopped into a chair and sat smiling and silent. Melissa found her expression difficult to read but finally said: "You look as if you've been to a mass rather than supper and a concert with a very personable young man."

"I feel a bit like that," Cassandra admitted, "it was a very beautiful concert."

"Hmm! It must have been," said her mother. "And Nicholas?"

"He really is a very special person. How's Pa?"

"Cantankerous as ever, but coughing a lot and needing the odd top-up of oxygen. It's a mercy we've moved him down here." Melissa was not unaware of her daughter's sudden change of subject but knew nothing would be gained by alluding to it. "He's very anxious to see Robert again. I told him how difficult it all was with the work going on and dinner as well as breakfast for a guest. He didn't seem very convinced."

"I'll ring Robert tomorrow; after all I'll probably see him on Sunday. We won't need to rush back to see to the workmen this time."

"Would you like to ask him to lunch?"

"Not really; it would be awkward because he'll probably be with his friend Samson. Maybe he could come for supper on Monday---or something. He could come and see Pa, anyway. I'll think about it. But it's too late to do anything tonight. I'm going to bed---unless you want me to do anything to help."

"No, no; I've had an easy evening with Nicholas out and only Pete and your father to cook for. I'm going up myself when I've done the shopping list. Goodnight; sleep well."

Lying in bed Cassandra pondered on Nicholas's confidences. ' I wonder,' she thought to herself, 'if Robert felt like this when I told him I'd vowed to be a virgin till I got married and he said: "I hold you as a thing ensky'd and sainted"; that's a bit how I feel about Nicholas. Though of course people who go into monasteries or convents don't always stay in them. And if they don't they probably come out in even more need of somebody to confide in.'

Cassandra fell asleep happy and slept very well.

40

After a latish breakfast in college and a short sojourn in their rooms Robert and Samson set out for the Oratory as usual on a Sunday. As they turned from the college into the next street they were aware of a female figure some distance ahead of them. She was wearing high heels and walking rather slowly.

"Isn't that Muriel Thwaites ahead of us?" asked Samson.

"Yes, I believe it is." Robert had felt rather shy of Muriel since their evening of wine and revelations and had managed to avoid speaking to her. He was inclined to hold back and maintain the distance between them but as he and Samson were both long-legged and progressing at a normal masculine pace they soon caught up with her.

"Hullo Muriel," Samson greeted her cordially, "are you going in our direction by any chance?"

"I should think that very likely, Samson, if you're on your way to the Oratory."

"You're looking very nice, Muriel." Robert felt that a compliment was more in order than a query. He also hoped it might compensate for his recent avoidance of her.

"Thank you, Robert. When I was young we used to dress up in our Sunday best to go to church, but perhaps it's not so usual now."

"Well, not in Catholic churches as far as I've noticed. You see all sorts, including bare arms covered with tattoos at one end of the scale, and a fair proliferation of jeans."

"I must admit I hadn't noticed the sartorial peculiarities of the congregation," Samson contributed, "but the clergy certainly dress up."

"Women don't wear hats any more, do they? I'm afraid I haven't got one."

"You see the odd one or two," Robert answered, "and a few mantillas, but you'll blend better without any head gear."

"Well that's a relief. I really feel quite nervous---isn't it ridiculous?"

"Not at all; I felt like that when I first came, but Samson's been a great help. Do sit with us if you like."

Muriel expressed her thanks in terms more moderate than her feelings as she trotted between the men with the best pace she could manage in her unaccustomed heels.

Once in church Samson left it to Robert to look after Muriel. Robert was not averse to this as he felt it was quite the best time and place for him to re-establish normal relations with her. He was also aware, if rather dimly and without deliberation, that it might not be entirely a bad thing for Cassandra to see him with Muriel. He set about explaining the mysteries of the mass sheet and the Latin/English mass book with more assiduity than was, perhaps, strictly necessary. Cassandra indeed, from her usual place further back on the other side of the church, saw them as soon as she sat down after her initial prayer, and as she continued to watch Robert bending over Muriel's missal rather than casting his eyes in her direction, she felt a proprietary qualm. This was not lost on her mother, who took in the whole situation with a sharp glance and a sharper interest. Nicholas, on the other side of Melissa, was too much immersed in prayer to notice Robert or anybody else.

In the courtyard after mass Muriel was introduced, although Nicholas was the only person unfamiliar to her, and they all went to the club-room to have a drink. Cassandra lost no time in talking to Robert. "Now that we've settled down and Pa's in his new room he'd love to see you. Would you like to come and have supper tomorrow?"

"You know I would. I was beginning to feel unwelcome."

"Oh Robert! Please don't say that. Things have just been so topsy-turvy and I've felt I had to help Mummy as much as possible as well as keeping up with pot production. Pa's found it disturbing too."

Nicholas broke into their conversation asking what they'd like to drink; he wanted to go on ahead and do the ordering.

"No, no let me," Robert immediately volunteered, "I'm sure it must be my turn."

They went on to the bar and Cassandra turned to Muriel and mentioned that she remembered her from the pot sale. "I hope your Christmas presents were a success," she continued.

"They were indeed, and I wanted to tell you so. All the recipients were delighted to have things so different, so beautiful and so useful. If they ever come to Oxford I'll bring them out to your pottery if I may."

Melissa joined in the pleasantries. "How very nice to see you again," she murmured blandly to Muriel.

"I suppose you wonder what I'm doing here," Muriel responded rather awkwardly, feeling unable to match Melissa's tone.

Melissa smiled. "Far be it from me to wonder what anybody's doing in church; there must be more mixed motives than there are admissions to them!"

Cassandra gave her mother a sideways glance, "Not to mention *ulterior* motives, Mummy."

"True, darling, but even ulterior motives can bear fruit. There are many benefits to be gained by coming to church;

meeting pleasant people being one of them. Wouldn't you agree, Samson?"

"Indeed yes," replied Samson, "and also furthering the acquaintance of pleasant people one has already met, if they're likely to be there."

"How long have you been coming here, Samson?" asked Muriel, to avert any possible attention from herself. That Samson understood her own motives she had no doubt.

"Oh, some years now; but Robert's only begun to attend quite recently. Not, of course, that I imagine anybody to be drawn on *my* account!"

"You underestimate yourself, Samson," Muriel protested, "your judgment is much respected and your enthusiastic appreciation of the music here is very compelling."

"Thank you, Muriel; your swift response does credit to us both!"

Robert and Nicholas appeared with the drinks, apologised for the length of the queue and the wait and sat at the table, Nicholas beside Cassandra and Robert beside Muriel. The conversation continued with a discussion of the music and Nicholas admitted that he found it irresistible even though he was, in fact, to attend mass at Blackfriars that evening, adding that he'd been invited to supper there afterwards. "Would it put you out terribly if I accepted?" he asked Melissa. "I'm very sorry I didn't mention it before."

Melissa was, in fact, more pleased than she admitted. Cassandra saw an opportunity to invite Robert to a kitchen supper and would have asked him then and there had it not necessitated speaking across Nicholas and Muriel. She eyed the latter covertly with some puzzlement, thinking that she looked rather better than usual; better dressed and more animated. 'I suppose she's dressed up to come to mass,' she thought, 'people do when they're not used to it.' Melissa, though still talking to Nicholas, was well aware of the interplay between the others, as of course was Samson, who was watching with detached interest.

The drinks finished, seconds declined, the party broke up. Leaving the table Muriel stumbled a little on her high heels. "Oh these shoes!" she exclaimed, "I can't think why I ever bought them!"

"I can," said Melissa soothingly, "they're very beautiful. But it's not a good idea to wear them here. Kneeling absolutely *ruins* one's shoes! Why don't you let us drive you back to college? We're with Nicholas because he doesn't trust our car, but there's room for one more. Nicholas!"

"Yes, can I help?"

Melissa explained and Nicholas of course agreed. Muriel was actually very glad to accept though in fact she barely had need to as it was all arranged for her. She had been dreading the walk as she knew her male colleagues would politely regulate their pace to hers and hers was embarrassingly slow. She sat in the back with Melissa, who insisted on putting her daughter in the front passenger seat.

"I have enjoyed meeting you properly," Melissa turned her charm on to Muriel, "and I do hope we'll see you next Sunday. We must arrange for you to come out to us with Robert and Samson for an informal lunch after mass one Sunday. I know you drive because you brought Samson to Cassandra's sale."

"Yes I do, but it's so impossible to park in Oxford that I really only drive out of it. But I'd love to come out to Huntsfield and see it in the daylight. Thank you."

Muriel alighted from the car, thanked Nicholas, went into her room in college and changed her shoes.

After lunch at Huntsfield Cassandra went to her room, rang Robert and invited him to come and have supper that same day and not wait till Monday.

Melissa relaxed over her coffee and *tiny* last glass and Fergus, after saying little during lunch asked "How was church?"

"Very interesting. That woman colleague of Robert's came for the first time. The one who teaches French."

"I was asking about the service, not the people,"

"The mass, you mean. You might at least try and get the terminology right. Are you enquiring about the music or the sermon or the general ambience?"

"I don't know. I wish I could come."

"It might be too much for you, combined with the drive there and back."

"I'd be all right if Robert was there. When's he coming again? Why hasn't he been here?"

"Probably because Nicholas has. Why don't you talk to *him*?"

"He's too pious for me. He crosses himself and bows his head and mutters something before meals."

"Does he? I've never noticed."

"He waits till you're not looking. I suppose he feels I don't count."

"Hmm." Melissa considered this with some interest. "That's a bad sign."

"What is?"

"Well, why do you think Robert treats you with such deference?"

"Because he's a nice chap and he likes me."

"You're not the only one he likes."

"Oh. No. You mean Cassandra."

"Quite."

Cassandra came in to announce that Robert was coming to supper that evening and that she'd cook it to give her mother a break. Fergus cheered immediately but announced his intention of having a rest so that he wouldn't be too tired later.

"So how is Robert?" Melissa asked. "Not entirely ousted by Nicholas, I gather."

Cassandra had to smile; there was no hiding much from her mother. "Not entirely." she replied.

"Preferable to have one's pleasures singly, of course," Melissa continued.

"Less complicated, certainly. Come to that, how's Jasper?"

"I'm glad you asked because he wants me to meet him in London on Friday and I said I would if you'd see to things."

"Of course I will. It's time you had a break. We'll be busy when the colonials---as you call them---come."

Melissa sighed; "sufficient unto the day---."

"Is the evil thereof," Cassandra finished.

***

Robert arrived early enough to talk to Rufus before supper and arrange to take him to the Oratory again, though he wondered privately whether his state of health would not render this impossible. Fergus, however, read his thoughts without difficulty and told him: "You seem to give me strength. But I mustn't be selfish ---I know I usually am---and keep you from your beloved; you must have some catching up to do." Robert went gratefully into the kitchen to help Cassandra with the supper. Melissa took the opportunity to go up to her own room, knowing that she'd be tempted to interfere with Cassandra's cooking if she stayed downstairs. "I'm going to relax in luxury and lie on my bed and read until I'm called," she said.

The mechanics of preparing a meal provided Robert and Cassandra with something of a bridge over the gap in their relationship, of which they were both acutely aware though it had never been overtly referred to. When the preparations were finished and they sat down to wait for things to cook Cassandra opened the conversation by saying: “How do you think Pa’s getting on?”

“Physically or spiritually?”

Cassandra smiled. “You are coming on, Robert; I don’t think you would have mentioned a spiritual dimension when I first knew you.”

“Knowing your father has done me a lot of good; he’s made me think about these things even more pressingly than you have. Leading somebody who’s more in the dark than you are gives you a lot of impetus, makes you feel on top of things in an odd sort of way. But since you ask, I think he’s better spiritually than he is physically. He wants to see the priest at the Oratory again but I doubt whether he’s strong enough.”

“The priest will have to come here; we can hardly take the oxygen in the car. Perhaps we could ask him to lunch and make it all less formal. But it would be nice if you were here too.”

“Do you really mean that?”

“Of course I do; Pa would appreciate it so much.”

“More than you would?”

“Oh, Robert, I know I’ve been busy and perhaps a bit---distant; but it was only for a week or so.”

“It seemed much longer, and further, than that.”

“I went to a concert one night.”

“Did you? Where?” Robert didn’t ask ‘who with?’ He didn’t want to be told.

“In Magdalen. It was a baroque concert; marvellous. You’ve never taken me to a concert.”

"I never thought of it; I didn't know you liked concerts."

"No. You only think of me as a potter, a maker of Oxford Pots. You forget I've got a degree in Latin and English---if you ever knew about it. You're always surprised when I know anything."

"You know a good deal more than my pupils do. But I'm not surprised, I'm delighted. I thought we were on the same wavelength. I don't go to concerts myself. I used to, but now I tend to listen to CDs and get on with my work at the same time. I'm sorry."

Robert looked so crestfallen that Cassandra felt for him.

"It's the way we met. It's that wretched bourdaloue. How can anybody take me seriously after seeing me in the market selling that thing? It must have coloured your whole perception of me."

"If it hadn't been for that we probably wouldn't have met at all."

"It's not your fault. It's probably just that people I've met here since treat me differently."

"In what way?"

"They realise I'm an educated woman---and ask me to baroque concerts!"

"I see. I thought you enjoyed *Charlie's Aunt.*"

"Of course I enjoyed it; you know I did. But it's the only thing we've been to; we just meet and eat. I need some intellectual stimulation. You live in a college with intelligent colleagues---."

"You wouldn't always think so," Robert murmured.

"Well there do seem to be some exceptions, that's true, but fond though I am of Pete he's not exactly as good a conversationalist as he is a potter and he *is* only sixteen. Oh, I'm sorry, Robert; I'm probably just taking out my general sense of frustration on you."

“Would you like to come to a college guest night dinner?”

“There we are; eating again. Yes I would, but I’d also like to go to a play or a concert. Even a film.”

“I’m sorry,” said Robert again. “I’ve been selfish. I’ve wanted to talk to you rather than listen to other things, I suppose. I’ll look up what’s on and we’ll go to something at least once a week. Will you forgive me?”

“Something’s burning! Help! I’ve been forgetting about the supper.” Cassandra rushed to the cooker. “So much for being snooty about food. Oh, I think it’s all right, just. Let’s get things finished and call the others, Ma and Pa that is, Pete’s had his.”

Robert immediately set about helping and decided the subject of forgiveness could, perhaps usefully, be deferred until later.

Melissa came in first after briefly telling Fergus to take a sniff of oxygen and not be in a hurry, but he was not far behind her. She sat down after pouring drinks all round and with every appearance of effortless pleasure began to relieve the tension she could feel in the atmosphere.

“So nice of you to come and help cook the supper, Robert, much appreciated. We’ve missed you over this last week of building and disruption, haven’t we Fergus?”

“Well *I* certainly have.”

“Nice seeing your colleague Muriel Thwaites at mass this morning,” Melissa continued, “she’s never been before, has she?”

“No, she hasn’t ever shown any interest before. I can’t think why she decided to come all of a sudden. She seemed quite worried about it and unusually dressed up for the occasion. I hardly recognised her when Samson and I saw her walking ahead of us. Strange, really. But of course

Samson does often talk about the beauty and variety of the music."

"How modest you are, Robert."

"I don't know anything like as much about music as Samson does and I don't feel very competent to talk about it."

"And of course Muriel Thwaites' attendance was due *entirely* to the music." Melissa was unable to suppress her smile or her irony.

Robert looked at her aghast, his fork poised in mid-air half way to his mouth. He thought of his bibulous evening with Muriel. His fork, still laden, descended to his plate. "Oh Lord!" he said, "How awful!"

"Not at all!" Melissa rejoined, "I'm inviting her to a Sunday lunch with you and Samson. She's a very pleasant young woman."

"Not young exactly," was Cassandra's comment.

"No; she's my age." Robert looked depressed.

"Very suitable," Melissa commented.

Robert stopped eating altogether. He'd always thought Cassandra's mother was at least non-committally on his side. It had never occurred to him that she might not consider him a match for her daughter. He felt deeply dismayed.

Fergus, who spoke less and thought more now that he found adequate breath rather harder to come by, looked at his wife narrowly. "I don't know what you're playing at, Melissa," he rasped, "but I don't think suitability is a very common reason for people to take to each other."

"Clearly not, Fergus, as I have learnt to my cost."

"Surely, though," Cassandra interjected, "it is a good reason."

"I'm very glad to hear you say so, darling." Her mother nodded approval. "You show a wisdom beyond your years.

Similarity of background, parity of age, complementary interests, agreement on religion and related matters, all these things are of enormous importance in a relationship; if everybody took notice of them there'd be far more stable marriages, far fewer divorces."

"Unfortunately, however," Fergus made himself heard, "the blind god tends to cut across all that."

"The what? Oh I suppose you mean Cupid; how classical of you. Well you're right, of course, blind is the operative word."

Robert listened in silence, feeling increasingly unhappy. The absent Nicholas loomed large in his mind and he reflected bitterly that in addition to that young man's possessing all the attributes detailed by Melissa it was certainly not necessary for a woman to be blind to find him attractive. Robert sighed audibly. Such a rival rendered him all too conscious of what he considered his own relative unsuitability.

"If love wasn't blind there'd be far fewer marriages in any case," Fergus averred. "Or they'd have to be the sort arranged by parents---and plenty of those end in disaster. Look at the Asians."

Robert felt a little cheered. "There are numerous examples from the middle ages, too," he said. "But then disparity of age was often a factor. The Church gave out warnings to parents not to marry their daughters off to rich old men."

"Chaucer's told some interesting stories on that theme," Cassandra contributed, "mainly the bawdy ones. They're probably the most popular."

"They are with most undergraduates, certainly." Robert and Cassandra went on with a discussion of the merits and demerits of these tales as he wanted to show his appreciation of her knowledge of them and she wanted the stimulus of such a conversation as well as the opportunity to upgrade what she considered to be her 'artisan image'. Their discussion was lively and of interest to them both. Fergus listened with satisfaction. Melissa was not entirely delighted. She had to admit to herself that Robert was not without merits, but she considered it beyond question that Nicholas had a great many more of them, and she noted with some dissatisfaction that the tension between Robert and Cassandra seemed to have evaporated. They became even further in accord when arranging for Robert to bring an Oratory priest out to see Fergus as soon as this could be organised, with Cassandra promising to see to the details by email. Melissa pondered on how to prevent her daughter from going to Robert's car with him and could only think of murmuring that she might need help with getting Fergus to bed as he was beginning to find even dressing and undressing quite a strain. But Robert immediately offered to help, either with Fergus or the clearing up or both, so that ploy failed to work.

When Fergus was safely in bed, with Robert's help, and the dinner things entirely cleared up, with Cassandra's help, Melissa sat alone at the table enjoying the comfort of a cigarette and a *very* tiny glass of port (which had been refused by the others) and tried to analyse her daughter's attitude to Nicholas in the light of her reaction to her evening out with him. It didn't seem to match anything in Melissa's experience. She was musing on this when Nicholas himself came in. He agreed to join her in a glass of port and asked if a new guest had arrived.

"No, they're not due quite yet. Why?"

"Oh, just that there's another car in the yard."

"Oh yes." Melissa was doubtful how much to say. She could hardly say nothing but was unwilling to admit to the presence of Robert's car in the yard and the absence of

Robert---and Cassandra--- from the house. "That's Robert's car," she said finally. Then, with what she considered a flash of brilliance, "they're arranging for Robert to bring a priest out to see Fergus, he's showing some interest in becoming a Catholic."

Nicholas was immediately attentive. "Really? I'd no idea. I would be very happy to talk to him about it. Robert's not a Catholic himself, is he?"

"No; but I think that's why Fergus is so willing to talk to *him.* They appear to have some fellow feeling. But tell me about your evening at Blackfriars. Was the dinner very Spartan?"

"No. I wouldn't say that; it was more than adequate. I enjoyed it. We didn't talk during the meal but there was stimulating conversation before and after, until we all went into the chapel for Compline. It's not quite like the Benedictines, but I do feel very much at home there."

Melissa smiled. "You're not thinking of joining them?" she asked more in jest than in earnest. Nicholas threw her a quick, questioning glance. "Did Cassandra---" he began suspiciously.

"No, no; Cassandra's never mentioned such a thing; I was merely making a not quite serious response to your obvious enthusiasm. I beg your pardon if I've spoken out of turn."

Nicholas looked at her indecisively; he moistened his lips and seemed about to reply when Cassandra opened the door.

"Hullo darling, how's your father?" Melissa asked blandly.

For a second Cassandra was astonished at the question, but she was quick enough to appreciate her mother's subtlety.

"Very tired, I think he's asleep now," she answered truthfully. "Hullo Nicholas. How was Blackfriars?"

"I found it both restful and stimulating, if that doesn't sound too impossible."

"Not at all; I understand perfectly. It must have been very satisfying."

Nicholas gave her an appreciative smile, which Melissa saw with interest. It almost looked, she thought, as if there were some complicity between them. She flicked her mind over the conversation she herself had been engaged in with him before Cassandra came into the room. "Ah!" she said aloud. It sounded like a sigh.

"Are you all right, Ma?" Cassandra looked at her anxiously. "You sound as if you're in pain."

"Thank you for your concern, darling. You don't want two sick parents to look after so I'll try to keep as well as possible. I daresay I'm just a little weary. I may not be as old as your father but I'm not as young as you are, either, so I'm bound to be slowing down."

"This is the first time you've shown any sign of it," her daughter responded.

"I do hope you don't find it too tiring looking after me," Nicholas broke in anxiously. "I could do a lot more for myself, you know. You've enough to do looking after your husband; and I could help with that, too, if you'd let me."

As Fergus seemed to have developed an antipathy towards Nicholas the latter's offers of help were a source of some embarrassment. Melissa had been afraid her husband's rudeness, which she suspected to stem in part from a suspicion that Nicholas was putting Robert in the shade, might deter him from paying attention to Cassandra. Cassandra, however, considered it might be useful to Nicholas to have some first hand experience in dealing with the dying and replied that it would be a good idea if the need arose. "I'll let you know," she promised, "if you're here."

"He can be very cantankerous, I'm afraid," was Melissa's warning, "and as to doing more for yourself, you're a model guest as it is."

Nicholas's polite disclaimers as he rose to leave the room were more genuine than is usually the case but Melissa could see how their ready and perfect expression could annoy a man like Fergus. When they were alone she asked Cassandra: "Do you really want Nicholas to do anything for your father? Of course it might put him off."

"Put Pa off the faith, you mean? Surely you don't want that to happen!"

"No. Put Nicholas off joining the Blackfriars. He might find he's not suited to talking to odd converts."

"Did he tell you…" Cassandra was aghast, "tell you about his vocation?"

Melissa smiled. "No. Don't worry. You must be the only one he's told. He gave himself away….with a little unconscious help from you. Somehow I don't think he'll go through with it. He's probably too idealistic."

Cassandra fell asleep that night pondering with renewed respect on her mother's powers of deduction. Melissa, also pondering on the disclosures of the evening, was not disinclined to congratulate herself on her accuracy in the case of Nicholas but her satisfaction was tempered with the sobering thought that she had signally failed to make use of her deductive ability when living with her husband.

41

On Monday the post arrived so late in the afternoon that Cassandra, very busy in the workshop, had no time to look at it until she'd showered and put on clean clothes for dinner. She came down to find a lull in the preparations and her mother indulging in a *very tiny* pre-prandial drink, with, of course a cigarette to go with it, so she sat down to keep her company and open her mail.

"I've actually got a *real* letter," she announced happily, " a real letter with handwriting on it! How exciting; and I think the writing looks familiar, but I can't place it." She slit it open with a handy knife and moments later exclaimed: "Oh great heavens above, I don't believe it!"

"Who's it from? What's the matter?" her mother asked anxiously.

"It's from Celestria, my friend at school."

"Didn't she become a nun?"

"Yes, but she's come out of the convent. She's at home with her parents. She wants to come and see me."

"Where do her parents live?"

"Somewhere in the wilds of Yorkshire, I think. Let's see the address. Hm; it doesn't mean a lot to me but it's definitely Yorkshire."

"She'll have to come and stay, then."

"Well she can, can't she?"

"Of course; we can easily get a room ready for her. It doesn't have to be *paying* guest standard, especially if she's used to the rigours of a convent."

As soon as Nicholas came in for dinner Cassandra greeted him excitedly. "You know my friend who became a nun, the one I was telling you I'd been thinking about lately?"

"Yes, I remember very well. Have you heard from her?"

"Heavens, Nicholas! I know you said you believe in telepathy and she was probably thinking about *me*, but surely it can't extend to your knowing I've heard from her!"

"Not exactly, but I'm not surprised. These things do seem to happen more frequently than can be explained by mere coincidence."

"Well she's come out of the convent. She wants to come and stay with me. Well, she said see me, but of course she'll have to stay."

"How exceedingly interesting; I'd very much like to meet her. What's her name, by the way?"

"Oh, didn't I mention it? Celestria."

"Celestria!" Nicholas savoured the name as he said it. "How beautiful. What a truly lovely name. I could lose my heart to it!" Then, remembering that losing his heart to girls' names was not entirely in accordance with his vocation, he added rapidly, "metaphorically, of course."

Cassandra, who was not sorry to hear Nicholas depart from his usual poise and precision, didn't try to stop herself laughing. "Well I'm very glad to hear that, Nicholas. You might be in rather a bad way if you lost it literally!"

Fergus shambled in and sat down heavily. After a gasp for breath he said: "What are you laughing about?"

"Oh, nothing significant. My school friend Celestria's coming to stay. I don't suppose you remember her."

"No, I don't. What a bloody silly name to saddle a girl with. Is she heavenly?"

"Well, she was a nun until very recently."

"How sickening; but what can you expect with a name like that."

Nicholas listened, somewhat aghast. It occurred to him that anybody instructing Fergus as a potential convert might have a very hard row to hoe. He said grace to himself hastily and added a prayer for Fergus, though he felt his resolution to speak to him about the faith somewhat shaken.

"Now, Pa!" Cassandra spoke in tones of not very serious reproof, "there's nothing particularly reprehensible about a girl having a try at being a nun."

"I think there is," Fergus averred, "these over-pious people make me feel sick. They put me off. That's what I like about Robert." He was interrupted by a fit of coughing, during which Melissa came in and begged them to start as she was seeing to the main course. Fergus didn't resume his discourse, feeling that he had made his point, but contented himself with a glower of deep dislike directed at Nicholas, who concluded that talking to potential converts had better wait until he'd had some training.

***

Cassandra telephoned Celestria the following day, having decided not to trust to the vagaries of snail mail, and was rewarded by an immediate and grateful acceptance of the invitation to stay. She arrived by train two days later and was met at Oxford station by Cassandra and also Nicholas, who had insisted on driving there to meet her. Cassandra recognised her immediately; she seemed no older than she had at school. Her hair, a light auburn, was very short, as she had joined an order where a full habit and veil were still worn; she looked young, vulnerable and quite strikingly pretty. She greeted Cassandra with open arms. "Oh I'm so happy to see you," she said, "it was tremendous fun going on a train but just a little scary; I haven't been on one for so long. I'm very grateful that you haven't forgotten me."

"Of course I haven't. I've thought about you very often, especially just recently for some reason. Nicholas says it's telepathy. Were you thinking about me? Oh this is Nicholas; how awful…I'm so excited I almost forgot to introduce you. Nicholas, Celestria."

Celestria coloured a little as polite how-do-you-dos were exchanged and lowered her head. Cassandra supposed she was rather out of the way of meeting young men, though come to that she'd never shown any interest in them when a teenager at school, unlike some of their contemporaries who'd seemed able to talk and think of nothing else.

Nicholas carried her suitcase and led the way to the car. Celestria demurred at sitting in the front with him but Cassandra insisted. "You want to be able to see Oxford properly; I see it very often."

"Even going in a car's exciting, you know!" Celestria was certainly showing every sign of real pleasure and responded with interest to the sights of Oxford pointed out by Nicholas, with the occasional interjection from Cassandra. Nicholas responded in his turn by taking a detour out of the usual way so that she could see some more.

"Oh, I'd no idea it was so beautiful!" Celestria exclaimed. "The colleges must be wonderful inside."

"I'll take you on a proper tour while you're here," Nicholas offered; "I'll be very happy to look at some of them in detail myself, and you must see the Sheldonian and the Divinity School and the Duke Humphrey." He went on to describe the glories of the city as they drove out towards Huntsfield and Cassandra, while happy that her friend was being so well received and was increasingly at ease, began to feel that she herself was taking a back seat metaphorically as well as literally.

Arrived at Huntsfield Celestria was equally enthusiastic about the beauty of the house and grounds, the fine views of the wintry landscape.

"Heavens, Cassandra! I'd no idea you lived in so magnificent a place! How modest you are about it! I only remember you in a nice flat in France."

"We inherited this quite recently, and there's still a great deal to do here. But your parents' address sounds very grand. Have they moved since you were at school?"

"Oh yes; they bought their present house just a short while ago. It's the old family place and my father took it over when his last uncle died. Nobody else in the family wanted it. I'm afraid it's rather large and gloomy and doesn't seem like home. My mother doesn't really like it either."

Nicholas insisted on carrying Celestria's case, not only into the house but up to her room. She seemed almost embarrassed. "Oh dear," she murmured, "I'm not used to being so pampered. Not that I don't appreciate it," she added hastily, " but I shall get quite spoilt at this rate."

Nicholas regarded her seriously; "I don't think anything could spoil you," he said. Celestria coloured brightly and looked first at the floor and then at Cassandra, who had led the way to her room.

"Thank you so much, Nicholas," Cassandra managed to sound just a little dismissive, "I'll show Celestria the bathroom and so on and we'll see you at dinner, when she's had a chance to brush up and rest after her journey."

"Oh yes; yes of course." Nicholas disappeared with a rapidity that looked almost gauche, very unlike his usual, faultlessly urbane, manner. Cassandra stifled a smile as she feared it might distress her friend, and proceeded with the mundanely necessary pointing out of the bathroom and loo. "Come down whenever you're ready and we'll have a nice coze in the warm kitchen before dinner. My mother should be back by then, too; she tends to go out shopping in the afternoon while my father's having a rest. I'll tell you all about it later."

Celestria in fact appeared in the kitchen after a very short time. Cassandra commented on her quickness and asked if she'd already unpacked.

"I haven't very many clothes, you see, or anything in the way of ornaments or make-up, so I can travel very light. But perhaps you could come and help me to choose some clothes while I'm here, I've no idea what's fashionable now; well acceptable even, I don't really aspire to fashion. But I know you have work to do and I don't want to be a nuisance."

"I'd *love* to go shopping with you and it's a good time because the sales are still on. I'm afraid I do a lot of clothes buying from charity shops myself so I might not be the best guide."

"That sounds like an excellent idea! I'm sure I'd be happier myself with charity shops. I've got my dowry back from the convent but I haven't thought about earning my living yet. I don't want to be dependent on my parents. Oh I'm so happy to be staying with you, Cassandra; it's just like picking up where we left off at school."

"Come to that, I haven't had a girl friend of my own age with me for what seems like years; my mother and I get on very well, but it's hardly the same thing."

"No indeed! You're very lucky, though; it can be a difficult relationship." Celestria gave a small sigh and Cassandra surmised that her friend was more than a little relieved to have found a haven, however temporary, away from home. She forbore to comment on this in any way but used the time to outline the story of her father's disappearance and sudden return, feeling it necessary to give some inkling of her parents' relationship and her father's illness. "He does seem to be interested in becoming a Catholic before he dies, however," she added. Celestria's interest in the story could hardly increase but her face took on a look of glowing happiness which told Cassandra that though she had lost her vocation she had clearly not lost her faith, something she had wondered, but would have hesitated to enquire, about. By the time Melissa returned with the shopping the girls had re-established their friendship and she could see that the visit was promising to be harmonious and successful. Cassandra was a little apprehensive about her father's attitude to their guest but Melissa welcomed her with the utmost graciousness, remembered her as a schoolgirl, praised her appearance, albeit with the delicacy of indirectness, and generally confirmed Celestria's remembered opinion that Cassandra was indeed fortunate in her female parent at least.

Nicholas came down early for dinner and made his way into the kitchen with offers of help and usefulness. Melissa suggested that he help the girls set the table, a task he undertook most willingly by immediately relieving Celestria of a tray she was carrying.

"We'll set for five," Cassandra told them, "my father likes to have dinner with us when he can; he says he sleeps better after that."

Remembering Fergus's comments on Celestria's name Nicholas was not entirely happy with this news and wondered if somebody ought to warn her. Realising it was hardly his place to do so he contented himself with mentioning: "he's not very well, you know."

"Yes, Cassandra told me; it's very sad, but I hear there's some hope of his being received into the Church before he dies. Oh dear! You may find that strange. I must remember that I can't always talk about such things now. I don't know….."

But Nicholas was looking at her with rapt attention. "Please go on," he said. "Did Cassandra not tell you anything about me?" Celestria shook her head.

"No; and I didn't like to ask."

Cassandra, who was continuing with the table setting while the other two were rooted to the spot and clearly too interested in each other to engage in mundane tasks, broke in with "I'm afraid I was far too involved with explaining, well trying to explain, my somewhat unorthodox parents to Celestria; I do apologise. Nicholas was at Ampleforth, Celestria, and it hasn't put him off the faith; quite the reverse, in fact."

"Thank you, Cassandra; very well put!" Nicholas was genuinely grateful.

Celestria's expression changed from anxiety to glowing happiness. "Oh, I'm so glad; I've often heard that Amplefordians keep their faith better than many people from Catholic schools. Of course I was in a Benedictine house myself."

"But you've left it!" a voice growled from the doorway. Nobody had noticed Fergus, who had in fact been there long enough to hear himself described as an 'unorthodox parent' and had remained quiet and attentive to hear what else might be said. There was a shocked silence. The heightened atmosphere engendered by the young people's apprehension of each other was shattered.

"And a bloody good thing too!" Fergus continued.

"Now Pa, you really are being tiresome---and rude."

"I only said 'bloody'," Fergus objected, "I'm usually a lot worse. Anyway, I meant it. What's a pretty young girl doing incarcerated with a lot of crabbed old maids?" He made his way over to Celestria and shook her by the hand. "How do you do, my dear. I'm very glad to see you here, anyway. I'd no idea you'd be so attractive. But Cassandra will tell you I'm impossible and my dear wife will probably put it rather more strongly. Can I sit down?"

Nicholas hastened to draw out a chair for him and received a growl of thanks delivered without the look of animosity Fergus generally tended to direct towards him. Dinner proceeded more smoothly and amicably than anybody other than Fergus could have hoped. Melissa and Cassandra were afraid he would be unpleasant to Celestria and embarrassingly intrusive. Nicholas shared their misgivings and was prepared to encounter hostility towards himself. Celestria was hardly surprised at the attitude already expressed about her vocation, she had encountered similar reactions before embarking on it, but she was very fearful of being asked to explain her departure from the Order. Fergus, however, fulfilled none of these fears. He merely asked Celestria whether she'd been to Oxford before and expressed the hope that she was comfortable in the house before relapsing into silence and contenting himself with enjoying his food and observing the others. He had not failed to notice that Nicholas and Celestria seemed absorbed in each other and was delighted to think that this portended the safe reestablishment of Robert Taylor as his daughter's accepted admirer.

42

During the following week Nicholas and Celestria became increasingly inseparable. They were kind enough to invite Cassandra on their tour of Oxford but she professed herself too busy with her pottery. The girls did manage to spend part of one day having lunch together in Woodstock and combing the charity shops there and in Kidlington with considerable success. Celestria was an easy size to fit and she found some bargain clothes in which she looked prettier than ever. Cassandra thought Nicholas was probably beyond any critical appraisal of her wardrobe but he could hardly fail to notice how her glowing beauty was enhanced not only by judicious dressing but by her pleasure in achieving this with so little expenditure and so much benefit to charities. Cassandra was almost equally happy. Shopping with another girl was a rare treat for her and she was able to regard Celestria's successes as if they had been her own. Envy was alien to her nature. Being an only child she had consciously missed the benefit of sharing and always rejoiced when she found an opportunity for it. Celestria was also sisterless, though she had a brother a good deal older than herself. "Oh it *is* such fun shopping with you Cassandra; I can't thank you enough for spending so much time with me," she said appreciatively.

One very pleasant evening was spent when Nicholas suggested going to a flute and harpsichord concert in the Holywell Music Room. Celestria insisted that Cassandra come with them and Cassandra insisted that Robert come too. He accepted with alacrity and found that he liked Nicholas a good deal better as the accepted escort of Celestria than he ever had before. Even his pedigree seemed less daunting. They were all very equally educated and Robert felt that his years in an Oxford College and even his age were an advantage rather than a liability. After the concert they all went to his favourite Chinese restaurant and discussed music and talked and laughed until almost midnight. Nicholas drank very little but the others all had enough to keep the conversation flowing without fatigue and Robert became sufficiently bold to comment on Celestria's charm and enthusiasm and normality…..though not in quite those words.

"Of course I knew Cassandra would have a very nice friend," he said, "but I must admit I was a little scared before I saw you. I've never met an ex-nun before; come to that I don't think I've ever met a nun at all! It is rather a disadvantage being brought up a Protestant!"

"Never mind, Robert," Cassandra consoled him, "you can make up for it now. Come and have supper with us tomorrow."

"Thank you; I'd love to. I'm only sorry not to be going back to Huntsfield with you all now. I have enjoyed this evening, but it seems strange not to be driving Cassandra home."

"At least it's meant you could be less inhibited about your alcohol intake," Cassandra laughed. "But I'll tell you what; one evening we can all go out and *you* can drive and then Nicholas can have a turn at drinking more than two small glasses of wine!"

Nicholas laughed. "Don't worry about me; I have more than that whenever I dine at Huntsfield. Your mother's so generous. I'm glad Robert's had a turn for a change. After all, he'll have to drive back to Oxford after dinner tomorrow."

A kind of pattern became established. During the day Nicholas and Celestria were together, sometimes merely walking round the grounds of Huntsfield talking to each other, but often going out into Oxford or the surrounding towns and countryside. They had neither of them explored the Cotswolds before and were very ready to admit that they greatly excelled the environs of Cambridge. "Not," Nicholas added, "that one spends a lot of time going round the countryside as a student; no car, for one thing, and no time for another." Nevertheless their having both been at Cambridge formed another bond between them.

Robert and Cassandra were both at work during the day but very often joined the others in the evening. They went to concerts, to plays, to films, and Cassandra found she was in fact enjoying Robert's company more than ever. He himself felt more alive and youthful than he had for years.

"You've done me so much good," he remarked to Nicholas and Celestria one evening over a meal they were all having together after a particularly good film. "I realise I was getting into a donnish, middle-aged---prematurely middle-aged---rut. Cassandra said we ought to go to things like concerts and she was quite right." He looked at her a little quizzically. "No wonder you were getting bored with me!"

"I wasn't really," she averred, "but I do enjoy these foursomes. We're rather isolated at Huntsfield and of course we've been very occupied just with making a living and getting the place organised. It's refreshing to go out with other people and there's always something of interest on in Oxford. We could even go to London to a play or an opera, couldn't we? The buses go all day and all night and make it very easy."

Cassandra had found that she had no difficulty in accepting the fact that Nicholas and Celestria had bonded from their first meeting. Greatly though she admired Nicholas she had not known him long enough or closely enough to feel emotionally attached to him. She had only felt a little deprived of Celestria's company, though she could not have afforded very much time to spend with her. Pete was an excellent assistant but could not be left to work on his own too often. She was, moreover, so delighted at her friend's obvious happiness that she could not wish for things to be any different. They did manage to spend another day shopping together, at sales and charity shops in Oxford, and talking in the car on the way home. Celestria had easily been persuaded to prolong her stay and she had become increasingly relaxed and confident. During their companionable car journey she even began to talk about the convent, a topic Cassandra found most interesting but would never have broached herself.

"I'm so happy here," Celestria began, "I don't think I've ever been happier. It's not as if I was miserable in the monastery---we call it that but I know everybody thinks monasteries are only for men, so we don't use it so much outside. No, I was contented there. I never intended to leave it. But I was told I had to."

"But why? Who by?" Cassandra could hardly believe anybody like Celestria could have been expelled from a convent, or anywhere else.

"Oh, not by anybody there; not by a human being. I was praying one morning at mass and very devoutly asking for the grace to work up to my final vows in the most suitable way when a voice in my head cut into what I was saying mentally and said 'You can't stay to take your final vows. You must leave and go out into the world again.' I was completely shocked. It was totally at odds with my own feelings and the prayers I'd been saying. I sat up and stared all round me. I was asked if I was ill. I could only shake my head. I felt I couldn't speak. As soon as it was possible I went to see the abbess and told her what had happened. I was afraid she would dismiss it as a delusion but she was very measured and sympathetic. She only told me to take a little time to think about it. I spent some days trying to act as if all was as it had been but found I was continually preoccupied and unable to concentrate on anything else. After a week I went back to the abbess and told her I had to go. It took a little arranging, of course, and my parents had to be contacted. I'm really grateful that the monastery made no difficulties about it."

"You must have been a model nun for them to know your motivation could be trusted."

"I don't know about that; perhaps they felt my continued presence might be disruptive. It must have been clear to see that I was no longer as I had been."

"I'm grateful that you've told me about it. Thank you for your confidence."

"I haven't told anybody else, except Nicholas of course. You know about his vocation; he said he'd confided in you."

Cassandra smiled. "I know what he *thought* his vocation *was,* but something tells me he's found a different one!"

Celestria smiled in her turn. "I won't deny it, however premature it may seem. Nicholas says it's obvious we're to marry and that that must be why I was told to come out of the Order. He thinks that's why he was inspired to come to Oxford to consider his own vocation. Otherwise we wouldn't have met."

"It's wonderful. It makes me think of pictures I've seen of St Joachim and St Anne with an angel hovering above them and joining them together."

"Oh Cassandra!" Celestria was quite shocked. "The parents of Our Lady! You shouldn't say such things!"

"Well surely it can happen even to lesser mortals, though not with quite the same results. Maybe a pope among the progeny, or a saint or two. It used to be said that marriages are made in heaven, but I can't say I've seen many that would make me believe it. I think yours might, though."

Melissa greeted the girls on their return and remarked that they must have done some very successful shopping as they both looked so glowing. In fact even Cassandra had forgotten about such mundane considerations and their purchases had to be retrieved from the car to be duly admired by her mother, who swiftly deduced that there must be some other cause for joy. She said nothing but watched for clues. The following morning two letters arrived for Celestria. One was from Yorkshire, "That'll be from her mother" Melissa deduced. The other was from Staffordshire. Melissa pondered on that one and concluded that it might be something to do with Nicholas as she knew he came from an old recusant family and there were a number of those in the Staffordshire area. She was right, of course. She handed the letters to Celestria when she and Nicholas came in from a day in the Cotswolds and they exclaimed simultaneously: "That's from my mother!" which made them both laugh. Melissa offered them a cup of tea and they sat down at the kitchen table.

"I don't know which one to open first," said Celestria. "Oh, perhaps the one from my mother and save the other till second because it's special. Though I don't know what my mother can have to say---apart from warning me not to overstay my welcome. Yes, I thought so. My poor mother; I'm afraid she doesn't quite know what to do with a failed nun."

"You mustn't think of yourself in that way!" Nicholas was quick to defend her.

"As a matter of fact I don't. I was meant to have just the time I did have in the monastery. It's my mother who sees it as failure. She wasn't pleased when I went in, but she seems even less pleased that I've come out. It must be very difficult for her."

"I think I know what's in *my* mother's letter and I'm glad you're reading it second." Nicholas looked beamingly pleased. Celestria opened the envelope.

"Oh how lovely! It's an invitation to stay! How *very* kind of her to ask me---and so promptly."

Cassandra came in from the workshop and was immediately told the news.

"Well I'm glad for you, Celestria; from what Nicholas has said about his family I'm sure you'll have a very happy time, but I hope you're not going too soon. I haven't seen enough of you yet."

"We could go at the end of next week, if that's all right with you, Mrs Marjoribanks," said Nicholas, deferring to Melissa.

"Certainly, my dears; and I may say I'm delighted at your very suitable and thoughtful manners. Nowadays one hears of a young man plus girlfriend simply turning up at his parents' house not merely with no warning but with no invitation from his mother. I do consider that very bad form."

Cassandra smiled ."I'm sure bad form is something of which you could never accuse Nicholas, Mummy, or Celestria either."

"No, indeed; but as we'll be preparing for the 'colonials' just when they're going to be away I'm afraid we might see rather a contrast."

"Oh dear! I'd forgotten. Well at least we'll be kept busy and not have too much time to miss them; otherwise it might be very sad."

Nicholas and Celestria smiled appreciatively at the compliment and Celestria said "Oh, but I'll miss you, too, especially as I'll have to go back to my parents' house afterwards, I suppose. Of course I'll ask my mother if Nicholas can come and stay there for a day or two."

"I've got an idea!" Cassandra suddenly exclaimed. "You know you told me you wanted to earn and not be dependent, Celestria?"

"Yes, that's very true."

"Why don't you spend this coming week finding a job in or near Oxford and then come back and stay here until, well, until you don't need it any more?"

"Oh that's a *brilliant* idea! I don't mind what I do; working in a shop or anything. Even being a cleaner. Standards of cleaning are very high in women's monasteries and I'm well used to it. But are you sure you'll have room for me? I'd have to pay, of course; I wouldn't consider it otherwise."

"We'll *make* room," Melissa spoke firmly. "There's *loads* of space in this house and the new bathroom down here takes the pressure off the upstairs ones. And of course we wouldn't be quite able to get another room up to paying-guest standard immediately so it would have to be much less expensive."

Nicholas was not quite so happy at the idea of Celestria working as a cleaner but was delighted at the thought that she would be able to stay in Oxfordshire while he continued with his sabbatical.

"I'm sure you'll be able to find something more suitable than cleaning," Nicholas protested, "and it would be wonderful to have you stay here. I couldn't bear the idea of you languishing in the wilds of Yorkshire for six months."

"Six months?" asked Melissa.

Nicholas looked a little sheepish. "Well, however long it takes, um, needs, um well maybe until I've finished my sabbatical."

Cassandra realised that he was thinking of six months ahead as the earliest possible marriage date but was not quite ready to announce that to her mother.

"It's not so *very* wild in Yorkshire," Celestria murmured.

"It sounds rather wild where you live," Nicholas countered.

Celestria sighed slightly. "I must admit it has been let go a bit, and there's almost no heating in the house. Not that there was much in the monastery, come to that, but I'd certainly much prefer to stay here."

"I think we ought to have a drink to that, and it's after six o'clock!" Melissa disappeared in the direction of the cellar while the others exchanged smiles of quiet amusement.

43

Samson Southey sat beside Robert at a rather sparsely attended dinner in college. Dons who were married or who merely had their own houses in Oxford tended to dine at home on ordinary evenings. Samson, however, was not vastly domesticated and preferred eating in college. He generally taught until just before dinner time, following the long-standing tradition of enjoying a glass of sherry with his pupils during the six o'clock tutorial.

"It was interesting to meet your ex-nun friend after mass on Sunday, Robert; a very pleasant and intelligent young woman, I thought. And how very sensible of Muriel to come again."

"Sensible?"

"Indeed. One can be more able to talk to people one expects to see there than in a college common room."

"She seemed to spend a good deal of time talking to Cassandra's mother; of course she wouldn't often see her in a common room. And she talked to you, too, Samson."

"Very true. You four young people---I suppose I must include you, Robert---spent most of the time talking to each other. You doubtless find the advent of the ex-nun a considerable advantage."

"Yes; it's been very pleasant for us all to go out together. Cassandra's been very happy going to concerts and films and so on. I've realised I was rather stuck in a donnish sort of life with too few outside interests. I don't really socialise much with couples, like the married people in college, though they or English Faculty colleagues occasionally ask me to dinner."

"Probably for you to meet some young woman they hope you might take an interest in, and therefore much less likely to invite you with your own young woman friend in tow."

"There usually are equal numbers of men and women, certainly, but they're all ages. Oh, hullo, Muriel."

Muriel brought her soup to the table and sat in the chair opposite Robert. "Robert! How unusual to see you at college dinner."

"Oh, I had to teach till seven. I've put off one or two tutorials lately and had to make up."

Robert racked his brains for some neutral conversational gambit. Since Melissa's revelation of Muriel's interest in him he had found her company a source of unease. Previously he would have been sufficiently unaware of her to say nothing at all without being conscious of any defect in his behaviour. Now he became somewhat self-conscious in her presence and felt it incumbent on him to take notice of her.

"Did you find it interesting to meet an ex-nun on Sunday?" he asked her. "I'd never met one before and I don't suppose you had."

"Really Robert! Have you never realised or merely forgotten that our Theologian colleague is an ex-nun?"

"Oh Lord! I never thought about it, somehow. But of course she's not....er...."

"Not an attractive young woman, I suppose you mean!" Samson finished his sentence for him.

"Like the one under discussion whom I'm sure you appreciate enormously," Muriel added.

"As, clearly, does the young man staying with the Marjoribanks," added Samson.

"Quite," said Muriel.

"They do seem made for each other," Robert agreed happily.

"Exactly," said Muriel.

Robert's extra teaching was in part due to his having arranged to take Fr D. from the Oratory to see Fergus and have lunch at Huntsfield. Melissa had lit a fire in the drawing-room and insisted on giving them coffee in there when they arrived. Fergus had been inclined to grumble and say he preferred the informality of the kitchen.

"Certainly not," Melissa had objected, "I can't possibly have you in there while I'm getting lunch."

"Well, what's wrong with my bedroom, come to that?"

"Practically everything. But don't worry, we'll put the oxygen discretely in the drawing-room. I'm sure Robert will see that everything goes smoothly, since you refuse to have Cassandra with you."

In the event Fergus, warmed by the fire, was more benign than might have been expected. After the usual pleasantries he started proceedings by holding up his dog-eared copy of the 50p Catechism and stating proudly: "You can see I've read it!"

"I certainly can," said Fr D. "Good work."

Fergus didn't deem it necessary to add that he'd in fact lost it for a day or two and discovered eventually that it was in his bed, which had more to do with its present state than constant reading.

"And how do you feel about the contents?" Fr D. continued.

"Absolutely fine."

"Do you believe all the articles of faith?" Fr D. went on to mention the important ones in detail. Fergus merely nodded at each of them.

"You do believe them?" Fr D. was a little anxious, not to say incredulous.

"I accept them," said Fergus. He took a sip of coffee and began to cough. The coughing was prolonged. His face took on an alarming shade of blue. Robert got hold of the oxygen and put the mask over his face. Still racked with coughing Fergus gasped the gas in and something like a normal colour returned, but he regained his breath with difficulty.

Father D. looked seriously alarmed. He could see considerable deterioration since their last meeting.

Fergus looked at him appealingly and managed to say: "Can't you let me in now, Father? You know, get it over with."

Fr D. winced slightly at the inappropriate language but supposed one must make allowances. If he were to require a more reverent attitude or wait until Fergus was unable to speak at all it might be too late. "Yes, I think I can," he said. "Would you like your wife and daughter to come in? It is a solemn occasion, you know."

"I'll fetch them." Robert left the room in search of Melissa and Cassandra. They returned with haste and some trepidation, Cassandra apologising for the clay on her clothes and Melissa asking if anything were needed. Fr D. said no, everything was in his bag, including a small phial of holy water from the Jordan. "I'd better do a conditional rebaptism," he said, "just in case."

Melissa sensibly gave Fergus another whiff of oxygen to help him through the proceedings.

Fr D. kissed the small cross embroidered on a long, narrow band of heavy silk, which he then suspended from his neck. Fergus looked puzzled.

"This is a stole. Priests wear one when administering a sacrament." He opened the phial of holy water, held it over Fergus's head and said: "If you have not been baptised I baptise you in the name of the Father and of the Son and of the Holy Spirit." The words were accompanied with the delicate pouring of three small spurts of water. Fergus was then anointed with holy oil. He was asked whether he repented of his sins---in case, as Fr D. paused to explain, he had already been baptised as a child and his sins were thus not washed away by the conditional rebaptism.

"I certainly do," Fergus replied, "all of them."

Fr D. gave him Holy Communion. The others knelt.

"Bread of heaven," said Fergus, "I always liked that hymn. I can die happy now."

Cassandra found herself dripping tears, looked in vain for a tissue and wiped her eyes on her clay-covered sleeve. Melissa, rather to her surprise, found her mouth trembling and her eyes wet. Robert felt profoundly moved in a way he had never before experienced.

Fr D. put away his stole and other apurtenances while the others remained kneeling, until Melissa rose to her feet and announced, predictably: "Well, this definitely calls for a celebration. Fortunately I've already got the glasses out, but I think an extra special bottle might be in order."

Robert gave Fergus another whiff of oxygen, Cassandra disappeared to wash and change, Melissa, in a very short time, brought in nibbles, an already opened bottle of wine and a dusty, cobwebby, 'very special one', which she invited Robert to open so that it could breathe a little while they drank the first one.

"Like the wedding at Cana," she said, "we'll keep the best till last!"

Before Cassandra came downstairs again Nicholas and Celestria appeared, looking guardedly through the open door of the drawing-room and apologising if they were intruding. Melissa welcomed them with almost fervent enthusiasm, seconded by Fergus himself, as they were told of his somewhat sudden and not entirely premeditated reception into the Church, and invited to enhance the celebration with their presence. Celestria embraced him and kissed him on both cheeks and Nicholas shook him warmly by the hand.

"Thank you," said Fergus. "Thank you all. I'm beginning to feel I really belong. It's a good feeling. I'm very happy."

Lunch was a jubilant occasion even though Fergus went to his room after the first course. Robert would have liked to spend the whole day at Huntsfield but had to take Fr D. to the Oratory and go to a meeting in college himself. During the drive back he found himself asking Father about the usual course of instruction in the faith and booking himself in. "I can't be the only one left out in the cold now that Fergus has stolen a march on me," he said.

"Let's hope, however, that your own reception is less sudden and dramatic!"

"Do you have many like that?"

"Perhaps a surprising number of death-bed ones, but often a week or two before the actual death. Of course that might be the case here; a number of people rally after being received, or even after receiving the last rites. The Provost tells a story about a woman patient in a mental hospital who was given the last rites seven times, and then eventually died without them."

***

College dinner was fairly full as it took place almost directly after the meeting. Robert was very eager to tell Samson about the lunch time events at Huntsfield. Muriel Thwaites, who seemed these days to sit near them more often than before, was within earshot. Robert had previously remarked to Samson on Muriel's frequent propinquity, but Samson had replied that nothing had changed apart from the fact that Robert now noticed it. Robert sighed, but when Muriel showed considerable interest in his narrative he was not unwilling to include her in the conversation. He felt he'd witnessed an event of such moment that he wanted to share it.

"They really are impressive, these priests at the Oratory. Fr D.'s probably younger than I am and yet he's so able to deal with people of all ages and he's got such a sane and almost matter-of-fact attitude to death. I do admire him."

"In his calling he must come across death not infrequently," Muriel remarked, "but it's not something people of our age and kind of occupation have a lot to do with these days. If we do it's all rather remote and sanitised and limited to funerals and memorial services. We don't have wakes round open coffins any more."

"I gather, however," Samson put in, "that death bed scenes are coming back into vogue with assisted suicides. They can be reliably planned beforehand and family and friends invited to attend. It does sound rather civilised. But of course one does have to go abroad and that must add to the expense. Still, I suppose it's possible to save on the funeral; those who've been present at the death probably won't feel the need to go again, especially if it's in a different country."

"I wonder," Robert pondered, "if it ever happens that the dying person gets into a panic at the last minute and wants the process reversed?"

"Even if they only called it off minutes before the injection, or whatever, was due it could be decidedly embarrassing," Muriel contributed. "Almost as bad as bilking at the altar! And speaking of weddings---."

"Please don't speak of Nigel's," Robert begged, "I can't face thinking about it at the moment. But I'm rather hoping to be invited to a much more suitable one in the not too distant future."

"More suitable in what way?" Muriel had a shrewd idea but wanted to hear more about it.

"Cassandra says it's a marriage made in heaven. Not that they've even announced it yet, but it's clearly a sure thing. Somehow it's a much more attractive prospect than a mere coupling accompanied by a display of expensive food and drink."

"I'm not sure that 'coupling' is quite the right word in the context, Robert."

"Oh Samson, you know what I mean."

"There was some rather special drink produced at the marriage at Cana," said Samson.

"True," replied Robert, "but apparently not expensive. I can't imagine they were charged for it."

Amid the general laughter Muriel said drily: "Congratulations Robert! It's not often anybody gets the last word when conversing with Samson!"

44

Nicholas and Celestria, with occasional comments from Melissa, were poring over the 'situations vacant' advertisements in the Oxford Times and The Lady.

"Though I see," Melissa remarked with disapproval, "the newspaper heading merely says 'jobs'. It's probably too much to expect that everybody can read a four syllable word these days."

"Look! Here's a job for 'cleaners to clean student rooms and bathrooms' in an Oxford college. 'The rate of pay is £6.46 an hour increasing to £6.63 after the NVQ qualification is obtained.' What on earth is an NVQ qualification?" Celestria was puzzled.

"From what I've seen of people working in most public places I should think 'not very quick' might be the answer," was Melissa's rejoinder. "But that's not a vast amount of pay for cleaning student rooms; it must be a ghastly job."

"I quite agree, and I can't bear to think of you doing it," said Nicholas.

"Perhaps it's the best way to get an NVQ," Celestria murmured "it seems to be rather necessary for lots of jobs, and I really wouldn't mind working in a college."

"No doubt you could offer it up as a mortification," was Melissa's comment, "but believe me life provides quite enough of those without our encountering them deliberately. Let's have another look at The Lady."

"This looks better," Nicholas sounded more hopeful, " 'carer wanted for retired surgeon, Oxford city, to prepare light lunch, companionship and some personal care.' I wonder how one prepares companionship?"

"That sounds really pleasant, apart from the style of writing, but how would I get into Oxford and back every day?"
"One of us could drive you to Woodstock to get a bus, or you could get a train or a bus from Tackley."
"I couldn't think of putting you to so much trouble. And there'd be getting back as well. You know, actually, there are quite a few live in jobs; perhaps that would be best. I ought to be independent and it would solve the whole travelling and accommodation thing. Look, what about this one: 'Friendly manor house, Oxfordshire, needs carer/housekeeper/cook for three elderly people. Full board and lodging, £5,200 pa' ."
"Nice to know the house is friendly, of course, and very important; but what about the people? And to be all those things for all three of them for £5,200 a year!" Melissa was not impressed.
"How much is that a week? Oh, £100 of course. That seems quite a lot just to spend on oneself without any other bills. I might try for that."
"What do you think this means?" Nicholas sounded genuinely puzzled. " 'Highly experienced and proactive full time housekeeper with old fashioned values needed in large formal house near Oxford. Team player and dog lover essential.' I thought 'proactive' had something to do with medicines; and do you suppose they run a cricket team? Or maybe football?"
Celestria laughed. "I'm happy with the old fashioned values---though it might depend how old fashioned. They weren't great in the eighteenth century. But I draw the line at team games!"
"I have heard of households where the menservants were expected to be useful in the lord of the manor's cricket team," Melissa commented, "but I wouldn't have thought

that extended to housekeepers! It might be interesting to find out more about it. Oh but here's a good one, 'nanny for five year old son non-smoker', heavens! That must be the child's only recommendation. One wonders how many nannies he's gone through already. Of course some children are absolute monsters; and who knows? He could even start smoking at any time!"

"I don't think I've had enough experience with children to be a nanny. I'm more used to elderly people. Some of the nuns were very old."

"But not sufficiently into second childhood to give you that sort of practice," Melissa suggested.

"No," Celestria agreed, "they were pretty alert mentally----and they were all non-smokers!"

Talking of smoking prompted Melissa to light a cigarette. "Strange," she said through the first spiral of smoke, "I've always heard that smoking helps guard against alzheimers!"

Eventually Celestria decided to apply to the 'friendly manor house', feeling rather doubtful about how highly experienced she was as a housekeeper and extremely doubtful about being 'proactive' as was deemed necessary in the 'large formal house'. She was given an appointment for an interview and driven there by Nicholas.

It was a large and rambling stone house, smaller than Huntsfield but covering a good deal of ground. The door was opened by a woman in her seventies with hair of an improbable shade of henna red and an accent of impeccable gentility. She led the way to a shabbily but comfortably furnished room where a woman some ten years older was sitting by a fire. It transpired that they were sisters, the younger one unmarried and the elder, Mrs Colman, with a husband, who also lived in the house but was less able to get about and sometimes needed help in moving from room to room.

Celestria asked how many hours of work would be expected and whether there was any other domestic help, since caring, cooking and housekeeping might be enough for one person in a house of such a size. They were told that a woman came in from the village to clean twice a week and that a gardener/chauffeur/handyman was also employed.

The elder sister looked piercingly at Celestria and asked "Why are you interested in this position? You don't sound like a domestic!" She listened attentively to the explanation, then turned to her sister and said commandingly: "Flossie! Tea!"

The younger sister rose obediently and Celestria offered to help her. This was declined both by 'Flossie' and Mrs Colman, and the latter continued to talk about the position, now apparently upgraded to that of 'companion help' on account of Celestria's accent and origins, though the duties and rates of pay remained the same.

Flossie, who was never introduced and whose surname remained unknown, returned with a rather dangerously unsteady trolley supporting a large tea-pot, milk, sugar, cups and biscuits. Nicholas and Celestria hastened to help rather than be waited on as Mrs Colman looked on approvingly and Flossie hovered about in a fluster of indecision as to whether they should be treated as visitors or domestics. Eventually she was given a little guidance on being commanded to show Celestria her proposed room in what "used to be the servants' quarters; different now, of course." Nicholas went too. He stood aghast at the sight of a very cold room, floored with aged linoleum, containing a bedstead of the kind usual in the more spartan boarding school dormitory, an upright chair, a chest of drawers with a mottled mirror hanging above it, and a washbasin.

"What about a wardrobe?" Nicholas asked.

"There's a chest of drawers," Flossie spoke as if that was surely adequate.

Celestria smiled. "I'm not used to luxury, Nicholas!"

Nicholas looked worried. "Where's the bathroom?" he asked.

Flossie looked triumphant: "It's very near!" she said proudly and led the way down a corridor. "Here!" She flung open a door at the end. "Bathroom!"

It was indeed a bathroom; a small narrow room with a bath in it and nothing else.

"What about a lavatory?" Celestria, reconciled to lack of luxury, did want to be reassured about necessities.

"Ah!" said Flossie. "You might as well see the kitchen while you're here."

Her hearers were somewhat at a loss as to the relevance of this statement especially as they were taken downstairs, along a corridor, through a maze of rooms described briefly in passing as "the scullery; the pantry; the larder; the kitchen" until they finally arrived at a door in a kind of lean-to along from the kitchen. This at last was the lavatory!

Nicholas and Celestria looked at each other and began to laugh.

"It wouldn't do to need to come here in the middle of the night!" Celestria giggled. Flossie regarded her with stiff disapproval. "You have a chamber-pot in your room, of course. But you'd better see the kitchen."

The kitchen, though dark with high windows, originally to prevent the servants from seeing out of them, was large and warm.

"Oh! an aga!" said Celestria. "I suppose it's run on coal."

"Yes. Richard sees to it."

"He's the handyman, then?" Nicholas queried.

"The chauffeur/gardener," Flossie replied a little haughtily. "But he does seem to like working in the house."

The upshot of the interview, if it could be so called, was that Celestria, despite Nicholas's pleas to think about it, agreed to take the position on a three months' trial basis. At Huntsfield they regaled Cassandra and Melissa with details of the visit. Cassandra was amused and Melissa rather aghast.

"Well," she said, "at least we can lend you some bits and pieces of furniture to make your room more comfortable; we may not be allowed to get rid of anything but there's no harm in lending."

Nicholas was full of gratitude and eagerly offered to help while Celestria protested that it really wasn't necessary and after all she was used to living in a cell in a nineteenth century building, which was listed for its architecture rather than for any pretensions to comfort. "Anyway," she concluded, " it sounds as if I'll be too busy to be in my room very much!"

Nicholas switched his mind with some difficulty from Celestria and her proposed employment and remembered to ask Melissa how Fergus was.

"He's been sleeping a good deal, but he does seem to have rallied a little. He wants to have supper with us all. He says he'll miss you when you go away. I won't have the courage to tell him Celestria's taking a live-in job! But before you go I'd like to ask the Oxford Marjoribankses to come and have a drink and celebrate Fergus's reception; I'm going to ask Jasper, too."

"How is Jasper, Ma? You've been very quiet about him lately."

"I have seen him in London, but his coming here did rather upset your father and I didn't want to be responsible for him dying of apoplexy or some related onset any sooner than necessary. But I think it should be safe enough if Jasper's diluted by some other relatives, and he can probably stay with them as well. Would you like Stephen to be invited too?"

"No, not specially. He could come if he were here anyway, of course, but not otherwise. He's asked me to a party at his house in London but I don't think I'll go; if all his friends seem as young as he does I can't imagine I'd enjoy it much."

Celestria and Nicholas were hardly included in this conversation but as, after polite thanks for including them in the drinks party, they were entirely occupied in talking to each other about their visits to their respective mothers and Celestria's subsequent residence in the 'friendly manor house', they were perfectly comfortable.

Cassandra returned to the shed to find Pete in a more than usually talkative mood.

"That young lady your friend and the lodger, they go out together a lot, don't they?" he commented.

"Yes, they really enjoy each other's company."

"He's got a very nice car, o'course; wouldn't you like to go out in it, Miss?"

"Well I have been out in it, Pete, and it's certainly a lot more comfortable and reliable than ours!"

"Yeah, but, don't you mind, like?"

"Well I would like a better car, certainly."

"I mean mind about your young friend going out with him."

"Why no, I'm really glad; I wouldn't have been able to spend anything like as much time with her myself. You know I have to keep working."

"Yeah, I s'pose so. Anyway, he's from somewhere up north, isn't he?"

"Yes, he lives in Durham."

"A long way north, is it?"

"Yes, you know, getting up towards Scotland."

"You wouldn't want to live up there, would you now?"

Cassandra laughed. "No, Pete, I don't think I would. A couple of years in deepest Devon have been enough to make me realise that I'd rather live in or near Oxford than anywhere else in the world."

45

Melissa's plans for the 'very small drinks party' to celebrate Fergus's reception into the Church were unusually successful, given the short notice. It was not a socially busy time of year and her explanation that the gathering had to happen as soon as possible because 'one never *knew'*, had the effect of deciding the invited guests to give it precedence. So Sir Felix and Lady Marjorie and Jasper were coming and Samson and of course Robert, and also Muriel Thwaites, whom Melissa had insisted on inviting despite Cassandra's slight surprise and queries as to suitability. Fr D was to come early in order to bring Holy Communion for Fergus as he was not well enough to go to church himself. He asked if he might bring the priest who served the Woodstock parish and introduce him.

"Now that was *not* my idea," Melissa told her daughter; "he'll probably expect us to go to mass at the Woodstock church and that I have no intention of doing."

"It could be a good idea if we can't get into Oxford at some time," Cassandra demurred, "and anyway he's probably in a better position to bring Holy Communion to Pa. We can't expect the Oratorians to come all this way all the time."

"I don't know why not; we always give them something to eat and drink."

"Really Mummy! I'm sure they're not desperate for either! It's not as if they're mendicant friars in the Middle Ages."

"No, they seem to live rather well and people often invite them out for good dinners. I saw one at Hartwell House one evening. I suppose you're right, we can't quite come up to that. Oh well, men always enjoy mousetraps."

"Shall I ask Pete if he'd like to come and help hand things round? He was awfully good at the pot sale. But of course he was involved in that because his pots were in it."

"That's an excellent idea; it'll save me getting him his tea."

"Perhaps we could stretch to a couple of jam doughnuts as a special treat."

***

Fergus professed himself well enough to join the drinks party after he had received Holy Communion and had a short rest and a good sniff of oxygen.

"I've been much better in the last few days," he stated happily, "I feel almost well sometimes."

Robert and Cassandra helped him deal with the oxygen mask but he waved his daughter away saying "No, no, you go and deal with the mousetraps, Robert can look after me, I'm less important!"

"Don't be so modest, Pa; after all it's your party!" But she left him to go into the drawing room with Robert. It was a little odd because he had in fact met hardly any of the people present at any time before, though Jasper and Sir Felix were actually relatives and he knew Samson Southey by name. Melissa introduced Muriel as Dr Thwaites.

"'Dr' eh?" said Fergus. "What sort of a doctor?"

"Only a philosophical one, I'm afraid," Muriel replied self deprecatingly.

"Hm. Not a bad thing to be philosophical; most of us need to be much of the time." He turned to glare at Jasper but remembered that he'd just received Holy Communion and ought to be in charity with all his fellow men. Besides, he thought to himself magnanimously, she'll need somebody to look after her when I'm gone. And on the whole he couldn't help deciding that Jasper actually looked like rather a nice chap. "Well of course," he said aloud, "Melissa would have good taste."

"Thank you, Fergus; I appreciate the kind compliment, though it's more than I might always give myself credit for!"

The sharp edge of this was perceived by Samson, who smiled distantly, but to the rest of the company it passed as a polite exchange. Melissa urged Fergus to sit down but he said he'd stand as long as he could so that he'd feel 'part of the party and not miss out on the mousetraps'. Cassandra came in bearing these, with Pete and bottles in her wake. Glasses were topped up, the plate of mousetraps emptied with speed, more food followed, Fergus managed to greet and speak to everybody and receive their congratulations. Muriel was a little nonplussed as she had never attended such a celebration before. Sir Felix and Jasper each handed Fergus a card, which he opened with enthusiasm. One read: 'Congratulations on your First Holy Communion'

"I know it's not entirely apt," said Sir Felix, "but I couldn't find a better one."

"Thank you; I like it," Fergus eyed it gratefully. It had a picture of the Sacred Host hovering above a chalice. "Look!" He showed it round and Cassandra put it on the chimney piece.

"It's better than the one I saw," she remarked, "it said 'congratulations on your graduation', I did think of getting it but the cap and gown on it didn't look right."

The card from Jasper read: 'Congratulations on your reception into the Church' and showed the kneeling figure of a young man with a priest laying hands on his head.

"Oh I like this one, too," Fergus was genuinely appreciative, "especially as the chap looks so young!"

"That's an excellent card, Jasper," said Lady Marjorie, "I've never seen one like it. Where did you get it?"

"In Westminster Cathedral, actually; apparently there's quite a lot of call for them these days."

"How very encouraging!" said his sister-in-law with satisfaction.

Fergus continued to go round the assembled company following the supplies of food and drink, but Cassandra noticed that he was beginning to flag and begged him to sit down.

"I do feel a tiredness coming over me," he replied gratefully, "but I'll go and lie down briefly if nobody minds. I'd rather do that. But you must get me up before people go; I'll want to say 'goodbye and thank you for coming'. Don't forget, now." Robert would have gone with him but he insisted on going alone.

"It's not as if I have to go upstairs now, thanks to my ground floor room."

He left the room slowly but clearly happily and the party continued. Father D. made a point of speaking to Muriel and asking about her subject and position in College. She responded by inviting him to a College dinner. Nicholas and Celestria enjoyed talking to Samson and Jasper felt freer to speak to Melissa now that her husband was out of the room, but she made a point of including Lady Marjorie in their conversation while Cassandra looked after Sir Felix and the priest from Woodstock, whom they had not met before and whom Melissa had mentally dismissed as well meaning and uninspiring. He and Sir Felix appeared to get on very well as they conversed about the game on the Blenheim estate and the standard of the shoots held there.

Eventually, when people had refused any more drinks and the second and third lot of mousetraps had disappeared Melissa decided to bring Fergus back, as she mentioned to all and sundry.

"Then perhaps we could just drink a toast to him ---a very tiny one!"

Shc was out of the room a little longer than might have been expected and came back alone looking pale and less festive. Into the gradual silence which greeted her entrance she said: "I'm afraid he's gone!"

Sir Felix, who had wrenched his mind with some difficulty from the description of a particularly successful day's shooting, asked: "Gone? Where?"

Melissa turned to him with the kindest of smiles, which showed no hint of her very private opinion the he was not the most intelligent member of the Marjoribanks family, and answered, "Well, I wouldn't have said so until very recently but in view of the reason for this evening's celebration I think we might venture to suggest Purgatory. What do you think, Father?" She addressed Fr D., who looked a little perplexed at an attitude he found outside his previous experience of the reactions of sudden widows.

"I think we ought to check."

Sir Felix stared "Check on Purgatory?" he queried.

"I'm afraid that's beyond our scope," Fr D began to recover his poise, "I mean check that he really has, er, gone."

"Oh please do!" Melissa was grateful. "You must be much more used to this sort of situation than I am." She led him and the priest from Woodstock to Fergus's room and left them there.

Celestria and Cassandra, with admirable presence of mind, went into the kitchen to make some coffee. Melissa returned to the drawing room and found that she was a little weak at the knees and needed to sit down. Robert poured her another drink. "At least you don't need to drive anywhere," he said, feeling that anything more to the point would be misplaced, not to say totally inadequate. He disappeared for a moment and came back with Melissa's cigarettes and an ashtray. "Go on," he urged as she hesitated, "nobody can possibly mind. You've had a shock."

"Oh Robert, thank you. I *am* grateful,"

Nicholas went into the kitchen to help Celestria with the coffee and tell Cassandra to go and sit with her mother. Pete, at the back of the kitchen feeding Treasure with the odd biscuit, (she'd already had some mousetraps and was pining for more), realised that something had happened. He was a little in awe of 'the posh guest and the young lady' as he described Nicholas and Celestria to himself, and decided to do some investigating rather than ask them. He went into the passageway in time to see the priests emerging from Fergus's room and hear them discussing the necessity of getting a doctor to sign the death certificate. They stopped when they saw him.

"Passed away then has he?" said Pete.

"He has indeed," Fr D. replied, " and a very good death, too."

Pete was puzzled. It was the first time he'd heard death described as 'good' in any way. He followed them to the drawing room and stood at the open door to listen while they elaborated on this theme.

"Marvellous!" Fr D was saying, "he'd just been received into the Church a few days ago and been giving Holy Communion a couple of hours ago. Then he's died suddenly but peacefully and painlessly and fully prepared. It's rare to see such a good death."

"He seemed almost to be getting better the last few days," Cassandra said in some surprise.

"That is very typical, actually, especially with cancer. I've seen it so often I tend to take it as the beginning of the end when the almost ebullient, euphoric stage sets in." Fr

D. spoke with some authority. Muriel Thwaites heard him with interest, wondering that somebody so young, certainly younger than she was, should be so familiar with death. Samson turned to her and observed that she was probably having an evening of unique experiences.

"Yes indeed," she replied seriously. "I should be reasonably knowledgeable about Catholicism, having read so much French literature, but it has quite a different impact when experienced at first hand."

"How do you find it?"

"Impressive, but alien; disturbing perhaps. I suppose it's outside my sphere."

"Robert seems to be coping admirably."

"Yes; he seems to belong." Muriel gave a sigh, then quickly covered it and asked "What do you think we ought to do? We must be the least related of anybody here, and yet it seems unfeeling simply to go away."

"I think we finish our coffee and then ease our way out with expressions of sympathy and offers of help, however redundant."

***

It was agreed that the funeral should take place after Nicholas and Celestria had been to stay with their respective parents because, "after all," as Melissa said, "we want as good a turn out as possible and there can't be many people who'll attend, even if he did have the good sense to die in the middle of his own party."

"Besides," Cassandra added, "we ought to advertise it far and wide so that people in France know about it, and his first wife and sons."

"Oh dear, yes. I'd forgotten about them. Fergus kept in touch and had their addresses and so on but of course they've all got lost. I don't even know where his first wife's living now. I don't believe Fergus knew."

"What was her name, by the way? I can't remember hearing it."
"Alison. Not my favourite name; but then it wouldn't be, would it."
"Has she married again?"
"I don't even know that. I doubt it."
"Could we somehow publish an appeal for her to get in touch with us?"
"Perhaps we could tack it on to the death notice and she could make enquiries via the undertaker."
They were interrupted by the telephone, which Melissa answered.
"Oh how very kind," Cassandra heard her say, "Yes please do." A minute or two later she replaced the receiver and turned to her daughter, saying
" Felix and Midge are 'in the area' as she put it, and asked if they could come and see us. Isn't that kind and thoughtful."
"It's one of the advantages of having a mobile, too. I somehow hadn't associated them with anything so modern."
They arrived very shortly afterwards and sat down happily in the kitchen with a cup of tea. "We wondered if you might need any help planning the funeral," Sir Felix enquired. "You'd be very welcome to have the wake at our place if it's going to be in the Oratory; otherwise it's a bit of a trek out here."
"Well we had thought of having it in the Woodstock church because it's so much smaller and wouldn't look so sparsely attended. Besides, there's a decent sized car park in behind it. Then we could all go to the Wolvercote cemetery and back here for the wake. It is a bit of to-ing and fro-ing, certainly, but all outside town at least."

Sir Felix showed signs of wanting to take over the organising while his wife quietly intervened to let Melissa do it. All was very amicable and civilised, but also rather roundabout and time-consuming and Cassandra was glad when Robert arrived to take her out of it. They walked about the grounds in companionable silence for a time until Robert asked Cassandra how she was feeling. She had shown very little emotion.

"When I'm in the house I feel strange; I have to keep reminding myself he's not there. Then when I realise he's not there I miss him. I don't think I feel sad; he had such a good death. But of course there's been quite a lot to do. And my mother's very matter-of-fact about it, at least on the surface. It's always hard to know what she's really feeling. But perhaps we'd better go in and see how they're getting on."

They re-entered the kitchen to find the discussion still continuing; Melissa was not impervious to the benefits of the Felix Marjoribanks' kind offers of help and it had also occurred to her that that could just possibly extend to some aid with the expenses. She was saying she'd talk it all over with Cassandra before deciding, just as Cassandra and Robert came in.

"After all, darling," she said kindly to her daughter, "blood is thicker than water and he was your father; besides, you were very good to him. As far as I'm concerned it was definitely water, and most of it under the bridge at that."

"It must have been a shock, all the same, and you're coping very well, but you must let us help if we can," Lady Marjorie said sensibly.

"Thank you. I appreciate your kindness more than I can say. And it was a shock because you know, in spite of myself, I was almost beginning to like him."

Chapter 47

Melissa and Cassandra were driving to Woodstock for Fergus's funeral.

"I'm so glad we reached this compromise," Melissa was saying, "it's better to have the requiem in a small church where we won't feel the emptiness and then go on to the cemetery, which is actually on the way to the Marjoribanks'. It is good of them to have the food set up there and provide somebody to see to it all. It would have been very difficult for us to do it all ourselves."

"And very expensive to get somebody in to organise it!" Cassandra commented.

"Very true, especially out where we are. As it is people can come on to the burial and then the wake."

"Or not, if they don't want to."

"I'm glad we've got Fr D. to do the mass; it is nice of him to come out here specially."

"Well, he did receive Pa into the Church. But the Woodstock priest is assisting."

They arrived early but the coffin was already there, having been in the church over night according to Catholic practice. Four large, dark candles were burning round it.

"I suppose we have to sit in the front row," Melissa sighed, "where we won't be able to see who's behind us."

"Poor Mummy! You do find that frustrating, don't you?"

"Yes I do, and especially today when I really want to know who's here."

"You'll see when we go out; nobody's going to leave before we do."

"It's not the same. Anyway, I'm sure we can turn round and greet people before the service actually begins."

“Well I know Pete’s coming; I wanted him to give out the booklets, or whatever you call them, but he was too scared, he said.”

“Oh dear, I’d forgotten about them.”

“That’s all right, one of the undertaker’s men is going to do it. They should be here now; I’ll get a couple for us.” Cassandra brought them back to the pew. “They’re quite good, aren’t they? I suppose we needed the map of the way to Wolvercote cemetery and north Oxford on the back. There won’t be many people to use them!”

“Oh, you never know. We don’t want people wandering about lost; besides, it’s an incentive to come to the burial, isn’t it?”

Sir Felix and Lady Marjorie arrived and came to sit behind them.

“Oh, do sit in the front pew on the other side,” Melissa begged them, “we don’t want it to look empty!”

Robert came in and sat immediately behind Cassandra and Muriel and Samson arrived shortly after and sat behind the Marjoribanks, while Jasper and, to Cassandra’s surprise, Stephen, came in and joined Robert. Celestria came and joined Robert, too, as Nicholas was to be server at the mass and had gone into the vestry. Cassandra was thinking that only Pete was yet to come when there was a sudden sound of a number of people arriving all at once. It was not easy to see who they all were, though Cassandra and her mother turned round as far as seemed reasonably dignified. The bell rang, everybody stood up and the mass began.

***

Melissa and Cassandra followed the coffin out of the church and stood in the pale sunshine.

"Thank goodness it's not raining," Melissa murmured, "there's almost nothing more depressing than a wet burial!"

As the other mourners emerged from the church she and Cassandra were surprised to see not only Pete, hardly recognisable in a dark suit, but also his mother and 'Uncle Morris' and his Uncle Kevin (electrics) and all the members of his family and friends who had helped with the building work at Huntsfield.

Melissa went forward to greet them: "How very, very kind of you to come!" she exclaimed as she shook hands all round. "And I do hope you're coming on to the burial and the reception, er, wake, er refreshments."

Pete's Uncle Morris was the spokesman. "Thanks, Missus. We'll just come to the burial if that's all right. Got to get back to work, like. Except Pete, maybe."

Pete shook his head. "No," he said, "I'll go back with me mum and Uncle Morris. Thanks, though."

A sudden form thrust through the group of Pete's friends and relations and vigorously shook hands with Cassandra and then Melissa, who barely managed not to say 'good heavens!' Instead she gasped "Ah! How---how good of you, Mrs Fraser!"

"Well I said to Raymond," Norah Fraser indicated her husband, who was as usual slightly in the background, "I said, 'Raymond', I said, 'we really must go because there won't be many people there and besides we know them quite well, Mrs Marsh and the girl, I mean.' And Nigel and Effie are supposed to be coming too, but they must have got lost or something. Oh, there's Robert. Did you see Nigel, Robert?"

"Well, not today. I realised he knew about it but he never mentioned that he was coming."

A car drew in to the lane leading to the church car park.

"Oh *there* they are!" The Frasers hastened to meet and chastise the latecomers, and Melissa had time and space to discern a couple of elderly women standing a little distance away in the company of the Woodstock priest. Cassandra, who was exchanging raised eyebrows and silent expressions of comic horror with Robert, had not noticed them. Melissa was about to approach them when the head of the undertakers came up to her and murmured in his suitably sepulchral tones: "Whenever you're ready to join the cavalcade to the cemetery, madam."

"Oh, of course!" Hiding her amusement at the description of their car as part of a 'cavalcade' and rather relieved at having an excuse to put off a longer encounter with the two strange women, Melissa informed the small congregation of the imminent departure and led the way to the car park, merely pausing to apologise for having had no opportunity to speak to the unknown attenders earlier and expressing her hope that she could make up for it later.

In the car park Robert urged Melissa and Cassandra to let him drive them in his car. "It'll be really slow behind the hearse," he persuaded, "and you might easily stall."

"Oh dear, I hadn't thought of that. It would be rather awful."

"I'd take you in mine," Nicholas also offered, "but it's a bit sporty for the principal mourners, as well as a bit of a squash."

"Oh, Robert's will be fine. You must go in front, of course, Mummy." Cassandra opened the passenger door for her mother. "We'd better set off; they may have a schedule at the cemetery."

"It can't be as bad as the crem.," Robert ventured, "people get into the wrong funeral there because they don't know which queue to join!"

"Wait a minute!" Melissa shot out of Robert's car and went to her own, "I've got to take my good shoes. I wasn't going to wear them in church---all that kneeling---or in a muddy graveyard. They're in a bag on the back seat." She retrieved them and they finally set off, to the not unduly obvious relief of the undertakers waiting in the hearse.

***

After the solemnity of the burial with its silences, hushed voices and sounds of the handfuls of earth thrown on to the coffin lid, the atmosphere in the Marjoribanks' north Oxford house was positively convivial. Melissa was happy, and a couple of inches taller, in her elegant shoes and Jasper was assiduous in looking after her. Robert and Stephen were competing to supply Cassandra with food and drink. Samson was reflecting that it often fell to his lot to look after Muriel and Muriel was regarding Melissa with some interest, wondering how she contrived to be so attractive at her age and wishing she'd had the courage to wear her own unaccustomed and uncomfortable shoes, which were the only ones she possessed that were in any way similar to Melissa's.

The doorbell rang and Sir Felix went to answer it as his wife and the help were seeing to the food.

"Ah!" he said to the two unknown women on the doorstep. "Do come in. I saw you at the church. You're friends of Melissa's, I presume."

"Not exactly," the taller of the two replied, "but I'd like to speak to her."

Sir Felix ushered them in to the drawing room and led them to where Melissa was standing. He was hesitating as to how to introduce them when Melissa greeted them with her usual understated charm.

"I'm so sorry I had no opportunity to speak to you earlier. Are you friends of Fergus's?"

"Hardly!" said the taller woman. "Don't you recognise me? I'm Alison Marjoribanks."
"Oh! How---!" Melissa was, unusually, at a loss for words.
" 'How you've aged' is what you were going to say, I suppose!"
"No, no. How awful of me not to realise. I do apologise. It must be such a long time since I've seen you. Not since the boys grew up, in fact. Are they still living abroad?"
"They are. I've told them of their father's death. They had no idea about it; nobody *else* had contacted them."
"It was not possible. Fergus went bankrupt and disappeared leaving a multitude of debts and I practically had to flee the country. Everything got lost."
Alison gave a tight little smile, which denoted satisfaction rather than amusement.
"I can't say I'm surprised. He must have found it difficult to keep up with the extravagance of a younger wife."
Melissa was inclined to bring up the subject of somewhat excessive maintenance paid out to an older one but considered such retaliation, however tempting, to be decidedly bad form. Instead she turned a winning smile on Alison's companion and said "How do you do; you will have gathered that I'm Melissa Marjoribanks."
Alison, somewhat riled at her failure to draw a retaliatory remark from her successor, murmured sourly, "Margaret Meldrum, my friend; we share a house in London."
"Well you must come and meet the rest of the family, as far as it's represented here. You won't remember my daughter Cassandra, of course, she's grown a good deal since you saw her last. Cassandra!" She led the way to where the young people were standing. "This is Alison, the

mother of your half-brothers, and her friend Margaret Meldrum."

Cassandra exchanged courtesies with admirable politeness, introduced Robert and Stephen, and wondered how the man who had married her mother could ever have married this woman, though it did occur to her that of course Alison must be almost as old as Fergus and hence about fifteen years older than Melissa.

There were ensuing introductions all round and something of a loss of conviviality fell on the party. It was, however, broken into by more arrivals, this time let in by the help, and immediately recognisable from the voices which preceded them as Norah Fraser and attendants.

"Well I must say, the directions on that map weren't very clear and there seem to be different streets with the same name round here. Oh, good afternoon Lady M, Sir Felix, reelly nice of you to have the reception here, even if it was hard to find. Quite a nice area, though; not reelly *grand* of course like Huntsfield House, but quite smart. You know our Effie and her partner, well fiancé now, don't you. They were too late for the funeral and of course Nigel's blaming Effie and she's blaming him."

"Be quiet, Mother," said Effie.

Nigel went up to Melissa and Cassandra and offered apologies and condolences in more or less the same breath. Norah Fraser was talking to her daughter and explaining what she'd missed.

"It reelly was the most strange sort of funeral, Effie, and there weren't any hymns, not even 'the lord's my shepherd'; I thought they always had that at funerals. And there was communion, only we were told we couldn't have any because we're not Catholics."

"That doesn't seem fair," was Effie's comment.

"No, that's what I thought. C. of E.'s not like that, is it?"

"No it isn't. Me and Nige went to a christening once and it was in the morning and everybody had communion, even the people that weren't with the christening party. I don't see why we couldn't have had communion at the funeral, if we'd been there."

This conversation was apparently intended to be private but as Norah Fraser and her daughter were not greatly given to dulcet tones or experienced in the use of *sotto voce* their voices were clearly audible all over the room. Nicholas, already in their immediate neighbourhood, turned to them and asked, with the utmost politeness, if they would really like to know the reason. Nicholas had a sound knowledge, imbibed from an early age, of the old catechism and its listings of such things as the seven spiritual works of mercy, one of which, 'instructing the ignorant' was rather a favourite of his.

Celestria, a little anxious about the suitability of such instruction in the present circumstances, said: "Oh, Nicholas, I don't think---." But Nicholas was already saying that only those in a state of grace could receive Holy Communion, which meant that many Catholics were not always able to do so.

"How do you mean?" Effie was, unsurprisingly, puzzled, but so taken with Nicholas's good looks that she was not unwilling to listen.

"Well," he continued, "suppose people are living in sin---,"

"Tee hee hee," Norah Fraser interrupted, "it's a long time since I've heard it called that!"

"Yes, living together when they're not married, or not married in the eyes of the Church because one of them is divorced and has an earlier spouse still living, they're in a state of sin, not in a state of grace. So they can't, or shouldn't, receive Holy Communion."

"Even if they're Catholics?"

"Absolutely. And of course there are numerous other sins which have to be confessed and absolved before the person is in a state of grace. So the same thing should apply to anybody receiving Holy Communion; but it doesn't happen in other churches."

"Nigel's divorced."

"You don't need to tell everybody that, Effie," her mother reinforced her statement with a sharp nudge.

"So we can't have communion even when we're married."

"Well I think you can in most Protestant churches."

"We don't go, anyway, so it doesn't matter, but thanks for telling me; are you a minister or something?" Effie was unwilling to relinquish Nicholas's attention and pleased to talk to him for as long as possible. Melissa, who had observed this exchange with interest and some amusement, reflected that Celestria's diversion of Nicholas from his priestly vocation was probably a very good thing. 'No wonder Fergus considered him too holy,' she thought, 'and rather off-putting.'

Effie, however, was showing no sign of being put off but her conversation with Nicholas was interrupted by her fiancé, who asked what they were talking about.

Nicholas introduced himself and Nigel did the same, indicating of course that he was Effie's fiancé. The subject of the previous conversation was lost in the course of general pleasantries and Melissa noted this with some relief, as indeed did Celestria, who made an immediate friend of Effie by asking about her wedding plans.

Jasper quietly enquired of Melissa if she needed any help in dealing with Fergus's erstwhile wife and promptly provided it by engaging her in conversation himself and making delicate efforts to ascertain the nature of her relationship with Margaret Meldrum. He was soon joined by Norah Fraser, who felt rather left out of the younger people's conversation and was not so immensely struck by Nicholas's looks as to consider that they made him worth listening to. As she said to Raymond later, "I mean, fancy talking about religion at a funeral! I don't think that's very nice, do you?" Deciding, however that Jasper did not look the type to talk about religion she had no compunction about breaking into his conversation with Alison Marjoribanks and Margaret Meldrum.

"I'm Mrs Fraser," she told them. Their conversation stopped abruptly. Alison Marjoribanks looked positively startled. Jasper, who immediately recognised Norah Fraser, not from having met her previously but from stories he had heard about her, recovered first.

"Ah, of course!" he said. "Your fame has preceded you."

"Pardon?" said Norah.

"I've heard you spoken of."

"Oh well of course we're quite friends of the family, the Huntsfield ones I mean; we've been there several times. And Cassandra's young man, that's Robert Taylor, he's going to be best man at our Effie's---that's my daughter's---wedding." She turned to Fergus's ex-wife. "And you're another Mrs Marsh, Marshbanks, are you, there seem to be a lot of them. And this is your friend, I've heard, and you live together; partners, are you?"

Alison Marjoribanks was too outraged to reply. Jasper didn't actually say 'fools rush in' but his expression said it for him. Margaret Meldrum found her voice and said: "We're *friends* not partners apart from the fact that we share a house; neither of our ex-husbands left us with enough money to live on alone in the part of London we want to live in."

"It's a smart part of London, is it?" Norah Fraser was interested to know.

"Not really; Islington. But at least it's not south of the river."

Norah's husband, who had been hovering on the outskirts of the gathering, came and joined them. "I think it's time we went, Norah."

"Oh I don't know," Norah was rather enjoying herself; she introduced him. "This is Mr Fraser, my husband." The others hastened to introduce themselves. 'Mr Fraser' was clearly somewhat ill at ease, however, and soon succeeded in detaching his wife from the group and approaching Nigel and Effie.

"What a pity," said Jasper, "I was finding that encounter most enjoyable."

The Frasers and their daughter and prospective son-in-law left together.

"What was that chap talking to you about when I came up to you?" Nigel asked his fiancée.

"Oh, I'm not sure; something about not having communion when you're not married."

46

The family, including Robert, who of course had to drive Cassandra and her mother back to Woodstock to retrieve their car, sat round the north Oxford Marjoribanks' table with an extra cup of tea and the remains of the refreshments. They were, unsurprisingly, discussing the funeral and its attenders.

"I suppose," Melissa ventured, "this might be rather literally described as a *post mortem*!"

"I'm glad to see you can take it so calmly," Lady Marjorie commented.

"Mainly thanks to you for holding the wake here. It was really remarkably successful, in spite of Fergus's ex turning up like Banquo's ghost!"

"You dealt with her superbly," Jasper was full of admiration, "so tactful and diplomatic. Of course the whole situation was greatly aided by the arrival of that incredible Fraser woman. She is a rare plant to be carefully cultivated and ought to be a *must* at any potentially difficult gathering. I appreciated her tremendously."

"I absolutely agree," Lady Marjorie was enthusiastic, "there'd be no dearth of conversation and everybody could swap stories and have a good laugh afterwards."

"Really?" Sir Felix was puzzled. "I just thought she was ghastly."

"Quite," said his wife, "and one often needs ghastly people at parties. It makes all the others feel superior. Before I give a party I pray that the guests will feel the better for attending; and a sense of superiority is a very good recipe for feeling all the better."

"I'm not sure that Alison Marjoribanks felt all the better," Cassandra ventured.

"Oh, I think the Fraser woman took her mind off Melissa," said Jasper happily. "Or possibly gave her the idea that that was the kind of friend Melissa had---which must have made her feel *very* superior!"

"I do rather wonder why she came," Melissa mused. "Curiosity, I suppose. Did she show any interest in you, Cassandra?"

"I wouldn't say so. She spoke to me very coldly. I would have liked to ask about my half-brothers but I don't suppose there's any point."

"I'm sure it must be possible to find her again and at least get their addresses," said Jasper. " We know she lives in Islington."

"Do we? How did you find out?" Melissa was intrigued.

"That marvellous Mrs Fraser extracted the information in a matter of minutes. I told you she was a rare specimen to be cultivated with care."

"You might not think so if you'd seen as much of her as Cassandra and I have!" Stephen interposed.

Robert laughed. "Unfortunately she's usually encountered by accident, but we'll have to ensure that you're one of the party in any anticipated situation, Jasper. Perhaps I could procure an invitation to her daughter's wedding for you."

"Ah! The one where you're to be best man. Now that *would* be a privilege indeed."

It was decided that Robert would take Cassandra back to Woodstock to collect the car and Melissa would be taken home by Jasper. Stephen also offered to take Cassandra back but was discouraged by his mother, who said she'd hardly seen him and wanted him at home for a change, and by Cassandra's obvious gratitude for her intervention.

"Well," Stephen gave way resignedly, "you must come to my party in London, anyway."

Cassandra smiled but gave no answer and was somewhat proprietorially escorted away by Robert. Once in his car she sighed and relaxed into the seat with her head against the head-rest.

"Thank you for everything, Robert, for all you've done."

"I haven't done anything!" Robert was genuinely surprised.

"I don't just mean today, though you have, you've been very supportive. I mean your being so kind to Pa and befriending him. Seeing you always made him happy; and actually, strange though it may seem, you were probably the person most instrumental in his becoming a Catholic."

"That really is the blind leading the blind!" Robert had to smile. "Well, I mean, it was."

"You weren't nearly as blind as you thought. And even apart from that you were patient and kind. Which is more than my mother could always manage."

"That's understandable; I had no previous involvement, no old scores to settle. Your mother was probably less acerbic than many women would have been in such a situation. And she did make an effort not to smoke in front of him and make him cough!"

They came to the church and Cassandra prepared to get out and drive her old car home. "Come back to the house and have a bite of supper with us, Robert; Jasper's probably there and I don't want to feel left out."

"I'd love to anyway. But Jasper's certainly not wasting any time."

"No; that's another thing, Mummy stopped him coming to the house when she knew that Pa got upset about it. I think she only saw him in London."

"Your mother's a great deal more full of the milk of human kindness than she pretends to be!"

Robert waited to see that Cassandra's car actually started and then followed her to Huntsfield. Jasper was indeed there but preparing to leave as he thought Melissa and Cassandra might want to be on their own.

"Thank you, Jasper, I appreciate your delicacy, but cast though I may be by others in the role of grieving widow I feel my inability to enact it with any conviction. It is, of course, a social stereotype to which one is expected to conform; which I would have done of necessity had we still been living in France, but I'm thankful we know so few people here that it's not obligatory. So do stay and have some supper."

Cassandra echoed her mother's invitation: "yes do; you see Robert's going to."

Nicholas and Celestria came in later and were more than a little surprised to find a rather convivial group gathered round the table. They had gone out with the express purpose of leaving the bereaved on their own. None the less they joined in as they were warmly invited to do and enjoyed the atmosphere of relaxation, it might almost be said of relief, that prevailed. When, however, they had departed to their separate rooms and Robert and Jasper to their respective dwellings and Melissa and Cassandra were in fact on their own, they sat on at the table and helped themselves to another drink and Cassandra smoked one of her mother's cigarettes.

"It's all very well for me," said Melissa as if continuing a conversation, "one can have any number of husbands---if one's silly enough---but it's not really possible to have more than one father. How do you feel about Fergus's death?"

"I don't feel sad, at least I don't think so. I'm relieved that it was such a good death and that he suffered so little and didn't even have to go into hospital. But perhaps it hasn't quite sunk in yet. There may be a sense of loss later. Actually I don't think I've ever really known anybody who's died; it's a new experience. When the house is full of paying guests everything's going to be different, too."

"It certainly will simplify matters as regards guests, not to mention that we've got a vacant, newly done up en suite room. Now all we need is for Treasure to depart this life; that really would be a relief!"

"Oh, Mummy! The place wouldn't be the same without her."

"No, darling, and I shall be very thankful when it's not!"

***

It was Celestria's last night at Huntsfield before her move to the 'friendly manor house' to become a carer/housekeeper/cook. Melissa put on a special dinner to which Robert was invited. Nicholas was clearly distressed at the prospective departure of his beloved, although to a very short distance away, and even more distressed at the thought of her subservient position and the amount of work it would entail.

"This is the last meal you won't have to cook," he observed gloomily; "it's really too much."

"I won't have to cook at weekends," Celestria countered brightly.

Nicholas was barely cheered. "I'll come and pick you up on Saturday mornings, and you won't have to go back till Sunday, will you?"

"No, you can stay here at weekends," Cassandra anticipated Celestria's probable anxiety about accommodation. "You can share my room if the rest are full, but I don't think they will be, not now that we've got Pa's room".

"But tell us," Melissa wanted to change the distressing subject of Celestria's departure, "how did you get on with the visits to your respective parents? We haven't had time to hear about it yet."

"We went to our house first," Celestria began, "and my mother looked rather puzzled to see us. She knew we were coming, of course, but she clearly was wondering why. My father, though, seemed to like Nicholas immediately and even insisted on lighting the fire in the main hall. It was terribly cold. I don't remember it being quite so cold, but I suppose I've got used to it being warm here. My mother doesn't seem to feel it. When my father lit the fire in the hall she asked how long we'd be staying. Fortunately we'd already arranged to go on to Nicholas's parents after a couple of nights. But the next day Nicholas asked to speak to my father and told him we wanted to get married, and really after that my mother was quite different. She sat down rather suddenly when we first told her and commented that we certainly hadn't wasted any time, but apart from that she smiled more than I've ever seen her and indicated that she was more pleased with me than at any time since I was born. She's even got big plans for the wedding."

"Will it be at your parents' house? The reception I mean."

"I don't really want it there. I haven't any feeling for it and besides, there's no Catholic church for miles."

"We'd actually like to have it in the chapel of my college in Cambridge and the reception in the college hall," Nicholas was enthusiastic, "but it's a long way for our families to come and we think they might not like the idea."

"Especially my mother!" Celestria murmured.

"But your father might come round to Nicholas's way of thinking; I'm sure he'd be glad to be spared too much involvement in the preparations," Melissa had a rather dim view of the interest most men took in wedding preparations. “What about your parents, Nicholas? How did they react?”

Celestria answered for him. “They were really wonderful; so warm and welcoming. I felt as if I’d known them for years. If they were surprised they didn’t show it. They’re even going to write to my parents and ask them to come and stay. But I hope if they return the visit and go to our house it’ll at least be when the weather’s warmer.

47

The post van drove into the yard as Cassandra was going towards the house for lunch. She took the thick wadge of papers from the hand of the driver as he stretched his arm through the window.

"Look!" she announced to Melissa, who was having a cigarette with a *tiny* pre-prandial drink at the kitchen table. "Here's a real letter with real writing on it! Who can it be from?"

"It looks more like a card than a letter." Melissa took it and opened it neatly with the aid of a knife. "Heavens! It's a wedding invitation from Mr and Mrs Raymond Fraser to the marriage of their daughter Euphemia Tracey to Dr Nigel Nelson Nethercott. Oh dear; is this the one where poor Robert has to be best man? Oh, I see it's in a church and the reception's in a hotel. Do we have to go?

"I think we must, if only for Robert's sake. Besides, if the card's anything to go by it might be rather lavish!"

"That's a charitable word for it!" was her mother's comment. "Look at the back. It seems to have a tear-off reply form. How very odd."

"Oh, something like that's normal these days. Some people don't know how to reply to invitations."

"But it's got RSVP on it."

"They don't know what that means."

"Oh dear. How dreadful. I didn't realise things had come to such a pass. But I don't suppose I've been to a wedding for years. None of our friends' children in France seemed to get married. They just lived with a partner. Cheaper for the parents, of course, but rather unsatisfactory, somehow.

Though I'm the first to admit that marriage can be a mistake."

"I'm afraid this one might be; you'd think Nigel would be more careful after making two mistakes already."

"Yes. You'd wonder why he bothers to get married."

"Perhaps Effie's mother has something to do with it; or Effie's mother's money."

"Do we have to use that awful tear-off or can we reply properly?"

"I don't suppose it matters. I'll do it if you like."

"Oh please; I'd feel awkward about it and anyway I'm a bit busy with our first alien guest arriving tomorrow."

"But everything's ready, isn't it? And really, he's not an alien, he's an Australian and if you remember, you said he sounded quite civilised."

"Did I? Well, we'll see. I'm glad the 'Hi!' Americans won't be here first."

***

A modest Vauxhall turned into the 'back yard' of Huntsfied House in a manner that could only be described as tentative. Cassandra watched from the workshop as her mother went out to welcome the driver, who uncoiled himself from the car and stood up to reveal a tall, bronzed, rangy man in his early fifties. His handshake with Melissa was accompanied by something between a bend and a bow and he merely said his name, Henry Acland, as he glanced at the house and grounds and took in the elegant figure of his hostess with every appearance of awed appreciation. Melissa's relief expressed itself in increased graciousness as she enquired after his journey and his luggage. From the workshop window Pete regarded the car with some disdain: "Not much of a car, is it, Miss? Only a year and a half old, though. Shall I help with his luggage?"

"Oh Pete, that would be kind. I don't want to meet him until I've tidied up a bit. But you'd better wash your hands."

By the time this was achieved the yard was entered by Nicholas's Alfa Romeo and Nicholas himself leapt out of it to help the new arrival. Melissa had the task of introducing him and Pete almost simultaneously, somewhat to the bewilderment of Henry Acland, who found the contrast between their respective accents a little difficult to account for, but who was none the less grateful for the extra hands and arms to cope with his rather formidable amount of luggage.

When Pete returned to the shed to remark that the newcomer seemed 'sort of shy, like, but quite nice,' Cassandra found she couldn't wait to find out her mother's reaction, so she washed hastily and went to the kitchen. Melissa was, predictably, sitting at the table smoking, but without a drink.

"Would you like a cup of tea, Mummy?"

"Well yes, actually; I must keep a clear head for the dinner."

"First take favourable?"

"Very. Seems impressed and appreciative. Said: 'Well! It's beautiful! I must say I never expected anything like this.' He seemed pleased that Nicholas was staying here too. I can't tell you how relieved I am!"

"Let's hope the Americans will be an equally pleasant surprise."

"I fear that's too much to hope for; but at least they'll be diluted."

Dinner went swimmingly with Nicholas and 'Dr Acland' finding plenty to talk about and clearly enjoying each other's company.

"It's a good thing, having a new guest now," Cassandra observed, "it should stop Nicholas worrying so much about Celestria. Poor girl; I'm afraid she won't be having such a pleasant dinner."
"At least she won't be sitting in silence listening to some far-fetched story of impossible holiness."
"Oh Ma! Some of the lives of the saints are really interesting. Take Maximilian Kolbe, for example."
"I've never heard of him."
"He was a priest and he died in a prison camp to save a man who had several children."
"When?"
"During the last war."
"Oh. Too recent for me. He can't have been a saint for long. He doesn't sound as interesting as Padre Pio. *He* could do levitation and bilocation and understand people's thoughts. He's credited with catching an airman whose parachute didn't open and bringing him safely to the ground."
"Really Ma! You are illogical! Talk about far-fetched stories of impossible holiness! Not that he hasn't a great following. He sounds like a medieval saint and yet he lived in the 20th Century."
"Well, I do remember enjoying that one. It's those saintly women who put up with impossible husbands that I can't stand."
Cassandra laughed. "Shall we see if they've finished their pudding?"
"That would be a good idea. And how about a complimentary little glass to celebrate the arrival of a civilised Australian?"
Melissa produced a bottle of Madeira as if by magic and they took it into the dining-room where the two men were

still talking animatedly. They both stood up as the women went in.

"Oh do sit down," Melissa purred, "we don't want to interrupt you but we thought a tiny drink might be appropriate to celebrate Dr Acland's arrival. It won't happen every evening."

"Oh that is kind," Nicholas was enthusiastic; "we've discovered we have a lot in common; Henry's a Classicist and we both do some of the same kind of teaching."

Henry Acland smiled and expressed his appreciation. "This is all so much more than I could have imagined," he said.

"Thank you; we're so glad to think you'll be happy here. But you must have been in England before."

"Only a long time ago, when I had a year here while I was working on my doctorate."

"You don't seem---" Melissa was about to say 'very Australian' but changed it to "er, to feel, er---"

Cassandra, afraid her mother was going to say 'out of place', broke in with "homesick", and continued with "I mean I hope you feel at home."

"Well I had an English grandmother. Of course a lot of Australians could say that, but mine was quite a forceful influence, especially on my mother, and she lived till she was ninety-five, so we saw quite a lot of her. I think we were brought up more 'English' than anything. We came in for a bit of stick about it at school. But I do feel at home here. I like the countryside, the gentleness of the landscape, the beauty of the old buildings, the villages. Pictures of England always appealed to me even when I was a child; it's wonderful to find that the things I saw in them are real."

"You must see as much as possible of the Cotswolds while you're here." Melissa still felt a little phased as to how to converse with a colonial. Cassandra made a mental note to tell her not to be patronising.

"I certainly intend to; and I'll be in an excellent position to do it from here."

Nicholas had some useful observations to make and the conversation continued, but Cassandra wished they'd left the men to themselves and hoped they might in future. She escaped to the kitchen as soon as possible and was soon followed by her mother.

"Oh dear," Melissa sank into a chair and lit a cigarette, "something tells me I didn't quite get that right."

"No; we should have left them to it, but never mind, at least we've welcomed the newcomer and shown him something about our set-up. And it was certainly a very good dinner."

Nicholas poked an enquiring head round the kitchen door.

"Oh do come in, Nicholas," Melissa spoke welcomingly "and tell us how Celestria's getting on."

"She sounds very cheerful but we've only had time for the briefest of conversations. I'm afraid she's working too hard. I can't wait to take her away from there. I'm determined to get on with the wedding plans. You're to be chief bridesmaid, of course, Cassandra. There are lots of children in my family so you'll have to keep them in order!"

"That sounds a little daunting; I didn't know things had progressed so far."

"I'm afraid I'm chivvying everybody into it. But enough about us; you're both looking weary. Is another guest too much for you?"

"It's just that I don't know how to treat him," Melissa sighed. "It's so different with you, somebody like us who'd be likely to stay on equal terms anyway. And I suppose I'm more used to Europeans than colonials. I think we'll be a little more distant in future. You won't mind, will you. You can always come in here and talk to us any time."

"He's a very nice chap and I can't imagine we'll have any problems getting on together. But you've got some Americans coming, haven't you?"

"Yes, in a couple of days. I'm not looking forward to it. They addressed us as 'Hi!' and really don't sound like our sort of people at all."

"Now, Ma, you know we can't afford to be like that!"

"Like what?"

"Judging people by their manners."

"How else can I judge them?"

"You shouldn't judge them at all."

"I can't believe that; sound judgment's an admirable quality; not that I can congratulate myself on having possessed it in abundance. I wish I'd had more of it when I was younger."

"One should judge by character, not superficial things like manners, which are different in different parts of the world anyway. Don't you think so, Nicholas?"

"The motto of one of the best schools in the country is 'Manners makyth man', but it must depend on what that actually means. Good manners really show consideration for other people and that can be expressed in different ways. I don't suppose you judge Pete by his manners, exactly, but you've often said he's a kind, good natured boy with real concern for other people."

Cassandra laughed. "Yes, that's true; but Pete himself seems to judge people almost entirely by the kind of car they drive. You come really high in his estimation, Nicholas, but poor Robert's regarded as very inferior! Still, you value Pete quite apart from his manners, don't you Ma?"

"Oh certainly, but we wouldn't ask him or his family to dinner. I think I'm just unhappy about people we expect to be on our social level showing that they're not---and having them to stay in our house. And of course colonials speak English---more or less---and we expect things of them that we wouldn't expect of, say, Chinese people for example."

"But you're agreeably surprised that Henry Acland's so uncolonial, aren't you, Ma? I'm afraid you made that rather clear."

"I know. I don't think I can get it right."

"I'm sure Henry was perfectly pleased with his reception," Nicholas spoke encouragingly, "he was happy to explain about his English grandmother. He must suffer from some Australians himself; he almost said so."

"Thank you Nicholas, that makes me feel better; let's hope he doesn't suffer from the Americans!

48

Melissa sat down after breakfast and stared into her coffee cup. Cassandra regarded her rather anxiously.

"What's the matter, Mummy?"

"The dreaded Americans are coming today," was the disconsolate reply.

"Oh Mummy! You only make it worse referring to them like that!"

"Not really. I'd rather be prepared than disappointed. I won't say 'dreaded' when they're here."

"No of course not; you don't dread things that have already happened! Do you want me to help you greet them?"

"No, but thank you. You need to get on with your work and it won't really do for you to emerge covered in clay; I can't have you take a whole morning off. But perhaps Pete could stay just clean enough to help with the luggage."

Melissa checked the prepared room more than once, decided to put some flowers in it as there was a woman coming, found nothing in the garden but a few sprigs of winter jasmine, reflected that at least there were numerous vases she could put it in. Unable to settle to anything she went over to the 'potting shed' as she amused herself by calling it, to speak to her daughter. Cassandra was throwing a large bowl. She looked up in surprise at her mother's entry; Melissa was normally meticulous about leaving her to work uninterrupted, but today her restless anxiety was almost palpable.

"It's all right, Mummy, I can do a simple one like this and talk at the same time. You shouldn't worry so much; it's not like you."

"I can't do anything to take my mind off it."

"Perhaps you could ring Jasper?"

"Certainly not! It simply wouldn't do. He'd think I was chasing him, and that's the very last thing I want him to think."

"I'm sure he'd be delighted. Can't you find something to ask his advice about?"

"I'd really like to go out and drive somewhere, even if it's only shopping; but I feel imprisoned."

"We'll have to get on with the flats; you wouldn't need to worry so much about what people are going to be like if you didn't have to feed them and look after them in the house, and you'd have far more freedom yourself."

"That's very true, but we can't afford it yet. Oh heavens! Look what a vast car! They must be here already."

Melissa hastened into the yard and Pete, interested to see the car, hastened to the window. Cassandra finished the bowl in time to stop the noise of the wheel and listen to her mother's first encounter with the new arrivals.

"Hi there!" she heard. "I'm Con; Con B. Weaver; you must be Cass." He spoke through the electrically opened window and didn't get out of the car.

"How do you do." Melissa spoke mellifluously, turning a smile of impeccable politeness on both the car's occupants.

"Hi, Cass, I'm Marlene," Mrs Con B. Weaver responded.

"Cas*sandra* is actually my daughter's name," Melissa took a deep breath and decided to begin as she meant to go on even if she had to use a designation she would never normally have employed, "I'm Mrs Marjoribanks."

"Wow! So that's how you say it: marsh banks. Reckon I might get bogged down in that, ha ha ha! Pardon the pun. Can't we call you by your first name?"

"I'm afraid I'm very English and old-fashioned; our other guests address me as Mrs Marjoribanks and I address them by their title and surname. Continental people of my generation use Christian names only for relatives and long-standing friends and some of our guests are continental." Here Melissa took another deep breath and added mentally 'well I hope they will be!' "I'm afraid," she went on aloud, "I can't possibly make an exception. It would be unfair to our other guests, even embarrassing. But do come round to the front door and up to your room. I'll get my daughter's assistant to help with your luggage. There seems to be rather a lot of it."

"Yeah, well Marlene likes to pack everything and I've brought a heap of stuff." Con B. Weaver descended from the large car and dragged a couple of huge suitcases from the back of it. "I'll wheel these round for a start, anyway, and then maybe we can just put them in the elevator."

Cassandra, watching and listening from the door of the shed, feared for her mother's composure and deemed it high time to send Pete out to help. Melissa was clearly relieved to see him, imperfectly cleansed of clay though he was.

"Ah!" she announced, "Here's a strong young man to help. This is Pete."

Pete gave a silent nod of acknowledgement and took one of the cases.

"Hi Pete!" Con B.Weaver greeted him. "We *can* call you *Pete,* can we?"

Pete nodded, looking puzzled.

"Well I guess that's a relief, anyway."

They progressed round the path to the front door and went into the impressive main hall. Melissa hoped it might be sufficiently impressive to counteract the Weavers' dismay when she summoned the courage to confess that there was no lift. Pete began to pull his appropriated suitcase up the stairs. Con B. Weaver looked round in anything but admiration.

"Where's---" he began.

"There's no lift, I'm afraid," Melissa interrupted.

"There's no what?"

"She means they don't have an elevator, Con," his wife explained.

"In a place this size?"

"It is a private house, not a hotel," Melissa rejoined.

"In the States a private house this size would definitely have an elevator."

"This house is some hundreds of years old."

"Yeah; I'm beginning to realise that." The strain of hauling his case up the stairs was sufficient to stifle any further verbal observation. They reached the Weavers' designated room as Melissa reflected thankfully that it was on the first floor, not the second; thankfully if only because the agony of initiating these new guests could at least be somewhat curtailed. The male guest released his suitcase and looked round.

"Is this it?" he said.

"Why Con," his wife spoke from the window; "the view's quite nice."

"Yeah, so what? Where's the telephone?" The last question was addressed to Melissa.

Before Melissa could reiterate that this was not a hotel Pete, angered by the guest's attitude and protective of 'Missus', found his voice and said "Haven't you got a mobile?"

"A what?"

"He means a cell phone, Con," his wife translated again.

"No, I don't. Not a British one. Ours doesn't work over here."

"They're really cheap. You can get one for about £10 and just pay for how much you use it. Tell you what, you can borrow mine till you get one. Then you won't need to worry Missus about it."

"Thank you so much, Pete, that's most kind and thoughtful of you," Melissa was not unaware of Pete's protective support.

"Now isn't that just darling of him, Con," Mrs Weaver was enthusiastic. "Thanks, Pete. I'd just love to borrow it to call my daughter in the States. Then you can tell us where to buy a British one tomorrow." Pete went to his room to fetch his mobile, showed Mrs Weaver how to use it---and how to top it up ---and departed to bring up some more luggage. By the time Melissa had explained the mysteries of the kettle, the tea tray and the location of the bathroom, not forgetting to point out that the *lavatory* was separate, Pete was back. She left him with the Weavers, hoping they might at least give him an American sized tip.

He came into the workshop some twenty minutes later waving a five pound note. Melissa was there, regaling Cassandra with a description of the 'still dreaded Americans'.

"Well," she remarked, "I think they might have done better than that after all your help. That man must be mean as well as utterly uncouth."

"It's O.K., Missus; the Aussie only gave me a pound. And she's really nice, the lady. Don't you let them get you down."

Melissa sighed. "I'm afraid they've got me down already, Pete. I admit the woman's less vile, but even she only faintly praised that superb view as 'quite nice'; imagine it! *Quite nice* when she's talking about a Capability Brown vista stretching to a clear horizon!"

"Oh, Ma!" Cassandra exclaimed. "I know about that; you mustn't take umbrage. I've had it explained; Americans say 'quite' when they mean 'very'. One of the Devon potters had an American boy staying and at almost every meal he'd say 'this is quite nice', in tones that sounded like surprise. When she couldn't stand it any longer she told him it was rude and he was really devastated that he'd got it so wrong. You see if I said 'quite devastated' I'd mean 'completely devastated', wouldn't I? It's very muddling."

"Why can't they speak English the way we do?"

"Well, it's due to foreign influences and time and distance. People in the north of England don't speak like we do, let alone people in Scotland."

"People like us do. Anyway I'm going to have a drink; I don't care how early it is."

Melissa was sitting at the kitchen table over a glass of wine that made no pretence at being tiny and smoking a consoling cigarette when the door opened to reveal Mrs Weaver, all smiles and friendliness, saying: "Hi! Can I come in?" She didn't wait for an answer before doing so, which was possibly just as well as Melissa would have been strongly tempted to give a negative one. As it was she stood up and advanced towards her guest to prevent her from coming any further.

"Is there something I can get for you, Mrs Weaver, er, anything you need?"

"Oh, do call me Marlene; nobody calls me 'Mrs Weaver' except my dentist. And thank you, I don't need anything right now but I was just wondering if we could have a bite of lunch some time soon because then we could have a rest and maybe get over our jet lag."

"It's dinner, bed and breakfast we provide; I don't expect to do lunches. I don't know that I've got anything suitable."

"Oh just a sandwich or something like that. Nothing special." Marlene Weaver's eyes wandered to the table, where Melissa's no longer consoling cigarette was still burning. "I see you smoke. My! Don't let Con know; he's really disapproving of smokers. We didn't reckon anybody'd still be smoking here."

"I think this house is big enough to contain it," Melissa replied coolly.

"I guess you're right. I never smelt it when we came in. Say--do you mind if I just have a little puff of one? Con'll never know about it if I use some chewing-gum after."

Melissa's momentary sympathy with Marlene Weaver all but vanished.

"*Chewing-gum!*" she repeated in tones of horror. "I've never allowed chewing-gum in the house."

"I won't put it on the furniture, honest I won't. But Con won't have me smoke and it really gets to me sometimes."

"I can certainly understand that. Oh dear; you'd better come and have a cigarette. Then I'll see about getting you and your husband something to eat---just this once. Have a drink, too."

"Oh you're really kind. I said to Con I thought you were probably nicer than you sounded. English people can't help being sort of off-putting; it's the way they speak."

In spite of herself Melissa began to think it might be difficult to dislike Marlene; in small doses and without her husband she might almost be companionable. But the husband was certainly a force to be reckoned with. Melissa sighed.

"I'm really sorry to put you to this trouble; you must let me know if I can help," Marlene spoke sympathetically.

"And I'm really grateful for the cigarette---and the drink. If you could buy me some, cigarettes I mean, and hide them away, I'll gladly pay for them."

"I'll get you some next time I go shopping. But now I'll find something for lunch."

"I'd better go upstairs; I don't want Con coming down to find me."

"I can have something ready in about twenty minutes; I'll show you where the dining-room is."

Melissa set the table and prepared some giant mushrooms with cheese and tomato on top and put them together with fried bread and crisp bacon. These were ready when the Weavers came down and even Con was not entirely unimpressed.

"This is quite nice!" he said in tones that sounded like surprise. Melissa was glad she'd heard her daughter's translation of the phrase and made an effort to believe in it, as she told her when they were having their own lunch together.

"I'm really sorry you had to give them lunch; and you needn't have cooked them anything," Cassandra was concerned.

"Oh, that wasn't so bad; easier than sandwiches."

"I'm so afraid it's going to be too much for you."

"I am finding it very painful but perhaps it's doing me good."

"You mean you're offering it up as a mortification?"

"I hadn't exactly thought of that, I'm afraid; no, I'm trying to see people beyond their manners as you said I should. It looks as if I'll have plenty of practice."

"We can both do with some practice before the Fraser wedding."

"Oh heavens, yes; when is it?"

"Very soon, actually."

"Yes isn't that peculiar? Wedding invitations usually come out months ahead."

"I rather suspect we were asked only when other people had refused and left some space!"

***

The Americans were down for dinner before Melissa had rung the gong.

"You're very welcome to sit down," she told them politely, " but I'm afraid meals are not actually ready until the gong's gone."

The Weavers immediately sat down at the places decked with napkins in rings, avoiding the two places set with pristine, shining white, starched napkins sitting under different rings. Melissa was rather proud of her starched linen napkins, of which Huntsfield House contained a plentiful supply.

"Oh, those places belong to our other two guests," Melissa hastened to point out. "They've used those napkins; yours are the unused ones under the rings. Of course if you want to sit there I'll just change the napkins."

This proved easier than having the guests change places. As Melissa departed towards the kitchen she heard Con B.Weaver say: "I can't get the hang of this place; it's not like any sort of a house I've ever been in but it's not like a hotel either."

"Really, that man!" she exclaimed to Cassandra, "He's so utterly ghastly. I can't imagine what Nicholas is going to make of him, or Dr Acland for that matter."

"I admit I'm tempted to listen at the door," Cassandra laughed, "but I hope Nicholas can tell us about it afterwards. Shall I ring the gong now?"

Nicholas and Henry Acland came down together, talking amicably. Cassandra put the starters on the table and Melissa performed the introductions, speaking of 'Dr

Forbes-Mowbray' and 'Dr Acland' and of course 'Mr and Mrs Weaver'.

"Hi!" the penultimately named replied, and immediately added "Con B.Weaver; call me Con, and this is Marlene."

"Henry", the quiet Australian responded and "Nicholas" followed soon after.

"Henry, eh? You sound like an Australian."

"Yes, I am an Australian."

"Yeah, I went there. Thought you were all called Bruce, ha ha ha!"

"Oh *no!"* Nicholas merely breathed the words but Con picked up the sound.

"What was that, Nick?" he asked.

"I was merely observing that by no means all Australians are called Bruce."

"No, I was jesting. And I don't think all the girls are called Sheila, either, only most of them ha ha ha"

"No, you're mistaken there," Henry interrupted the laugh as soon as possible. "*A* sheela is a girl; it's a common noun, not a proper noun."

Con looked uncomprehending but Nicholas was immediately interested: "I didn't know that before; clearly a sort of folk derivation, 'she' with 'la' added. Fascinating. And by the way," he added, turning to Con, "my name is Nicholas and I am *never* called 'Nick'. I think that must be understood."

"Yeah, well I don't blame you; my granddad used to say 'Old Nick' when he meant the devil. 'Nicholas is a bit of a mouthful, though."

"Oh now Con," Marlene spoke for the first time, " I think it's really pretty; sort of soft and refined."

"Yeah, well I'd better not say what it sounds like to me---" Con seemed about to embark on another of his guffaws but was swiftly interrupted by Henry.

"How do you spell *your* name? I've never heard it before; C-O-R-N, Corn, is it?"
"It doesn't have an R in it."
"Really? That's how we'd spell it. C-O-N sounds quite different, as in *con*man."
"You mean a cahnman? I guess I wouldn't do too well in that line; I'm too straightforward. And anyway it's different; my name's Cawn."
"Yes," Henry persisted, "like the grain."
"Nah, that's corrrn; that does have an R in it."
"We'll call you Cawn, then, shall we? Unless you'd prefer to use the name beginning with B; you said Con B. Weaver, didn't you?"
"Oh, yeah well, that's just B., there's no name to it, it's just an initial."
"How unusual!" Nicholas expressed interested astonishment, "is that how you were christened?"
"I guess I never was christened; my parents didn't do religion a lot. I guess my granddad put them off it."
Con B. Weaver took a mouthful of food and the conversation languished. Henry and Nicholas exchanged glances of sympathetic amusement, but the object of their suppressed mirth was mercifully unaware of it and had in fact enjoyed being the centre of attention for the previous few minutes. The others decided to continue the conversation they'd been engaged in when coming down the stairs together. As this was a common feature of high table talking even Nicholas felt no guilt about it and Henry was merely relieved to have silenced, however temporarily, the new arrival, who reminded him all too forcibly of many of the inhabitants of his native land. He reflected that there must be plenty of similar people among the English, but somehow one seemed less likely to encounter them. Cassandra, coming in to remove the

plates, was relieved to find Henry and Nicholas conversing happily and without interruption.

When the pudding had been eaten Marlene helped bring the plates out. Cassandra tried to dissuade her but was surprised when Melissa said: "It's all right, darling, Mrs Weaver just wants a faggie; isn't that so?"

Marlene responded with a nod and a guilty smile. "You see," Melissa went on, "her husband disapproves, so she has to be secretive about it."

"Heavens!" Cassandra was more amazed at her mother than at this information, which was unsurprising. "Won't he come looking for you?" she added, to disguise her near astonishment at Melissa's friendliness to the new guest.

"No, he's really tired, he likes to do just nothing after a meal. I should be safe."

Melissa passed her packet of cigarettes to Marlene, who took one gratefully, lit it and inhaled with obviously deep delight.

"Gee, thanks; I really appreciate this; I'll pay you back when I get some. It drove me wild to see all the duty frees at the airport and not be able to buy any."

"Are many American women so subservient to their husbands?"

"So….? Oh, I get it; well I guess not, really, but almost everybody's against smoking in the States so I'm kind of outnumbered all round. My daughter doesn't know I smoke, either, and I don't want Con telling her."

"She's very much her father's daughter, is she?"

"Oh, Con's not her father; it's a second marriage for both of us. Well no, it's Con's third but he doesn't really count the second one; says it was just a brief mistake. Come to think of it he's got a friend over here getting married for the third time; we're going to the wedding, that's partly why we came over early."

"Oh, that should be pleasant; where is it?" Melissa expressed polite interest.

"Well it was going to be in a college in Oxford. I can't remember the name of it. But anyways they've changed it to a hotel now---Great Gables Hotel it's called. I'm real disappointed it's not in a college. Con's friend's a professor and he wanted it in his college."

"It wasn't Chester College, by any chance?" Cassandra felt she knew the answer.

"Now I think that might be it. Why, do you know it?"

"Is the friend's name Nigel Nethercott?"

"You don't mean you know him too! My, isn't that amazing. He sent us that Gazette newspaper with your advertisement in it, but we didn't realise he knew you. He never said."

Melissa and Cassandra exchanged glances, which contained the query of how much to reveal about their knowledge of Nigel in general and his wedding in particular.

"Oh," Melissa countered, "that's hardly surprising; he may not have even realised that we took paying guests. I expect he just knew this was an attractive area. We don't really know him at all well; he's a colleague of a friend of Cassandra's."

"He and Con got on great when he was in the States on a sabbatical. But I'd better go up now; I don't want Con wondering where I am. It's nice to talk to you and thanks for the cigarette. Have a good evening."

Left alone, Melissa and Cassandra looked at each other somewhat wonderingly, both feeling a little lost in an unfamiliar situation.

"I think I need a cigarette, too," said Cassandra. Melissa pushed the packet across the table. "Are you really coping with them, or just pretending? Don't you mind her coming into the kitchen?"

"I don't think I do, somehow. I was horrified at first, but I can't help thinking she's actually quite a nice woman. It's a while since I've talked much to a woman my own sort of age. I began to feel it a little when Celestria was here; I suppose it made me feel old seeing you girls together."

"Oh dear. I hope you didn't feel left out. You know Lady M.---Midge--- of course."

"I don't see her very often, she's as busy with good works as I am with housekeeping and besides, she's got a nice husband."

"That certainly seems to be more than one can say for Mrs Weaver!"

"That's probably why I'm finding I almost like her. A husband who's a friend of Nigel Nethercott's can't conceivably be nice…even if we hadn't already discovered that for ourselves."

"It's funny we didn't feel like telling her we were also going to that wedding. I wonder why we didn't?"

"I'm afraid," Melissa simultaneously exhaled a puff of smoke and a sigh, "it was fear of being overwhelmed by too much mateyness. It's not nearly as bad as I thought it would be but I can only take a little at a time."

49

On Friday evening Nicholas almost bounded into the kitchen with the news that he'd be picking Celestria up directly after breakfast the following morning.

" I know," Cassandra smiled, "she rang me last night; but she did say she'd go back for the night and not stay here as I had thought she was going to. Can't you persuade her?"

" I'm hoping to; she could stay in Fergus's room, couldn't she?"

"Yes of course. Why doesn't she want to be here?" Melissa queried.

"You know her: she doesn't want to give you any trouble."

"But it would be trouble for you to have to drive her back and then pick her up again on Sunday morning," Cassandra protested, " and besides, I want to see as much of her as possible. Do you think I dare ring her on her mobile and try to persuade her?"

" Of course you must, darling," Melissa insisted, "she'll surely be able to answer while she's clearing up after dinner. And would she like to have dinner here tomorrow evening and meet our new guests? It might be interesting for her to know who we're talking about when we mention them, as we can hardly fail to do."

"That would be nice, especially as we're going out to explore the Cotswolds during the day."

Cassandra did manage to speak to Celestria at the third attempt. "I know you must be awfully busy; can you manage to talk now?"

"Oh dear!" came a breathless voice, "I've been talking to Miss Flossie about the weekend. There seems to be a lot to organise before she can take over. I really feel I should be here to do the breakfast on Sunday."

"But you're supposed to have the whole weekend off! Surely they managed all right before?"

"She's been counting the eggs; she seems to think I've used too many."

"All the more reason for you to be away and not able to use any more!"

"I feel I need to justify----"

"Now that's not sensible. They're very lucky indeed to have you there, and they're more likely to appreciate the fact when they have to do without you. Anyway, I miss you dreadfully and want some opportunity to talk to you, especially as Nicholas will be taking you out all day."

"Well-----"

"That's settled, then, and you can have Pa's room as your own and we'll just leave it from week to week and not even change the sheets!"

With a few more words it was agreed and Cassandra handed the telephone to Nicholas while she and her mother tactfully found other things to do at a suitable distance. After finishing the call he came to speak to them, showing a small measure of happiness and a large one of anxiety.

"I hate to have her working there," he said, "even if she does have the weekends away. She's too diligent and scrupulous; they'll take advantage of her. We must arrange the marriage as soon as possible so that I can look after her. And we haven't even decided where it's to be." Nicholas sank into a chair by the kitchen table and put his head in his hands.

"You'll be able to discuss it tomorrow, don't worry." Cassandra spoke consolingly. "And you know, if Celestria could cope with all that time in a convent---monastery---she must be tougher than she looks."

***

Nicholas could hardly down his breakfast before setting off to fetch his betrothed. He was gone before the Weavers had even emerged from their room. Cassandra and Melissa tempered their sympathetic amusement with some puzzlement as to how to arrange the evening's dinner. Should Celestria and Nicholas eat with them in the kitchen or should they brave the 'colonials' in the dining-room?

"Can't we just ask them which they'd prefer?" Cassandra suggested.

"They'd have to say they'd rather be with us," her mother countered.

"I expect they probably would, anyway."

"True, but then Celestria wouldn't have a chance to meet our guests and know who we'll be talking about, and besides, I'm rather unwilling to leave that nice Dr Acland on his own with the 'dreaded Americans!"

"Oh Ma, you don't dread Marlene any more, you know you don't."

"Not entirely, but she is still something of a mixed blessing."

***

Celestria of course demurred at the idea of having dinner with the guests as did Nicholas, but they eventually gave way in response to pleas for the protection of Dr Acland, whom Nicholas both liked and respected and to whom he was by no means averse to introducing his fiancée with very excusable male pride.

"It's time you had an engagement ring," Melissa murmured, looking at Celestria's unadorned hands. "Let me lend you one you can use in the meantime."

"Oh, I couldn't! It's not important---I never thought of it." Celestria was embarrassed at the idea but Nicholas supported it.

"I'm having a family one remade for her," he said, "but it will take time and I'd really like her to wear a ring now; I want everybody to know it's official."

Melissa went upstairs and returned with a quite large selection of rings including one containing a delicate sapphire. "This is a little small for me," she remarked, "but it might just fit you."

Celestria found it a little difficult to put on but the application of liquid soap eased its passage.

"That's excellent; it looks beautiful and won't come off easily and get lost," Cassandra commented approvingly.

Nicholas was delighted at Melissa's kindness and happy to have his proprietary status made apparent, though of course he was convinced that no adornment was in any way necessary to enhance the beauty of his betrothed! Poor Celestria was almost too overcome by the novelty of so much attention to be able to murmur appropriate thanks and appreciation. Melissa suddenly realised that dinner would be late if she didn't force herself to concentrate on mundane matters, and told the engaged couple to go and sit in the dining room now that they were suitably armed to meet the Americans.

Dr Acland joined them first and showed just the right degree of interest in Celestria, which calmed the self-consciousness she was a little unhappily aware of. The Weavers were another matter, however. Con B. flicked his eyes over her with more than a hint of the salacious and Marlene launched into ecstacies about rings and romance. Perhaps fortunately this began to bore her husband and he interrupted with the snide comment: "Well I just wish your precious daughter would get herself engaged; you'll never get her off at the rate she's going."

"Oh now, Con, she's not that old and anyways people get married older these days."

"Yeah; if they get married at all. Mostly they just shack up together. Does that happen much here? Maybe not. What about Australia, Henry?"

"Yes, I'm afraid so. Sometimes a couple live together for years with no children, no commitment, and then the chap goes off with somebody younger, marries her and has a family and leaves the older woman behind with nothing, not even the possibility of having a family herself. Of course it can be worse when there are children, but the same could probably be said of married couples who divorce.

"Yeah, well, at least with divorce there's alimony. I should know, I've been divorced twice."

"I'm sorry, I didn't know." Henry was apologetic.

"It's no big deal in the States; happens to a lot of people. Marlene's been divorced too."

"I don't think this is a very nice thing to talk about when we've got a young engaged couple here, Con."

"Oh I dunno. Some people feel glad to think there's always a let out if things don't work out right---eh Nick, er Nicholas?"

"I can't imagine anybody embarking on marriage with such feelings," Nicholas replied stiffly, "but if they do, and they go through a Catholic marriage service, the marriage is not a valid sacrament and can be annulled."

"You don't say? I thought Catholics never got divorced."

Nicholas was about to launch into an elucidation of the Catholic position when Celestria said softly "I agree with Mrs Weaver; I'd rather talk about something other than divorce."

All three men looked at her with surprised respect. It was as if they had hardly expected her to be able to speak and were almost astonished when she did. Celestria was insufficiently accustomed to the society of men to realise that this is a not uncommon phenomenon. She would have ample opportunity to get used to it, however, as a don's wife in Durham. There was a silence, broken by Marlene, who said "Thank you, Celest, I'd rather talk about weddings. When's yours going to be?" This utterance surprised nobody, of course, but it had the effect of making the men switch into a conversation among themselves; even Nicholas, who might be supposed to have an interest in the matter, detached himself from it in the company of others of his own sex.

After dinner Celestria went gratefully into the kitchen to talk to Cassandra and her mother while Nicholas lingered a little in conversation with Henry Acland. She had barely begun to answer their interested 'How was it?' when a voice at the door said: "Hi there! I don't want to intrude, ladies, but---"

"Of course! Come in Marlene; you'll be wanting your cigarette. Come and join me." Melissa made way for her guest at the table after taking the 'special packet' from a drawer. "Have a drop of wine to go with it. The girls won't want any." The girls were indeed at the other end of the table already engaged in the most animated conversation. Melissa realised that she was glad of an excuse to leave them to themselves without any necessity of feeling that they ought to include her.

"I feel I'm intruding," Marlene apologised again "I didn't realise---" but Melissa interrupted her to express gratitude for her company.

"No really, you're not intruding. The girls want to talk to each other and I feel rather *de trop*, I mean in the way, when they're together. I appreciate having a woman my own sort of age to talk to once in a while. You've got a grown up daughter yourself, of course, so you know what

I'm talking about." Melissa smiled graciously and hoped she hadn't put too much emphasis on 'once in a while'.

"You're so kind; I never thought you were going to be so nice when we first met you. Even Con says you're a really good cook, and that's a lot from him." Marlene puffed happily at her forbidden cigarette and Melissa responded "I'm glad you find I'm nicer than I look!"

"Oh gees, I never meant that; I mean you look terrific, well maybe just a bit scary. It's more the way you sound, I guess, but I'm getting habituated. Tell me, though, what I ought to wear to this wedding we're going to. In the States weddings are usually in the evening these days and this one's in the afternoon."

"It's a while since I've been to one in England but we used to wear a smart dress or coat and skirt---er, suit---and a big, important looking hat."

"Wow! I don't have a hat; well, not that kind. You don't wear them with evening dress."

"Well it's true not everybody wears a hat now; I've seen pictures of women, especially young ones, with gauzy looking shapes stuck on the side of the head. Personally I think they look rather silly. But I must admit that large hats have the disadvantage of coming off in a wind or even if a couple of women greet each other with the obligatory kiss. Wide brims discourage proximity. It's ridiculous, really, to go on wearing them. But I know what we can do: buy a copy of *Hello* and look at the pictures of wedding guests in there, or perhaps even *The Tatler*; though of course they're both quite likely to be a bit over the top."

"I guess you're thinking what to wear to that nice young couple's wedding, Nicholas and Celest, is it?"

"Celestria. Yes, yes indeed, we'll be going to that of course." Melissa remembered that she and Cassandra had not mentioned their attendance at the Nigel and Effie wedding to Marlene and she now felt a little awkward about admitting it. How to explain why she'd said nothing about it before? She decided to brave it. "As a matter of fact," she continued, "we're also going to the one you're here for."

"No! You don't say! I thought you said you didn't know Nigel?"

"It's because Cassandra's been going out with his best man, Robert Taylor, and she feels he needs support. We've only just been asked; I think they waited until they had some refusals before they put us on the list."

"Well I can't say how happy I am that you'll be there; I thought we wouldn't know anybody, and with English people not being that friendly we might not be very comfortable. Anyways, you and me had better plan together and make certain we don't wear the same thing."

Melissa considered this a rather unlikely eventuality but to avoid replying she offered Marlene another cigarette and a 'tiny top-up' of her drink.

"Well, thank you, but really *very* small; I don't want to be inebriated. Thinking about weddings makes me so sentimental. They're just so special."

"Some are, perhaps, but with so many coming to grief these days it's not always easy to feel optimistic about them. Didn't you have any qualms about entering on a second marriage?"

"Any--- ?"

"Any anxieties. Were you so sure it would work out better with your second husband than with your first?"

Melissa was genuinely curious to know whether Marlene's ex could possibly have been worse than her present husband, and if so, how she'd ever found the courage to venture on matrimony again.

Marlene looked dreamily through a wisp of smoke and sighed “Well I guess if we think it’s all right at the time we reckon it’ll go on being all right, and anyways we’re too busy with the arrangements to worry about anything else much.”

50

Cassandra replied to the Nethercott/Fraser wedding invitation using the tear-off attachment. It seemed the most appropriate thing to do. She was surprised into wondering whether she'd done the wrong thing a few days later, however, when her mother called her to the telephone saying 'Mrs Fraser' wanted to speak to her.

"Hullo?" Cassandra said doubtingly into the receiver.

"Oh, Cass Andrea, this is Mrs Fraser. You know, Effie's mother. She's so glad you and Mrs Marsh---banks are coming to the wedding and she wants you to come to her hen party. We're, I mean she's, having it quite early, well quite soon, so as not to be too near the wedding."

"Oh, that's terribly kind of her, but really---I mean---she hardly knows me---er, surely she can't want---"

Norah Fraser was not to be put off. "Well it's you being the best man's girlfriend you see; and besides you live in a reelly nice place and Sir Felix and Lady M. are relatives of yours so I mean you're quite suitable. Now about picking you up, we'll have the limo come for you at 6.00 o'clock because it's got to get to Birmingham."

"To *Birmingham!*"

"Yes, to a club in Birmingham. Well you see Effie's got friends in Birmingham because we used to live there and she wanted to go out like they used to when they were teenagers."

"But when is it?"

"Oh, didn't I say? On Saturday week. So that's all settled then. And make sure you're ready on time. Goodbye." The telephone gave a loud kplock and Cassandra was left holding the receiver and glaring into it as if it was responsible for her astonishment. With surprising presence of mind she decided she must find out Norah Fraser's number so that she could ring back with reasons for being unable to accept the invitation, if it could be called that. She dialled 1471 only to be told that 'the caller withheld their number'.

"Oh Lord above, what on earth shall I do?" she gasped aloud as her mother came into the room.

"Darling! Whatever's the matter?" Melissa voiced her concern. "What's happened? You're pale as a ghost. Sit down and have a drink. Here." She eased her daughter into a chair and put a glass of wine in front of her. "Now tell me what's upset you. Is it Robert?"

Cassandra began to laugh weakly. "No, no. Nothing like that. It's quite ridiculous. I don't know whether I'm more angry or amazed. That Mrs Fraser's demanded that I go to her daughter's hen party."

"Oh dear! I suppose she wouldn't take no for an answer."

"She didn't even give me time to answer. Simply told me when 'the limo' would pick me up."

"The *limo?* Does she mean 'limousine'?

"Oh no! I mean No I can't bear it. Oh spare me; can it be a *stretch limo?*"

"You don't mean one of those great long things Arab sheiks transport all their wives in?"

Cassandra gave a groan and put her head in her hands. "I fear!"

Mother and daughter looked at each other and began to laugh.

"Well you know, darling," Melissa managed finally, wiping her eyes, "it could be quite fun to see what those things look like inside. And I don't think anybody can see into them from outside, so it's not as if you'd be recognised by somebody we know."

"You're not trying to tell me I ought to *go*!"

Melissa took a long draw on her cigarette, blew out an elegant spiral of smoke and said *"I* would!"

***

So Cassandra, on the relevant Saturday, and despite Robert's protestations and apologies 'for having got her into something so appalling', sat ready and waiting for 'the limo' to pick her up. As it was not quite six o'clock her mother felt she had a perfect excuse for waiting with her, and Pete, who had been alerted to the event, was in the shed with eyes and ears primed for signs of the car's approach. Three minutes before six there was a sound of somewhat fluty honking from outside the front door.

"Oh dear!" Melissa murmured; "they clearly consider the back yard inappropriate!"

Pete shot out of the shed and was round at the main entrance before Cassandra and her mother reached the front door. "She's just coming," he informed the uniformed driver in tones of what he considered to be suitable formality. Melissa opened the front door and gasped to Cassandra, who was standing behind her: "I don't believe it! It's *pink*!!"

Pete was grinning with delighted pride. "It ain't half posh, Miss! Cor! Good thing they didn't come into the yard; mightn't have got out again it's so long."

Cassandra was too involved in the difficult conquest of a desire to giggle to make any answer but her mother, coming down the steps to see her off, murmured: "I'm *so* glad you're going, darling, I wouldn't have missed this for *any*thing!"

Inside the vast vehicle Cassandra was found a seat on the shiny silver upholstery that stretched all along one long side, opposite a lighted area containing a glittering array of decanters, glasses and all the necessary ---and unnecessary---appurtenances for providing drinks. Effie Fraser, from a dominant position, waved a casual hand and announced: "This is Cass; she's our best man's girlfriend."

The eight other girls responded variously with 'hullo' or 'hi' and there was even one 'pleased to meet you', the speaker of which went on to ask "Do you live here?"

Cassandra admitted that she did.

"Wow! But you can't live in all of it."

"Oh, no. We don't use the top floors."

The other girls were all silent, focussing on Cassandra, who deemed it wise to continue "And we let rooms."

Another, younger, girl enquired "Is that boy your brother?" As the limo had already progressed some distance 'that boy' was no longer in sight but as Pete was obviously meant Cassandra anticipated that his position in the household would be in question. It didn't occur to her simply to say 'no' without any addition so she added "He's got a room in the house." Then, hoping to deflect attention from herself she asked the questioner "Do you live in Oxford?"

"In Kidlington," was the reply. "Not the Garden City, mind; we live in a Close with really nice, new houses. I work in the same place as Eff, only of course she's older than me, and so does Kerry, over there, and Charlene." Kerry and Charlene nodded agreement. "What do you do?"

"I'm a potter. I make pots."

"Flower pots?" Charlene looked puzzled.

Effie intervened. "No she doesn't, Charl, she makes piss-pots. Don't you remember all that about her in the paper, her and her mum selling them in the market and people complaining and somebody called the police?"

"Wow! Was that you? Yeah I remember that. And you had your picture in the paper and all."

"It was a long time ago; I hoped people had forgotten about it."

"I wouldn't want to forget about having my picture in the paper!" Charlene was not unimpressed.

"It was one of those piss-pots you gave me for Christmas, wasn't it Eff?" Kerry giggled.

"Yeah, have you used it?"

"No. My mum thought it was for putting gravy in and when I told her what it *was* for she thought it was really disgusting. But my Nan said it was a good idea because she used to have just an outside toilet and that pot would have been easier to use at night than the sort they kept under the bed; a chamber she called it. But my mum shut her up because she didn't want people to think she'd lived in a house without a proper inside bathroom."

"Urgh! I wouldn't want to pee in it and then have it in the bedroom all night; it'd smell something awful."

"Don't be silly Lisa," Effie told Cassandra's original questioner, "you just throw it out the window."

There were multiple giggles as to the fun this would be, especially if you could pick out who was underneath.

"I bet you use yours, Eff, don't you?"

"Yeah, quite a lot. Saves going to the bathroom and interrupting things. Nigel says it really turns him on, seeing me use it."

"You're a cool one, I must say," Kerry continued. "I wouldn't have the nerve to try it on Kevin. He might be shocked."

"Oh well," Effie assumed an air of superiority, "Nigel's older, you see; more experienced. Besides, he's educated and educated people don't get shocked about things. That's what he says, anyway." She turned to Cassandra. "What does your Robert think about it? I bet he likes seeing you use it!"

Cassandra remembered using similar words to Robert about his supposed wife on the occasion when she first saw him and sold him a pot. Filled with mortification at the dreadful memory she felt herself growing hot from the neck up and was not comforted by the laughter of the other girls and their cries of "Ooh look how she's blushing! I bet she's thinking of things she's not going to tell us about!"

"That'll do now girls; it's not as if she knows us," Kerry interrupted kindly.

"Well, she's the one who invented the pot," Lisa spoke defensively, " she doesn't need to get all up-tight about it!"

"It'd be a good idea to have one in here now," Charlene piped up. "You didn't think to bring one did you Effie?"

"No I did not; don't want you girls spilling pee all over the limo---we'd have to pay compensation and it costs quite enough as it is. Let's help ourselves to a drink. What do you all want? There's gin, whisky, brandy, cherry brandy, crème de mente---oh, practically everything; don't have beer, though, or you might want to use one of those pots, and it's not as if there was any chaps here to enjoy watching!"

The laughter subsided as the drinks were distributed and Cassandra, uncharacteristically, decided that she needed a brandy on ice to fortify her for the rest of the evening; or, if that was too much to hope for, at least the rest of the journey.

"That's right," Effie encouraged her. "Have a double."

As Cassandra took it thankfully she noticed that her hand was shaking. It was all so utterly awful. She began to hate her mother. It was all her mother's fault; not just making her go on this ghastly outing but starting the whole business of that frightful, awful Oxford pot. She'd never live it down. What would Celestria think if she knew about it? What would Nicholas think? She felt totally overcome with shame and disgust and only wanted to hide away and cry. She took a sip of the brandy, which turned into a gulp as the limo went over a bump. It didn't make her feel any better. She decided to drink it quickly and go on to gin. There didn't seem to be any wine. The other girls were busy talking about their boyfriends, all of whom everybody seemed to know. Cassandra was not sorry to be left out of the conversation, which became increasingly ribald as the drinks reached a third round.

The limo drew up to a smooth stop. They had arrived. Where they had arrived was a mystery to Cassandra, though it looked like a particularly garish nightclub. "Where are we?" she asked the nearest girl, who told her the name. "What is it? A nightclub?"

The girl, it was Charlene, giggled. "Better than that," she answered, "it's a male strip club! See the big pink sign, it says 'The ultimate girls night out'." Cassandra barely had time to amuse herself with their status as 'ultimate girls' before her companion shrieked "Ooh, here comes another hen party!"

Another limo, white this time, drew up behind them and an excited group of young women hurled themselves out of it, shrieking and screaming. They were all wearing wide white satin sashes proclaiming HEN PARTY in crimson capitals.

"Come on Eff," Charlene nudged their hostess "get out our sashes; we can do better than that lot."

"Oh, okay. I was going to wait till the local girls arrive but we can put them on now. They're pink with silver letters on, like the limo." As Effie began to hand these round there was a banging on the door, which was opened to reveal four more young women, all in the top end of the BMI scale, shouting greetings with a volume of noise that belied their number. Effie called out their names above the din but the only one Cassandra could catch was what sounded like 'Sherry'.

"We've got something for you, too, Eff," Sherry announced, and out of a large bag she drew a short white veil with a kind of coronet attached. "Come on, put it on, you've got to wear it so everyone'll know who the hen party's for."

Effie was gigglingly happy to obey and Cassandra could see that the centre of the 'coronet' sported an embracing couple in pink plastic. "Oh *heavens!"* she said aloud. Sherry turned to her appreciatively.

"Yeah, great isn't it? I'm Eff's cousin and we wanted to give her something hot. I'm Sherry."

"Sherry? Is that your real name?"

"Yeah but you're sposed to spell it C-h-e-r-i-e. It's French, you see. You're new, aren't you? I don't think I've seen you before."

"I'm the best man's girlfriend."

But Sherry---or Cherie---was too busy admiring her cousin's headdress to listen. She did, however, turn to Cassandra again when the general stampede to get into the club began. "Come on!" she urged, "you don't want to miss anything!" Despite her doubts as to the truth of the statement Cassandra had no option but to follow.

51

They were met at the door, on what looked like a rather stained red carpet, by an over-developed young man in very tight jeans and a black bow tie; nothing else. The interior presented a weird combination of shadow and glare. Cassandra mused that it looked like Milton's Hell: flames but no light. All around were tables full of varying numbers of mainly young, sometimes not so young, women. The decibel level was high. Drinks were ordered. The lights went down, a group of young men, all clad like the one at the door, came on the stage and began to wave flaming torches in rhythmic circles to the accompaniment of harsh music. It was not unskilful and certainly showed off the physique of the men to advantage. In spite of herself Cassandra found it fascinating. The other girls were mainly talking among themselves; they'd seen it all before and were more interested in anticipating the exciting acts to come. Cherie kindly explained this to Cassandra.

"You not been to a club like this before?"

"No, I haven't." Cassandra didn't admit to having been ignorant of their existence.

"Don't your friends have hen parties, then?"

"Well I don't think any of them have got married yet."

"No, well, lots of people don't. They'd rather spend the money on other things. But I mean you look sort of respectable and quite old."

Charlene, hearing this from across the table, interrupted with "She's not that respectable, Cherie, she makes piss-pots and sells them in the market!"

"You're having me on, Charle, I don't believe you."

Fortunately the uproar which greeted the end of the act on the stage drowned any further attempt at conversation and ensuing shouts of "Where's the strippers? Let's have the strippers!" took up the general attention. In response to this an elegantly---and fully---dressed young man took centre stage and, to a suitable musical accompaniment, began to remove his tie. Cassandra gazed in amazement as he imported into this elementary, everyday action a most erotic suggestiveness. By the time he came to unbutton his shirt, with the lowest button necessitating the unbuckling of the belt of his trousers, the audience of shrieking females had reached fever pitch and Cassandra felt herself being carried along with the general hysteria. Little strands of objective reason crept in occasionally; how interesting that now women should be watching a man displaying his body in this way when men have been watching women do it for heaven knows how many centuries. No wonder he's ---well he was--- wearing trousers; it would be impossible to slip out of tight jeans so elegantly. He was down to a small, bulging garment, which could scarcely be called underpants. He turned his back on the audience and inched the covering down slowly and provocatively, then turned round again, to increased shrieks from the floor, and tantalisingly fingered the remnant of covering over the prominent genitalia. At last! The final garment came off. There was a flash as of fireworks and the lights dimmed, glared and dimmed again and the stage was empty.

Amid the uproarious applause Cherie turned to Cassandra. "Are you all right, love?" she enquired kindly. "You look as if you was going to faint. Well, he is gorgeous, isn't he? Wow! Later on they come round the tables and talk to us and you can really see them close to, know what I mean. There's some clubs where there's a swimming pool and you can go in swimming with them; but they haven't got one here."

"Heavens! You don't mean---?"

"No, you have to wear a bathing suit. Mind you, not always easy to see what happens under water, is it?" Charlene gave Cassandra a nudge to accompany her giggle.

The evening wore on; as Charlene had predicted some of the men came round the tables and showed themselves off to the seated girls at (very) close quarters, their obvious attributes at eye level. Cassandra tried to preserve an objective attitude by musing that it was probably no worse than Elizabethans wearing codpieces, but she found it embarrassingly distasteful none the less. After one of these visitations Cherie left her to go and talk to some girls at another table and a small, palely pretty girl came and took her place. Cassandra had not noticed her before.

"Do you mind if I sit here?" the girl asked. "I'm Sarah. I can see you're different."

"Oh dear, I hope I don't, er, oh," Cassandra floundered "I mean, in what way?"

"Well, you're quite thin, for a start."

"So are you, come to that," Cassandra had to smile, "in fact you've hardly been visible! You're with the Birmingham girls, of course."

"Yes, I live here. My partner's Effie's cousin so that's why she asked me. I had to come. But really when you're not single and you've got a family this sort of thing isn't something you want."

"Oh you've got a family?"

"Yes, a little girl. She's four."

"Are you older than Effie? I wouldn't have thought so."

"About the same age, but she's not got children, and I don't think she's been in this relationship that long. Have you got a family?"

"No, I'm not married. Oh!" Cassandra immediately realised that her instinctive reaction to the question was hardly tactful to the questioner. “I mean I’m not in that sort of relationship. I never have been.”

“Aren’t you the best man’s girlfriend?”

“Well yes, I suppose I am; that is, I’ve been going out with him but he’s not what you’d call my partner.”

“Don’t you want him to be?”

Cassandra didn’t answer. She was beginning to feel rather unsteady and to find the effort of concentration something of a burden. She turned to focus on Sarah with difficulty.

“Don’t you?” Sarah repeated.

“Sometimes I do; sometimes I don’t know.”

Sarah sighed. “It’s always like that,” she said, “if you let yourself think about it.”

Preferable though the company of quiet Sarah was to that of the other girls, who were becoming increasingly raucous and repetitive, as indeed was the whole club and its entertainment in general, Cassandra longed desperately for the evening to be over, little though she relished the journey home. There was nothing to do but drink and she was mortally afraid of passing out completely if she drank much more. At last they spilled into the street to pile into the limo again, all of them decidedly unsteady, stumbling into each other and finding it uproariously funny. Cassandra was knocked sideways by one of the larger, fatter girls and would have lost her balance had she not fallen against another equally large one. Charlene found this particularly amusing.

“Oi! Look at Lady Piss-pot! She’s as bad as the rest of us! Never mind, love, you can sleep some of it off in the limo!”

Jostled into a seat at last Cassandra was very glad to close her eyes; she would have liked to close her ears as well, as the raucous conversation---if the high pitched, disjointed sentences could be called that--- was more unavoidable and obtrusive even than in the club. She escaped involvement by feigning sleep and after hearing a few comments on her state of drunkenness she actually managed to doze. She woke only when the limo stopped and she received a hefty nudge from her neighbour.

"Wake up, love, we're at your place!"

"Not passed out, has she?" Effie queried. "God, I hope not. Nigel told me to look after her."

Charlene pulled Cassandra to her feet. "No, she's all right; she can stand up. Come on love, I'll take you to your door. Have you got a key?"

With an effort Cassandra replied "Yes, but not for the front door; I need to go round to the side."

"Good job I'm holding on to you then." They emerged from the limo and Cassandra almost fell as she was dragged over the ground by Charlene, who then shouted at top pitch "Come and get on the other side, somebody; she's well unsteady!"

Cassandra would have liked to point out that Charlene was not the firmest of props but Cherie saved her the trouble by tumbling out of the vehicle and shouting "Look who's talking! You're all over the place yourself, Charle; never you mind, love, I'll help you." This was a signal for uproarious laughter both inside and outside the pink and silver monster and Cassandra was sufficiently *compos mentis* to register the extent of the noise in the otherwise soundless grounds and to groan as she envisaged the reaction of guests in the house.

"What's the matter, love? Going to be sick?" Cherie asked sympathetically as the three of them weaved a serpentine way round to the side door. Cassandra ventured to say she didn't think so.

"Just a bad head, is it? Bet it'll be worse tomorrow!" Charlene remarked comfortingly.

"Don't be silly, Charle, it's tomorrow already!" More laughter hit the high decibel register as Cassandra found her key and opened the door. She managed to say good night and thank you as she much more thankfully went inside. The laughter was still audible as she entered the kitchen and collapsed into the nearest chair----then got up quickly and rushed to the sink, just in time. She was wiping her mouth with kitchen paper and running a strong stream of water to clear the evidence when her mother appeared.

"Oh dear," Melissa exclaimed " was it so very, very awful?"

"I think," Cassandra managed to reply as she stumbled to a chair and sank into it, "I hope—-that it's the worst night of my life!"

"If it is, darling," her mother observed as she exhaled a delicate plume of smoke drawn from a cigarette which seemed to have materialised out of thin air, "if it is, then you'll be a most unusually fortunate woman!"

52

Cassandra managed to go to the 11.00 o'clock mass with her mother on the morning after the hen party in spite of a throbbing head and a very nasty taste in her mouth. The latter, as she remarked to Robert when they sat in the club room after mass, was probably mental as well as physical. Robert was full of sympathy and regret.

"I'm so sorry," he kept saying, " it's a concomitant of this ghastly wedding that I'd never considered; I feel so responsible letting you in for it; I should have been with you."

"Don't be silly, Robert, you couldn't have come to a hen party! It would be like me going to a stag party. Anyway, it's my mother's fault. She said I ought to go, didn't you, Ma? Thought I might find it interesting!!"

"I would have gone myself if they'd asked me," Melissa countered. "I find it fascinating. Now that women are supposedly liberated they're behaving just like men at their worst. Perhaps they're just showing that they're human beings too."

"Not all men behave like that, I hope."

"No, Robert, nor all women, of course. But I can't help thinking how cramped we were when I was that sort of age. I didn't go through all the pre-wedding stuff myself, of course, but I had to go along with people who did. They had the most dreadful girls-only evening parties called 'showers' where everybody brought useful presents for the bride to be. The boredom of watching her undoing endless parcels of patty tins and oven gloves was indescribable. One poor girl was given a scrubbing-brush and a bar of sandsoap, which made her look decidedly depressed. I'm afraid I took a certain amount of pleasure from it at the time. It made a change. It says something for the evening when I tell you it was the most exciting thing that happened. I would have *much* preferred a male strip club!"

"I must admit you would have managed it better than I did, Ma." Cassandra preferred not to tell Robert that the worst thing had been the other girls' reaction to her and the awfulness of being called 'Lady Piss-pot'.

"Yes, darling, I think I would; I'm not so serious-minded as you are and of course I'm more worldly. You would have been more at home in Celestria's convent."

"I hope you're not thinking of that!" Robert looked alarmed.

Cassandra had to laugh at his consternation. "No, Robert, one awful evening hasn't quite driven me out of the world altogether, but if I had to choose between going to such an event every week and going into a convent the convent would win!"

***

"You know, darling," Melissa said to her daughter as they were having a cup of coffee after lunch, "it's awfully important who one's husband's friends are. Married couples' friends always go in the male line, so to speak, and the wives have to get on as best they can. You don't seem to have met any friends of Robert's apart from that frightful Nigel; and of course you've never met any of his family."

"Nigel isn't Robert's friend; he's never liked him. He just didn't know how to refuse to be his best man---and he's been regretting it ever since."

"Has he any other friends, ones he himself counts as friends I mean?"

"Well there's Samson Southey."

"Oh yes, true. An oddity, but definitely worth while."

"And he gets on very well with Nicholas."

"Whom he met through you, of course. Yes, that's probably a good sign. They'll be living in Durham, however. Of course he has colleagues; it can't be so necessary to have friends if he can meet and talk to colleagues whenever he wants to. Of course that woman Muriel might be considered a friend, I suppose. Not as much of one as she'd like to be, poor thing."

"*Muriel?* You don't think she's carrying a torch for Robert, surely! She's really quite *old!*"

"Yes, darling, quite; about as old as Robert in fact. I don't like American expressions as a rule but I have to admit that one's useful, and certainly less inelegant than most. And of course she's enamoured of Robert, it's too utterly obvious. You must remember his startled reaction when I pointed out that that was why she'd been to mass at the Oratory."

"No, I don't remember. I think you're making it up. If Robert was so startled he can't have had any idea about it, so it can't be obvious. She seems more interested in Samson from anything I've noticed."

"That's obviously *faute de mieux*! Not that it matters; it's Robert's friends we're talking about not his female admirers. It might be interesting to see how he gets on with his colleagues at the wedding; I suppose a good many of them will be there."

"I don't know. Robert says the married ones only dash in and out of college at lunch time, if then, and don't really mix in very much."

"And I suppose there are more unmarried women than unmarried men. In my generation intellectual women were generally considered to be practically unmarriageable."

"Oh I don't think that's the case now; almost all the girls I was at university with are married. But of course they're not Muriel's age."

Melissa smiled. “Poor Muriel!” she said.

***

Cassandra took the first opportunity she could find to give Celestria an account---slightly expurgated---of the hen party. It was not very easy as of course she was inseparable from Nicholas whenever she had any time away from her job. There was one fortunate Saturday evening, however, when her betrothed simply had to attend a college dinner and the two girls were able to be together. Celestria was much less amazed at the idea of a male strip club than at the stretch limo.

“Oh, yes,” she responded to the information. “I remember one of the postulants talking about that sort of thing. She said it was what decided her to come into the convent. She didn’t stay, though.”

“Why do you think she left?”

“A vocation should be something more positive than a mere dislike of the world. She was just trying to find herself. I hope she has, now.”

“I told my mother and Robert that if I had to choose between going to parties in male strip clubs and going into a convent the convent would win every time!”

Celestria smiled. “But fortunately you don’t have to choose. I can solemnly promise you that I am *not* intending to have a party like that! In fact not any sort of party. Apart from you I’m not really in touch with girls my own age.”

“You could try contacting the ones in the convent and invite them to a special night out!”

They both laughed. “Oh yes, why not. Reverend Mother might be delighted to let them go and have an evening off herself. I can just imagine it. But seriously, Nicholas isn’t going to have a stag party either; it’s not his sort of thing at all.”

“Has Nicholas got a lot of friends?”

"I don't really know; I've never thought about it. He speaks more of his family than anybody else, and one or two people in Blackfriars. His brother's going to be his best man."

"I don't know any friends of Robert's either, except Samson Southey. And of course I've never met his family. Do you think it matters? My mother does."

Celestria was silent for a time, concentrating on the question. "I was very happy to meet Nicholas's family," she said finally, "but I don't think it would have mattered if he hadn't met mine. I can't imagine we shall be seeing a great deal of them. In fact, I don't think it would have made any difference if neither of us had had any family at all. But perhaps I've become too detached after being in the convent. I probably don't know enough about living in the world."

"I'm beginning to wonder if *I* do! After that terrible hen party I consider myself an innocent---and not even abroad! I must have led a far more sheltered life than I realised. But seriously, should I meet Robert's family before I decide whether to marry him?"

Celestria looked shocked. "You must be very unsure if you think it would affect your decision."

"Yes; I am unsure. It's not like you and Nicholas, but then I don't think many people are. You must be very unusual, very particularly blessed. There can't be many women who come out of a convent and almost immediately find the man they know they want to marry. I'd envy you if I weren't so happy for you."

"Is Robert not the man you know you want to marry?"

" How can I tell? My mother must have thought she wanted to marry my father. She cut herself off from her family and her faith to do so, and she never stops saying what a terrible mistake she made."

"She should have known it would be a mistake if she went against her faith. Nothing can compensate for that. You know we had a guest house at the convent. People could come and stay there and attend our services and so on. We didn't generally mix with them much but I did do a stint helping the sister in charge and she told me quite a lot about the kind of guests she'd met. I spoke to a few of them myself, too. They were often divorced women. I remember one in particular who'd married a Protestant and given up her faith. It hadn't worked out at all well and in fact he'd left her. She got an annulment and then went round the country lecturing to other people on how to do the same. But of course you wouldn't have any problems like that with Robert. He seems very interested in becoming a Catholic himself."

"That's true, and he'd certainly never go against my faith. It's not as if he's unsuitable in any way, well, perhaps apart from his family."

"If that really matters to you you will have to meet them. Then perhaps you can take a large sheet of paper and write down the *pros* on one side and the *cons* on the other. But honestly, if you're in any doubt---"

"Yes, I know, 'if in doubt don't'! I believe Protestants, the old-fashioned sort, used to open the Bible at random, shut their eyes and put down a finger and trust that the sentence it lighted on would tell them what to do."

"Poor things," Celestria shook her head sadly. "They have some very strange ideas about the Bible. But actually their own reaction to what they read in it could perhaps bring out what they really felt."

There was the sound of a car in the yard and Celestria looked up eagerly. "That must be Nicholas!"

"Don't tell him what I've been saying, will you," Cassandra asked anxiously, "he might be shocked at how I feel about Robert. He's so sure about you. I know he wouldn't understand."

"No, no; of course I won't say anything. I would never betray a confidence, not even to Nicholas."

Nicholas, who had left the dinner at the earliest possible moment in order to return to Celestria, came in happily, accepted a cup of coffee and barely noticed Cassandra's absence when she disappeared and left him with his beloved.

The telephone rang in the kitchen as Cassandra entered it. "Oh, Robert, hullo! I thought you were at a dinner."

"Yes I was; Nicholas was there too but he left without staying for coffee or after dinner drinks. I daresay he's back with you by now."

"He is indeed. I've just left him with Celestria in the sitting-room."

"I wish I was there with you! Well, not necessarily in the sitting-room. Outside in the car would do very well."

"Oh dear!" Cassandra gave an involuntary sigh.

"What's the matter?"

"I wish I was like Celestria."

"Well I don't. I'd rather have you just the way you are."

Cassandra sighed again. Robert was concerned. "Something *is* the matter isn't it? Tell me."

"I think, well perhaps, I'd like you to take me to meet your family."

"Ah."

"Not if you don't want to, of course."

"Term time is difficult."

"Yes. During the vacation would do."

"Oh, right; yes certainly, we can talk about it later. But I wish I could see you now. Can I drive out?"

"Robert! You must have had far too much to drink at a college dinner to be able to drive!"

"I'm perfectly able to drive; I just wouldn't pass a breath test."

"So of course you can't come out now." Cassandra found herself wishing he could but felt somehow inhibited from saying so. The conversation ended a little unsatisfactorily. Robert was so distressed by it that he went out of his room to walk aimlessly round the college gardens. He was not able to fathom the complex causes of Cassandra's discontent and quite erroneously related it to his own recurrent jealousy of Nicholas. He suspected that Cassandra was really in love with him and wishing she were in Celestria's place. That she should simply be desirous of emulating Celestria's sureness of feeling, her complete sense of the rightness of what she was doing, was something he could not be aware of. He muttered to himself as he walked, almost blindly, over the sloping college lawns in the outer garden, "he's younger, better looking and better off. Of course she likes him better." He stumbled over a projecting tree root and almost fell. "Damn!" he said aloud. "Damn damn damn. Hell and damnation and—-"

"Robert!" a female voice made him wince uncomfortably. "Have you hurt yourself?"

He wanted to answer no, he hadn't hurt himself, he was just hurt, really hurt, hurt all over, but as he realised immediately that the voice belonged to Muriel and as he felt very chary of allowing himself to weep, however metaphorically, on Muriel's shoulder as he had once done before, he answered no, he'd merely tripped on a tree root and been annoyed at its interrupting his train of thought.

"Not a very pleasant train of thought from the sound of it," was Muriel's response. Robert wondered uncomfortably how much more he'd actually uttered aloud and how much more Muriel had heard. Blast the woman;

why couldn't she shut up, mind her own business, go away and leave him alone. It was all he could do to prevent himself from telling her to. Fortunately it was too dark for her to see his expression. "Would you like to.....?" she began but Robert was in no mood to let her finish.

"No!" he almost shouted. "No. I wouldn't!" And he stomped back to his room at a speed she couldn't match.

Cassandra, meanwhile, had searched the books in the house for a Bible, finally found one and carried it upstairs to her room.

53

In his bedroom Robert undressed rapidly, threw his clothes on the floor, got into bed and slept for a couple of hours, after which he awoke moaning and miserable. He was seized with pangs of guilt and remorse; guilt for having drunk too much at the dinner; remorse for his rudeness to Muriel. 'If I hadn't drunk so much I could have driven out to see Cassandra; Nicholas didn't drink, of course---*he* rushed back to see his beloved. He does everything right. I do everything wrong. Does Cassandra feel about him the way I feel about her? And the way I treated Muriel! Does she feel about me the way I feel about Cassandra? Hell and damnation! The way, the way, the way's all blocked. Why does Cassandra want to see my family? Because she's thinking seriously about me? No. Because she wants an excuse to break things off altogether and my family will provide it.'

Robert moaned again, considered ringing Cassandra on her mobile, decided against it 'it would only make things worse' and continued to indulge in self-inflicted misery.

Cassandra, meanwhile, sat on her bed, closed her eyes, opened the Bible and placed a finger on the open page. Eagerly she looked at the small print to see what it revealed. It was not very conclusive. 'The righteous perisheth, and no man layeth it to heart' she read. "Oh dear! Does that mean poor Robert's dying of love for me? No, I don't think so, though it's amazing how long that sort of thing persisted in all kinds of literature, from the Princess of Cleaves to Barbara Allen. Nobody can believe in it now. I'll just have another go and see if I can turn up something clearer." The next revelation could be considered more successful. 'He brought me to the banquet' Cassandra read, 'and his banner over me was love.' Had she been able to see Robert tossing on his bed she might have been more inclined to trust the first turn up; even so it made her think of his kindness and his care of her; his help with her father, his consideration for her mother. She even felt ungrateful for having complained that he took her to so many meals! Almost automatically she reached for her mobile and telephoned his number.

When his phone rang Robert grabbed it in a panic. "Cassandra! What's the matter?"

"I just suddenly wanted to speak to you. I thought you sounded unhappy and I was worried about you. Are you all right?"

"I am now."

"You weren't before?"

"Far from it!"

"I wish you were here."

"You don't mean that."

"I think I do."

"I could be there with you all the time if you'd let me."

"Yes."

"Yes?"

"Yes."

Robert gave a sound between a gasp and a sob. "Do you mean it? Do you really mean it? You won't wake up tomorrow and say 'no'?"

"No."

"I'll come and see you tomorrow, first thing, before breakfast, before you've had time to change your mind."

As early in the morning as she considered reasonable Cassandra knocked softly at the door of Celestria's bedroom. She was rewarded with an immediate "Come in!"

"I'm really sorry to disturb you so early," Cassandra apologised.

"Oh, you're not disturbing me; I'm used to waking up early after years of it in the monastery. And I don't sleep late in my present job, either, I can assure you. I'm very happy to see you. Come and sit on the bed."

Cassandra did so. "It worked!" she whispered.

"Worked?"

"Yes. It really did."

Celestria smiled. "Something must have, clearly. You're looking much happier than you were last night. But I would be grateful for just a little more explanation."

"The Bible!"

"Oh, Cassandra! You don't mean you opened it and shut your eyes and….."

"No, I shut my eyes and then opened it and put a finger on it."

"What did it say? I mean, what did you read?"

Cassandra produced a slip of paper on which she'd written the relevant sentences. Celestria studied them with a slight frown.

"Don't you think they're apposite?" Cassandra asked a little anxiously.

"The second one is, certainly; but you knew that already."

"I think it just made me realise it."

"Yes, perhaps it showed you how you really feel. But you know it is rather a superstitious practice. You won't make a habit of it, will you?"

"I don't suppose I'll ever do it again. I think it concentrated my mind, more than anything." Celestria sympathised and congratulated and said kind encouraging things and generally rejoiced in Cassandra's obvious happiness. She realised that she had very little experience of such situations and that her own must be unusual. One should not generalise from one's own situation, she thought, especially when it was decidedly out of the ordinary. She had not infrequently been involved in discussions when there were objections raised concerning the suitability of unmarried priests to give advice to married couples. The answer had been that they were far more likely to look at the problems of marriage objectively than were married men or women, who were bound to be influenced by their own experience.

"You're looking pensive," Cassandra said a little anxiously. "Do you disapprove of my using the Bible?"

"I'm sure it hasn't done you any harm," Celestria smiled. "But I don't think any magical or should I say supernatural significance should be attached to it. After all, you've known Robert quite a lot longer than I've known Nicholas."

"But you had a supernatural experience in being 'told' to leave your religious life! I've said before that your marriage seems to have been made in heaven. I'm afraid consulting the Bible is the nearest I'm likely to get to that!"

Robert was a good as his word. He drove into the yard at Huntsfield just before 8 a.m. As it was Sunday, preparations for breakfast were only just under way. If Melissa was startled to see him at such a time she gave no hint of it and merely asked him whether he'd like tea or coffee. Cassandra entered the kitchen a moment later, to be greeted with a big hug and a whispered "You haven't changed your mind?"

She emerged from the hug and said impishly: "Not so far!"

Breakfast over and cleared Robert drove Melissa and Cassandra to mass at the Oratory. He'd telephoned Samson to explain his whereabouts. Samson had seemed unsurprised and merely remarked that he wondered whether Muriel would be going. Robert had replied that he hoped not, to which Samson made no reply.

As they had arrived together Robert sat with Cassandra and Melissa while Samson sat in his usual place, further down on the other side. Robert glanced at him covertly, hoping not to see him joined by Muriel. Despite his almost all-consuming happiness in Cassandra's acceptance of him, which had at first erased the previous night's unfortunate encounter from his mind, Samson's mention of her had brought it unpleasantly back to him and Muriel was quite the last person he wanted to see. He closed his eyes and said a fervent, silent prayer. When he looked up again he was dismayed to see the subject of his petition just about to enter the pew where Samson was sitting. "Oh dear!" he said aloud. Cassandra, engrossed in her own prayers, didn't notice, but Melissa was quite aware both of his words and the direction of his gaze. 'Oh dear indeed!' she thought. 'Poor Muriel!'

After mass Melissa waited outside for Samson and Muriel to emerge and invited them both to lunch. "Only something very simple, we don't give the guests lunch and Nicholas and Celestria have gone out."

"I suppose they're going to Blackfriars this evening," Samson suggested.

"Really, Samson," Robert addressed him rather tersely, "you do seem to know everything about everybody."

"Thank you Robert; an undeserved commendation….if it is one. I merely know that Nicholas likes Blackfriars, is not particularly enamoured of the earlier family mass and would never miss mass on a Sunday."

"You sound like Sherlock Holmes, Samson." Muriel smiled appreciatively.

"Dear me, no. Far too active. Mycroft Holmes would be more my style."

Amid general agreement that Mycroft was indeed more appropriate, especially as he was considered to be even more intelligent than Sherlock, it was also agreed that Muriel and Samson would be happy to come to lunch at Huntsfield and would collect Muriel's car from college for the purpose. Cassandra was puzzled at her mother's apparently unpremeditated invitation. Robert was not sure whether to be aghast or relieved. As they drove back the two women were discussing what to have for lunch and he had leisure enough to decide that relief was the better option; it would be preferable to encounter Muriel in company rather than in college where she might easily find an opportunity to speak to him alone; it would in fact be less embarrassing and easier in every way. He found himself wondering whether Melissa were not, in her own way, almost as astute as Samson.

On their way into the house, as Melissa went on ahead to 'see to the lunch' Robert had a chance to exchange a hug and a kiss with Cassandra and ask whether they could announce their engagement immediately. Warmly though Cassandra responded she was a little wary of an immediate announcement as such. "Do you think it's appropriate?" she queried. "Shall we wait till Celestria and Nicholas come in? Well, maybe if it comes up….." She was conscious of feeling different, feeling something more for Robert than she had ever felt before. She looked up at him and suddenly gave him a spontaneous hug and rested her head against him.

Robert was so moved as to be almost tearful. "You've never done that before!" he said, "never looked at me like that before!"

"No. I've never felt like this before; it's different."

"How, different?"

"It's as if I've been standing on the steps of a swimming pool and fearing to go in because it might be cold; and now I have actually gone in and I find it deliciously warm and soothing and exciting all at the same time."

Poor Robert was no longer able to hold his tears back. He held Cassandra close and wept into her hair and managed to murmur that he'd never been so happy.

Unbeknown to the two lovers, they were being observed by Pete, who was at the open window in the potting shed, where he'd been doing some work of his own. Fortunately they were far too involved with each other to hear him give a particularly loud and prolonged sniff.

***

Busy though Melissa was preparing lunch in the kitchen she could hardly fail to notice that Robert and Cassandra were clinging to each other in a way she'd never observed before. She stopped stirring the pot on the hob, carefully turned off the heat and said "Well?"

Robert only managed to say "I…we…" while Cassandra murmured "We're getting married, Mummy, and can we have one of the flats upstairs? When it's ready, I mean."

Robert found his voice, "I want to pay to have it done, of course. That's if you think it would be a good idea."

Melissa smiled graciously. A better way to her heart would have been hard to find. She had a running vision of an elegant and attractive apartment, which would be available for renting out when Robert and Cassandra had children and needed a house of their own. Her doubts about Robert's family were temporarily put on hold as she mentally resisted any tendency to contemplate the necessity of having them to stay. "I think it would be a *very* good idea; excellent in fact. Cassandra can continue with her work and still perhaps help me with the guests when really necessary, while you two can live independently in your own space."

There was a ring at the doorbell. "Good heavens, our guests! I'll just have to explain why I'm behind with the lunch, and of course we'll have to have a *special* celebratory drink!"

She went to the door as Robert and Cassandra looked at each other with slightly wry smiles.

"Trust Mummy to solve things," she said, "it'll all be done without our having to say anything."

"Actually, you know, I think I'm rather grateful."

As Muriel and Samson were ushered in to the accompaniment of Melissa's apologies for a delay in producing the lunch "because these two have taken it into their heads to tell me they intend to get married. So you must come and sit down and have a celebratory drink and lunch will be a little later and a little simpler than planned!"

The guests were hardly able to express their congratulations before being swept into the drawing room as Robert and Cassandra busied themselves with glasses and Melissa produced a dustily impressive bottle, which Robert was required to open, and a surprising array of nibbles.

"Some of these might have been the first course," Melissa murmured as she proffered prawns and taramasalata, "but it's just as nourishing to eat them in one's fingers now."

The preliminaries and the ensuing lunch passed with apparently effortless ease as plans for the top floor flat were discussed and Melissa offered to show Muriel this interesting region and something of the rest of the house. Leaving the others to a second cup of coffee the two women proceeded on their tour, Samson having of course seen it before. Muriel was immensely impressed with the number and size of the rooms and the superb views visible from every one of them. As Melissa had sensed, she felt diminished by the news of Robert's engagement. She had never quite given up hope that it would not come about and her witnessing of Robert's obvious distress on the previous evening had encouraged her. She had in fact lain awake for some hours imagining situations in which she could provide him with comfort. She had attended mass that morning more than half expecting him to be sitting in his pew dejected and wretched. A qualm had seized her when she saw him sitting with Cassandra and her mother. She gave a sigh, which Melissa noticed without comment. As if to cover it she said: "This really is a very great house; you must be very happy in it."

"Yes and well, not exactly no, but with some reservations. It's a lot of work and we have to have paying guests in order to live in it in any comfort. Of course it should be easier with Robert in the family. At least he earns a steady income; Cassandra's and mine are somewhat less secure. He's perhaps not everything I could wish for my daughter but I suppose nobody ever would be and the situation as a whole is certainly satisfactory."

Muriel wondered with some surprise what more Melissa might have to wish for in a son-in-law, but was strangely comforted by hearing Robert being a little down-graded, and was oddly even more comforted by the grandeur of the house and the prospects it offered. It made Robert's preference of Cassandra less diminishing to herself. She could put it down to material things with which she could never compete being a relevant factor; she need not see it only in terms of her being less physically and personally attractive. Not that she could accuse Robert of being a gold-digger. On the contrary he would be making a very significant contribution to the household, but there was no doubt that marrying into such a family, with such connections, could not fail to confer status, however much one might affect to disregard it.

They returned to the drawing-room, where the others had finished all the coffee and Samson was making signs of willingness to depart. Muriel said all the right things about the beauty of the house and the suitability of the top floor for conversion into particularly attractive flats and she and Samson took their leave and drove away. The yard and its exit were negotiated without any attempt at conversation and Samson showed no inclination to break the silence. Muriel was not so entirely happy with her own thoughts as to wish to be shrouded in them all the way back to Oxford and ventured to remark that that was all very pleasant, wasn't it?

"I'm interested that you should say so, Muriel. It does you credit."

"Why? Didn't you enjoy it?"

"Oh, certainly. The food was excellent. Mrs Marjoribanks is an extremely competent woman."

"What about the rest of it?"

"Young people in love, in fact any people in love, tend to be a little tedious, even more so when love has been declared and one is expected to rejoice with them while feeling at the same time that they are too totally preoccupied with each other to render one's presence in any way necessary---or even noticeable. You were fortunate in spending some time going over the house with Mrs Marjoribanks."

"That was certainly pleasant and interesting, but it hardly does me credit to say so."

"You wouldn't like to live in such a house yourself? Or indeed in such a situation?"

Muriel was aware that Samson's use of the word 'situation' did not refer to place but chose to ignore it.

"I can't imagine it; I fear I may have become institutionalised....and I'm certainly accustomed to living within walking distance of the centre of Oxford."

"You are certainly accustomed to leading your own life precisely as you want to. For a person of settled habits and not in the first flush of youth to have to alter their life by continually consulting the wishes and interests of another person ....not to mention the possibility of several ensuing persons with irregular habits and noisy demands....is a consummation by no means *entirely* devoutly to be wished!"

"There's certainly some truth in that. Do you suppose Robert's thought of it?"

"Of course not."

"Oh dear. Well, but you know, Samson, he'll still have a room in college, even if it's not the suite he's in now, and come in to teach and have meals and go to meetings and so on. And I think marriage is less disruptive for a man than for a woman, especially if she has children, even though modern husbands are expected to give much more help and be far more involved than formerly."

"Possibly; though I know of dons who have simply moved into college and stayed there until their offspring were old enough to stop waking up at night and disturbing the household."

"That's quite dreadful!"

"But by no means unheard of. Consider yourself fortunate, Muriel."

"Thank you, Samson. Perhaps I should."

"After all, nobody is going to tell you these days that your failure to have children will result in your being forced to lead apes in hell, as Beatrice suggested."

“You mean it was considered to be one’s own fault, one’s own choice, if one didn’t marry and bring up a family?”

“So it would appear.”

“At least that’s preferable to being considered a miserable old maid, left on the shelf!”

54

Nicholas and Celestria were delighted, though hardly surprised, at the news of Robert and Cassandra's engagement. Nicholas was too distressed at the necessity of parting from his beloved at her place of work that evening to be more than cursorily congratulatory and Celestria of course had prior knowledge. Cassandra informed Pete in the workshop the following morning by telling him that the expertise of his older male relatives would be needed again as part of the top floor was to be made into a flat for her and her husband. Unbeknown to Cassandra, Pete had also had prior warning of a kind and his responding sniff was rather less dismissive and prolonged than the one he had indulged in as an unseen spectator the previous evening.

"You won't be giving up work, will you Miss?"

"No, of course not, Pete. I'll be working just the same. Only perhaps I won't have to work quite so hard. I might be able to give you more to do and pay you a bit more."

"I'm OK like, now, Miss. Yeah, but I see what you mean. Will he get a new car, do you reckon?"

"I hadn't thought of that, Pete, but I suppose it's possible. He might even get me one!"

Pete's face brightened for the first time. "Cor! That'd really be something like! Yeah, that'd make it all right!"

Cassandra was relieved at Pete's approval, of which she'd had some doubts. A disapproving atmosphere in the workshop would have been decidedly trying. She was less prepared, however, for the gushing congratulations of Marlene, who had somehow gleaned the information by dinner time that evening and had an extra cigarette over an extra drink with Melissa in the kitchen on the strength of it, while bombarding her and Cassandra with a mixture of queries about the proposed venue, clothes, number of attendants, and information about other nuptials she had attended, including her own. She was only stopped by the sound of male footsteps, which she took to be those of her spouse come to look for her. She jumped up suddenly, the picture of guilt, holding out her half-smoked cigarette in a panic. Cassandra took it from her and said kindly: "Don't worry, I'll pretend it's mine." The kitchen door did not open, however, and only the voice of Con B.Weaver was apparent on the other side of it. "Marlene?" it queried, "are you in there?" Marlene responded by hurrying out and was heard, along with departing footsteps, informing her husband of the news of Cassandra's engagement. In the kitchen she and her mother exchanged relieved glances, but the footsteps suddenly stopped and Con's voice could be heard a few decibels louder than usual.

"Marlene!" it said, "I can smell cigarette smoke!"

"Oh gee I'm sorry, Con, I guess it's on my clothes. They smoke in there, you see. Well, it is their kitchen."

"Yeah, well you see your clothes is all you get it on! You see how *nasty* it is?"

The footsteps recommenced and gradually faded into the distance.

"I really can't understand how that woman can be so enthusiastic about marriage!" Cassandra commented.

"Perhaps the enthusiasm is merely about weddings," Melissa replied, "that might explain why Americans seem so prone to having rather more than one each."

When Robert arrived the following afternoon Cassandra, hearing his car, almost ran out of the workshop to meet him and greet him with a hug and a kiss. After responding eagerly he held her at arms length and said seriously "You've never done that before!"

"No; I don't think I have. It's very strange. I feel altogether different. I've…..I don't know….well …..let go. Do you mind?"

"Mind? Mind!! I'm positively ecstatic. You won't change after we're married, will you?"

"You never know. I may become sickeningly clingy and you'll find it utterly boring."

"That I can *not* imagine."

Pete's sniff from the shed window was loud enough to be clearly audible to Cassandra, if unrecognised by Robert, but she laughed happily and led Robert inside, holding his hand.

Melissa gave a slight sigh as they entered the kitchen.

"Oh Ma! Have I been neglecting you? Do you want some help? Are you tired?"

"No darling, no more than usual. I'm just thinking about practicalities. How soon can we start on your flat? Shall I invite Robert's parents to come and stay? Where shall we put them if I do? Am I to put the engagement notice in The Times? Where and when is the wedding to be? How…." Melissa was about to continue with 'on earth are we going to afford it' but thought better of it and said "I mean *who* …er, who's going to give you away?"

Robert sat down and laughed, comically making brow-mopping movements. "Oh dear!" he said happily, "what a catalogue! But we *had* thought of the flat if not quite all the other things."

"There's one important detail you haven't mentioned," Cassandra broke in with a mischievous grin, "who's going to be the best man? Because if it's going to be Nigel Nethercott I think I'll have to turn round half way down the aisle and flee the church!"

"I really haven't given the matter any thought at all," Robert admitted, "but I can quite safely assure you that it will most certainly not be Nigel!"

"Well of course, darlings, you haven't thought of all these things yet; I'm sorry to bombard you, but I don't suppose you want a long engagement and one must be practical. I think, Robert, if I may say so, that your parents should be informed before we do anything about the notice in The Times."

"Surely we don't need that anyway, Mummy. It's hardly important."

"It's customary and traditional, darling, and I do rather feel that marriages seem almost *clandestine* without it; and that's unlucky. I should know!"

"*I'd* like to put it in," Robert spoke enthusiastically, "I want everybody to know about it. But you're right, I must tell my family first. Then *after* it's in I'll take Cassandra to meet them."

Melissa smiled graciously. She was aware that Robert felt the need to bind Cassandra to him as far as possible before she met his family. She well remembered one of her contemporaries telling her, over a rather longer series of drinks than was entirely conducive to discretion, that she would *never* have become engaged to her husband had she met his family beforehand!

"How very sensible, Robert. Quite the right way to proceed." Melissa's smile became a little wry; she was very relieved that the expense of the notice in The Times would not be hers but her fears as to the suitability of Robert's family were not diminished by Robert's obvious reluctance to have Cassandra meet them.

***

In the Senior Common Room after lunch, which Robert had attended perforce, as he had a heavy teaching day and could not, therefore, spend much of it with Cassandra, he was approached by Richard Holdsworth, whose interest in the details of other people's lives compensated for a lack of anything interesting in his own.

"So, Robert," he smirked as he sat on the window seat beside him, "I hear congratulations are in order!"

"Oh, and where did you hear that?" Robert was surprised, though not ungratified, that the news had spread so soon.

"Well at lunch. I was at the other end of the table from you. I don't suppose you noticed."

"No. I was a bit late. I had a tutorial from 12 to 1.00."

"I was sitting opposite Muriel Thwaites and the Theology Fellow. You know, our ex-nun. She was grilling Muriel about her going to mass at a Catholic church, I forget what they called it."

"The Oratory, probably."

"I thought it was some fancy saint's name, but never mind, she was saying to Muriel 'isn't that the church Robert Taylor goes to?' She sounded a bit snide, like as if she was suggesting that Muriel had a not very religious reason for going…ha ha ha!"

Robert reflected that he had always found Richard's laugh particularly irritating, but he was anxious to hear more. "And?" he queried.

"Well Muriel just looked sort of, well, bland and said 'Oh yes, he does; so does Samson Southey, and the young woman Robert's engaged to.' So of course anybody who heard said 'oh, Robert's engaged, is he?' Not that they seemed much interested. They didn't even ask who to. They just went on talking shop. Who is it to, anyway? I bet it's that Oxford Pot girl, isn't it? I remember *her*... ha ha ha …mind you she's quite a looker. I wouldn't have thought you had it in you; just shows, you never know.

Well, congratulations, anyway." Richard got up and lumbered away, still laughing his irritating laugh.

Robert decided that he must nerve himself to write to his parents immediately, for unlikely though they were to hear the news of his engagement from anybody else, it seemed unfair that they should not be at least among the first to know of it. Since he had lived in College his communications with them had generally been only of the most basic kind; how were they keeping; whether he was coming home for Christmas; when would he be arriving; what would they like him to bring. Once at home he tried to be helpful and quiet, feeling that he had very little in common with his family, and that he should say as little to make this apparent as possible. He considered their minds uninformed, their interests limited, their opinions biased. They went to church only to attend weddings, carol services, and…increasingly… funerals, though they would have been deeply offended if anybody had suggested that they were not Christians. They had an inbuilt, instinctive, totally illogical suspicion of Jews and Catholics, especially Catholics. Robert groaned as he thought about it. Cassandra's religion was so much a part of her.

Absorbed in thoughts of his family and mentally composing a letter to his parents, Robert made his way back to his room. Writing (they were not on email) would be preferable to telephoning he decided; it would give them time to adjust their reactions and he could say what he wanted to say without being interrupted. Doubtless they would want to ask questions. At his desk he sat down with a blank sheet of College writing paper in front of him. After five minutes he had written nothing but the date. Writer's block was not something he normally suffered from but he realised suddenly that he balked at writing 'Dear Mother….and Dad' as he knew that addressing one's female parent as 'Mother' would not go down well with Melissa, or probably with Cassandra either, even though she wouldn't show it, and 'Mum and Dad' was not much better. 'Oh lord', he moaned to himself, 'what an idiot I'm being. It's not as if *they*'re going to see the letter. I'm just totally inhibited by the thought of what I'll call the parents when I take Cassandra there.' He picked up his pen again and wrote firmly: 'Dear Mum and Dad'. After a pause he continued: 'You may be surprised but I hope you'll be pleased to hear that I'm engaged to be married. It should be in The Times under 'forthcoming marriages' in the next day or two. Cassandra's mother, Mrs Melissa Marjoribanks [pronounced marshbanks], is rather keen on that sort of thing and I must admit I quite like the idea myself. I want it all to be very definite and official.

'Cassandra is unusually beautiful and very talented; she's not only a potter but also has a university degree. I'm sure you will like her.' Robert paused and muttered to himself that he didn't care if they didn't like her, as long as they didn't show it; he then considered that it would be impossible for *anybody* to dislike Cassandra…though he wasn't so sure about her mother. However, that bridge could be crossed later. He continued 'She is very anxious to meet you'… no, I'm the one who's anxious, he thought, but they won't realise that… 'and it would be very nice if you could write to her, Ma,' (Oh, no, I mustn't use *Ma*) he crossed it out and substituted *Mum,* 'and invite her to come and stay; with me, of course. And if she does come and stay we'll have to go in separate rooms because Cassandra is a very devout Catholic and has very high principles.' There! I've got in about her being a Catholic; they can hardly object to her having high principles, can they?

Robert put down his pen, sighed deeply and indulged in reflecting that this was the most difficult letter he'd ever had to write. His usual flowing style had totally deserted him and he felt completely at a loss for anything else to say. Well then, I won't say anything else, he decided; so he finished off with a paragraph expressing the usual hopes for his family's health and well-being and signed it 'With much love, Robert.'

Three days later Robert received an answering letter from his mother. He picked it up from his pigeon-hole on his way to lunch and lingered over the meal rather longer than usual to put off the moment when he would have to open it. He sat beside Samson and Muriel and the Theology Fellow, ex-nun Frances Walsingham, sat opposite them. Now that he was officially engaged he felt more comfortable with Muriel. She could have no expectations of him and if she was 'carrying a torch' she was at least, he reflected, managing to hide its light under a bushel. Frances Walsingham opened the conversation.

"So, Robert, I hear you're engaged to be married."

"Yes; it should be in The Times tomorrow." Heavens, Robert thought, I hope I don't sound as smug as I feel!

"Well I gathered it was no secret. The girl's a Catholic, I presume."

"She is indeed, but I don't know why you should presume it."

"Because you've been going to mass, of course."

"Samson's been going to mass too and he's not engaged to a Catholic, are you Samson?"

"There are other possible reasons for attending such services, Frances. But I have often observed that spinsters tend to have a penchant for entertaining romantic notions. Wouldn't you agree, Muriel?"

"Only if you exclude me from their number, Samson."

Frances Walsingham regarded Muriel narrowly. "I don't see why he should," she remarked rather pointedly. Then turning to Robert she asked "Going to join your girl in the faith, then?"

"I'm certainly going to take instruction," Robert replied happily "and I hope they'll see fit to let me in. I'd like to have a proper wedding in the Oratory."

"Oh well, I suppose that's as good a reason as any. What does you family think about it?"

"I don't know yet; I only told them a couple of days ago. In fact I've just picked up a letter from my mother. I'll read it after lunch. By the way Samson, what do you call your parents, since you've been grown up I mean, that is, how do you address them?"

"My parents were not very young when I was born and so have unsurprisingly not been addressed at all since they were buried quite some time ago. But when they were alive I called them Ma and Pa, or sometimes Mater and Pater."

"You never called them Mamma and Papa though, did you, even when you were a small child?" Muriel was interested.

"No, I didn't; but I believe that's what they called their own parents and my father later addressed his male parent as Sir."

Robert was glad the discussion went on into derivations and continental practices and that he was not asked about his own usage. Such considerations had never caused him concern before but now he was increasingly aware of the fine distinctions that were important to people like Cassandra's mother. He had too sensitive an ear and too much regard for the subtleties of language to be able to ignore them or even to consider them unimportant. But it was one thing to acknowledge their importance in literature and quite another to deal with them in real life situations. He decided to forego coffee in the SCR and to brave the opening of his mother's letter without any further delay. He went back to his room, made himself a cup of instant coffee, took up his paper-knife and applied it to the envelope. He groaned as he opened it. The letter was written on lined writing paper. Of course he knew his mother used such paper…his father almost never wrote letters but would certainly demand lines when he was forced into doing so…but he had never previously thought that it mattered. Now he did. He could only think of Cassandra's reaction if his mother wrote to her on similar paper. If nothing else she would be unwilling to show it to her own mother. The actual contents of the letter concerned him less. 'It can't be right to think like this', he told himself, 'but in some ways it's a mercy. It does show how much I've become detached from my family. It must happen to a lot of first generation university people even if they're only there for three years; and I've been living in Oxford for a great deal longer than that.' He sighed again and began to read:

Dear Robert,

Well, what a surprise. Your dad can hardly believe it though we'd always hoped you'd get married and not be a crusty old bachelor. I said to him I'd begun to wonder if something wasn't up when you went to that Roman Catholic service at Christmas. Of course your dad doesn't much like the idea of her being a Catholic but she does sound a nice type of girl and that's more than you can say for most of them nowadays. I'll write and ask her to stay if you give me the address. I can clear out the spare room for her though I don't know where I'll put everything because we do store a lot of stuff in it; still I suppose if she's a potter she won't be used to anything very grand. Not that I know any potters, but I don't think they're moneyed people, are they? If her mother wants an announcement in the newspaper she must be really keen to have you in the family. It makes it very official so you can't get out of it. Of course I don't mean you want to, but you never know. Last time you were engaged you pulled out of it. Mind you I wasn't sorry; I never did like her. I thought she was really stuck up. Anyway, better luck this time.

Love

From

Mum.

Robert put down the letter with a long sigh. He considered it not very tactful of his mother to remind him of Charlotte, though he need hardly feel guilty over that failed engagement. Their parting had been very mutual and Charlotte had indeed made it apparent that Robert's family had not come up to her expectations. He had been closer to them then and more inclined to be defensive. He had also been much less sure of his feelings for Charlotte or of hers for him. She had wanted to better herself, to marry upwards, which could hardly be said of Cassandra. Robert looked again at his mother's letter, closed his eyes, then took up his pen with some alacrity as he had what he considered a brainwave. He thanked his mother for her kind letter ('not that it was, particularly' he thought) gave her Cassandra's address and suggested that she send her a card rather than an actual letter when inviting her to stay.

55

Cassandra duly received a large envelope, containing an equally large card, in the post a few days later.

"Who can this be from?" she murmured as her mother handed it to her at lunchtime. "The postmark's illegible, as usual."

"Only one way to see", her mother responded, handing her a knife.

Cassandra drew the card out with some difficulty as it was adorned glassy sparkles. "Heavens!" she exclaimed, "it's an engagement card."

"Well I suppose you must expect such things now; I've seen them in various shops. Of course they didn't exist in my time. Who's it from?"

"Dorothy Taylor. Oh! It's Robert's mother."

"It's certainly a generous size."

Cassandra didn't answer; she was scanning the written contents of the card. "She's invited me to go and stay….with Robert of course."

"Well, that's all very right and proper. Does she sound pleasant?"

"I'm not sure. It's a bit…..guarded." Cassandra read the card again. Melissa lit a cigarette, looked at the ceiling and said nothing. After some minutes she drummed a rhythm on the table with her fingers. Cassandra looked up as if suddenly aware of her mother's presence.

"You don't want to show it to me?" Melissa queried.

"I'm not sure."

" One can't be too fussy these days. I promise not to utter a word of criticism. After all, who am I to talk?"

"All right; here you are." Cassandra handed the card to her mother, who read, murmuring the words: " 'Dear Cassandra, Robert's Dad and I are very pleased about Robert being engaged and we're looking forward to meeting you. Would you like to come and stay for a day or two next time Robert comes? I'll do out the spare room for you and Robert will have his own room; I've always kept it for him. Hoping to see you soon, Yours sincerely, Dorothy Taylor.' Well, really, darling, there's nothing to complain about. There's very little space on a card, especially one that says 'Congratulations on your engagement' in large letters, and she has said all the right things. A friend of mine got engaged and the day after it was in The Times her fiancé's divorced mother descended on them without warning and tried to make her son break it off. Think what that was like to contend with!"

"What happened?"

"Oh, it only made him all the more determined and when his mother realised she was beaten she took off in high dudgeon and had nothing more to do with them for years. She refused to go to the wedding. Which was a relief to everybody, of course."

Robert was greatly relieved to hear that his mother had sent a card and also that Cassandra seemed happy with its contents and had responded with a polite letter of thanks. There could of course be no question of staying with his parents until after the end of term, and there was Nigel's wedding to be faced first. He was inclined to consider that more of an ordeal. His speech was yet to be written and the more he thought about it the more impossible it seemed. Samson had totally refused to help him and he even considered the possibility of asking Muriel. While he was unwilling to go out of his way to do so he was increasingly tempted to mention it when she sat next to him at lunch the following day. It was partly, indeed, because he felt he should talk to her and was rather at a loss as to what else to talk about.

"Er…you know I've never managed to get out of being best man at Nigel's wedding," he began.

"I do indeed! I'm sure we would have heard about it if you had managed!" she replied.

"Well I seem to remember that you once offered to help me…"

"To help you compose your speech? Yes, I believe I was silly enough to do that. Are you going to hold me to it?"

"Not if you don't want to, of course, but if you were to have any ideas…."

"I'll give it some thought and send you an email if I come up with anything. It might be quite fun."

"The only things I can think of are quite funny, but not the sort of funny I could possibly use at a wedding!"

Muriel laughed. "That I can well imagine! I fear I may have the same problem, but I will try to produce something acceptable,"

"It's awfully good of you. I really am grateful."

***

That evening Robert, who was of course at Huntsfield, made the mistake of mentioning to Cassandra that Muriel was going to help him compose his dreaded wedding speech.

"Oh indeed? Did you ask her to?"

"Well no; well not exactly. She offered."

"You must have been talking to her about it."

"I did originally; a long time ago. It must have been when I first knew about it."

"But you must have been talking to her about it again."

"She was sitting beside me at lunch and, frankly, I couldn't think what else to talk to her about."

"It hasn't occurred to you to ask me to help you with it!"

Robert was silent, it had indeed never occurred to him.

"Don't you realise," Cassandra continued, "that you've asked me to be your wife, 'to be a help meet for you', a 'helpmate' in other words, and that it *should* have occurred to you?"

"But….but you hardly know Nigel."

"True; but I know Effie a good deal better than you do and it might be safer in the circumstances to talk about his good fortune in marrying Effie than about any other aspect of his character!"

"You certainly have a point there! But can we make out any sort of case for regarding Effie as 'good fortune'?"

"Probably only the most literal one, I'm afraid. Her parents do seem to be well off. But you can hardly mention that! Never mind; I'm sure you'll think of something….or Muriel will!"

Robert was mortified. "I'm sorry," he murmured, looking so crestfallen that Cassandra was almost inclined to pity him, "I've got a lot to learn. You'll have to help me do that. You'll have to help me in a great many ways. Please forgive me. I have to pretend I'm clever when I'm teaching but I can obviously be very stupid. How can I make it up to you?"

Cassandra smiled. "I won't demand that you go out and kill a dragon or capture a castle but don't worry, I'll think of something!"

Early the following morning Robert received two emails, which had obviously arrived overnight: one from Muriel and one from Cassandra. He was so afraid that Cassandra's might say she'd changed her mind about marrying him that he decided to skim through Muriel's first. It was not very long.

'Dear Robert,

I've been thinking about your wedding speech and can only come up with clichés like "Yet for a man may fail in duty twice And the third time may prosper" or simply "third time's lucky", neither of which would go down very well, would they? I find I can't think seriously about Nigel! There's something ridiculous about him that inhibits rational thought. But perhaps I shouldn't say that in case you have decided to return the compliment and have him as your best man!

It's altogether too daunting a task to say anything positive, I'm afraid. We're always being told that love is blind and no doubt if it wasn't there would be far fewer marriages, apart from forced ones; but how three women could possibly be so completely sightless as to be willing to marry a clumsy philanderer like Nigel is more than I can fathom.

Sorry to be so little help; but the subject has even less appeal than I imagined.

Best of luck anyway,

Muriel.'

Robert read the email with some relief. He would be pleased to tell Cassandra truthfully that Muriel had been absolutely no help at all. He said a quick prayer and got Cassandra's email up. It was long. He scanned it eagerly and with increasing pleasure and admiration. It was not dismissive, as he had feared it would be. It was a draft of a speech.

Robert darling,

How about something along these lines?

'It is usually expected that a best man will talk about the bridegroom's youthful follies and reveal hitherto hidden misdemeanours for the amusement of the assembled company. I intend to depart from this supposed norm; first because I have known Nigel only in his recent years of undoubted maturity and secondly because from any accounts of his youth that I have been able to glean I have gathered that he was not only a sober and diligent student but also that he was always so much in the company of members of the gentler sex that he was never tempted to any indulgence in the indignities of laddish behaviour.

So I intend to talk about Nigel's present and, as far as conjecture makes reasonable, his future. Both are surely happy subjects. We can all congratulate him on winning the affection of his very lovely [ugh! But don't let it show in your voice] bride Effie. Effie! A very propitious name. Did you know that it was an Effie, Effie Allen, who composed the famous piece known as Chopsticks? We need not dwell on another well-known Effie, Effie Ruskin, some time wife of the art critic, who eventually had her marriage annulled on the grounds of non-consummation. I'm sure we need have no fears of such an outcome of *this* marriage [for all that none of Nigel's other wives have had any children…but don't put that in!]

No, let us consider the origin of the name and its very much more glorious associations. It is, of course, short for Euphemia as we know from hearing its present possessor say her full name in the course of the moving ceremony we have all witnessed today: 'I, Euphemia Dawn Daphne, [I can't remember the extra name, but you can see it on the invitation] take thee…' Euphemia! Or 'well said' as it means in the original Greek, or 'well spoken' or even, especially in Scotland, where of course the Fraser family hails from, and where the name is better known than in this country, it can mean 'well-renowned, well spoken of'. For Euphemia was, indeed is, a very important saint in the Eastern Church; she has a cathedral dedicated to her and two feast days. Her relics attract numbers of pilgrims. [I'm not sure if that should go in; the association of Effie with relics is too much of a stretch!] She was martyred for her faith.

Now of course I am not suggesting that Nigel has married a saint in the theological sense of the word, nor that his bride can in any way be considered a martyr, but I am inclined to suggest that most women have saintly qualities which are much more rarely to be found in men. They need to be saintly to put up with us, to tolerate our many failings and still go on loving us. We should look up to them and value their judgment and their good opinion throughout our married lives. I must be forgiven for stating the obvious and telling Nigel what I'm sure he knows already, [try to say it as if you mean it] but I can, I hope, be forgiven when I say that I have recently become engaged to be married and that I am sincere in wishing Nigel and Euphemia all the happiness which I feel so sure of achieving myself.'

No doubt you can think of a lot more but at least it cuts out the impossible task of talking about Nigel's past without referring to his failed marriages. It may sound a bit donnish but they ought to expect that. Anyway, let me know what you think.

Fondest love,

Cassandra xxxxx.

PS I don't actually remember if Effie really has a second and third Christian name; they just seemed all too appropriate! But I do know her first name is Euphemia because she was named after a childless aunt of her father's, who promised to leave her some money if she was given that name. She implied that it was worth it!

xx C.

Robert read and reread the email. He had, he realised, never actually seen anything other than short text messages written by Cassandra and very few of those, as they almost always communicated by telephone. He was not merely impressed, he was almost shocked, shocked into regarding her in a completely new light. He felt humbled and contrite; he realised that he had never appreciated her adequately. Nonetheless, he felt a glow of satisfaction in his choice and half subconsciously congratulated himself on his perception in picking such a paragon. Of course he would alter the speech somewhat, but the idea of it was brilliant. He sent Cassandra a deeply appreciative and complimentary email, not omitting to mention the feebleness of Muriel's response, and even having the good sense to forbear any suggestion of his intention to make alterations in Cassandra's effort. He in fact finished with a declaration that he would need her help in finishing it off. This Cassandra received with a happy smile and an even happier conviction that her fiancé was, despite his comparatively advanced age, not incapable of learning.

56

After breakfast the following Saturday Marlene put her head round the kitchen door, whisked herself into the room and exclaimed in tones of mingled apology and excitement: “Aw gees I’m really sorry to intrude so early but I just do need a cigarette to get me through today with all this happening, I mean the wedding: it’s all so special and I’ve bought two outfits and I don’t know which to wear and I reckon you can help calm me down.”

Melissa stifled a sigh and brought out the required panacea. Lighting the cigarettes for herself and Marlene and regretting that it really was too early for an accompanying drink she ventured to remark consolingly that it was probably not necessary to decide on dress for several hours yet. Marlene rattled on about her alternative garments amid requests for advice about the weather. “I mean, it’s this climate. Now in the States it’s hot at some times of year and cold at others and there’s heating and air conditioning and you know what it’s going to be like from one day to the next, but here you don’t know even from one hour to the next. So I don’t know what to do. What do you think I ought to wear?”

“I think most of us will have decided on that in advance and we’ll simply go through with it and brave the weather as it comes. We are rather used to doing that. Why don’t you leave your decision until after lunch and then put on whatever seems most comfortable?”

“I thought you’d have some real good advice; you’re so *collected!* I wish I was more like that.”

A voice from somewhere in the distance was heard calling “Marlene? Where are you?” Marlene stubbed out her cigarette with guilty speed. “Lawks! There’s Con! I thought he was outside having a walk around. He doesn't much like walking, though." She left the kitchen hastily and called out in answer only when on the other side of the door. "Here, Con. I was just trying to find out about the weather."

"There's no finding out about the weather in this goddam country," the answer came from not far away, "you should know that by now."

Notwithstanding the vicissitudes of the English climate Marlene was already sitting, resplendently arrayed in a flowing garment of many flowers and many colours, in the Emmaus College chapel when Cassandra and Melissa arrived there. Con had apparently hustled her out of the house while they were getting themselves ready so she had had no opportunity for last minute consultation.

"It would be politic to sit beside them don't you think?" Melissa murmured.

"Politic?" Cassandra was puzzled.

"We must keep our guests happy; well, as happy as possible. We want good reports of our hospitality."

"Really, Mummy, you must have an even more ulterior motive than that; but all right, we'll sit beside them. I hardly think we'll know many people here."

Melissa moved into the pew beside Marlene, whispered commendations of her attire, congratulated her on wearing a hat and settled down to read the service booklet. Cassandra was aware that her mother was reacting to its contents with barely muffled exclamations of disgust but decided that the safest course was to show a determined interest in the other members of the congregation and inhibit a sharing of comments until a more suitable opportunity.

The chapel filled; the organ played; Nigel and Robert stood up to await the arrival of Effie and her attendants.

The music suddenly changed to the well-known pom pom p-pom of *Here comes the bride---* ("Well *really!!")* Melissa was heard to whisper with the force of a soda siphon---and Effie progressed triumphantly down the aisle on the arm of her father.

The music stopped and the service began. Melissa had already muttered disapproval at its being the full marriage service and not merely a blessing, so she contented herself with casting her eyes up to the vaulted roof and assuming an expression of pained resignation. Cassandra was impressed by the beauty of the liturgical words and listened with interest, while Marlene dabbed her eyes with a colourful tissue and hoped to be suitably affected. With the clergyman's homily, however, the atmosphere altered. People began to take notice and continued to do so with increasing astonishment. He was talking about flying buttresses.

"Now these, as such an educated congregation is sure to know, have the property of counteracting the downward thrust of the heavy walls of a building by providing stabilising upward thrusts. Now such upward thrusts are, similarly, what must be provided to stabilise a marriage." He paused, pressed his hands together, cast his eyes skywards, or at least roofwards, as the sky was not visible, for a few seconds and then brought them down to rest benevolently on the bridal couple. "Upward thrusts," he repeated, "*upward thrusts!"* I strongly recommend that these should not be lacking in *your* marriage, Nigel and Euphemia. Never be stinting in your upward thrusts, but, at the same time, see to it that some of your thrusts are spiritual, not merely physical……"

The worthy man continued in the same vein, clearly quite unaware of the stifled sounds denoting the suppressed mirth of members of the congregation. Mouths that were not actually open in incredulous astonishment were covered by hands attempting to hold in guffaws or giggles. Nobody had completely recovered even by the singing of the last hymn, which was of course *Jerusalem,* and it was rendered with a particularly cheerful enthusiasm. The ensuing photographs of the wedding party and groups of guests outside the chapel were often commented on in later years as looking quite uniformly and unusually jolly.

The Four Gables Hotel, or as Effie's mother always referred to it 'the venue', was lavishly decorated and brightly lit. Guests progressed slowly past the reception line and were duly supplied with champagne ("Fizzy wine!" remarked Melissa *sotto voce*) and canapés. Marlene remained close, clearly afraid of being lost in the crowd, though in fact the guests who had attended the service were joined by only a small number of extra people as the younger element were to come after dinner to a dance in the evening. Cassandra had been relieved to see that very few of the hen party girls were present.

"Isn't it lovely!" Marlene had dispensed with the coloured tissue and was making do with a paper napkin.

"Hmmm." Melissa's tone was opaque.

"What do you think of Effie's wedding dress?" Cassandra asked, feeling that some attempt at conversation was in order.

"Most unsuitable," Melissa did not moderate her tone of disapproval.

Marlene looked shocked. "Oh! Don't you think she looks nice in it?" she clearly expected the answer 'yes'.

"If there were more of her *in* it and less of her *out* of it she might qualify for some degree of niceness!"

Marlene tittered. "Aw, you're so clever! I'd never think of saying that. Isn't your mother clever, Cass—andra?"

"I'm afraid some people might call it acerbic; but not unamusing. Oh here's Robert at last; he's had to be with the wedding party. Robert, I'm afraid my mother's being a little critical."

"I can't say I'm surprised! Have you ever heard anything like that homily?"

"Well I must say," Marlene was beginning to show the effects of two unaccustomed glasses of champagne, "I did think it wasn't very nice for a parson to be talking about things like that, and in church, too. I mean, that's more kind of what a best man puts in his speech, isn't it?"

"I can assure you it's not going to be in this best man's speech! Oh, Cassandra; I'm so sorry; it's all so awful."

"Actually, Robert, I'm finding it rather interesting---and Ma's being so acerbic about it I can't help laughing to myself, though I just hope she doesn't offend too many people. I'll try to keep her from saying anything utterly outrageous until we get home!"

Con B. Weaver loomed up from the depths of the room, where he'd been hovering near the champagne. "C'mon, Marlene, we gotta find our table; it's time to siddown."

Lists were consulted. Predictably, Con and Marlene Weaver and Melissa and Cassandra were on the same table. There was also a Professor Highsmith and his wife and a Mr and Mrs Ashley-Jones.

Oh gloom and despondency!" Melissa was heard (Cassandra hoped only by her) to murmur. "Husbands and wives are not merely on the same table but *next* to each other!"

"Never mind, Mummy, at least it doesn't apply to either of us!"

Professor Highsmith lost no time in introducing himself to Melissa.

"Are you a friend of the bride or the groom?" she asked as she surveyed him coolly.

"I'm the head of the Geography Department and I taught Nigel and was his D.Phil. Supervisor. What about you?" He forebore to add that she seemed an unlikely adjunct to either party, but feeling that some other question was necessary to avoid bluntness he continued, rather uncertainly, "family friend?"

Melissa resisted the temptation to say "Hardly!" and replied that her daughter, she indicated Cassandra, was engaged to the best man. "He wanted us here to support him. He hasn't the most enviable task at a bridegroom's third wedding."

"Well he can hardly fail to do better than the clergyman, even if he's planning to say something on the same lines!"

"He assures us that he's not. But really, I'm amazed that there was such a full service for a third marriage when *both* Nigel's previous wives are still alive. Poor Prince Charles had to be content with a mere blessing."

"Oh I believe anything goes these days, with the clergyman's consent. This old chap's a retired college chaplain, very High Church and otherworldly. Nigel's first two weddings were in the Registry Office so they're not thought to count."

"You must be kept quite busy going to Nigel's weddings!"

Professor Highsmith laughed. "Let's hope this is the last. It's obviously the most expensive, if nothing else."

"That," Melissa pronounced with some emphasis, "may augur well for its continuance, especially as maintenance payments are more often to the ex wife than to the ex husband."

Cassandra, meanwhile, was talking to Mr Ashley-Jones. He seemed to be a business acquaintance of Effie's father's.

"I see you're wearing an engagement ring," he said.

"Well yes, the best man is my fiancé." Cassandra didn't deem it necessary to mention that it was a temporary ring, lent by her mother for the occasion.

"I'm glad to see it. Not enough young people getting married these days; living in sin, most of them."

"I don't think it's called that nowadays."

"No it isn't, more's the pity. There might be less of it if people weren't so squeamish about calling a spade a spade."

Despite her own views on the subject and her own vow to have no sex outside marriage Cassandra was sufficiently of her generation to find an older man's explicit condemnation rather shocking. Nevertheless she felt some reply was necessary.

"Well," she managed after some hesitation, "I do remember a friend of my mother's saying he had a son-in-law and a sin-in-law; but he seemed to regard it as rather a joke."

"He was more fortunate than I am; I have two of the latter variety and I do not regard it as any kind of joke." Mr Ashley-Jones thrust a fork into his mouth with what looked like a dangerous ferocity.

"Well perhaps they'll become sons-in-law eventually, it's not unusual. Have they been together long?"

"Far too long. I have no hope of them regularising their situation. They even have bastards."

"Bastards?" The literal use of the term was so unusual that at first Cassandra did not appreciate its significance in the context.

"Oh! Oh but…really….I mean…er do you mean your daughters' children?" Cassandra dared not say 'grandchildren' in case of an even more angry reaction.

"Unfortunately yes."

"How old are they?"

"I hardly know. I don't see them."

"That's very sad."

"It is indeed."

"Can't you just make the best of it and enjoy a happy relationship with them anyway?" Cassandra was averse to any pretence at sympathy with this angry man's views.

"Too late. They've made it very clear that they don't want to see me. They consider their attitude perfectly right and acceptable and mine unrealistic and outdated. But I suppose you have similarly licentious modern views and are already living with your fiancé even if you do intend to get married yourself?"

"No I don't as a matter of fact; but then I'm a Catholic and I believe in the teachings of the Church. I don't expect people to have my views if they haven't got my faith."

Melissa, who was apparently not quite as impressed with Professor Highsmith as he was with her, and who was thus able to keep an ear on Cassandra's conversation as well as her own, felt it was time for a little rescue work. As Mr Ashley-Jones was stating with some force "I'm not a religious man myself; religion's got nothing to do with it. Some of the so-called religious people are the worst….." Melissa broke in with "Dear me! You seem to be having an unusually serious conversation for such a social occasion! Do tell us about your work, Mr…er…Ashley, I know we've heard it's something very impressive…."

"Well, of course I have largely retired," Mr Ashley-Jones responded with a predictable change of manner.

"No! Really? I would never have thought so," Melissa gave a remarkably good impression of genuine surprise and as her target beamed contentedly and launched into a description of his prowess in the field of business Cassandra sat back with relief and silently blessed her mother's expertise. Con B.Weaver had been about to embark on a monologue of agreement as to the evils of religion in general and religious people in particular but was quite unable to compete with Melissa for the attention of Mr Ashley-Jones, so took it out on his wife instead. As she had heard it all before and was far more interested in the various modes of dress displayed by the other women in the gathering it washed over her quite harmlessly.

The speeches, when they came, were to many a welcome relief from the necessity of making conversation. Cassandra found herself decidedly anxious when it came to Robert's, partly because it would not be pleasing if he failed to include at least a modicum of her suggestions and partly because she feared his sense of humour would get the better of him and he'd be tempted to say something outrageous. She had, of course, never heard him teaching or lecturing and she was immediately impressed by his command of his audience. He was very clearly audible---more than one could say for most of the speakers---and very arresting. Whether the listeners fully understood what he was saying was not entirely clear, but listen they did, as the stillness and hush testified. He declared the beauties of the name Euphemia with a passionate conviction and was equally convincing regarding the excellence of Nigel's choice. Even Melissa later admitted that despite prior knowledge and better judgment she had, for several minutes, almost believed him! The final accolade came, however, after the dinner with the arrival of Effie's hen-party contingent and their many and certainly various partners. Cassandra was nearby when Charlene and Sherry (alias Cherie) approached the bride and slapped her on the back and called her 'Ef'. She responded with some dignity. "I don't want to be called that any more," she said almost haughtily, "it's just childish. I never liked my name before but I do now. Robert's shown it's really special. He says it means 'well-spoken' and as well as that it means 'well spoken of', you know, respected, looked up to. Besides I'm a married woman, aren't I? Mrs Euphemia Nethercott. It makes me feel different." Ignoring her friends' disbelieving response of "Cor! Hark at her!" she sailed into the body of the room to greet her guests with something approaching graciousness.

57

Marlene was, of course, in the kitchen for a sneaky smoke and a *critique* of the wedding immediately after breakfast the following morning.

"Well I must say I thought it was really lovely," she breathed huskily with an exhalation of fumes, "and your Robert's speech was truly beautiful. I mean, there was only one thing in it that was the least little bit ---well, you know, what you expect in a best man's speech--- but all the rest of it could have been said in church. It was a lot better than that parson."

"I must admit I was impressed," Melissa replied musingly, "it was totally unexpected in every way and genuinely interesting to listen to. I can't imagine how he thought of such a clever way to avoid the pitfalls of dealing with a bridegroom's third marriage. Did you know how he was going to deal with it, Cassandra?"

Cassandra put a hand over her mouth to hide her involuntary smile; "I did have some idea about it, yes," she replied ambiguously, "I'm sure he'll be pleased to hear that it was appreciated."

"Even Effie seemed to acquire something resembling dignity after it," Melissa continued, "I heard her telling people she wants to be called 'Euphemia' in future. But I can't imagine that's likely to last."

"I'm afraid she'll have to acquire some new and different friends if she's to have much hope of it!" Cassandra spoke feelingly.

***

Robert expressed surprise when some of his colleagues, few of whom had been at the wedding, enquired about it with interest.

"Really Robert," Samson said with some severity, "considering how long and how much we've heard from you about your agonies of anticipation, your surprise at our interest in the outcome is somewhat misplaced. Would you not agree, Muriel?"

"I would indeed," Muriel agreed, "but I have heard on a slender and indefinite grapevine that in fact Robert's speech was quite brilliant ---albeit in a donnish sort of way---and amazingly inoffensive and arresting. However did you manage it, Robert?"

Somewhat stung by Muriel's tone and very imperfectly aware of the feelings which caused it Robert decided that she needed putting in her place and replied "I really can't take any credit for it; it was almost entirely Cassandra's doing. She's so sensitive and so able and yet so modest that one hardly realises how very intelligent she is. She has a degree in English and Latin, you know, as well as being a skilful and creative potter!"

Sensing that this might be a veiled revenge for her own refusal to help Robert and feeling more aware than ever before that he was totally lost to her, Muriel lowered her eyes and gave a slight, involuntary shiver. Quite unaware of her reaction, Robert was happy to listen to Samson, who remarked "I'm delighted to hear of your appreciation of your fiancée's abilities, my dear friend. Lacking though I am in personal experience I am convinced, as an onlooker who sees most of the game, that this is a good basis for a successful marriage."

Robert beamed his appreciation and determined to report this happy observation to Cassandra as soon as possible. The only shadow on his general contentment was the anticipated visit to his parents. Looking round his colleagues he realised that those with whom he was best acquainted were single and could hardly be expected to provide precedent or advice. He finished his lunch with some haste and went back to his room to ring Cassandra and combine reported praise for her ability with setting the dates for the stay in Eastbourne.

***

Term finished and the sojourn which Robert anticipated with considerable misgivings and Cassandra with considerable interest was sufficiently imminent to necessitate packing. Robert's was achieved with very little trouble; Cassandra's took rather more time and attention, although her wardrobe was still fairly limited despite some profitable visits to charity shops. Her mother insisted that she take at least two bottles of wine.

"I don't think they drink wine very often, Ma," Cassandra demurred.

"That's beside the point," was Melissa's response; "you and Robert are likely to be the ones who'll need it!"

At mid-morning the following day Cassandra was ready and Robert arrived to collect her. Seeing the car come into the drive Pete emerged from the shed to say goodbye and assure her of his diligent attention to work in her absence and his willingness to 'look after Missus'. "Have a safe journey, now," he added. "Not got a new car yet, though, has he? Never mind, I reckon that old thing'll get you there. Not that far, is it."

Melissa came out with another bottle of wine, which she insisted that they take "just in case you need it. You can keep it in the car as a standby."

"Oh Ma," Cassandra suddenly felt anxious, "I feel badly about leaving you to do everything by yourself."

"Nonsense, darling. I shall manage perfectly well. In fact Marlene's offered to help me. She says I've been so kind she wants to make it up to me. Can you believe it?"

"Yes I can. She must have learned to be thankful for very small mercies---and you've given her some quite big ones. I'm really glad she's here."

"Actually, darling, I think I am, too. Don't worry about anything. I'll be thinking of you. Goodbye."

They set off. Robert sighed. "I'm sorry this is deemed necessary," he said unhappily.

"You mustn't be! And of course it's necessary. You know *my* mother and you knew my father as well as anybody did; we can't get married with your parents only meeting me, for the first time ever, at the wedding! Besides, I haven't seen the sea since I moved to mid Devon quite a while before we came here and I'm dying to smell the salty waves and hear the seagulls. It'll be my first holiday for years. And I've never been to Eastbourne before."

"It's not the most interesting place on earth."

"It is the seaside; something I almost never experienced even when I was a child."

"Well at least that can provide a safe topic for conversation."

"Are there unsafe ones?"

"I'm afraid there might be; but we'll try to avoid religion and racism."

"Those can be dangerous topics anywhere."

Robert sighed again. "You're so sensible, you'll probably cope better than I will. I'm afraid I feel a kind of heaviness descend on me whenever I go home. It's certainly not bracing as such places are supposed to be. But I'll try to concentrate on you and the salt and the seagulls."

Cassandra laughed. "Well, I'm looking forward to it. How far is it?"

"About 130 miles. It takes between two and three hours. But we'll stop somewhere for lunch. We're not expected till this afternoon."

"I'll look at the map and see where we're going through or by. I didn't have time before. I spent too long on Catholic churches in the area. Let's see, um---um Eastbourne, ooh! I hadn't realised, it's very near Brighton. I've always wanted to go to Brighton."

"What a good idea! We'll go one day. We can look at the Lanes and their amazing antique shops and go to the Pavilion."

"Why Robert, that sounds really exciting; why didn't you tell me about these things before?"

"I suppose I don't exactly associate them with my parents' house."

"Well of course people who live so near don't go doing touristy things like that; but I'd be thrilled to go."

Robert felt considerably cheered. He realised that there would be no necessity for them to vegetate perpetually in the company of his parents; Cassandra's interest and enthusiasm would make expeditions very feasible.

They had a reasonable journey, considering the vagaries of the M25, and an extremely pleasant lunch and by the time they arrived in Eastbourne and drove into the street where stood his parents' semi-detached house, he was in a happier and more optimistic frame of mind than he would have believed possible. The house was small, neat, clean, tidy and unrelievedly ugly. It was, Cassandra considered as she took in its size, its shape, its flat blandness, impossible to associate it with Robert. Robert himself watched her anxiously for signs of disapproval or, he feared, even disgust, but he could detect only interest.

"I don't suppose you've ever seen a house like this before," he ventured.

"What? Oh, I must have. Not in France, though, nor in Devon, come to that. It looks newer than I expected to see in Eastbourne; I always thought it would be more Victorian."

"Some parts of it are, certainly. Oh! There's my mother, she must have seen the car. I'll take the bags."

Mrs Taylor was indeed standing outside the open front door though she didn't advance to greet her son and prospective daughter-in-law. Cassandra decided to take the initiative and relieve Robert, as far as possible, of his obvious anxiety over the encounter. She went forward ahead of him, held out her hand and said "Hullo Mrs Taylor, I'm Cassandra. I'm so happy to meet you." Mrs Taylor, somewhat thrown by this unexpected approach, simply said "Oh. Very nice. Come in out of the wind it's quite cold. Oh, hullo Robert." Robert gave his mother a brief kiss on the cheek and volunteered to show Cassandra her room and put her bag in it.

"All right then, and we're in the lounge when you come down. I'll put the kettle on."

Robert couldn't forbear wincing at the mention of the 'lounge' but he also blessed the happily universal Englishness of the kettle and the clearly ensuing cup of tea. They went up the stairs to the spare room. "Heavens," Robert exclaimed as they entered it. "I hardly ever see this room and when I have seen it it's been so full of stuff that not much else has been visible. I can't think where it's all gone."

"Oh dear; your mother must have been to a lot of trouble. It's very kind of her."

"There's still not a great deal of room, I'm afraid," Robert murmured. Indeed the double bed and the large, triple-mirrored dressing-table left little walking space. "It's hardly what you're used to. I hope you'll be able to manage."

"Really, Robert! I haven't lived in Huntsfield House all my life. I went there from a small, unheated flat above a general store in Devon. Now let's go downstairs and have some tea."

Robert's mother was wheeling a trolley from the kitchen when they went down.

"Can I help with anything?" Cassandra asked.

"Oh no, no thank you, I've got everything on here I think." Mrs Taylor seemed just a little flustered. "Come on Dad," she said as she entered the lounge, "here's Robert's intended; you haven't said hullo yet." Mr Taylor put down his newspaper but did not rise from his armchair.

"This is Cassandra," said Robert.

"Well, I didn't think it would be anybody else." He viewed Cassandra with a stare rather than a smile and continued "Pleased to meet you."

"And I *you*," Cassandra responded, with a smile of considerable brightness.

"Do sit down," Robert's mother murmured, as she poured milk into four china teacups. "I'm sure you'd like some tea."

"Oh yes, please," Cassandra skilfully combined a grateful smile at Robert's mother with a 'don't say anything' look at Robert who, she knew, had been about to expostulate that she didn't take milk.

"I hope your room's all right for you," Mrs Taylor ventured.

"Oh yes indeed; it's really lovely. I do hope you haven't been to a lot of trouble."

"Well nobody's stayed in it for a while so it was a good reason to have a proper clear out and once I got started I really enjoyed doing it. I found quite a few things I'd forgotten about and threw away a few more."

"Oh I know just what you mean; I found things when I was clearing out my flat in Devon, and I hadn't even been in it so very long."

"Robert says you live in a big house."

"Yes, it was left to us. We take paying guests or I don't know how we'd live in it."

"Well I must say I'm glad I've never had to do that. Hard work and no privacy, I should think."

"Oh you're quite right. My mother works very hard. I try to help but of course I have my own work to do. I feel rather guilty about leaving her for a few days; but I must admit I've really been looking forward to this holiday. I love being near the sea and I've never been to Eastbourne before. And of course I wanted to meet you."

Mrs Taylor smiled appreciation and even Robert's father showed a glimmer of interest.

"Where do you go for your holidays, then? Somewhere foreign, I s'pose." He finished with the faint hint of a sniff.

"Well, my parents used to live in France, though I went to school in England. Holidays were usually spent just going home, as far as I remember. And I haven't really had any since I finished university. I hope Robert's going to take me to Brighton; that's a place I've always wanted to see. Once I've had a good look round Eastbourne, that is. I'd like to see Beachy Head and the red and white lighthouse, and the famous pier, too, of course."

Robert's father began to show signs of mellowing. "Well, I'm sure all that can be arranged, can't it Robert? What about tomorrow; then you could go to Brighton the next day, Sunday."

"Well of course we'll have to go to mass on Sunday. I thought….."

"What? Even when you're on holiday?"

"Certainly," Robert replied firmly. "Cassandra's interested in going to Our Lady of Ransom; it's listed Grade II and quite a famous building."

" Don't think I've ever heard of it, have you Dot?"

"Course I have, Dad. You can't miss it. Right in the middle of town it is. That great big one---sort of spread out."

"Hmph! Never knew it was called that. Where's Ransom, anyway? Why call it that when it's in Eastbourne?"

Robert cast his eyes skywards and looked as if he were in danger of explaining but Cassandra answered swiftly "I'm not sure, really; I've never been to a church called that. I'll try and find out on Sunday."

Robert's mother eyed her with a steady look of appreciation and something like awe. "That's right," she said, "you and Robert go there on Sunday morning and then we'll have a nice Sunday dinner here at home when you get back."

"Oh, thank you. That does sound nice. The main mass is at 11 o'clock so we'll come back straight after it, won't we Robert?"

"What? Oh yes. But perhaps now we could go out for a bit of a walk; we've been sitting down all day."

"Can't we just help your mother with these dishes first?"

"Oh no, dear, that's not necessary. Besides, I always wash these things up myself; they're from my bone china tea-set, you see. But I expect you know about these things; Robert says you make crockery."

"Pottery, Mother." Robert spoke brusquely.

"Yes, I do. And I appreciate nice china. It's lovely to drink out of. I think it makes the tea taste better."

"I quite agree. I've never got used to those thick mugs lots of people have now. They make marks on the furniture, too."

Robert was showing signs of impatience and holding out Cassandra's coat for her to put on. "I'll drive to the sea front and then we can walk along and see what there is to be seen." His mother closed the front door behind them. Robert heaved a sigh of what sounded like relief and made for the car, settled Cassandra into it and sank into his own seat with another sigh.

"Robert dear, do relax! I've never seen you so tense."

"Well now you know; this is what it does to me. I can't help it. You're being so nice. It must be a dreadful effort."

"The only effortful thing is trying to disregard you being on tenterhooks. I've been given a room done out especially for me; I've had a very good tea …"

"Poured onto unwanted milk," Robert broke in.

"I prefer tea with milk if it's strong and most people serve it like that. I do wish you'd known me when I was a student and when I lived in Devon. I'm not like my mother, you know. I've actually seen much more variety of life than she has and lived among all sorts of people. I value kindness more than anything."

"My father's not particularly kind."

"It can't be easy for him to have a son who's excelled as you have. It must make him feel defensive. At least he hasn't gone off and disappeared and left his family impoverished as mine did."

"No, it's true your father's behaviour was probably much more reprehensible; but I liked him a good deal better than I ever remember liking my own father. Your father seemed to like *me*; my own never did….and still doesn't."

"Perhaps most people feel a grudge against their parents, or at least one of them. Even Celestria, who I always think of as the most exemplary person I've ever known, seems to want to stay as far away from her mother as possible."

"I think *you're* the most exemplary person I've ever known. The more I know you the more I admire and love you."

Robert stopped the car, but it was some little while before they emerged from it to walk along the sea front.

Chapter 60

At Huntsfield House Melissa was finding Marlene's desire for cigarettes, conversation and company to be increasing to the extent of tiresomeness, presented as it was under the guise of helpfulness, which made it difficult to escape. They were in the kitchen, where Marlene was reorganising a drawer full of spices into a neat, alphabetical order, when the telephone rang.

"Oh, Jasper! How nice of you.....yes, I'm managing quite well despite Cassandra's absence. I do have some help from a kind guest." Marlene, though pretending not to listen, was unable to suppress a satisfied smile. Melissa was tempted to tell Jasper to ring later but he was talking with a volubility that brooked no easy interruption. He seemed determined to take advantage of Cassandra's absence by coming to stay and help Melissa himself. She let him continue as she swiftly considered the pros and cons. One of the pros was the dilution of the company of Marlene.

"Oh Jasper…well really…yes, I'm sure you can cook; well, certainly, help with the shopping would be rather a boon…. What? This evening? Tonight? Oh well, if you're sure; that really is very kind. I'll see you at about six, then." Melissa hung up and turned to look at Marlene, who was peering into her drawer arrangement with somewhat exaggerated concentration. “People are so kind,” she murmured to the back of Marlene’s head, “that was an old friend insisting on coming to help me while my daughter’s away. At this rate I shall be almost better off than when she’s here!”

“That’s just dandy! I’ve really wondered…I mean I’d’ve expected you to have a friend…well of course I know it’s not long since your husband passed away…”

“Well, he’s a relative, actually, a relative of my late husband’s, though quite distant.”

“Not a married man, though?”

“Not at the moment.”

“Does he smoke?”

“No, but he doesn’t mind me smoking. He does have a cigar after dinner occasionally. Don’t worry.”

Marlene gave a sly smile. “Don’t you worry, either. I won’t stick around too much when he’s here!”

Jasper duly arrived at a little after 6.00. He brought flowers, wine, chocolates and 200 of Melissa’s favourite cigarettes. “I thought you might need a little sustenance,” he replied to Melissa’s protestations, “after all, I don’t suppose we’ll be able to go out to dinner.”

“I haven’t quite got your room ready, I’m afraid, but it won’t take more than a minute or two.”

“Which room?”

“Well, it was Fergus’s.”

“Oh. Do I have to sleep there?”

“Are you worried because he died in it?”

“Hardly. In a house as old as this quite a few rooms must have had people die in them. Of course I’ll put my things in it, but….”

“Now Jasper, that’s enough. I thought you were here to help me, not to wear me out. We can talk later and you can deal with my defences then! For now you can just put your things in that room and then come and be useful by helping me with the dinner."

Marlene had disappeared discreetly soon after Jasper's telephone call, but not so discreetly that she hadn't kept the drive in view. Her husband was spending the day in the library and she had little else to do. She watched Jasper get out of his car and unload his case and some of the presents for Melissa and she longed to hear their ensuing conversation. She was impressed by Jasper's appearance and obvious generosity but she might have been disappointed by Melissa's response. She sighed and decided to have a wander in the grounds and keep her eyes and ears as unobtrusively open as possible.

Jasper proved to be more of a help and less of a hindrance in the kitchen than Melissa would have given him credit for. Although she had visited him in London they had always gone out, so that the cooking of a meal together was a new experience. To Melissa it was, in fact, a new experience altogether. Her husband had certainly not, she reflected, been remotely kitchen competent.

"Really, Jasper, you might be quite an asset once you've found out where everything is in this rather primitive kitchen! In fact you seem to have found out a great deal already."

"Oh, there's no end to my talents! Would you like me to show off my skill as a waiter as well? I'm not too sure how I'd succeed there though."

"No I think you'd better stay in here. I don't quite know how to explain your presence. I've told Marlene….the American woman I mentioned to you….you were a relative, but I don't think she believed me. And I certainly don't want any crass remarks from her unlovely husband. Then of course there's Nicholas. Oh dear! I should have thought of all this before. I'm not a frec agent with all these people in the house."

Jasper chuckled. "Rather fun, really. Makes me feel young and daring!"

"I can't feel anything till this dinner's over and done with. I'll set the table while you keep an eye on things."

The dinner was predictably excellent. Nicholas helped bring out the dishes after the last course and was duly introduced to Jasper. "Oh I'm so glad you've got help and company while Cassandra's away," was his immediate comment. "Celestria's been quite worried about you coping on your own. I must tell her. She'll be really relieved." Melissa smiled as she realised that she need have no worries as to Nicholas's reaction to Jasper's presence, everything as far as he was concerned revolved round his beloved.

Marlene was so tactful that she even went without her post-prandial cigarette in order to leave Jasper and Melissa alone and Melissa felt almost guilty for her not infrequent impatience in Marlene's company, relieved as she was to sit down and enjoy her own meal in relative peace.

"I'm sorry we've had to wait to eat, Jasper, but it's better than gobbling it in between courses."

"Oh, absolutely. I'm not used to eating early anyway and I want to have leisure to talk to you. It's the first time I've been here with your daughter away. I know there are a lot of other people, but they don't matter very much, do they?"

"Nicholas Forbes-Mowbray does; he seems almost family. Though he's so totally involved with his betrothed he only sees other people as they relate to her."

"How do you mean?"

"Well, if he thought this was an immoral household he probably wouldn't let her stay here. I think she's actually much more reasonable, even though she is an ex-nun."

"If we got married I could stay here without being immoral."

"Really, Jasper, you're not even divorced yet. And even if you were I couldn't marry you and still be a practising Catholic; and I've been down that road once, to my sorrow. I've no intention of repeating the experience. I've seen too many people who repeat a pattern of mistakes and never learn from them."

"Surely I could get an annulment now my wife's turned into a lesbian!"

"That I don't really know; but I do know you have to be divorced first and then it can take an awfully long time."

Jasper gave a great sigh. "Why is it so many people make mistakes?" he asked.

"They have to make too many decisions at too early an age, or they did in our generation. They were pressurised into marrying in their twenties, especially women, and the whole of the rest of their lives depended on the choice they made then, when they had very little experience of the world, or of anything else, come to that. It's not so bad now. They can leave it till later and they can earn a living and be relatively independent. So even though they still make mistakes they're not so likely to be stuck inescapably in a miserable marriage. But then of course there are a lot more divorces."

"How do you feel about your daughter's proposed marriage?"

"Robert's kind, thoughtful---well, reasonably, he needs some training---and dependable. He does love Cassandra very sincerely. She'll be happy with him as long as she doesn't fall in love with anybody else, and as long as she can tolerate his family. I wonder how she's getting on with them. She hasn't rung me so either she's had no opportunity or it hasn't been too dreadful."

"You haven't met them, have you?"

"No, and I suppose I should invite them to stay. Oh dear!"

The telephone rang. "Oh Cassandra darling; I've been wondering how you are. How is it?" Jasper made to leave to room but Melissa motioned him to stay. She did more listening than talking and that for a very short time. "She's either in danger of being overheard or conserving her telephone's battery," said Melissa as she replaced the receiver. "But she does sound cheerful. After all, she's not going to have to live there."

"It's not quite what you would have wanted for her, is it?"

"No, I'm afraid not; but who am I to talk? She's much less socially critical than I am and perhaps she has more of the right values. A university education should make a difference. Women of my generation met so few people outside their own class. But enough of this. There's work to do."

There was indeed, and it was some time before Melissa and Jasper could retire to their *separate* rooms, despite Jasper's protestations.

Marlene, overcome with an almost equal degree of curiosity and craving for nicotine, listened to her husband's satisfactory snoring, got up and put on her bath robe, crept downstairs, passed the ground floor bedroom in which Jasper was also snoring, went into the kitchen, found her cigarettes, sat at the table and smoked contentedly, disappointed as she was that Melissa was apparently not making as much of her friend's company as she might have.

***

Robert and Cassandra also retired to separate rooms, each with a sense of considerable relief that initial encounters had been without incident. Robert was more than ever lost in love and admiration of Cassandra and just as much as ever at odds with his parents. He lay awake musing on their difference from himself. 'I wish I could believe I was a changeling,' he thought. 'But nowadays it's only a matter of being adopted or swapped with another baby in a hospital. And I wasn't even born in a hospital.' Robert sighed, turned over, turned over again, thumped his pillow and turned that over, felt extremely sorry for himself, decided he'd have a completely sleepless night…..and fell asleep almost immediately.

Cassandra, feeling pleasantly and healthily tired after her unusual exposure to sea air, decided that Robert's parents were perfectly tolerable, wished Robert could be less tense and nervy in their presence, anticipated a day in Brighton with considerable pleasure and fell asleep before she'd finished saying her prayers.

Robert's parents, slower in their movements and mental processes, lay down rather later. "Well, Dad," Dorothy Taylor said questioningly as she heaved her second leg into their bed, "what do you think?"

"What do I think about what?" Of course he knew 'about what' but he was not very accustomed to the speedy exchange of ideas, nor particularly inclined at any time to make things easy for other people.

"What do you think of her, Robert's girlfriend…well, fiancée?"

"Why? What do you think?"

"She does seem nice. Not too posh; I thought she might be. Still she only makes pots, doesn't she; it's not as if she's a doctor or a lawyer or anything like that and her mother's got a lodging house, even if it is big."

"Our Robert'll do what he wants to anyway. Too bad if we don't like it. Pity she's a Catholic."

"Yes. They're bound to get married in a Catholic church. It'll all be in Latin and we won't know what to do."

"As long as they don't expect me to wear one of those monkey suits….."

"You'd look very smart in one, Dad." Mrs Taylor spoke a little wistfully. "You dress up really well, you know you do."

Her husband made a dismissive noise and turned on his side so that she didn't see his grin of satisfaction.

58

Robert insisted on setting out for Brighton as soon as breakfast was over the following morning. He had breathed a sigh of relief when Cassandra happily accepted tea, as coffee would have been boiled milk and water poured on to instant granules. Robert told her as much when they were in the car and safely on their way.

Cassandra sighed. "Robert," she said a little sternly, "I wish you would stop thinking these things matter. They're mere fashion. They differ in different countries and cultures. I often think Our Lord must find it pitifully funny when they're regarded as important."

"I'm sure your mother thinks they're important," was Robert's reply. "Moreover, it's not just that way round. My parents and their friends have no patience with anybody who does things differently from the way they do them. They'd be shocked at anybody serving coffee with cold milk, or drinking it with no milk at all."

"Quite. And they'd be shocked at the amount my mother drinks and the fact that she smokes and some of the language she uses. Let alone some of the things she says. So it just shows you how little such things matter. Now let's decide where we're going first and have a happy day of discovery. I'm dying to see the Pavilion. And just think about it: I'm sure the Prince Regent knew all about tea and coffee, but what an absolutely awful person he was!"

It was a very happy day and even included some shopping when Robert insisted on buying Cassandra a handbag she'd admired in a shop window. "Now this," she told him, "really will impress my mother. I don't think I've ever had a proper, good handbag before, and she thinks men are hopeless at shopping. Actually I'm quite impressed myself! But I also think it would be a nice idea to buy some flowers for your mother. I'd like to, anyway."

Robert was aware that his mother was not particularly keen on having flowers in the house as, if she ever thought about it at all, she considered they encouraged spiders, but he was unwilling to point this out to Cassandra and thought a little grimly that it would do his mother good, anyway. He merely demurred that he didn't know where to get any. Cassandra suggested a supermarket as florists were so prohibitively expensive.

"What about lilies?" she asked. "Does your mother like them? They're nearly always available."

Robert's willingness to agree to anything Cassandra suggested was not entirely due to his lack of knowledge of flowers, though he was a little apprehensive about his parents' reaction. The lilies were purchased and carefully carried back to Eastbourne on the back seat. Arrived at the house, Cassandra carried them in and had sudden misgivings when she realised that their size was somewhat out of proportion to the dimensions of the house. Huntsfield might well need sizeable flowers; they were not so appropriate in a low-ceilinged dwelling of narrow dimensions and limited space. There was, however, nothing to be done about it but present them to Robert's mother, who immediately appeared somewhat flustered.

"Oh dear! What can I do with them? I don't know what I can put them in. I mean, they're big enough for a church, aren't they?!"

"I'll deal with them," Cassandra said hastily, "I can soon cut them down a bit. Then perhaps I could put them in a water jug or, or a jar, if you don't mind. Robert can help me."

Robert's father, presumably out of curiosity, emerged from the sitting room and eyed the unfortunate flowers, which seemed to have vastly increased in size and volume since they entered the house.

"What's this then? Getting ready for a funeral are we?"

Robert turned on him sharply: "What do you mean by that?" he asked.

"Always make me think of funerals, flowers like that. All they're good for really, isn't it? They smell like latrines, too."

"They were intended," Robert replied icily, "as a present for my mother. But I now think the best thing we can do with them is to put them in a bucket of water in the back porch and then take them to Cassandra's mother; *she* will appreciate them!"

Robert's father gave a loud laugh and returned to the sitting room while his mother, with a sigh of obvious relief, agreed that that was certainly the best thing to do. Neither of them seemed to be aware of the acidity in Robert's voice or of the implied comparison with the manners and taste of his fiancée's parent. His father was too pleased with his own wit and his mother too thankful to be relieved of an unmanageable intrusion into her normal domestic arrangements.

The incident did nothing to relieve Robert's tension, however. Having deposited the unappreciated lilies he went into the sitting room, glared at his father, went out again, went into the kitchen, went out again, leapt up the stairs two at a time, knocked on Cassandra's door, found her talking on her mobile, went downstairs again, went back into the kitchen, told his mother not to get them anything for dinner as he was going to take Cassandra out.

His mother was puzzled. "Do you mean tomorrow?" she asked. "Aren't we going to have dinner here when you've been to church? I'm sure that's what we said."

"No, I do not mean tomorrow, I mean tonight; the *evening meal!*"

"Oh is that what you mean. But I've got it nearly ready."

"It's barely six o'clock."

"Yes, that's right. Then we can settle down for the evening by half past seven and watch the telly with everything cleared up. You know your father likes to do that. So do I, really."

"I'm afraid we're not used to eating so early and we don't want to watch television."

"But you've been out all day!" Robert's mother found his attitude inexplicable.

"Yes, and we'll be out all evening too, so please just do as you always do and don't think about us." Robert's tone sounded more as if he'd said 'leave us alone; don't interfere with us.' He was as unable to hide his anger as his mother was to comprehend it. Cassandra came down the stairs and Robert turned from the kitchen door to say "Come on; we'll go out now. I want to take you to dinner in one of the hotels on the sea front---they're quite a time capsule."

"Oh, I didn't know---am I dressed all right? Those hotels look very grand."

"Of course you are. You always are."

"Well I'll just fetch my coat ----and my new handbag to add lustre to the occasion!"

Robert could literally not wait to leave the house. "I'll see you in the car," he called over his shoulder as he made for the door. The car seemed to him like freedom; it was not particularly large but felt more spacious than his parents' home. Sinking into the driver's seat he began to breathe more freely as he leaned his head back and relaxed his shoulders. By the time Cassandra came to the car he was almost calm but he didn't move as she eased herself into the passenger seat. She snapped her seat belt into position and regarded him anxiously.

"Are we late for something, Robert, that you hurried out, or is it just.....?"

Robert sighed deeply, took her hand and murmured "Yes it's just, just so appallingly awful. I can't stay in that house. I can't bear to be in the same room as my father. Then I feel almost as bad in any of the other rooms. It's worse than ever. After spending a day with you the contrast's so frightful. You can't possibly want to marry me after this." To their mutual consternation Robert began to sob convulsively. Cassandra put her arms round him as best she could but he was tense and unyielding. She murmured to him that she loved him more than ever, that she understood how he felt though he had no need to feel so, that they could go home immediately after breakfast tomorrow if he felt so unhappy, that *of course* she wanted to marry him. The sobs subsided a little and Robert clasped Cassandra and put his head on her shoulder. She stroked his hair and kissed him. "Oh dear," he said at last, through tears rather than sobs, "oh dear oh dear oh dear I'm so sorry; so sorry about everything. What can I do?"

"Well," said Cassandra with more relief than she showed in her voice, " you can let me drive to one of those great, grand, glorious hotels and we can both go in and have a very large drink and then possibly some dinner....because we can't stay out here for too many hours."

Robert managed a small smile. "Can we book a room there and stay all night?"

"Actually, Robert, that's something I really would very much like to do, so I think perhaps we'd better get married as soon as we can before I break my long held vow of premarital chastity. And next time we come here, when we *are* married, we *will* stay in the hotel."

***

The interior of the hotel was as high and wide as its exterior proportions promised. Robert approached the receptionist and enquired about drinks and dinner. She looked from him to Cassandra and back and appeared doubtful.

"Dinner is available, isn't it?" Robert asked brusquely.

"Oh yes; but I think you'd better have it in the Adelphi Restaurant. I mean this one, well it's just ordinary food and I'm sure you'd like something a bit more special, wouldn't you?"

"Yes I suppose we would, really."

A waiter was summoned and they were shown into a vast room, elaborately lit and curtained. The menu was in French and contained numbers of not very meaningful terms preceded by 'à la'. They decided on something done to prawns for the first course and a mysteriously decorated lamb for the second. Although they were the only people in the over-spacious room they waited quite some time for the food to arrive. When it did, in elegant silver bowls, Robert began to laugh.

"Good heavens!" he exclaimed, "It's nothing but prawn cocktail! I thought that went out in the early sixties. I hope this pink stuff isn't that terrible sauce called Rose Marie or something."

"Well never mind," Cassandra smiled placatingly, happy that he could be taken up with such things, "I've heard prawn cocktails spoken of as something belonging to the period and people of *Abigail's Party:* pathetically pretentious and totally unacceptable; but I've never actually tasted one. I'm very interested to see if they're as awful as they're made out to be."

"I'm afraid they really are!" Robert had tasted a spoonful of his and made a wry face. "And it is that ghastly pink sauce I've always detested."

Cassandra tried a spoonful of hers. "I see what you mean," she murmured. "The prawns are all right but this sauce ruins them. The shredded lettuce underneath isn't very attractive, either. Oh well, we can scrape the prawns as much as possible and leave the rest."

Robert was gloomily inclined to think they'd never be able to cleanse the unfortunate shellfish enough to make them palatable.

"Yes we can, I've got some moist tissues in my bag, we can use those. There's nobody else here to see us." She fossicked in the new handbag, found the tissues, handed a couple to Robert and began to wipe her prawns individually and put them on her side plate. Robert did the same as they both laughed somewhat guiltily and kept an eye on the door to guard against the reappearance of the waiter. By the time he did come back all the prawns had disappeared and the wet tissues were hiding in the folds of the large, thick napkins reposing on their laps.

"We can think about what to do with these when we leave," Cassandra had murmured. "It won't matter by then. And you never know, we may need to wipe the lamb, too."

The lamb was brought in not only by the large, portly, apparently head waiter but also by a younger assistant as they carried one dish each: a plate with an imposing silver dome on top of it. These the waiters placed simultaneously before the diners and then, with a similarly simultaneously choreographed flourish, raised them into the air and bore them away. Revealed on the dramatically uncovered plates was, as Robert immediately exclaimed with a chuckle of laughter, "meat and two veg!"

Cassandra was equally amused though she did say "Actually we are doing them a slight injustice: it is meat and *three* veg. There's a pile of potato and one of mashed parsnip and then this shredded cabbage. And the meat and gravy look very palatable. It won't need wiping. But heavens! If this is their 'special' food whatever is the 'ordinary' like?!"

"It must be fish and chips or burgers, or maybe fish fingers and baked beans." They went through a repertoire of similar dishes and enjoyed the comical contrast between the surroundings and the food on offer.

"I think," said Robert finally, "if we do stay here when we're married, we won't actually eat anything but breakfast; that might be the safest."

As it turned out, however, the puddings, though dressed up in French names, were happily English and really rather good and Robert and Cassandra left the large, imposing edifice a great deal more cheerful than they had been on entering it. The stifling pretensions of its grandeur went some little way to reconciling Robert to the narrow confines of his parents' house; at least they could not be accused of pretending to be what they were not.

59

Sunday's breakfast went as smoothly as Cassandra had hoped and she and Robert set of as soon as possible after it to find a parking place at or near the church of Our Lady of Ransom. This achieved, they filled in time by wandering round the area, one of the more attractive in the town, before going into the church, which gradually filled up with the usual kind of congregation of elderly people and young families and a sprinkling of ages in between.

"It won't be like The Oratory, I'm afraid," Robert murmured.

"No; more like the church I used to go to in Devon," Cassandra responded, "with clappy-happy hymns and lots of lay participation. But you can't have been to many services like this, surely."

"I just meant no Latin, actually. I didn't know about the hymns."

"It's quite a good test really. All very well for an intellectual to be converted by going to high masses at The Oratory, with Palestrina and Haydn and Mozart, but these provincial parish churches can be off-puttingly basic. Something of a triumph of faith over aesthetics if you can cope with it."

***

The service was much as Cassandra had predicted but tempered by the genuine enthusiasm of the congregation and the singing of a not incompetent choir. Robert found it a new experience, very different from the Anglo-Catholicism of his youth, and not un-appealing. On the way out Cassandra searched the shelves of books and pamphlets to find some explanation of the use of 'Ransom' in the church's dedication. There was none to be found so she decided to ask the priest, who was standing outside to greet and speak to people. It would be usual for him to make a point of speaking to visitors. Fortunately he seemed delighted by the question.

"How nice to find somebody interested!" he beamed. "It's from a Spanish saint, St Peter Nolasco, who had a vision of Our Lady in the early 13th Century. She told him to found a religious order dedicated to the ransoming of men taken prisoner by the Moors, even by means of the men in the order giving themselves in exchange if necessary. The devotion to Our Lady of Ransom became widespread in Spain and France and Sicily and in fact she's the Patroness of Barcelona. But where are you from? ---- Ah, Oxford! No wonder you show an interest!" The priest seemed eager to converse further but was besieged by several members of his congregation and perforce turned his attention to them.

"Nice chap!" said Robert as they departed. "You know I really enjoyed that. It's all very much alive and even some of the children seem involved and interested. Did you know anything about Our Lady of Ransom before?"

"Not a thing. But you could go on learning about the saints forever. There have been quite a lot of them in a couple of thousand years."

Cassandra was glad to see that Robert's mood had lightened considerably and she had hopes that lunch would pass off without too much tension. There was likely to be some anti-Catholic flak from Robert's father, but she was used to dealing with that. Her own father had by no means been above it and it seemed to be built into the majority of English non-Catholics of that generation, especially the men. Younger people tended to lump all practising Christians together as weirdos to be despised or, at best, tolerated with pity. That didn't prevent them from attending churches for funerals, weddings or even occasionally christenings, but to go for a mere Sunday service was considered excessive, while to go every Sunday positively fanatical.

Back at the house, lunch (Robert refused to call it 'dinner') smelt ready and appetising. Mrs Taylor rejected any help with dishing up and insisted that they sit in the living room with 'Father' until everything was on the table. Fortunately that didn't take long, as nobody knew what topic of conversation to introduce and a somewhat strained silence ensued. At the table, however, it was easy for Cassandra to make appreciative comments about the delicious lunch and remark on its superiority to the meal at the very grand hotel. Mrs Taylor was happy to join in a discussion on the pretensions of such places, though not without a gibe at the extravagant foolishness of people who patronised them, and Robert and Cassandra hoped that references to their churchgoing might have been warded off. But hotels could not be talked about indefinitely, especially by people who rarely went to them, and Robert's father predictably came out with "How was the lady from Ransom, then? Did you find out where it is?"

"Oh yes, I asked the priest about it," Cassandra replied with every appearance of eagerness. "He told us it's not a place, it really does mean 'ransom' as in paying somebody to release a prisoner or a victim of kidnap." She told the story of the Spanish priest's vision and the Order he'd founded to save men captured by Muslims. She omitted 'Moors' and 'Saracens' as sounding too historical and obscure. It was a fortunate choice. Robert's father was considerably more intolerant of the adherents of Islam even than he was of Spanish Catholics -----after all, you couldn't expect Spaniards to be anything else-----and was so impressed by the idea of the ransom that he managed to ignore 'the lady' who suggested it. Cassandra noted this with some private amusement and reflected inwardly on the typical maleness of such an attitude. Her mother had often said "have a man act on a good idea any woman's suggested and he'll always believe he's the one who thought of it!" 'I must remember to tell her about it when I'm home,' she thought. 'Still, it does show the Church has a more appreciative attitude to women than it's often given credit for: a lot of good ideas are attributed to Our Lady.'

Mrs Taylor was impressed to hear that the church had been full with a number of young families present and Robert reminisced about the Anglo-Catholic church they'd attended when he was a child. "I used to like going to that," he said.

"Yes, we met a lot of nice people there," his mother concurred, "it's a pity we moved away."

Robert forbore to mention that there might have been nice people in another church and the rest of the meal proceeded without controversy. Nevertheless, he was greatly relieved when it was over and they could gather up their luggage, rescue the offending lilies from the outer darkness of the back porch, say goodbye and drive away.

The journey was pleasantly uneventful; it was too early for most weekenders to be returning home and there were almost no heavy lorries on the roads. Melissa was happy to welcome them back before it was even time for a drink. She admitted to having missed them and tactfully asked no questions as to what the visit had been like. It was not until after they had had dinner and Robert had departed that she and Cassandra settled happily in the kitchen to discuss it.

"I'm deeply grateful for the lilies, of course," Melissa began, "but I certainly hadn't expected you to bring me anything. What did you give Robert's mother?" The story of the distressful flowers was related.

"Oh dear! That really is considerably worse than could have been anticipated; but Robert should have known better than to buy them."

"I almost think he did it on purpose; his parents annoyed him so much in general that he seemed to want a specific excuse to be really angry with them."

"Were they so very ghastly?"

"No, I don't think so. His father clearly feels terribly upstaged by Robert so he's inclined to be rather aggressive. But after all, we have managed to cope with Con B. Weaver, who has much less excuse to be unpleasant."

"So you think you can tolerate them as in-laws?"

"Rather better than poor Robert can tolerate them as parents, actually!"

"You love Robert enough to compensate?"

"I think I love him even more because he's shown how vulnerable he is and made me feel very necessary to him. I don't think I've ever felt necessary to anybody before."

"That's all very well until you have children; you'll feel very necessary to them, at least until they're grown up. And you've always said you want a good-sized family. You don't want a dependent husband as well."

"Don't try to put me off, Ma; I do want to marry Robert. We won't be living near his family ---and we have decided that if we have to go there again we'll stay in a hotel!"

***

Robert returned to his college feeling that he loved Cassandra more than ever but with some anxiety as to her long-term reaction to their visit to Eastbourne. He wondered how much she would tell her mother about it. As to her mother's reaction he was astute enough to have little doubt. When his telephone rang his heart jumped with a momentary fear that it would be Cassandra telling him it was all off. It was Cassandra, but she was telling him to come as soon as he could with ideas on the best way to plan their top floor flat so that they could have it ready to move into as soon as possible and organise their wedding accordingly.

60

The work on the top floor flat proceeded apace. There was, after all, nothing structural to be done, only the fittings for a kitchen and a bathroom to be put in and the decorating of a sitting room and two bedrooms. There was another room, which could be used as a study, but that was hardly a priority as Robert would still have a room in college and Cassandra had her workshop. The wedding had been planned for a week after Nicholas and Celestria returned from their honeymoon, several months away, but Cassandra began to feel that it was rather pointless to wait for so long. Robert came for dinner that evening and they then went to inspect the work done on the flat. Pete's friends and relations were seen to have been doing a very good job, with no dawdling.

"This is very impressive," Robert commented. "Not that I know a great deal about such things, but surely we could start thinking about buying some furniture."

"There is quite a lot in the house," Cassandra demurred.

"Wouldn't you like some of your very own; things you've actually chosen?"

"Well it would be very pleasing to choose for once and not just make do; but it would be so expensive."

"You're not to worry about that. I've been working for years and living in College and spending remarkably little. Let's go and look at some on Saturday."

"It would be fun! And Robert, do you think we could get married *before* Nicholas and Celestria rather than after? They're almost certainly going to get married in Durham and we could go to their wedding as a married couple, which would really simplify things, like where we stay and so on. It wouldn't matter if I was a 'matron of honour' rather than a 'bridesmaid'!"

"Do you mean it? Truly? Nothing could please me more. How about tomorrow?"

"Don't be silly, Robert, and yes I do mean it. Let's go down and talk to Ma about it now."

As Melissa was talking, or rather listening, to Marlene in the kitchen while they smoked their companionable cigarettes Robert and Cassandra had to join them for a drink. Marlene was bewailing the fact that she and Con would soon be leaving Huntsfield House and that she would miss it and Melissa so much.

"I don't know how I'm going to be able to manage it," she repined, "I mean just being in the house with Con---and no cigarettes!"

Melissa was of the opinion that the situation would be totally unmanageable but merely said "Surely you'll be pleased to see your daughter, however."

"Yeah, well, she and Con don't get on that greatly."

"But she doesn't actually live with you, does she."

"No, I wish she did, but it wouldn't work out. You're so lucky having your girl here with you and all getting on so well. And you two are going to live here when you're married, too, aren't you?" She turned to address Robert and Cassandra. "When's that to be?"

"Well actually we're just about to discuss that with my mother." Cassandra gave up hope of any tactful departure by Marlene, who was clearly clinging to precious moments of congenial company for as long as possible. "We've decided to put it forward to just a few week's time, directly after the end of term. After all we only want something small and simple."

"Why, I wish I could be here for it! How soon is that? Maybe I could persuade Con……That's if you'd ask us, of course!"

Robert and Cassandra had to make conscious efforts to control their features into the kind of blandness that prevented them from looking aghast, but Melissa thought quickly of Robert's parents and speculated that Marlene and Con B. Weaver would be extremely useful companions for them and render them considerably less conspicuous than they would be if standing as it were alone. She immediately invited Marlene to the wedding in the warmest terms and pressed her to persuade her husband to stay as long as might be necessary in order to attend it. Robert and Cassandra abandoned any attempts to hide their astonishment but were at least relieved to realise that Melissa would present no opposition whatever to their wedding taking place as soon as reasonably possible. Deciding that any discussion of actual dates was probably not feasible on this occasion they retired to Robert's car, where they discussed Melissa's reaction.

"She's obviously playing at something, but I can't think what," said Robert in genuine puzzlement.

Cassandra sighed. "I once told Ma that the word 'ulteriority' should be invented just for her; she's almost always got an ulterior motive for anything she does; but I can't imagine what it is this time."

By the time Cassandra went back into the house the kitchen was empty so she had no means of solving the problem of her mother's behaviour that night. She went to sleep to dream confusedly of interesting sofas sold by shopkeepers with ulterior motives.

After breakfast the following morning, when Marlene had been taken by her husband on some unusually mutual expedition, Cassandra asked her mother to explain her surprising willingness, not to say her uncharacteristic eagerness, to invite them to the wedding.

"Well darling, if they stay longer they'll pay more and we'll need money for the reception and so on and we haven't really any more paying guests in the pipeline."

"Hmm! I think there might be more in it than that! You know Robert's happy to pay for most of it and when we're paying rent for the flat you won't need guests so badly."

Melissa smiled a smile of secret satisfaction but said nothing.

"Well anyway," Cassandra continued after waiting in vain for an answer, "we at least gather that you're happy for the wedding to go ahead as soon as we can arrange it."

"Oh, absolutely; the sooner the better. Where do you want it, in the Oratory?"

"We haven't really discussed it at much length, but we're not going to invite many people so they might look a bit lost in that big church; and if the reception's here it's quite a long way away. Why don't we have it in the Woodstock church? I think Robert wants it well away from his college so that he doesn't have to ask Nigel and Effie….er, Euphemia….and one or two other people who are better left out of the picture."

"Will that include poor Muriel, I wonder?"

"Oh Ma, you always call her that……"

"Not to her face, darling," Melissa interrupted.

"Of course not, but you know what I mean. I can't believe she's as unfortunate as you make out. And she might be asked to the wedding because Samson's going to be Robert's best man and she's quite a friend of his. Who do *you* want to ask? Apart from Marlene and Con of course!"

Melissa took no notice of Cassandra's sarcasm. "I really can't think of anybody, apart from the Oxford

Marjoribanks lot. Shall we ask Sir Felix to give you away?"

"Wouldn't you like me to ask Jasper?"

"No, indeed I would not! It might give him ideas."

"I think he's got plenty of those already."

"Well they don't need to be encouraged."

"But we'll ask him to the wedding, surely."

"Oh yes, we can go as far as that."

"Will he stay here?"

"No, I think not," Melissa replied decidedly. "We'll already have Nicholas and Celestria, and what about Robert's parents? We'll have to invite them to stay. But if his siblings come they can stay somewhere else."

"We'd have enough room for them though, wouldn't we?"

"Possibly; but it's too many people to feed and look after, especially when we're having the reception here as well."

"Oh yes, of course. And we mustn't forget Con and Marlene!"

Cassandra took care to 'discuss' the wedding plans with Robert, rather than merely inform him of them, but as he'd given the matter very little thought and was easily guided into total agreement it came to the same thing. He was more interested in providing suitable furniture for the flat and in deciding what sort of car he was going to give Cassandra as a wedding present. She had, in fact, already consulted Pete for advice about that and had made up her mind to acquire one of the larger hybrid cars, which, besides being big enough to carry boxes of pottery, were so eco-friendly and cheap to run, but she thought it better to delay mentioning it until the decisions about the wedding had been fully digested.

61

So everything came about as planned. The wedding invitations were sent out, with instructions that men were to wear suits, not morning dress. Con B. Weaver was greatly relieved at this as he did not want to wear 'one of those English monkey suits' but Marlene was a little disappointed as she'd thought he'd look very distinguished dressed up like that and besides, it would really make something to talk about when they went back to the States and showed the photographs to all their friends.

As the wedding was to take place so soon it was not felt necessary to invite Robert's parents to stay at Huntsfield House beforehand and Marlene was confidentially requested by Melissa to look after them and keep them happy, most particularly at the reception. She did this with such thoroughness that they were almost entirely prevented from talking to anybody else, much to Robert's relief. In fact, his parents themselves, who found the Weavers very congenial company, were completely content to be monopolised by them. Robert's siblings had already had holidays planned and were therefore unable to come at all, (or so they said), and his parents were so awed by the grandeur of the house and its surroundings, not to mention Melissa's aspect and accent, that they felt a great deal more comfortable with unrelated Americans. Cassandra noticed this with considerable approval and a realisation of her mother's motive in pressing Con and Marlene to stay. There was, she decided, a good deal to be said for 'ulteriority' after all.

Jasper offered to give Cassandra away but Melissa told him she had already asked Sir Felix and that it would hardly be suitable to change anything. He did, of course, come to the wedding, as did all the Marjoribanks family, which made the small church in Woodstock very suitably full.

Cassandra looked her most beautiful in a white satin dress with a high neck and long sleeves, very different from the bare from the breast up style of contemporary fashion. To her surprise the young men present all admired it vociferously---'that gorgeous dress', 'that wonderful dress' was heard on all sides.

The reception was equally successful. There were some excellent canapés and time given to digest them while everybody sat down and listened to the speeches. Samson Southey was a somewhat unusual best man and his eloquence admirable if unsurprisingly donnish. The majority of his audience found him rather more impressive than comprehensible. If the younger people were a little inclined to be restless they were very soon cheered by the arrival of the serious food: bangers and mash! They were too subdued to utter very audible whoops of delight but their relief and enjoyment were manifest. Marlene and Robert's mother were a little shocked at the choice of food but Con and Robert's father were so enthusiastic that their wives soon came to the conclusion that it was worth a bit of what they considered to be vulgarity to keep the men in a good temper.

When Cassandra, accompanied of course by her bridesmaid Celestria, who was wearing a shorter version of the bride's dress and looking more ethereally angelic than ever, went up to change into the 'going away' outfit her mother had insisted on her having, Jasper took the opportunity to implore Melissa to marry him. As this tended to happen fairly frequently she was ready with her negative response. She generally managed to find a new one to each proposal. This time he stressed his ability to pay for everything so that she wouldn't have to work with paying guests any more.

"Thank you, Jasper, but with Robert and Cassandra taking a flat upstairs I'm considerably better off already."

Jasper's next idea, however, surprised even Melissa.

"I know!" he said suddenly, "I'll take the flat next to theirs when it's ready. I need a place away from London. That would solve a lot of problems."

"It might cause more problems than it would solve! But really Jasper, this is *not* the most propitious time.....and here comes Cassandra now. They're about to set off."

"Do you know where they're going?"

Melissa laughed "To Hartwell House, of course, but I don't know where after that."

"I wish it was you and me!"

Melissa turned away and Robert and Cassandra said goodbye to the assembled company, who followed them into the yard where Cassandra's suelte new car was parked. Before getting into it the bride threw her bouquet to be caught, predictably, by Celestria.

Arrived at Hartwell House, where Cassandra rather reluctantly allowed a porter to park the car for them, they were shown into a particularly large and beautiful room. Robert turned to his bride and said soberly "You know I'm very glad now that we never stayed here before....that you wouldn't.....It's all so much more special now. But there were times when I thought it would never happen. I thought you might have preferred Nicholas."

"Oh Robert, Nicholas is very nice and very good and suitable for a Celestria; but like the prince in Much Ado, he's far too fine for any day but a Sunday. I want a husband for every day of the week....and I'm very happy to think I've got one."

11519872R00335

Printed in Great Britain
by Amazon